THE NEW TWILIGHT ZONE

21 TALES BY THE GREATEST SCI-FI AND DARK FANTASY WRITERS OF OUR TIME

Edited by Martin H. Greenberg
Introduction by Alan Brennert

MJF BOOKS

NEW YORK

Published by MJF Books
Fine Communications
Two Lincoln Square
60 West 66th Street
New York, NY 10023

Library of Congress Catalog Card Number 95-81601
ISBN 1-56731-083-4

Acknowledgments

"Introduction: Two Years in the Twilight Zone" copyright © 1991 by Alan Brennert

"Shatterday," by Harlan Ellison; copyright © 1975 by Harlan Ellison. Reprinted by arrangement with, and permission of, the author and the author's agent, Richard Curtis Associates, Inc., New York. All rights reserved.

"Healer," by Alan Brennert; first published in *The Magazine of Fantasy and Science Fiction*. Copyright © 1988 by Alan Brennert. Reprinted by permission of the author.

"Nightcrawlers," by Robert R. McCammon; copyright © 1984 by Robert R. McCammon. Reprinted by permission of the author.

"Examination Day," by Henry Slesar; copyright © 1957 by HMH Publications. Reprinted by permission of the author.

"A Message from Charity," by William M. Lee; copyright © 1967 by Mercury Press, Inc. First published in *The Magazine of Fantasy and Science Fiction*. Reprinted by permission of the agents for the author's estate, the Scott Meredith Literary Agency, Inc., 845 Third Avenue, New York, New York 10022.

"Paladin of the Lost Hour," by Harlan Ellison; copyright © 1985, 1986, by The Kilimanjaro Corporation. Reprinted by arrangement with, and permission of, the author and the author's agent, Richard Curtis Associates, Inc., New York. All rights reserved.

"The Burning Man," by Ray Bradbury; copyright © 1976 by Ray Bradbury. Reprinted by permission of Don Congdon Associates, Inc.

"Wong's Lost and Found Emporium," by Wiliam F. Wu; copyright © 1983 by TSR, Inc. Reprinted by permission of the author.

"One Life, Furnished in Early Poverty," by Harlan Ellison; originally appeared in *Orbit 8* (edited by Damon Knight) and copyright © 1970 by Damon Knight. Copyright reassigned to author August 5, 1971. Copyright © 1971 by Harlan Ellison. Reprinted by arrangement with, and permission of, the author and the author's agent, Richard Curtis Associates, Inc., New York. All rights reserved.

Contents

Introduction:
Two Years in the Twilight Zone

ALAN BRENNERT

ART'S DELI IS A BUSY, NOISY, NEW YORK–STYLE DELI ON Ventura Boulevard in Studio City, a favorite lunch spot for the hundreds of people who work at nearby studios—from NBC, Disney, and Universal to CBS-MTM Studios, only a few miles down the street—and an unlikely place for the first story conference of the revival of *The Twilight Zone*.

But at the time—August 1984—CBS had yet to assign offices to the two men it had charged with reviving Rod Serling's classic—Phil De-Guere and James Crocker. Phil was in Paris, finishing up what would be his last episode of *Simon & Simon* for Universal, while stateside Jim was starting the ball rolling, contacting prospective writers. I was flattered to be the first writer approached, though Jim and I had met only once or twice before in passing. I'd written several episodes of *Simon* for Phil. He knew of my background in fantasy, and suggested Jim contact me.

It was in this crowded deli with the high signal-to-noise ratio that I pitched Jim several stories. The one that he bought—"Her Pilgrim Soul"—became the first story purchased for the new *Twilight Zone*. At the same time I gave Jim a half dozen short stories I thought merited adaptation, the most prominent being Harlan Ellison's "Shatterday."

"Harlan hasn't been doing any TV work for a while," I cautioned, "so I don't know if he'd be willing to adapt it, but I think it would make a perfect *Twilight Zone*."

"If he doesn't adapt it, but we can get the rights," Jim asked, "would *you* be willing to adapt it?"

I said, "Sure." I'd done an adaptation of Harlan's before—a script for an AFI project that never panned out—so I assumed he trusted me. But I told Jim it was Harlan's story and he should have first shot. My interest was just in seeing it get done.

Well, by the time this got to Harlan it had become transmogrified to "One of our writers, Alan Brennert, wants to adapt 'Shatterday,' " to which Harlan responded, "Alan's a good friend, but if anybody adapts

1

'Shatterday' its going to be me, and I don't even know if I want to sell it to you.''

I won't recount the meeting that followed—Harlan has done it far better, many times before—but as I understand, it consisted largely of Harlan and Phil yelling at each other, something both of them enjoy and excel at. About three days later, Phil called Harlan and asked if he'd like to be a creative consultant on the series.

Phil DeGuere is an opinionated, vocal, and stubborn man, but unlike many other producers with those same qualities, he is also intelligent, a good writer, and not afraid of dissenting opinions. He saw in Harlan someone just as opinionated and stubborn as himself, and hired him not *despite* but *because* of that. When I agreed to be executive story consultant, it was partly because of Harlan's involvement.

Any producer who sat and listened, as they had, as Harlan lambasted many of the stories they'd bought, then actually invited him on board, was unique, to say the least. And after my deal was cut, Phil stated his philosophy to me quite clearly: ''I've got very strong opinions,'' he said, ''and I will do everything in my power to bring you around to my way of thinking—just as *you* can do everything *you* can to bring me around to *your* way of thinking. If you win, fine. If I win, even better.''

Sounded fair to me.

And so began what was the most exciting, satisfying, and companionable experience I have ever had in television. *The Twilight Zone* will always have a special place in my heart and memory; by way of introduction to this book of stories culled from our two years on the air, let me tell you what it was like working in the Twilight Zone.

Television is like any other industry—there are as many ways to create a show as there are personalities to interact. Some shows are run with iron hands by strong-willed creator/producers who establish parameters, block out stories, even rewrite staff writer/producers. This can work out very well if the person at the top is intelligent and talented. It can work out very badly if the person is an idiot and a fraud. (And no, I'm not going to name names. It's called libel.)

Despite his strong opinions and personality, Phil DeGuere established early on an atmosphere in which we all felt free to tell him *exactly* what we thought. If, as he was wont to remind us on occasion, ''This is not a democracy,'' neither was it a dictatorship. Jim and Phil asked all the staff writers (Harlan, me, and, very soon afterward, Rockne S. O'Bannon, whose script ''Wordplay'' Phil and Jim had found in the slush pile and snapped up weeks before Harlan and I arrived) to write memos on each script and story in development. There were frequent, and frequently strident, differences of opinion. A later reader of some of these memos was quoted as saying that they seemed to reflect ''a lot of strong oarsmen rowing in different directions.'' I'm a bit baffled that he seemed to think this was a drawback. Of course we were strong oarsmen, and often, yes, we *were* rowing in opposition to one another. But it was in that very opposition that we found direction, we found our voice—and we found it not by appropriating someone else's, but through exploration and argument. Given the choice of being surrounded by a group of strong-minded individuals with imagination, or another group with a uniformity of vision but low aspirations, I'll take the former any day.

At one point, for instance, Harlan called me in frustration about a particular story he loathed and couldn't get killed—a story that either Phil or Jim liked a great deal. I pointed out to him that this series didn't reflect his taste, it didn't reflect *my* taste, it reflected his taste *and* mine *and* Phil's and Jim's and Rock's. Harlan muttered something and hung up, then called back ten minutes later. "You know," he said, "you're right. I've been an outsider in this business for so long, I've forgotten what it's like to be part of a group. I can get awfully egocentric sometimes."

"We all get egocentric sometimes," I said.

"Yeah, well, me more than most," he said, with a laugh. And now I *knew* I was living in the Twilight Zone.

People forget that the original *TZ* was not a one-man show. Rod Serling's vision guided the series, but Richard Matheson and Charles Beaumont between them wrote about three dozen shows, many based on previously published stories by both men: stories that existed before Rod Serling invented the Zone.

What Serling was—in addition to being one of the greatest television writers of all time—a canny producer who brought individuals with their own talents and visions into his playroom, and let them run loose. Over time the series seems to be a homogenous whole, but look closely and you'll see that there were at least three very distinct subgenres of *Twilight Zone* stories—humanistic parables like "Eye of the Beholder" or "Changing of the Guard," most of them written by Serling; darker, moodier pieces like "The Jungle" and "Shadowplay," hallmarks of Beaumont's writing; and inventive, plot-driven stories which, as Marc Scott Zicree has put it, are so involving that you have to keep watching to find out *what happens next,* and those were and are the domain of Richard Matheson.

That was what we were attempting, as well, and the very idea of the five of us—each of whom had his own particular passion, his own stories he wanted to tell—hewing to some formula, was anathema to us. Harlan had avoided television for years, and I had turned down every story editor job offered me since a disastrous staff experience four years before. We weren't going back into the series grind just to work on a formula show. And so, as with the original *TZ,* it soon became clear that each staffer on *TZ2* had his own subgenre that he excelled in (though was not necessarily limited to), and a consensus began to form about what the new *TZ* would be like.

We had a great deal to live up to, and we knew we could not do it by trying to compete with what Rod Serling had done. It had been twenty years since the original *TZ* left the air—twenty years of reruns, twenty years of increasing sophistication on the part of the audience, an audience weaned on the kind of O. Henry endings Serling loved, an audience who expected that kind of twist ending—yet would be able to spot one coming a mile away. We realized how difficult it would be to sustain that kind of story for a half hour, and how impossible it would be to do it twice a week, every week.

Nor, as I've said, did we have any particular desire to *do* that sort of story every week. It seemed to us that the best way we could honor Serling was *not* to imitate him. If there was anything Rod Serling respected, it was originality. By doing our own show, by telling the kinds of stories we had always wanted to tell but never been able to tell on television—as Serling had used the *Zone* to say things he could no longer get across on conventional television—we were following in his tradition, but not mimicking his style. And when we did do a "traditional" *Twilight Zone* story, it either had to have one hell of a kicker—as in, say, Jim Crocker's "A Little Peace and Quiet"—or be short enough so that we were one step ahead of the audience, instead of three steps behind. Stories like "Examination Day" and "A Small Talent for War" had good punches at the end, but had we been forced to expand them to half-hour length, those punches wouldn't have just been telegraphed, they'd have been subspaced.

Harlan put it best, I think: "We're doing *Twilight Zone, Book II,*" he would tell reporters. *Twilight Zone,* in other words, as we hoped Serling himself would have been producing it, had he been alive—not a simulation, but an evolution.

If in the long run "our" *Zone* leaves behind any kind of legacy, it will probably be in the writers we discovered or developed. The most obvious example is Rock O'Bannon, already well on his way to superstar status as the author of the movie *Alien Nation,* and having made his directorial debut on his original screenplay *Fear,* starring Ally Sheedy and Lauren Hutton. But we can also take pride in having purchased the first professional scripts from Donald Todd ("The Uncle Devil Show"), and Ron Cobb and Robin Love ("Shelter Skelter").

J. D. Feigelson is a talented writer/producer/director who had numerous longform credits before *TZ*—ranging from the genre piece *Dark Night of the Scarecrow* to the three-hour historical drama *Houston: The Legend of Texas*—but to this day the story that came out closest to his original vision was the charming and funny vignette "The Little People of Killany Woods.'' He also did a superb job adapting and directing Ray Bradbury's ''The Burning Man.''

George R. R. Martin's first television script was ''The Once and Future King,'' and on the basis of that we brought him on as staff writer, then story editor. Later he became a writer/producer on *Beauty and the Beast.*

Michael Cassutt had written a few sitcom scripts and sold a science fiction novel, *The Star Country,* to Doubleday. I brought him in to pitch. He did a smashing job on ''Red Snow,'' and we hired him as staff writer second season. (He has since been executive story editor on *Max Headroom* and writer/producer on *TV 101* and *WIOU,* and has recently published a new novel, *Dragon Season,* from Tor Books.)

Martin Pasko and Rebecca Parr's ''Cold Reading'' was one of our best-received comedies. They became story editors the second season, and went on to write for *Max Headroom, Simon & Simon,* and *Roseanne,* among many other shows.

And with directors like William Friedkin, Martha Coolidge, Joe Dante, Wes Craven, Paul Lynch, John Hancock, and Tom Wright, we had an atmosphere of excitement and expectation—the conviction that we were doing something special, something that might or might not succeed, but least we were being *allowed* to try something more ambitious than conventional, formula television. Actors were eager and pleased to appear on the show; I can think of only two instances of ''stars'' exerting their ego on the scripts. We treated actors and directors with respect, and they in turn treated the scripts with respect.

CBS development executive Carla Singer by and large let us have our heads and do what we wanted to do. There were only two or three stories that I recall she nixed, one of them being J. Neil Schulman's ''Profile in Silver,'' which we later rammed through after we'd been reassigned to Current Programming—and which Carla now admits came out wonderfully. It is rare that you find a program executive in this town who (a) trusts creative people to do their job, even 95 percent of the time, and (b) will admit to a mistake afterward. Carla Singer deserves a great deal of credit for the quality of those first thirteen episodes.

Understand: I am not saying that everything we developed during that time was brilliant, by any means. We did our share of clunkers but, as I've said elsewhere, by God they were *our* clunkers: either stories that one or more of us championed against dissenting opinions (I tried to get ''Opening Day'' killed about twelve times, but every time I thought I'd finally driven a stake into its heart the damned thing would rear up from the dead yet again) or stories we all liked that turned out less than wonderful on film (my own ''Healer,'' for instance, which was acted and directed so badly I took my name off it). We had our disasters, but they weren't the result of network interference, only our own lapses in judgment or skill. And that, I put to you, is unique in television. For better or worse, those first thirteen were *our* shows, and we shoulder the blame as well as the credit.

Production started in March of 1985, and soon all of us—even those of us like Harlan and myself who'd sworn we would never become producers—were in the thick of production. The logistics of doing two or three stories per hour were staggering. *Darkroom,* which in '81 had used the same format, had had two units shooting simultaneously—something we would later be forced to do, but at the start we had only one unit. That meant prepping a new show with a new cast, new director, new sets and locations, every four to five days: while we were in production on one segment we were in *pre*-production on the next, and writing/ polishing the one after that. Because of that ravenous production maw and frenetic schedule, there was simply too much for Phil, Jim, and line producer Harvey Frand to handle by themselves, and a wonderful thing happened. The writers stepped into the breach.

Harlan remembers how, at a pre-production meeting for "Gramma," the art director, asking what Gramma's bed should be like, looked to Phil—who looked to Harlan. It suddenly dawned on him that because he was the writer, they naturally assumed he would be the best judge of how a story should be realized—a view shared by Phil and Jim, themselves writers. It was they who created an atmosphere in which the script was regarded as sacrosanct; in which I felt free to go down to the wardrobe department to check on the costumes for "The Star," discover with horror that they'd rented spacesuits from Western Costume left over from *Tom Corbett, Space Cadet*—bubble helmets, so help me God—and, after seeing my pallid face, hear the costumer ask, "Well, we were thinking of tinting them. What color should we tint them?" Before I knew it, I was helping redesign the spacesuits.

When Bruce Willis, an energetic and dedicated actor, yelled so loud the first day of shooting on "Shatterday," that he gave himself laryngitis, it was Jim and Harlan who spent two days on the dubbing stage with Bruce, months later—*looping every line in the show.* (Harlan recalls how, on the second day, he came directly from the airport where he had just scooped up his soon-to-be-wife Susan Toth off a nonstop ten-hour flight from London. Susan, of course, had no idea who Bruce Willis was— *Moonlighting* hadn't begun airing in England—and, exhausted from the long flight, she fell dead asleep in the middle of one of his line-readings. If Bruce minded, he never showed it.)

When the Grateful Dead's original score for "Shatterday" turned out less suitable than hoped, I was on the dubbing stage with Phil from three in the afternoon to one in the morning, pulling apart music tracks— dropping a percussion track here, keeping a bass track there. It was my first experience in post-production and I discovered, much to my astonishment, that I loved it—and that there's nothing quite so satisfying as seeing your work through to the end. Later, by the time we were doing the Christmas show, we were all doing post-production as a matter of course. I remember going into a sound studio in North Hollywood to work on sound effects "spotting" (placement) just as Rock O'Bannon and Martha Coolidge were finishing the spotting on "Night of the Meek". Rock and I handled "But Can She Type?" together, then he left and I did "The Star." And when narrations were recorded, Rock, Jim, Harlan, or I were there to direct Charles Aidman's reading. And Charlie, a wonderful man and a joy to work with, would then proceed to give us *exactly* what we asked for.

But perhaps my fondest memory from *The Twilight Zone* is of sitting on a dubbing stage in Hollywood listening to the music cues come up for "Her Pilgrim Soul." This was a very personal story for me, a good-bye to a woman I'd loved very much, and I had been involved in its production from casting to rehearsals to the music spotting session with William Goldstein. And now I sat listening to Bill's music come up—a sweeping, romantic, bittersweet melody perfectly suited to the story. I kept telling the sound engineers to bring up the music and play down the sound effects, which astonished the arranger (in television and films it's usually the music that takes a backseat to the sound effects). I remember a lovely moment in which a particular music cue came up and seemed faintly wrong—a second or two before or after the five-year-old Nola grabs the holographic ball Kevin has fashioned for her. "Move it back," I suggested, "so the cue comes just as the ball falls into her hands." They did, and it suddenly felt exactly right.

This was no act of genius on my part. Had he been doing it alone, our sound effects supervisor, Steve Zansberg, would probably have done the same thing himself. But he didn't, I did. I had the opportunity to shape the final form of the film, a remarkable opportunity for a writer in either television or film. Jim and I had edited "Pilgrim" together, and thereafter, with our crack team of editors—including Tom Pryor, Noel Black, Gary Blair, and Greg Wong—I usually edited my own as a matter of course, alone or in collaboration with the director.

God, it was fun. And so swept up were we in the exhilaration of it all—so remote did our previous television experiences seem—that we thought it would go on forever.

Well, it didn't, of course, and there are probably as many theories why as there are produced episodes. For what it's worth, here's the one that makes the most sense to me.

The new *Twilight Zone,* like its predecessor, had always been intended as an adult program. It was developed specifically as a ten-o'clock show, and given the latitude of that later time period, we developed stories we never would have, had we been doing even a nine-o'clock series. "Examination Day," "Gramma," and "Nightcrawlers," to name a few, were written, produced, and directed for a ten-o'clock audience. Some of our scripts, by CBS's lights, were too intense even for *that* hour; Henry Slesar and Jim Crocker's adaptation of Florence Engel Randall's "The Watchers," for instance, was such an uncompromisingly bleak look at a Bernhard Goetz-like future in which everyone in New York packs a gun, that the network never did approve it. Which was why we were so stunned and appalled when then–CBS programming chief Harvey Shephard announced that *The Twilight Zone* would, come fall of 1985, be appearing on Fridays at *eight o'clock*.

I recall several of us standing on the balcony outside our offices at CBS-MTM, all looking rather poleaxed. Fridays traditionally had low viewing levels, but Fridays at *eight* the tube was controlled by kids. Would CBS try to water down the show to make it suitable for the whole family? If they did, none of us would be sticking around to watch. But the word soon came down from on high: *don't change a thing*. Keep on doing exactly what you've been doing. The catchphrase of the moment: *We're giving eight o'clock back to the grown-ups*. For the first time in years, they argued, a network was slotting adult programming in what had long been considered "family viewing hour."

Well, this sounded high-minded and noble enough to convince ourselves that perhaps Harvey had a point. And, in any event, there wasn't a whole hell of a lot we could do about it—CBS owned the show, and they could place it anywhere they damn well pleased.

After the first thirteen episodes were developed, we had been shunted over to Current Programming, which turned out to be a lot more like Real Television than the first thirteen had been. Our main network liaison there was a genuinely well-intentioned man, but he had no background in fantasy—he was far more comfortable with, say, *The Equalizer*. Still, his notes were generally minor, and we had very little interference compared to the average series. We continued to shoot the shows we wanted to, and when we suddenly became an eight-o'clock show, the pressure to soft-pedal the scripts never did develop. Our only problems came from Program Practices, who had their doubts, for instance, at using the word "copulate" in "Her Pilgrim Soul"—even if we *were* quoting Yeats. (We won that one, quoting Leviticus as precedent.)

Our premiere—on Friday, September 27, 1985—won the time slot with a thirty share, and garnered, to our great relief, generally positive notices. But perhaps the most satisfying thing about the reviews—those and later ones—was that our attempt not to mimic Serling was perceived by more than one critic as being faithful to Serling's vision.

Daily Variety wrote:

"Comparisons between today's 'Zone' and the show presented by Serling would be manifestly unfair because this is another time, another era in TV, and there is no Serling to guide the venture. But those who have inherited his concept have been faithful to his idea, and the initial episode reflects a fidelity to the premise of 'Zone' . . . Revivals of past TV successes are usually disastrous, but those who put together the new 'Zone' have done so with loving care and an obvious respect for the original.''

The *Los Angeles Times* was not enamored of "Shatterday" (well, the *New York Times* liked it) but loved "A Little Peace and Quiet," and, comparing it to the premiere episode of another anthology series, said of Jim Crocker's script: "Are you listening, Steven Spielberg? Now *that* was an amazing story." (I think Jim bought several hundred copies of that day's *Times*).

Over the course of the season, the positive reviews continued, from both genre and nongenre sources: *Cinefantastique* wrote that "science fiction and fantasy is alive and well on television thanks to a writing staff that knows and loves the genre," while *TV Guide,* in an article comparing *TZ2* to *TZ1*, observed that the fundamental differences between the shows lay in the anxieties of each era; *TZ2,* wrote Gary Christenson, portrays "characters facing personal dilemmas, people looking for love and acceptance, wrestling with what they are and what they've done . . . In the *Twilight Zone* of old, society was the heavy. In today's version, we meet the enemy and he is us." Not entirely true of *TZ1*—Serling did more than his share of such stories—but certainly an apt description of *TZ2.* Overall, he concluded that "special effects abound in the new series, but the folks behind the new *Twilight Zone* do not let visuals rule. They have learned well Serling's tried and true recipe for great fantasy television: Place one everyday individual in a situation conjured from the primal anxieties of the audience. Suspend temporarily the known physical laws of the universe. Use actors and writers who can bring plausibility and depth to the story. Throw into each episode a smidgen of topicality and *voilà*—a classic TV series.''

Flattering words, indeed. The ratings, alas, did not reflect mass agreement on the part of the Nielsen families.

For the first four weeks we had won the time slot, and displayed every indication of being a hit. Then, with episode five—"If She Dies" and "Ye Gods"—ratings began to slip; that week we lost the time slot to *Webster,* which is humiliating enough, but worse was our liaison's analysis of the situation. In typical dumbheaded network fashion, he decided that "Ye Gods" had alienated the audience—that people came to *The Twilight Zone* for chills and eeriness, not comedy—conveniently ignoring the fact that viewer drop-off occurred *before* the segment even started to air, and that some of Serling's original series had included comedic shows. He laid down the law: no more comedies. (How I slipped past "I of Newton," I still have no idea.) "Ye Gods"—a funny, delightful script by Anne Collins—became the scapegoat.

What did, in fact, cause that sudden drop-off in viewers? Everyone has his own theory, but the most bittersweet, from his perspective, is Phil's. The previous week, Phil's adaptation of Robert R. McCammon's

"Nightcrawlers," directed by William Friedkin, solidly won the last half hour of the time slot . . . and the following week we plunged from twenty-five-plus shares to a twenty-one share, losing the time slot to *Webster.* The audience, according to this theory, gave us a good sampling those first four weeks . . . then watched, horrified, as rotting zombie soldiers, conjured up out of a Vietnam vet's guilt and grief, laid waste to a small diner, blowing away just about everything in their path . . . all at 8:30 P.M. "I think they just decided, 'Well, if this is what we can expect from this show, forget it,' " Phil speculates, not without a certain bemused angst.

"Nightcrawlers" was unquestionably one of our strongest episodes, and Phil and Billy Friedkin have every reason to be proud of it. But because it played two hours earlier than it by rights should have, it may well have signaled the death knell for the series—viewers deciding they'd rather watch the harmless fluff of *Webster* or the sanitized violence of *Knight Rider* instead.

And who can really blame them? *TZ2* should *never* have been scheduled as an eight-o'clock entry, not given the intensity and adult nature of many of the episodes *already in the can.* Whether CBS actually thought they were "giving eight o'clock back to the grown-ups," or whether they simply didn't have anything else to put in that time slot—studios with hits on a network often have guarantees of favorable slots, and an in-house show like *TZ* can easily become a sacrificial lamb—we'll never know. But this much I'm certain of: putting us on at eight was the first body blow for *Twilight Zone* as a prime-time entry.

On the other hand, there's Mike Cassutt's theory: that there are, bottom line, only about fifteen million viewers out there interested in watching an anthology show—an audience that would make a cable or syndicated series a runaway success, but in the vaster (though rapidly shrinking) arena of network television, too small to keep an anthology on the air.

As the ratings slipped, CBS began to scrutinize the stories more closely. Our network liaison was, as I've said, not a fundamentally imaginative man; he felt more comfortable with formula shows, and so, by God, he managed to invent a formula for what was supposed to be the quintessentially *non*-formulaic program. A *Twilight Zone* story, he decreed, was one featuring "an ordinary person in an extraordinary situation." Each episode had to have a person *entering* the Twilight Zone— eliminating, then, any kind of strange future society like that of "The Watchers." Our liaison, while quoting us chapter and verse of what a good *Twilight Zone* was, was woefully ignorant of the show's tradition. By his narrow and restrictive standards, Serling could not have done episodes like "The Four of Us Are Dying" (no ordinary person there), or "The Eye of the Beholder" (the viewpoint character in that one turned out be as biased in her worldview as her society's). While "ordinary person/extraordinary situation" *was* a classic plot of the old series, it was by no means the only one.

Meanwhile Harlan, about to make his directorial debut on his adaptation of Donald Westlake's "Nackles," ran afoul of network censors and wound up leaving the show (for the full story, see Harlan's article, "The Deadly 'Nackles' Affair," in the February 1987 issue of *Twilight Zone Magazine*). This was certainly a blow to morale, as well as a personal disappointment to all of us who had worked with Harlan the past year; and with the share points still hovering around the low twenties, we decided—like an underdog political campaign with nothing much to lose—to just go ahead and do what we wanted to do, as best we could, and to hell with whether we were picked up for another season. In the latter half of the first season we produced as many episodes to be proud of as we had in the first half: "Red Snow," "Dead Run," "Profile in Silver," "The Library," and "Cold Reading" among them.

We also produced our share of stinkers, as well, notably "Welcome to Winfield," "The Leprechaun-Artist," and "Take My Life, Please" (bad scripts we never should have green-lighted in the first place), and "Button, Button" and "Monsters!" (good scripts mauled by bad directors, bad production, bad acting, or all three). But again, they were *our* stinkers: we were and are quite willing to take the rap for them. All in all, the first season of *Twilight Zone* was indeed as "uneven" as many critics have charged—but in a medium in which being "even" most often equates with being mediocre, I'll opt for unevenness.

The nature of an anthology show makes it a crapshoot: some weeks, yes, you'll wind up with a "Welcome to Winfield"; others, a "Paladin of the Lost Hour." *No* anthology series, from the original *TZ* to *The Outer Limits* to *Studio One*, has *ever* been consistent. And that, to me, is the appeal of them, as a viewer and as a writer. When they're bad, they're bad, but when they're good, they're better than anything else in episodic television—because each episode reflects a personal vision, an individual passion.

But with the surprise renewal for a second season, that freedom to succeed brilliantly or flop spectacularly was denied us. Our liaison now reassigned to "Vice President in Charge of In-House Programming" (which, since we were CBS's *only* in-house series, really meant "Vice President in Charge of *The Twilight Zone*"), CBS clamped down—and, leveraging the bad ratings and skin-of-our-teeth renewal against us, sought to impose their will on us. Rather than live with the low ratings, let the show run a few years, and then sit back and rake in the syndication money (which they would not have to share with any studio), they chose to try to make *Twilight Zone* a ratings success. However, they didn't have the vaguest idea of how to go about this. They asked for "provocative material," but when we gave it to them, they rejected it. They didn't want "small" stories, they wanted pieces with a "larger" point of view, then rejected one tailor-made for their needs.

Of all the staffers that second season, George Martin fared the best in terms of getting good scripts actually approved by CBS and into production: "The Once and Future King," "The Toys of Caliban," "The Road Less Traveled." Michael Cassutt got one script—"The Card"—produced. Rock did "The Storyteller," for which he would later be nominated for a Writers Guild Award, and a remake of "The After Hours" which only reflected CBS's lust to turn the show into a pointless retread of Serling's original. Marty and Becky, though they wrote several scripts, didn't get any on the air. I fared a little better with two: "Time and Teresa Golowitz" and "Voices in the Earth."

Still, it was frustrating to see a plethora of good stories rejected for arbitrary reasons. Despite offers to promote me to writer/producer, I quit the show in September of 1986. I would've stayed on, content to write a fraction of the material I had first season, if not for a conversation with our network liaison. I'd written an adaptation/treatment of an old short story of mine, "A Winter Memory." It was another "small," people-oriented story, the kind that CBS kept trying to avoid that second season, but the liaison had said to me, in effect, "Look, X is okay, but I'm not comfortable with Y. If you change Y to Z I'll approve the story."

Well, this seemed an arbitrary change, to my mind, but X was what was really important to me—it was the emotional core of the story, the dilemma of a man who's never done anything with his life suddenly flooded with other people's memories, and the pain and beauty it brought to him. So I said, what the hell, I'll change Y to Z. I handed in a new outline, and CBS came back with, "Great, we love it. Now get rid of X."

Our liaison had, in short, done to me exactly what another division of CBS, Program Practices, had done to Harlan over the "Nackles" affair—a bait-and-switch routine. I hung up the phone, and knew that if I stayed on I would wind up producing other people's stories, not mine. If that was the road I'd wanted to take, I would've taken it years before. I'm a writer, first and foremost, and my interest in producing lies primarily in safeguarding my work through the production process.

Moreover, our liaison's duplicity showed me quite clearly that I could never trust him; life is too short to feint and spar with such people. So I quit, although Phil asked me to adapt Tom Godwin's "The Cold Equations," to which we had finally succeeded in obtaining the rights after two years. I agreed, did the script, waited as it was about to go into pre-production—

And CBS promptly punched our ticket.

In all fairness, much of the pressure to formulize the show and make it a ratings success stemmed from massive internal injuries at CBS itself. The network had just fended off a takeover attempt from Ted Turner, but at stiff economic cost. And it was CBS itself, no studio, that was bank-rolling a very expensive *TZ*. My image is of Lawrence Tisch staring at a balance sheet in New York, looking at the ratings, at our budget, and asking, "Why the hell are we spending $1.4 million an hour on something that gets an eighteen share?"—and we were history.

What kind of history remains to be seen; clouding the issue, unfortunately, is the form in which that work will be available for posterity.

We all knew that cutting the hour *Zones* into half hours was, economically, an inevitability. All those who work in television know that their work will be trimmed—sometimes drastically—for syndication; Serling himself once said that he found it too painful to watch his shows after they'd been cut for local commercial time. We were relatively lucky: the man in charge of the job, Tom Pryor, was one of our own best editors, and both he and his assistant, Paul Levin, showed real concern for the integrity of the stories. Phil DeGuere also had involvement in the re-edit, and Mark Shelmerdine, who supervised the job, very kindly allowed me input in the re-editing of my own episodes. The series distributor, MGM/UA, had given Mark, Tom, and Paul a ridiculously short amount of time to assemble the sixty-four half hours. And they did, I think, the best job possible under the circumstances.

The reason for the rush job was to get the package—including thirty as-yet-unproduced new episodes to be shot in Canada, written and produced by a different staff—sold into syndication at the NATPE convention. The irony of this is that as soon as the people behind this made-for-syndication *Zone* had used our episodes to sell their series, they began bashing our show to promote their own—claiming we had "strayed" from Serling's original vision, and that their series would be "more humanistic" rather than centering on "special effects and explosions." In contrast, those of us on *TZ2* freely acknowledged our debt to Serling, but we had neither the inclination nor the bad form to impugn a show to which we owed our very existence.

These sorts of changes were, as I say, to be expected. What none of us anticipated was the sucker punch MGM/UA delivered to us *after* the editing.

The producers of *TZ3* claim that Charles Aidman was too costly to retain as narrator. Be that as it may, because of the new narrator for the new episodes, some pinhead at MGM/UA decided that the package needed "uniformity," and it was decided to *re-dub the sixty-four off-network half hours* with the new narrator. When I first learned of this—not from anybody at *TZ3*—I immediately called Paul Levin, arranged to see "Charity" . . . and was horrified to hear a perky, peppy, and, in my opinion, utterly inappropriate announcer's voice delivering what is probably my favorite of all the narrations I wrote.

It was not just a matter of my personal preference of Charles Aidman

over Robin Ward, who is doubtless a fine person and dedicated professional. Technically it was a bad mix—the voice was just laid atop the
production track, the echo filter was up too high, the timing of his reading did not even *follow* that of the original. The producer in me was as
offended as the writer; this was obviously a rush job, even more so than
the editing.

As for the rationale of "uniformity," I think a greater imperative was
simple greed: if MGM/UA had left Charlie Aidman's voice on all the
shows, they would have had to pay him residual payments as per the
SAG contract. Canadian residuals, on the other hand, are a fraction of
the cost of American ones—and so MGM/UA saves a bundle. In the
process, of course, they deface the work—but that's to be expected. All
they care about is that they have their ninety-four half hours, a solid
syndication package. MGM/UA were no strangers to self-amputation,
having already lopped off, bit by bit, everything from their film library
to their entire studio lot; one more bit of mutilation was surely no big
deal for them.

This is one reason why the book you hold in your hands is so welcome
to those of us who labored on *TZ:* it contains, with only two regrettable
omissions, nearly all the short stories we adapted on *Twilight Zone* between 1985 and 1987, and as such, is a fitting testament to our intentions
and accomplishments during that period.

Even before Harlan, Rock, or I joined the show, Phil DeGuere had
purchased—before its publication in J. N. Williamson's *Masques* anthology—Robert R. McCammon's story "Nightcrawlers." The purchase of
short stories for adaptation is the most sensible way to produce an anthology program, but oddly, only a handful of series have done it to any
degree. Serling clearly saw the wisdom of this, having bought many fine
stories to adapt for the original *Zone,* probably more than *Thriller* and
Outer Limits combined. The reasoning, to us, seemed eminently sound:
why buy half-baked ideas from writers with no grasp of the genre when
you can mine a vein of classic literature?

It was also cost-effective: Phil and CBS worked out a deal whereby
TZ would buy the television rights to a story for three years, produce an
adaptation, and have the right to broadcast that adaptation in perpetuity,
while at the same time *film and television rights would revert to the
author* after three years, and he or she could sell it all over again, say,
to *Tales from the Darkside.* Lest you think this latter possibility unlikely,
there *is* ample precedent: William M. Lee's "A Message from Charity"
was produced by public television in Pennsylvania years before our version (if there's anybody out there with a copy of it, by the way, I'd love
to see it); Tom Godwin's "Cold Equations" was done on BBC in the
sixties before we bought the rights to it; and at least one story I know
of, Stanley Weinbaum's "The Adaptive Ultimate," had no less than *three*

television productions (on *Studio One, Science Fiction Playhouse,* and *Tales of Tomorrow,* the latter scripted by Ted Sturgeon), *and* was made into a classically bad B-movie called *She-Devil.*

The fee for story purchases was generally no more expensive than what we would pay for an original story. The fact that this is a cheap and workable alternative is demonstrated by the fact that *Tales from the Darkside,* with budgets as low as $110,000 per half hour, was able to use adaptations for a large portion of its episodes. So whenever you hear someone talking about how "difficult" or "expensive" it is to do adaptations, that usually translates as: *the producer doesn't like to read.* Prose, that is. Most television producers recoil at the sight of a short story as they might a scorpion, and promptly hand the loathsome thing over for "coverage"—synopses written by "readers."

Because I started out as, and continue to be, a prose writer, my biases were clear from the outset; and I had the heady experience, those first few months, of dramatizing some of my favorite stories: Harlan's "Shatterday"; the aforementioned "Message from Charity," which I'd yearned to adapt ever since reading it at age seventeen in Terry Carr's *New Worlds of Fantasy #3;* the recent Hugo, Nebula, and World Fantasy Award nominee "Wong's Lost and Found Emporium," by William F. Wu, and stories by Greg Bear and Arthur C. Clarke. Harlan adapted Stephen King's "Gramma," Rock did Sturgeon's "Yesterday Was Monday," and frequently a freelancer would come in with one—as Steven Barnes did with Bob Silverberg's "To See the Invisible Man," or David Gerrold with Sturgeon's "A Saucer of Loneliness"—and we would buy the stories for them to adapt.

Except where permissions were impossible to obtain—e.g. Stephen King's "Gramma" and Sidney Sheldon's "Need to Know"—this anthology contains all those stories. All appeared first as short stories, then as scripts, with three exceptions. Richard Matheson's "Button, Button" was actually first written for the original *Twilight Zone,* but never produced. Years later, Matheson took the idea and turned it into a short story, published first in *Playboy* and then, fittingly, in *Rod Serling's Twilight Zone Magazine.* He then rewrote his original script—an hour in length—for the revived *Zone,* and we proceeded to screw it up. Network interference, dreadful acting, direction that turned the point of the story 180 degrees around from what was intended—you name it, it happened. Richard's pseudonym, "Logan Swanson," appears on the filmed episode, but the short story appears here as the author originally intended.

Another story originally broadcasted pseudonymously was, as I've mentioned, my own "Healer." I subsequently took the basic idea, expanded upon it, and published it under my own name in *The Magazine of Fantasy and Science Fiction,* and it is included here, as an apology, of sorts, for the ghastly botch that made it to the air.

And, lastly, there's Harlan Ellison's "Paladin of the Lost Hour." The chronology on this one is a bit baroque, so bear with me. Harlan wrote it as an original, handing in his story treatment in December of 1984; then, before going on to the script, he turned the treatment into a short story, publishing it in Terry Carr's *Universe* anthology, and *then* adapted the story into a script. So does this make the episode an original, or an adaptation? I have no idea. I get headaches just thinking about it. The short story won a Hugo Award; the script, a Writers Guild Award. So by any reckoning, it deserves inclusion in this volume.

The Twilight Zone will be remembered by all of us as a high point in our careers . . . and not just for the freedom it afforded, or the camaraderie of the production. Even now, four years after it left the air, I encounter people who, upon learning I worked on *TZ*, start to recount an episode they loved—recount it the way my generation can recite the plots of ''Walking Distance'' or ''The Midnight Sun.'' People remember individual stories in a way they would never recall specific episodes of, say, *Hunter*. Because the viewers were not responding to a formula, not reacting to a cast of continuing characters—they were moved by a *story*— a specific, stand-alone story that stuck with them, that didn't just vanish between their synapses five minutes after viewing it.

In an age when trilogies, quatrologies, and dectalogies mirror the reading public's television-weaned sensibilities, having done stories that people *remember* is no small flattery. We were grateful for the chance to do them, and happy that they are appreciated, on tape or in memory, by those who saw them. Now we direct your attention to the stories that served as the basis for many of our most memorable episodes. We owe a vast debt to writers such as William M. Lee, Theodore Sturgeon, Robert R. McCammon, Ray Bradbury, Joe Haldeman, Henry Slesar, Parke Godwin, et al., and we're pleased to acknowledge their very significant contributions to *The Twilight Zone*.

SHATTERDAY
Harlan Ellison

TELEPLAY BY ALAN BRENNERT

AIRED SEPTEMBER 27, 1985

STARRING BRUCE WILLIS

i: Someday

NOT MUCH LATER, BUT LATER NONETHELESS, HE thought back on the sequence of what had happened, and knew he had missed nothing. How it had gone, was this:

He had been abstracted, thinking about something else. It didn't matter what. He had gone to the telephone in the restaurant, to call Jamie, to find out where the hell she was already, to find out why she'd kept him sitting in the bloody bar for thirty-five minutes. He had been thinking about something else, nothing deep, just woolgathering, and it wasn't till the number was ringing that he realized he'd dialed his own apartment. He had done it other times, not often, but as many as anyone else, dialed a number by rote and not thought about it, and occasionally it was his own number, everyone does it (he thought later), everyone does it, it's a simple mistake.

He was about to hang up, get back his dime and dial Jamie, when the receiver was lifted at the other end.

He answered.

Himself.

He recognized his own voice at once. But didn't let it penetrate.

He had no little machine to take messages after the bleep, he had had his answering service temporarily disconnected (unsatisfactory service, they weren't catching his calls on the third ring as he'd *insisted),* there was no one guesting at his apartment, nothing. He was not at home, he was here, in the restaurant, calling his apartment, and *he* answered.

"Hello?"

He waited a moment. Then said, "Who's this?"

He answered, "Who're you calling?"

"Hold it," he said. "Who *is* this?"

His own voice, on the other end, getting annoyed, said, "Look, friend, what number do you want?"

"This is BEacon 3-6189, right?"

Warily: "Yeah . . . ?"

"Peter Novins's apartment?"

There was silence for a moment, then: "That's right."

He listened to the sounds from the restaurant's kitchen. "If this is Novins's apartment, who're you?"

On the other end, in his apartment, there was a deep breath. "This is Novins."

He stood in the phone booth, in the restaurant, in the night, the receiver to his ear, and listened to his own voice. He had dialed his own number by mistake, dialed an empty apartment . . . *and he had answered.*

Finally, he said, very tightly, *"This* is Novins."

"Where are you?"

"I'm at The High Tide, waiting for Jamie."

Across the line, with a terrible softness, he heard himself asking, "Is that you?"

A surge of fear pulsed through him and he tried to get out of it with one last possibility. "If this is a gag . . . Freddy . . . is that you, man? Morrie? Art?"

Silence. Then, slowly, "I'm Novins. Honest to God."

His mouth was dry. "I'm out here. You can't be, I *can't* be in the apartment."

"Oh yeah? Well, I am."

"I'll have to call you back." Peter Novins hung up.

He went back to the bar and ordered a double Scotch, no ice, straight up, and threw it back in two swallows, letting it burn. He sat and stared at his hands, turning them over and over, studying them to make sure they were his own, not alien meat grafted onto his wrists when he was not looking.

Then he went back to the phone booth, closed the door and sat down, and dialed his own number. Very carefully.

It rang six times before *he* picked it up.

He knew why the voice on the other end had let it ring six times; he didn't want to pick up the snake and hear his own voice coming at him.

"Hello?" His voice on the other end was barely controlled.

"It's me," he said, closing his eyes.

"Jesus God," he murmured.

They sat there, in their separate places, without speaking. Then Novins said, "I'll call you Jay."

"That's okay," he answered from the other end. It was his middle name. He never used it, but it appeared on his insurance policy, his driver's license and his social security card. Jay said, "Did Jamie get there?"

"No, she's late again."

Jay took a deep breath and said, "We'd better talk about this, man."

"I suppose," Novins answered. "Not that I really want to. You're scaring the shit out of me."

"How do you think *I* feel about it."

"Probably the same way I feel about it."

They thought about that for a long moment. Then Jay said, "Will we be feeling exactly the same way about things?"

Novins considered it, then said, "If you're really me then I suppose so. We ought to try and test that."

"You're taking this a lot calmer than I am, it seems to me," Jay said.

Novins was startled. "You really think so? I was just about to say I thought you were really terrific the way you're handling all this. I think you're *much* more together about it than I am. I'm really startled, I've got to tell you."

"So how'll we test it?" Jay asked.

Novins considered the problem, then said, "Why don't we compare likes and dislikes. That's a start. That sound okay to you?"

"It's as good a place as any, I suppose. Who goes first?"

"It's my dime," Novins said, and for the first time he smiled. "I like, uh, well-done prime rib, end cut if I can get it, Yorkshire pudding, smoking a pipe, Max Ernst's paintings, Robert Altman films, William Goldman's books, getting mail but not answering it, uh . . ."

He stopped. He had been selecting random items from memory, the ones that came to mind first. But as he had been speaking, he heard what he was saying, and it seemed stupid. "This isn't going to work," Novins said. "What the hell does it matter? Was there anything in that list you didn't like?"

Jay sighed. "No, they're all favorites. You're right. If I like it, you'll like it. This isn't going to answer any questions."

Novins said, "I don't even know what the questions *are!*"

"That's easy enough," Jay said. "There's only one question: which of us is me, and how does *me* get rid of *him?*"

A chill spread out from Novins's shoulder blades and wrapped around his arms like a mantilla. "What's *that* supposed to mean? Get rid of *him?* What the hell's *that?*"

"Face it," Jay said—and Novins heard a tone in the voice he recognized, the tone *he* used when he was about to become a tough negotiator—"we can't *both* be Novins. One of us is going to get screwed."

"Hold it, friend," Novins said, adopting the tone. "That's pretty muddy logic. First of all, who's to say you're not going to vanish back where you came from as soon as I hang up . . ."

"Bullshit," Jay answered.

"Yeah, well, maybe; but even if you're here to stay, and I don't concede *that* craziness for a second, even if you *are* real—"

"Believe it, baby, I'm real," Jay said, with a soft chuckle. Novins was starting to hate him.

"—even if you *are* real," Novins continued, "there's no saying we can't both exist, and both lead happy, separate lives."

"You know something, Novins," Jay said, "you're really full of horse puckey. You can't lead a happy life by yourself, man, how the hell are you going to do it knowing I'm over here living your life, too?"

"What do you mean I can't lead a happy life? What do you know about it?" And he stopped; of course Jay knew about it. *All* about it.

"You'd better start facing reality, Novins. You'll be coming to it late in life, but you'd better learn how to do it. Maybe it'll make the end come easier."

Novins wanted to slam the receiver into its rack. He was at once furiously angry and frightened. He knew what the other Novins was saying was true; he *had* to know, without argument; it was, after all, himself saying it. "Only one of us is going to make it," he said, tightly. "And it's going to be me, old friend."

"How do you propose to do it, Novins? You're out there, locked out. I'm in here, in my home, safe where I'm supposed to be."

"How about we look at it *this* way," Novins said quickly. "You're trapped in there, locked away from the world in three and a half rooms. I've got everywhere else to move in. You're limited. I'm free."

There was silence for a moment.

Then Jay said, "We've reached a bit of an impasse, haven't we? There's something to be said for being loose, and there's something to be said for being safe inside. The amazing thing is that we both have accepted this thing so quickly."

Novins didn't answer. He accepted it because he had no other choice; if he could accept that he was speaking to himself, then anything that followed had to be part of that acceptance. Now that Jay had said it bluntly, that only one of them could continue to exist, all that remained was finding a way to make sure it was he, Novins, who continued past this point.

"I've got to think about this," Novins said. "I've got to try to work some of this out better. You just stay celled in there, friend; I'm going to a hotel for the night. I'll call you tomorrow."

He started to hang up when Jay's voice stopped him. "What do I say if Jamie gets there and you're gone and she calls me?"

Novins laughed. "That's *your* problem, motherfucker."

He racked the receiver with nasty satisfaction.

ii: Moanday

He took special precautions. First the bank, to clean out the checking account. He thanked God he'd had his checkbook with him when he'd gone out to meet Jamie the night before. But the savings account passbook was in the apartment. That meant Jay had access to almost ten thousand dollars. The checking account was down to fifteen hundred, even with all outstanding bills paid, and the Banks for Cooperatives note came due in about thirty days and that meant . . . he used the back of a deposit slip to figure the interest . . . he'd be getting ten thousand four hundred and sixty-five dollars and seven cents deposited to his account.

His *new* account, which he opened at another branch of the same bank, signing the identification cards with a variation of his signature sufficiently different to prevent Jay's trying to draw on the account. He was at least solvent. For the time being.

But all his work was in the apartment. All the public relations accounts he handled. Every bit of data and all the plans and phone numbers and charts, they were all there in the little apartment office. So he was quite effectively cut off from his career.

Yet in a way, that was a blessing. Jay would have to keep up with the work in his absence, would have to follow through on the important campaigns for Topper and McKenzie, would have to take all the moronic calls from Lippman and his insulting son, would have to answer all the mail, would have to keep popping Titralac all day just to stay ahead of the heartburn. He felt gloriously free and almost satanically happy that he was rid of the aggravation for a while, and that Jay was going to find out being Peter Jay Novins wasn't all fun and Jamies.

Back in his hotel room at the Americana he made a list of things he had to do. To survive. It was a new way of thinking, setting down one by one the everyday routine actions from which he was now cut off. He was all alone now, entirely and totally, for the first time in his life, cut off from everything. He could not depend on friends or associates or the authorities. It would be suicide to go to the police and say, "Listen, I hate to bother you, but I've split and one of me has assumed squatter's rights in my apartment; please go up there and arrest him." No, he was on his own, and he had to exorcise Jay from the world strictly by his own wits and cunning.

Bearing in mind, of course, that Jay had the same degree of wit and cunning.

He crossed half a dozen items off the list. There was no need to call Jamie to find out what had happened to her the night before. Their relationship wasn't that binding in any case. Let Jay make the excuses. No need to cancel the credit cards, he had them with him. Let Jay pay the bills from the savings account. No need to contact any of his friends and warn them. He *couldn't* warn them, and if he did, what would he warn them against? Himself? But he did need clothes, fresh socks and underwear, a light jacket instead of his topcoat, a pair of gloves in case the weather turned. And he had to cancel out the delivery services to the apartment in a way that would prevent Jay from reinstating them: groceries, milk, dry cleaning, newspapers. He had to make it as difficult for him in there as possible. And so he called each tradesman and insulted him so grossly they would *never* serve him again. Unfortunately, the building provided heat and electricity and gas and he *had* to leave the phone connected.

The phone was his tie-line to victory, to routing Jay out of there.

When he had it all attended to, by three o'clock in the afternoon, he returned to the hotel room, took off his shoes, propped the pillows up

on the bed, lay down and dialed a 9 for the outside line, then dialed his
own number.

As it rang, he stared out the forty-fifth floor window of the hotel room,
at the soulless pylons of the RCA and Grants Buildings, the other dark-
glass filing cabinets for people. It was a wonder *any*one managed to stay
sane, stay whole in such surroundings! Living in cubicles, boxed and
trapped and throttled, was it any surprise that people began to fall apart
. . . even as *he* seemed to be falling apart? The wonder was that it all
managed to hold together as well as it did. But the fractures were beginning to appear, culturally and now—as with Peter Novins, he mused—
personally. The phone continued to ring. Clouds blocked out all light
and the city was swamped by shadows. At three o'clock in the afternoon,
the ominous threat of another night settled over Novins's hotel room.

The receiver was lifted at the other end. But Jay said nothing.

"It's me," Novins said. "How'd you enjoy your first day in my skin?".

"How did you enjoy your first day *out* of it?" he replied.

"Listen, I've got your act covered, friend, and your hours are numbered. The checking account is gone, don't try to find it; you're going
to go out to get food and when you do I'll be waiting—"

"Terrific," Jay replied. "But just so you don't waste your time, I had
the locks changed today. Your keys don't work. And I bought groceries.
Remember the fifty bucks I put away in the jewelry box?"

Novins cursed himself silently. He hadn't thought of that.

"And I've been doing some figuring, Novins. Remember that old Jack
London novel, *The Star Rover?* Remember how he used astral projection
to get out of his body? I think that's what happened to me. I sent you
out when I wasn't aware of it. So I've decided I'm me, and you're just a
little piece that's wandered off. And I can get along just peachy-keen
without that piece, so why don't you just go—"

"Hold it," Novins interrupted, "that's a sensational theory, but it's
stuffed full of wild blueberry muffins, if you'll pardon my being so forward as to disagree with a smartass voice that's probably disembodied
and doesn't have enough ectoplasm to take a healthy shit. Remember the
weekend I went over to the lab with Kenny and he took that Kirlian
photograph of my aura? Well, my theory is that something happened and
the aura produced another me, or something . . ."

He slid down into silence. Neither theory was worth thinking about.
He had no idea, *really*, what had happened. They hung there in silence
for a long moment, then Jay said, "Mother called this morning."

Novins felt a hand squeeze his chest. "What did she say?"

"She said she knew you lied when you were down in Florida. She
said she loved you and she forgave you and all she wants is for you to
share your life with her."

Novins closed his eyes. He didn't want to think about it. His mother
was in her eighties, very sick, and just recovering from her second se-

rious heart attack in three years. The end was near and, combining a business trip in Miami with a visit to her, he had gone to Florida the month before. He had never had much in common with his mother, had been on his own since his early teens, and though he supported her in her declining years, he refused to allow her to impose on his existence. He seldom wrote letters, save to send the check, and during the two days he had spent in her apartment in Miami Beach he had thought he would go insane. He had wanted to bolt, and finally had lied to her that he was returning to New York a day earlier than his plans required. He had packed up and left her, checking into a hotel, and had spent the final day involved in business and that night had gone out with a secretary he dated occasionally when in Florida.

"How did she find out?" Novins asked.

"She called here and the answering service told her you were still in Florida and hadn't returned. They gave her the number of the hotel and she called there and found out you were registered for that night."

Novins cursed himself. Why had he called the service to tell them where he was? He could have gotten away with one day of his business contacts not being able to reach him. "Swell," he said. "And I suppose you didn't do anything to make her feel better."

"On the contrary," Jay said, "I did what you never would have done. I made arrangements for her to come live here with me."

Novins heard himself moan with pain. "You did *what!?* Jesus Christ, you're out of your fucking mind. How the hell am I going to take care of that old woman in New York? I've got work to do, places I have to go, I have a life to lead . . ."

"Not any more you don't, you guilty, selfish son of a bitch. Maybe *you* could live with the bad gut feelings about her, but not me. She'll be arriving in a week."

"You're crazy," Novins screamed. "You're fucking crazy!"

"Yeah," Jay said, softly, and added, "and you just lost your mother. Chew on *that* one, you creep."

And he hung up.

iii: Duesday

They decided between them that the one who *deserved* to be Peter Novins should take over the life. They had to make that decision; clearly, they could not go on as they had been; even two days had showed them half an existence was not possible. Both were fraying at the edges.

So Jay suggested they work their way through the pivot experiences of Novins's life, to see if he was really entitled to continue living.

"*Every*one's entitled to go on living," Novins said, vehemently. "That's why we live. To say no to death."

"You don't believe that for a second, Novins," Jay said. "You're a misanthrope. You hate people."

"That's not true; I just don't like some of the things people *do.*"

"Like what, for instance? Like, for instance, you're always bitching about kids who wear ecology patches, who throw Dr. Pepper cans in the bushes; like that, for instance?"

"That's good for starters," Novins said.

"You hypocritical bastard," Jay snarled back at him, "you have the audacity to beef about that and you took on the Cumberland account."

"That's another kind of thing!"

"My ass. You know damned well Cumberland's planning to strip-mine the guts out of that county, and they're going to get away with it with that publicity campaign you dreamed up. Oh, you're one hell of a good PR man, Novins, but you've got the ethics of a weasel."

Novins was fuming, but Jay was right. He had felt lousy about taking on Cumberland from the start, but they were big, they were international, and the billing for the account was handily in six figures. He had tackled the campaign with same ferocity he brought to all his accounts, and the program was solid. "I have to make a living. Besides, if I didn't do it, someone else would. I'm only doing a job. They've got a terrific restoration program, don't forget that. They'll put that land back in shape."

Jay laughed. "That's what Eichmann said: 'We have a terrific restoration program, we'll put them Jews right back in shape, just a little gas to spiff 'em up.' He was just doing a job, too, Novins. Have I mentioned lately that you stink on ice?"

Novins was shouting again. "I suppose you'd have turned it down."

"That's exactly what I did, old buddy," Jay said. "I called them today and told them to take their account and stuff it up their nose. I've got a call in to Nader right now, to see what he can do with all that data in the file."

Novins was speechless. He lay there, under the covers, the Tuesday snow drifting in enormous flakes past the forty-fifth floor windows. Slowly, he let the receiver settle into the cradle. Only three days and his life was drifting apart inexorably; soon it would be impossible to knit it together.

His stomach ached. And all that day he had felt nauseated. Room service had sent up pot after pot of tea, but it hadn't helped. A throbbing headache was lodged just behind his left eye, and cold sweat covered his shoulders and chest.

He didn't know what to do, but he knew he was losing.

iv: Woundsday

On Wednesday Jay called Novins. He never told him how he'd located him, he just called. "How do you feel?" he asked. Novins could barely answer, the fever was close to immobilizing.

"I just called to talk about Jeanine and Patty and that girl in Denver," Jay said, and he launched into a long and stately recitation of Novins's affairs, and how they had ended. It was not as Novins remembered it.

"That isn't true," Novins managed to say, his voice deep and whispering, dry and nearly empty.

"It *is* true, Novins. That's what's so sad about it. That it *is* true and you've never had the guts to admit it, that you go from woman to woman without giving anything, always taking, and when you leave them—or they dump you—you've never learned a goddamned thing. You've been married twice, divorced twice, you've been in and out of two dozen affairs and you haven't learned that you're one of those men who is simply no bloody good for a woman. So now you're forty-two years old and you're finally coming to the dim understanding that you're going to spend all the rest of the days and nights of your life alone, because you can't stand the company of another human being for more than a month without turning into a vicious prick."

"Not true," murmured Novins.

"True, Novins, true. Flat true. You set after Patty and got her to leave her old man, and when you'd pried her loose, her and the kid, you set her up in that apartment with three hundred a month rent, and then you took off and left her to work it out herself. It's true, old buddy. So don't try and con me with that 'I lead a happy life' bullshit."

Novins simply lay there with his eyes closed, shivering with the fever.

Then Jay said, "I saw Jamie last night. We talked about her future. It took some fast talking; she was really coming to hate you. But I think it'll work out if I go at it hard, and I *intend* to go at it hard. I don't intend to have any more years like I've had, Novins. From this point on it changes."

The bulk of the buildings outside the window seemed to tremble behind the falling snow. Novins felt terribly cold. He didn't answer.

"We'll name the first one after you, Peter," Jay said, and hung up.

That was Wednesday.

v: Thornsday

There were no phone calls that day. Novins lay there, the television set mindlessly playing and replaying the five minute instruction film on the pay-movie preview channel, the ghost-image of a dark-haired girl in a gray suit showing him how to charge a first-run film to his hotel bill. After many hours he heard himself reciting the instructions along with her. He slept a great deal. He thought about Jeanine and Patty, the girl in Denver whose name he could not recall, and Jamie.

After many more hours, he thought about insects, but he didn't know what that meant. There were no phone calls that day. It was Thursday.

Shortly before midnight, the fever broke, and he cried himself back to sleep.

vi: Freeday

A key turned in the lock and the hotel room door opened. Novins was sitting in a mass-produced imitation of a Saarinen pedestal chair, its seat treated with Scotchgard. He had been staring out the window at the geometric irrelevancy of the glass-wall buildings. It was near dusk, and the city was gray as cardboard.

He turned at the sound of the door opening and was not surprised to see himself walk in.

Jay's nose and cheeks were still red from the cold outside. He unzipped his jacket and stuffed his kid gloves into a pocket, removed the jacket and threw it on the unmade bed. "Really cold out there," he said. He went into the bathroom and Novins heard the sound of water running.

Jay returned in a few minutes, rubbing his hands together. "That helps," he said. He sat down on the edge of the bed and looked at Novins.

"You look terrible, Peter," he said.

"I haven't been at all well," Novins answered dryly. "I don't seem to be myself these days."

Jay smiled briefly. "I see you're coming to terms with it. That ought to help."

Novins stood up. The thin light from the room-long window shone through him like white fire through milk glass. "You're looking well," he said.

"I'm getting better, Peter. It'll be a while, but I'm going to be okay."

Novins walked across the room and stood against the wall, hands clasped behind his back. He could barely be seen. "I remember the archetypes from Jung. Are you my shadow, my persona, my anima or my animus?"

"What I am now, or what was I when I got loose?"

"Either way."

"I suppose I was your shadow. Now I'm the self."

"And I'm becoming the shadow."

"No, you're becoming a memory. A bad memory."

"That's pretty ungracious."

"I was sick for a long time, Peter. I don't know what the trigger was that broke us apart, but it happened and I can't be too sorry about it. If it hadn't happened I'd have been you till I died. It would have been a lousy life and a miserable death."

Novins shrugged. "Too late to worry about it now. Things working out with Jamie?"

Jay nodded. "Yeah. And Mom comes in Tuesday afternoon. I'm renting a car to pick her up at Kennedy. I talked to her doctors. They say she doesn't have too long. But for whatever she's got, I'm determined to make up for the last twenty-five years since Dad died."

Novins smiled and nodded. "That's good."

"Listen," Jay said slowly, with difficulty, "I just came over to ask if there was anything you wanted me to do . . . anything *you* would've done if . . . if it had been different."

Novins spread his hands and thought about it for a moment. "No, I don't think so, nothing special. You might try and get some money to Jeanine's mother, for Jeanine's care, maybe. That wouldn't hurt."

"I already took care of it. I figured that would be on your mind."

Novins smiled. "That's good. Thanks."

"Anything else . . . ?"

Novins shook his head. They stayed that way, hardly moving, till night had fallen outside the window. In the darkness, Jay could barely see Novins standing against the wall. Merely a faint glow.

Finally, Jay stood and put on his jacket, zipped up and put on his left glove. "I've got to go."

Novins spoke from the shadows. "Yeah. Well, take care of me, will you?"

Jay didn't answer. He walked to Novins and extended his right hand. The touch of Novins's hand in his was like the whisper of a cold wind; there was no pressure.

Then he left.

Novins walked back to the window and stared out. The last remaining daylight shone through him. Dimly.

vii: Shatterday

When the maid came in to make up the bed, she found the room was empty. It was terribly cold in the room on the forty-fifth floor. When Peter Novins did not return that day, or the next, the management of the Americana marked him as a skip, and turned it over to a collection agency.

In due course the bill was sent to Peter Novins's apartment on Manhattan's upper east side.

It was promptly paid, by Peter Jay Novins, with a brief, but *sincere* note of apology.

HEALER

Alan Brennert

TELEPLAY BY MICHAEL BRYANT

AIRED OCTOBER 11, 1985

STARRING ERIC BOGOSIAN, VINCENT GARDENIA,

ROBERT COSTANZO, YOAQUIN MARTINEZ

THERE WAS ANOTHER DISTURBANCE IN THE CITADEL TO-
day; Ta'li'n saw it from his hidden room in the temple atop the Pyramid
of the Sun—a short, bloody skirmish between followers of the Old Order
and proponents of the New. The latter were armed not merely with clubs
and daggers, as in the past, but with atlatls, as well—spears tipped with
gray or green obsidian points—and Ta'li'n noted with sadness that the
followers of the Old had taken up weapons of their own: daggers, slings,
a few knives edged in black obsidian. The confrontation was more evenly
matched than previous ones, and briefer; both sides dispersed upon ar-
rival of the Priests' Guards with atlatls of their own, the two factions
leaving a bloody trail both north and south along the broad, two-mile-
long avenue that bisected the City—a road that would one day, Ta'li'n
thought ruefully, be aptly known as the the Avenue of the Dead.

Past, present, and future all seemed to be fighting for dominion over
the priest's soul. The past was a glorious lure, a dangerous seduction on
which he could not afford—yet could not avoid—dwelling. From up here,
the City was still beautiful, still vibrant, the undisputed capital of a
continent; not even the Maya had built a home as large, as populous, as
this city which the Aztecs would rechristen Teotihuacán—whose true
name would be as obscured by time and history even as its temples, its
pyramids, its courts and its palaces would be covered over by mounds
of dirt and tangles of guayule scrub. But now, at this moment, it was
still alive, some twenty square miles of it, and he could see, from this
tallest pyramid at the center of the City, the ceremonial platforms lining
the broad, expansive Avenue; the Pyramid of the Moon to the north;
the—what would they call it, centuries from now?—the Temple of Quetzalcoatl, to the south. The frescoes and facades blazed with vivid colors—bright reds, whites, golds—and the marketplace thronged with
merchants and traders from as far away as the Gulf Coast, bartering for
the City's famed obsidian, or its Thin Orange pottery. Ta'li'n's people
had lived here, in peace and prosperity, for nearly seven hundred years;
and staring out now at the City, the rioters no longer in sight, business
as usual being conducted in the Great Compound, it was easy to believe
that it would continue so forever. But the present, that eternal Now, was
as dangerous a lure as the past; only the future mattered, as terrible and
unfathomable as it was, or would be.

Returning to his meditation, and to the peyote that induced it, he
placed another of the mescal caps on his tongue; it burned, sharply, for

several moments, then all sensation was lost as the vision took form behind his closed eyelids. For an instant he hoped that this time, perhaps, the future would show him a different face, a kinder countenance—

But it was the same vision: always the same. The City, center of light and peace for six and a half centuries, in flames. The Temple of X'l'o— the god renamed Quetzalcoatl by those who would follow—would be stripped of its color, the plumed serpents adorning its face reduced to dun reflections of their present glory, and the City itself, the thousands of private dwelling places . . . all that, set to the torch. A fire that would burn for days, turning nights into a kind of constant dawn, a flickering orange glow that could be seen as far away as Oaxaca. Pillars of black smoke would rise from one end of the Avenue to the other, eclipsing even the massive presence of the sacred mountain, Tenan, for centuries the home of the water goddess, X'la'n—or Tlaloc, as she would be known.

Tlaloc. A strange name, he thought, invented by they-who-would-follow; yet somehow the idea that they would never know her true name, nor even that of the City itself, gave him odd comfort as he watched that city's destruction—better, perhaps, to be an object of anonymous mystery, than of indifferent notoriety. He did not care if such thoughts seemed stoic, or overly philosophic; he had seen the vision too many times, these past months, to spare any more tears for it—especially now that the event itself, the reality of it, was so frighteningly close.

If he was to save any of his golden city—to preserve any of its achievements, these past six and a half centuries—he would have to act, soon.

A drifter lay sleeping at the mouth of the alley, a two-day-old *Times* wrapped around him like a blanket, a rain-soaked carton for his pillow; if he heard or felt the rat scuttling at the tattered cuffs of his pants, he gave no indication of it—no more notice than he gave the short, somewhat feral young man at the far blind end of the alley. Dark-haired, bony, with a build more likely to be called wiry than strong, Jackie Thompson nervously tugged on the straps of the rope harness as he slipped it over his stooped shoulders; he hated this thing, hated the way the straps cut into his skin no matter how many layers of clothing he wore—he still had rope burns under his arms from the last time he'd used it. Nervously glancing toward the mouth of the alley and the lighted street beyond, he reeled in the twenty feet of rope and fingered the rusty grappling hook at its end; he knew it was too dark for anyone to clearly see him from the street, but he couldn't help it, couldn't help the pounding of his heart or the sweat on his palms or the small twitch at the corner of his eye. Even after fifteen years of second-story work, he had to take deep breaths, had to ignore that small mocking voice inside that told him he was no good at this, that he was a loser and a screw-up and a putz. Rubello's voice, sometimes; sometimes, his own.

It was probably only his stubborn defiance of that voice that had kept him in this business, all this time; that even now made him raise the grappling hook and, winding up like a swarthy Mickey Mantle, let it fly—up onto the roof of the two-story museum. It landed with an unwelcome clang, but Jackie was too busy trying to stifle a cry of pain to pay it any mind—he'd wrenched his shoulder, still tender from the fall he'd taken last month, that botched jewelry job on Fairfax. Doing his best to ignore the pain, he yanked on the rope, just enough so that the hook snagged on an outcropping of ledge; then, gingerly testing its hold, he took the rope in two hands and began slowly ascending the brick wall, half expecting his luck to unravel along with the rope—relieved and a little amazed when he actually made it to the second-story window.

He took a glass cutter from his jacket pocket, placed a small suction cup on the bottom half of the window, and began cutting a hand-sized half oval in the glass. Earlier he'd broken into the museum's alarm box and rigged a parallel circuit at the junction controlling this wing of the building; now, as he gripped the suction cup, pulled out the half oval of glass, and reached inside to raise open the window, that parallel circuit was telling the alarm system that everything was just copacetic, that the perimeter alarm on the window was intact and the sensors under the plush museum carpeting were likewise undisturbed as Jackie clambered inside. He slipped off the rope harness and left it dangling—uncomfortably resembling a noose—from the roof; taking out his flashlight, he began to make his way through the deserted museum, the red wink of motion sensors in far corners noting his presence, but unable to get their warning past the bypass circuit Jackie had installed. At the same time he'd been careful not to place the circuit board *too* far downline: shunting the downstairs alarms out of the system could potentially have attracted some attention.

Still, for all this, he felt no less nervous. He'd breached the museum, as intended, in the Mesoamerican wing, the section his sources had told him was least patrolled, most remote from the guard station on the ground floor. Padding silently through, he swept his flashlight beam from side to side, illuminating statuary too large to transport: a reclining porcelain figure of Chac Mool, the Aztec rain god; a fresco, bright even after the bleaching of centuries of sun and dust, of the water goddess, Tlaloc; a bronze metalwork of Quetzalcoatl, the Feathered Serpent—

A phone rang.

Jackie stopped dead. The ring was muffled, distant, from downstairs; after another short ring, someone picked it up, and he could hear the indistinct drone of someone's voice—a guard, obviously—talking.

Suddenly impatient, he began casting about for something small, something he could snatch and grab and get the hell out of here. He stopped at a glass display case, and in the wash of his flashlight he saw a bronze plaque: TEOTIHUACANOS RELIGIOUS ARTIFACTS, CA. 650 A.D.—

COURTESY MUSEO NACIONAL DE ANTROPOLOGIA, MEXICO CITY. Inside were half a dozen objects, none larger than ten inches across: a mask made of some dark green stone, with slits for eyes and a broad, flat nose; some sort of gray vessel in the shape of a jaguar's foot, one of its six claws broken at the joint; another jaguar, this one a black obsidian figurine; a stone model of a Teotihuacanos temple, with its distinctive, four-tiered *talud-tablero* style.

Dimly he was aware that the voice downstairs had ceased; he stood, frustrated, at the display case before him and swore silently to himself.

All the research he'd done on the museum's collection was doing him damned little good just now. He had assumed, naively, that the more valuable artifacts would be identifiable by their material—gold or jade, say, easy to recognize, easy to carry. But none of these looked particularly—

A door shut, downstairs, followed hard upon by the sound of footsteps—ascending stairs.

Jackie's first instinct was to run, but that mocking voice within him would surely torment him later should he leave without something to show for his efforts. He swung his flashlight along the display case again—

And this time, his attention was caught by a polished oval stone perhaps two inches high, flashing a lustrous green in the lamplight; it looked marbled, with black highlights. Jackie's heart raced faster. Jade? Yes, of course; it had to be. Hurriedly he jimmied the lock on the display case, lifted the glass cover—

And an alarm sounded throughout the museum.

As the klaxon began its shrieking alert, Jackie's bladder chose to empty itself at the same moment. Oh, Christ, he thought. He thought he'd gotten the full scope on the system, but in his caution not to disable *all* the alarms, he must've placed the circuit not downline *enough;* he'd accidentally left the systems functioning in this room. *Damn* it! He'd fucked up royally this time—he had to get *out* of here. He snapped up the smallest object in the case—the oval stone, burnished like metal and yet, somehow, not metal—and bolted out the room, frantically retracing his path. Behind him he heard the sound of footsteps pounding up the hardwood stairs, then softening as they took to the thick museum carpeting. He felt a wave of relief—prematurely—as he reached the window through which he'd first entered; he opened it again, started to reel in the rope harness—

"Hold it!"

Jackie whipped around to see a security guard silhouetted in combat stance in the doorway, a .38 gripped firmly with both hands, pointed directly at the fleeing thief. Jackie froze for an instant, then, panicked, forgot about the harness, spun round and started to clamber out the window.

The guard fired.

Straddling the window, Jackie took the bullet in the abdomen and cried out in pain; that and the velocity of the bullet's impact sent him pitching sideways out the window. The world turned upside-down, there was a fire in his stomach and he was falling, two stories, the ground somehow *above* him, a thin cord of blood streaming out of him like a vapor trail—

He plummeted twenty feet to the ground, a messy fall broken inadequately by a couple of garbage cans and a mound of rancid trash. Stunned and in shock, he caught a glimpse of the guard poking his head out of the window above, then vanishing. *Move,* Jackie told himself. *You've got to move.* The lancing pain in his stomach intensified as he staggered to his feet; it became unbearable as he took a step forward, nearly buckling on what was probably a broken ankle. But something propelled him forward, something sent him stumbling down the alley, around a bend, and into another alley; in one hand he still unconsciously clutched the jade stone he had stolen, while with the other he sought to hold his lacerated skin together, a blood streaming out between his fingers as he stumbled on. Oh God, he thought, oh Jesus, please, please help, I'm sorry, I'm sorry, please *help* me . . .

There were sirens now, and above the roofs of nearby buildings, the red flashing corona of police cars drawing closer. Finally, in an alley behind a dry-cleaning store on Figueroa Street, the pain became too much; he could go no farther. He slumped behind a low wall separating this store's parking lot from the next, he held his hand uselessly over the bleeding wound . . . and, soundlessly, he began to weep, and to pray: Jesus, oh Jesus, I'm *sorry,* I'm an idiot, I'm a thief, but please, let me *live*—I'll get it right, next time, I swear, just let me live, oh sweet Christ, just let me *live*—

Slowly, he became aware of something other than the pain in his stomach, or the throbbing in his ankle. He became aware of a growing warmth in his right hand . . . a soothing warmth that he soon felt, as well, in his wounded abdomen, a warmth that blotted out the pain. He looked up at his balled-up hand . . . and saw *light,* a pulsing white glow leaking out from between the fingers of his fist. Oh God, he thought. Was he dying? Don't you see white light when you die? He uncurled his fingers long enough to see the stone—no longer jade-green, no longer marbled, but white-hot, like the heart of a star—yet he felt no pain, no scorching heat, just . . . warmth. There, and in his stomach. Dazed, he closed his fist around the stone once more, not understanding but waiting until the warmth totally obliterated the pain; then he got to his feet and began running, still holding his side, still clutching the stone, afraid to let go of either. He ran strongly, as strongly as you can on a broken ankle, and within minutes he had made his way through the maze of alleys and side streets of downtown Los Angeles, losing himself amid the homeless who peopled its quiet corners.

When he was far enough away from the sirens and the police cars, he leaned up against a brick wall and, for the first time, looked down at himself. Slowly he took his hand away from the blood-soaked sweatshirt he was wearing; the warmth had dissipated, but the pain had not returned. He rolled up his shirt, steeling himself for what he was certain he would see—

And instead saw . . . nothing. No gaping bullet wound, no powder burns, no blood . . . just smooth, unbroken skin. As though he'd never been shot at all.

Stumbling half from disbelief and half from his swollen ankle, he made his way to a pay phone and fished in his pockets for a quarter to call Harry. Harry would come, and pick him up, and then he'd be safe. Harry was always there. Harry would always be there. He found the quarter, dropped it into the slot, and stabbed, a little dazedly, at the touchpad; and as the dial tone was cut off by the click of connection, Jackie exhaled a long breath—allowing himself to believe, at last, that he might live, after all . . .

Even the shadows of the sacred Tenan offered little relief from the blistering sun; Ta'li'n felt drained, light-headed, after his long ascent up the steep slopes of the valley. Or perhaps it was the sight of row upon row of failing crops, maize and beans and squash dying on the vine, that made him sway and teeter; he stopped, turned, and looked back down into the valley, seeing terrace upon terrace of irrigation canals lying parched and dry. For centuries Tenan, and the rain goddess, X'la'n, who dwelled within, had provided water to this thirsty land, these otherwise infertile slopes whose crops fed the hungry City below. X'la'n had shaped the volcanic mountain in such a way as to capture the rainfall, to channel it into a stream that fed the canals. The dwelling structure at the valley floor—home to the hundreds of farmers who tilled this land, and the priests who administered them—was adorned with a brightly painted façade, nearly all the bas-relief statues carved in the squat likeness of the water goddess. The correct rituals were still performed each day, the just and proper offerings made in Her honor; but the canals were still dry, and the sound of the river that ran inside the mountain—once a constant, mighty rumble—was now just a thin whisper on the wind.

One of the administrator-priests from the dwelling below drew abreast of Ta'li'n; he had followed at a respectful distance, and now stood beside his superior and offered him a small jade figurine in the shape of the goddess. The high priest closed his eyes, wrapped his hands around the small carved devotion, and prayed.

He stood, motionless, silent, for a full minute—until a brief cooling around him caused him to open his eyes. He looked up; a gray storm cloud pressed low over the valley, blocking the sun, so near it seemed to touch Tenan itself. For a brief moment the priest allowed himself to hope, and, hoping, closed his eyes once more, hands tighter around the talisman as he continued his prayer. It seemed like hours before the first raindrops, carried on the southerly breeze, brushed his face; he opened his eyes again—but far from feeling joy at the light mist that had fanned across the valley, he felt only misery. He had conjured similar mist before, with this talisman, once even a steady rain that had lasted nearly twenty minutes—but what he had been praying for was a cloudburst, a downpour that would split the skies with thunder and fill Tenan, and the canals, with water. He had prayed that the crops might be restored, the exodus from the starving city halted, the unrest within it quelled. And instead he received a light mist which was passing even now . . . the storm cloud dissipating in the hot, dry wind, exposing the brutal sun.

He had prayed, yet known his prayers would be fruitless: he had seen the future, and it contained neither rain nor food—merely ash and flame. The other priest had observed such failures before; he looked respectfully away, to the west, where the sun was falling into the abyss from which it climbed, triumphant, every morning.

"I shall take this," Ta'li'n announced suddenly, weighing the jade figurine in his hand, "back to the temple, where I might consult the Tonalpohialli." It was a lie—the Tonalpohialli, which the high priests used to predict the coming cycle, had yielded the same bleak answers as the peyote—but a convincing one. "As you wish," the administrator said hopefully—then turned and headed down the terraced slopes, to carry a glimmer of false hope back to his fellows.

Ta'li'n hefted the small devotion. The talisman still worked, up to a point; the power vested in it by the gods still lingered. But it, and the two or three others like it used so successfully over the centuries, possessed not nearly enough power to replenish the barren canals. Only the gods, working through the talismans, could do that.

He turned and looked down at the City; the Great Compound was crowded not just with merchants and traders, but pilgrims drawn to the City's great shrines—hundreds of them making the journey each year, to worship and to honor. They called the City "the home of the gods"— would continue to call it that, the priest knew, even in its nameless future—and yet—

And yet there were other cities—Oaxaca, Xochicalco, El Tajin—and other cultures—the Zapotecs to the west, the Mayans along the Gulf, even the warlike Toltecs to the north—rising in ascendancy across the continent. Was it possible—could it be that—

The priest shivered, despite the oppressive heat.

Could the gods have found another home?

Harry Faulk was an owlish man in his late fifties, with thinning brown hair, watery eyes set deep beneath arched eyebrows, and a cast to his face that made it seem as though he were always frowning: as though gravity and age had permanently turned down the corners of his mouth, making the creases and wrinkles of his face look forever disapproving, or cynical. Certainly he was frowning when he picked up Jackie at the corner of Figueroa and Temple; he helped the younger man, who could barely take a step without pain, into the car, then looked at him—at the ankle swollen to the size of a grapefruit—and sighed heavily. "We'll stop at a 7-Eleven," he said, shifting the gears of his dilapidated Oldsmobile, "and pick up some ice for that ankle." He turned his gaze to the road as he swung left onto Temple, toward the Harbor Freeway. "But first let's put a little distance between you and wherever you were." The car swung onto the freeway on-ramp, and Jackie felt himself relax, at last, as the Olds merged into the anonymous stream of cars heading north on the 110, carrying him safely and forever away from police cars, from flashing lights, from gunshots in the dark.

Jackie told him where he'd been and what had happened—omitting the gunshot and the wound, the bloody traces of which couldn't be seen in the dimness of the car; omitting, too, the aftermath, the stone, the healing—and Harry's face grew even more disapproving than usual. "Christ," he said in disgust. "How many times have I told you, museums aren't worth the trouble. Half the stuff's too big to carry and the other half's too hard to move once you've boosted it." Just ahead, the Harbor split in two, on the left becoming the Pasadena Freeway, on the right, the Hollywood. Harry veered to the right.

"No more museums," Jackie promised distantly. His hand, hidden from Harry's view, still clutched the stone, no longer white, no longer warm—a deceptively cool, green stone. He wondered how he would tell Harry about it, and what had happened back in the alley. Harry would never believe it—he could hardly blame him for that—but there had never been any secrets between the two of them, and Jackie was not going to start now, not when he'd been given this second chance . . . a chance he wanted desperately to share with his friend.

Harry Faulk was the closest thing to a father Jackie had ever known; his own father was a dream, a memory of beard stubble and big, callused hands holding his son aloft—a lingering scent of after-shave or cologne, and that was all. He had left when Jackie was four, and to this day, Jackie could not recall his face. Jackie and Faulk had first met, briefly, ten years ago, back when Jackie was a runner for Joseph Rubello; three years later, Jackie found himself sharing a cell with Harry at Vacaville, the younger man serving ten months for burglary; the older, a year and a half for mail-order fraud. When Harry got out, Jackie found him a cheap one-bedroom in the two-story, yellow stucco courtyard apartments on Fountain, off Highland Boulevard in Hollywood, where Jackie had already taken up residence. Since then, they'd executed a succession of seldom risky but only marginally profitable swindles, scams, and the occasional burglary—usually enough to pay for food and rent, but not

much more. And on their sporadic solo efforts—like Jackie's, tonight—
there was an unvoiced, unwritten understanding between them: if either
made that big score first, he would cut the other in.

Harry took the Highland exit off the freeway and headed toward a
convenience store a few blocks north of Hollywood and Highland. He
dug in his pocket for change. "I got a buck in here for some ice," he
began. "I'll stop and—"

"Forget the ice," Jackie said suddenly. It had just occurred to him
how he would convince Harry of all that had happened this night. "I
won't need it."

"What the hell's wrong with you?" Harry said. "You got an ankle
the size of an emerging nation, you might've broken it—"

"I did break it," Jackie said. "I felt the bone snap."

"Then we get you some ice, take you to an emergency room and get
that taped or splinted or whatever the hell they do, and—"

"I *won't need it,* Harry," he insisted doggedly. Somehow Jackie convinced him that he wasn't in shock, wasn't delirious or drunk or stoned,
and got him to take him not to the nearest hospital, but home—finally
by lying, by telling him that the security guard at the museum saw him
hobble away and that showing up at an ER with a broken ankle might
not be such a good idea just now. "Okay," Harry allowed. "We'll wait
till tomorrow, find a private doctor. But we still stop for some ice."

Back in Jackie Thompson's bleak little single apartment, with its
scuffed linoleum floors and its foam rubber couch that doubled for a bed,
Harry Faulk watched as the young man showed him the green marbled
stone he had stolen; watched as Jackie closed his fingers around it, then
cupped his other hand around his broken, swollen ankle; watched as light
spilled out from between the fingers of Jackie's fist, and as the swelling
began to perceptibly shrink before his eyes. He stood, transfixed, as
Jackie, eyes shut, seemed to concentrate . . . seemed to *will* the swelling
smaller and smaller . . . until, finally, the white light faded, Jackie took
his hand away from his foot . . . and Harry stood staring in awe and
disbelief at the perfectly normal, unbruised, unswollen ankle. Jackie
stood up and grinned; not only could he stand without support, he even
danced a few giddy tap steps, to Harry's utter astonishment.

"Jackie . . . how in the *hell*—"

Jackie told him, then; all of it. And now, no longer in the concealing
darkness of the car, Harry could see Jackie's bloodsoaked sweatshirt,
which rolled up to reveal absolutely nothing—nothing, certainly, to account for the dark, mottled stain on Jackie's shirt. And Harry began to
believe. Not in the way Jackie believed, but the power of the stone, that
he began to accept. He asked if he could hold it a moment, and as he
turned the stone over in his hand, staring at it in wonder and dawning
realization, he said softly, "My God, Jackie. You realize how much
something like this is *worth?* We could have every goddamn hospital and

research center in the country down on their *knees* for this—we could set our own *price—''*

"No," Jackie said, with a steel and a suddenness that surprised him as much as it did Harry, who looked up, startled. Jackie lowered his voice. "I struck a . . . a deal, back in that alley. To . . . change . . . if I got out of there alive.''

"A *deal*?'' Harry said derisively. "With who? God?''

"Maybe,'' Jackie said. "Why not?''

Faulk sighed, seeing his friend's determination, and backed off.

"Okay. Fine,'' he said. "No more burglaries. No more scams. Man, we won't *need* any of that penny-ante shit if we sell this. Look: it's simple. We find some doctor with a Beverly Hills address to front for us, he brokers the rock and gets a commission; by the time the buyers find out it's stolen property, they won't care. They'll hush it up, and we'll be set for life.''

"If they hush it up, they won't go public on it, and it won't reach the people it needs to reach,'' Jackie said adamantly. "They'll keep it to themselves, Harry. They'll test it, and X-ray it, try to figure out ways to duplicate it—and if that doesn't work, they'll keep it to themselves and use it to cure billionaires with lung cancer. That oughta be worth a new wing to the hospital, eh? Or how about Alzheimer's? Two wings and a parking structure. Maybe even—''

"So what the hell,'' Harry snapped, exasperated, "do *you* want to do with the damn thing?''

Jackie hesitated only a moment.

"I want to use it to heal people,'' he said quietly.

Harry stared at him in disbelief.

"Jesus H. Christ,'' he said softly.

Ta'li'n did not tell the other priest-rulers of his plan; they were too busy squabbling among themselves, arguing how best to appease the gods, how to put down the uprisings and nullify the proponents of the New Order. The dissension that was tearing apart the general populace had spread to its ruling elite, and Ta'li'n knew there was no way he could stitch the Council together any more than he could avert the coming catastrophe. So he set about on his own course, quietly procuring as many of the sacred talismans as he could, hoping to preserve, at least, some small part of his culture.

He secured the amulet of Pe'x'r, goddess of fertility, a necklace of polished obsidian chips strung on a fine gold strand; barren women wore the necklace for seven days and seven nights, and their husbands made love to them on the seventh and last night, planting the seed that invariably took root where none could grow before. He acquired, discreetly, the cloak of Ya'n'l, god of springtime, of renewal, a god known also in Oaxaca as Xipe Totec; at the spring rites, Ta'li'n often wore this cloak himself, helping to celebrate and honor the renewal of the land. And he obtained the small golden figurine of Qo't'l, the fat god, bringer of luck and prosperity, entrusted for times to families beset by death or ill omen: the small figure squatted on the hearth of the accursed family, speaking, it was said, in its own tongue to the spirits of misfortune that plagued the home, convincing the demons to move elsewhere.

Each of the relics and talismans still possessed the power invested in them at the time of their creation, when they were kissed by the breath of the gods on the hot, dry ceremonial platforms lining the central Avenue. Ta'li'n tested each one before he locked them away in a chest in his private chambers.

Pe'x'r, Ya'n'l, Qo't'l, X'l'o—all the major deities were represented, save for X'la'n, the plumed serpent, whose talismans were beyond even Ta'li'n's political authority; some of the more recent, and more sanguinary, additions to the pantheon like Za'd'e, god of the curved knife; and H'ue'na, god of medicine and health, healing and well-being. For this last talisman, the priest would have to seek out the healer, Ch'at'l—and for that reason he suspected that procuring this one would be almost as difficult as obtaining the serpent's. If not more so.

The Shrine Auditorium was packed to capacity tonight, as it was each night, three times a week; Jackie peered out from the wings, holding back the curtain to make the narrowest of slits through which to see the crowd. It never failed to amaze him, the size and the reverence of the audience, the low whispers in which they spoke, as though afraid to speak too loudly their hopes and hurts; and it never failed to frighten him, either, as he scanned the line of supplicants, noting their disabilities or deformities, wondering at those whose afflictions were not readily apparent, and realizing that they had come here to see *him*—that for most of them, he was their last best hope, their final recourse along a torturous path of pain and disappointment.

Tonight he saw three people in wheelchairs, one ravaged by the blight of Lou Gehrig's disease, the other two paralyzed from the neck down; behind them stood a small girl, thin, emaciated, with no hair, obviously the result of a chemotherapy or radiation treatment that had not worked; and half a dozen men and women with the gaunt, wasted look of AIDS victims. Jackie knew that for every one of these sufferers who would leave tonight weeping with joy at their miraculous recovery, there would be at least two who would leave disappointed, or buoyed with false hope; the stone was not, he had learned, infallible, and it was difficult to predict which ailment or which sufferer would be healed by it. To date, Jackie had failed to cure anyone of AIDS, and had only arrested, not eliminated, the growth of several cancers—turning malignant tumors to benign, and at least one case of leukemia into remission. Viral and neoplasmic diseases like these were most resistant to the stone's power; it had better luck dealing with simpler, though no less crippling, ailments, as though those were the ones it was originally designed to treat: bacterial infections, metabolic and nutritional diseases, "mechanical" trauma caused by physical injury—paralysis, muscular and skeletal damage. The stone could cure arthritis, but not MS; gangrene, but not, say, chemical poisoning . . .

Like that first day, six months ago; that first morning, in Lafayette Park, when a scared, nervous Jackie had shuffled into the park, stood on an outcropping of rock, and, the stone hidden in one hand, began calling out to the homeless people scattered—sleeping, eating, talking to one another or talking to themselves—around the park. "My name is John," he told them, using a name he had not heard since his mother died, years before, "and if you're hurting, I can help you." They thought he was a nutcase at first, of course, and ignored him—until one old woman, perhaps a quart low herself, stumbled up and asked if he could do anything for the bursitis in her left hip. Jackie gently put a hand to her hip—so tiny and frail, he was almost afraid to apply too much pressure—palmed the stone, keeping his hand behind him so no one might see the glow as he closed his eyes, trying to will this woman well again . . .

And succeeded. And then, all at once, it seemed, they were upon him: battered, hurting people with arthritis, or cataracts, or emphysema, and so busy was he in healing them that he didn't notice until an hour into his labors that there were now news cameras trained on him, videotape whirring away and a news van from Channel 11 parked on Wilshire Boulevard . . . brought there, Jackie later discovered, by an anonymous tip from Harry. He'd called all the local stations, and though the three network affiliates ignored him, independent KTTV had sent a team; as soon as the cameras started grinding, Harry was there, shepherding the supplicants as he would do on a much larger scale later on: "Brother John will see you all," he'd said, Jackie hearing the designation for the first time; "Wait your turn, sisters, brothers, wait your turn . . ."

Jackie wasn't comfortable with the title, nor with the religious trappings of all this—the Church of the Brotherhood, as they came to call it—but Harry had convinced him that it was the only way the public could accept what he was doing. It was probably the shrewdest move of Faulk's career: after the recent, bitter disappointments and breaches of trust by so many evangelists and faith healers, at the appearance of one who could actually *deliver*—one whose results were, in fact, verified by baffled physicians—people flocked to Brother John, happy to finally find one man of God worthy of their faith. And Jackie had to admit he liked it; for a man who had never in his life been treated with even the most minimal respect, this newfound adoration was . . . intoxicating.

"Jac—John?" Harry's voice, behind him. He turned, amused as always to see Harry looking so respectable in his smartly tailored gray three-piece suit. "Better get ready," Harry suggested. "We go to floor in five minutes."

Jackie nodded and went to his dressing room, where a petite young woman applied his makeup for him; before leaving, he checked himself in the mirror, impressed at the man he saw reflected back at him: his hair neatly trimmed, his tendency toward five-o'clock shadow even at noon artfully concealed by the makeup, his cream-colored suit impeccable and tasteful. For the first time in his life, he could look at himself without the slightest hint of self-disgust, without hearing that inner mocking voice harping at him, belittling him. For the first time in his life, he could actually feel proud—of himself, and of what he was doing.

"Brothers . . . sisters . . ." He could hear Harry, always and ever the advance man, warming up the crowd. ". . . If you think no one cares . . . if you think no one can help you . . . you're wrong."

Jackie left the dressing room, waiting in the wings as Harry finished his introduction, feeling a rush of excitement and anticipation as he listened. "We don't pretend to be infallible," Harry was saying reverently. "That's reserved for a higher power than ours. But we can try. We can try to take away the pain, and we hope you'll let us." A susurrus of voices from the crowd murmured eager agreement. Harry went on for a while longer, delivering the pious homilies and righteous platitudes the audience seemed to demand, finally concluding with, "My friends, I give you . . . Brother John."

A burst of heartfelt applause greeted Jackie upon his entrance; it never failed to move him, to expunge his doubts and get the adrenaline surging. As usual, Harry had handpicked the line of supplicants that stretched from the lip of the stage, up the aisle, to the back of the auditorium—there were only so many people they could treat in a two-hour telecast—with the simpler cases, the rheumatics, the deaf, the vision-impaired, up front. That way they led the hour with immediate and tangible successes, and by the second hour, they could afford the occasional failure or non-visible healing (cancer cures, being internal, didn't make for especially good television). Jackie disliked the artifice of it, but knowing the limitations of the stone, it was necessary . . . though Harry liked it, because the more dramatic the cure, the bigger the "love offerings" the next day, and Jackie was constantly fighting to keep the quieter, less showy sufferers on the bill at all.

The first person in line was a classic Faulk choice; yet the moment he saw her, Jackie could hardly fault Harry for it. She was a ten-year-old girl, with pretty green eyes and limp blond hair, sitting in a wheelchair; behind her, her mother hovered nervously, her eyes pathetically searching Jackie's face as he turned to them—a silent, desperate plea that Jackie had come to know only too well. He purposely averted his gaze from the mother, squatting down to look in the little girl's eyes; she looked self-conscious, embarrassed, but had none of her mother's reek of desperation.

"Hi," he said softly. His body mike picked up even the faintest of whispers and made them echo in the vast auditorium.

"Hello," the girl replied tentatively.

"I'm John. What's your name?"

"Amanda," the girl said with a shy smile.

"How long have you been in that chair, Amanda?" Jackie asked gently.

The mother answered for her: "Almost three years, Brother John. She was . . . hit by a car. They never did find the driver . . ."

Yes, of course. Multiple sclerosis, muscular dystrophy, they were more problematic; Jackie's success rate with them was low. Harry would never put one of them on first. Simple spinal break, that was better, more potentially dramatic. Jackie sighed inwardly. Right now, he didn't care; right now he just wanted to make this little girl well.

"The driver," he told the girl's mother, "will answer to God's judgment. All that concerns us here is Amanda." He reached up, one hand palming the green marbled stone, and laid his hands lightly on her legs. "Don't be afraid," he said, smiling. He slid one hand—the one clenching the stone—behind Amanda's back, touching her spinal column. The stone didn't have to be in contact with the afflicted area to function, but this served to hide its glow from the audience and the camera. They had decided, when they'd made the transition to television, that the glow would seem too phony, give skeptics a chance to claim they were just using fancy video effects—so Jackie either hid the stone, as he was doing now, or covered it with a black felt cloth inside his cupped hand, which damped the glow without diminishing the warmth, the power.

Jackie closed his eyes and began to concentrate. "Dear God," he said softly, "help this child. Help her walk again . . ." Harry was always trying to get him to make his speeches more flowery, more pious, but the words sounded unnatural to Jackie; *help me* or *help her* seemed sufficient for the occasion. He felt the stone growing hot in his hand, felt that warmth spreading through his clenched fingers, then beyond—

"Mommy," he heard the girl say, "it feels *hot*—"

"It does?" The mother's voice was full of hope. "Honey, are you sure?"

"God's love is warming her," came Harry's voice, booming and sententious. "Praise be!" The audience chanted in unison: *"Praise be!"* Jackie tried to ignore it, tried to concentrate on nothing but the task before him—for the briefest of instants he felt something shift, felt something seem to fall into place in Amanda's back, and then the stone began to cool. When the heat was totally dissipated, Jackie opened his eyes. He drew his hand from behind her back, pretending to wipe perspiration on his jacket, but in reality pocketing the stone; then he took the girl's hands in his, smiled, and began to stand. "Stand with me, honey," he said gently. "You can do it."

The girl came to her feet, tentatively . . . Jackie let go of her hands . . . and she stood. Unaided. The audience cheered. Amanda took a step forward, away from her wheelchair, a look of wonder and delight on her face. The audience roared. "Praise God!" Harry shouted. *"Praise God!"* the crowd bellowed back, filling the auditorium with their cheers. The mother embraced her daughter, and then the daughter, spontaneously, ran to Jackie, and hugged him round his waist. Jackie, genuinely moved and pleased, stroked the girl's hair—

Only to find Harry, a moment later, hustling the little girl and her mother offstage as quickly as possible, to make way for the next supplicant . . .

At the end of the evening, an exhausted Jackie left the stage to wild applause and exuberant cries: "We love you, Brother!" they shouted, and Jackie felt drained but happy, depleted but exultant. "Praise the Lord!" Then, finally, Harry took the podium to deliver his fund-raising pitch: "On behalf of Brother John, thank you for coming tonight. And those of you watching at home—won't you take a moment to count the blessings in your life, and perhaps share some of them with others? Anything you can give, to do the work He has charged us with, would be deeply appreciated. God bless you all, and good night."

That night and the next morning, the phones in the Church's small offices off Cahuenga Boulevard rang incessantly with credit card pledges, even as an overworked staff opened letters containing checks, money orders, dollar bills, and sometimes even pennies from a child's piggy bank.

Jackie had his misgivings about all this, but the fact was, it did cost money to rent the shrine, lease video equipment, hire technicians and, most expensive of all, purchase air time on the two hundred fifty TV stations across the country that carried the program. By now Harry and Jackie had moved from their dive on Fountain to a pair of pleasant town houses just above Sunset; to Jackie the modest condos were palaces, but Faulk, it developed, took a broader view.

The day after the broadcast, Harry drove his new white baby Mercedes down Sunset to an office building a few blocks east of Vine. It was a twenty-story, steel-and-glass tower, and Jackie thought they were going there to a restaurant, for lunch; but the elevator instead delivered them onto a deserted floor filled with empty offices, plush carpeting, and stacks of boxes containing what seemed to be personal computers, phone systems, and office equipment. "Welcome," Harry announced, "to the new headquarters of the Church of the Brotherhood."

Jackie's jaw dropped. He'd put all the financial dealings in Harry's hands, but *this*— "The whole *floor?*" he said, with quiet astonishment.

"Five floors," Harry corrected him, "and the penthouse. C'mon. Let's take a look at our new home."

Numbly, Jackie followed him to the three-thousand-square-foot pent-house that perched atop the tower. This was in better array than the offices downstairs; Jackie followed, dazed, as Harry led him through a home the like of which he had never imagined he'd see in his lifetime. There was a huge living room with a three-cornered, sixty-foot wall of windows overlooking the city: to the east, the mirrored facade of the Bonaventure Hotel, five glassy cylinders dwarfed by even higher struc-tures, gleamed in the afternoon haze; to the west, Beverly Hills sprawled lazily from Sunset to Pico, stands of palm trees marching down wide, immaculate streets; west of that, the sleek towers of Century City shim-mered in the heat and the smog, seeming, in tandem with the skyscrapers of downtown, to bracket the Basin.

Off the living room was a formal dining room already furnished with sleek Scandinavian tables, chairs, and hutch; beyond that, a state-of-the-art, fully equipped kitchen with three microwaves and a cooking island the size of Catalina; down a T-shaped corridor, a cluster of four bedroom suites. Harry's and Jackie's were at opposite ends of the corridor, each one enormous, with breathtaking city views, full baths, and small kitch-enettes off the bathrooms.

Jackie sank, stunned, onto the soft king-size bed in his room, but Harry grinned and pulled him to his feet. "Tour's not over yet," he said, leading Jackie to a private elevator that took them to the roof—and an Olympic-size swimming pool surrounded on all sides by majestic views of the city.

"Jesus, Harry," Jackie said softly. "We're not actually going to *live* here?"

"Why not? 'Appearances'? It's legitimate, we use five floors for office space, and the rest—hell, who's going to begrudge a few luxuries to a man who's helped so many people?"

Jackie felt uncomfortable; he didn't know whether he wanted to be convinced or not. "Why do we need so much money?" he asked. "Ninety percent of the people who contribute won't even be able to get on the show, just by sheer weight of numbers. Not that the stone could handle so many, anyway, but—"

"I'll give you one very good reason we need so much money, my friend," Harry said soberly. "You and I, we don't have the cleanest of slates in the world. You have any idea how many of our old pals from Vacaville have turned up lately? In need of funds?"

Jackie started. "You've been paying blackmail?"

"Pin money. Most of them are so stupid, they ask for a hundred thousand, I bargain them down to fifty, they go away happy. It's the reporters who're more savvy; they ask for more, and I have to deliver."

"Oh, shit, Harry, maybe we should forget this whole—"

"Don't be an idiot. This *was* your idea, wasn't it? *You* wanted to heal people, right?"

"Yeah, but—all this—it doesn't seem—"

"Fair?" Harry said. "For a man who's made cripples walk . . . made the blind see . . . the deaf hear? Why the hell shouldn't you have a few creature comforts? After all the shit-holes you've lived in, after all the good you've done in the last year—you're telling me you don't deserve a decent *home,* for the first time in your miserable life?"

Jackie wavered. In that moment of hesitation, Harry put a hand to his back, started walking him along the pool, the two of them taking in the city below. "Besides," he said, "I think we can eliminate the danger of extortion, with a little grease applied to the right wheels. Our records, our convictions, our downtime—the only place it really exists is in the state computers, right?"

Jackie began to see where this was going. "You want to bribe somebody to go in and wipe out our records? How the hell much will *that* cost?"

"Not as much as you'd think." Harry smiled. "I've done a little checking. Seems the deputy commissioner of prisons for the state of California has a wife, with cancer. Terminal. I think a deal could be struck . . ."

Jackie said nothing. He looked out across the dazzling blue swimming pool, toward downtown; from up here, that night in the alley—all the nights in all the alleys—seemed utterly remote. He felt safe. When was the last time he'd felt safe? He couldn't remember. He didn't care. Harry was talking about profit margins and satellite time and promotional items. He listened to Harry, he nodded, and he did not protest.

The healer lived in a dwelling identical to those of the majority of the City's inhabitants: single-story, white-walled buildings of adobe brick, each compound containing some thirty apartments clustered around a central atrium; there were no windows in any of the apartments, but no walls facing the center court either, only hanging curtains that most of the day remained open, admitting sunlight into the comfortable rooms. At the entrance to the compound, a doorkeeper greeted Ta'li'n with a solemn nod, respectfully stepping aside to let him pass. The laughter of children carried out on a gust of wind, and the priest felt a twinge of pain, knowing how soon that laughter was to end.

Most courtyards had at their center a small brick temple, a miniature of the ones atop the great pyramids, each one adorned with the likeness or symbols of a particular god; this one, understandably enough, was an altar to H'ue'na, god of medicine. Around the fringes of the atrium, small children chased one another, laughed and giggled; at the priest's approach, they hushed momentarily, but as he made his way to Ch'at'l's apartment, they quickly resumed their games.

Outside the healer's room—its curtain drawn, for the moment—some half a dozen people lingered in a casual line, each injured in some way, or visibly ill. Ta'li'n hesitated, weighing the extent of their afflictions; but told himself he could not let that sway him. He pushed aside the curtain and entered the healer's apartment.

Ch'at'l was seated on a pillow in the middle of the sparsely furnished room, eyes closed in concentration, his left hand on the stomach of a woman who looked to be about five months pregnant. The room was lit only by candlelight, but even in the dimness the priest could see a distinctive glow—a pure, white, pulsing light that spilled out from between the fingers of the healer's right hand. He seemed not to notice Ta'li'n's entrance, or if he did, paid it no mind. The priest kept a respectful silence, watching the old man for some moments, then letting his gaze drift to the bright frescoes painted on the plaster walls: pictures of running children, laughing women, crying infants, strong and vibrant men. Ta'li'n had almost forgotten how uniquely beautiful the healer's quarters were; each apartment was adorned with similar murals, but Ch'at'l's burst with life and health and light, even in this semidarkness.

After several minutes the glow in Ch'at'l's hand subsided, and the healer opened his eyes and nodded with satisfaction. "The child will be fine," he told the woman, who exhaled a long breath of relief. "The birth canal was twisted; askew. It is repaired. The birth will occur, now, unimpeded."

The woman hugged him gratefully, and as they stood, Ta'li'n saw how small the old man was—perhaps five feet tall, with browned, leathery skin taut over a brittle skeleton. If height were a measure of authority, Ta'li'n would have had no problem fulfilling his task. But not even the authority vested in him by his robes was sufficient to intimidate this frail old man.

The woman left the room, and only then did Ch'at'l look up to greet his visitor. "Most Holy. Good day," he said, with deceptive humility. "Is there an ailment that plagues you? How may I help?"

Ta'li'n found himself straightening, mustering as much authority as he was able. "No ailment," he said. "I—have need of the stone."

The old man blinked his large, black eyes, eyes set deep in a lined and furrowed face; his bald head seemed somehow too large for his frail body. "I do not understand," he said, but something in his tone made the priest feel that he did understand, that he was somehow expecting this. "If there is no ailment, why then do you have need of the stone?"

"The Council," Ta'li'n lied, "requires it for a ceremony. It will be returned to you when we are done."

"I am not to join in this . . . ceremony?"

"No."

The healer looked at him with those black, penetrating eyes. "I have been entrusted with this stone," he said quietly, opening his hand to reveal the green marbled stone in his palm, "for over sixty years, and not once has it left my sight.'' He met the priest's gaze evenly. ''I do not take my trust lightly.''

''No. No, of course not,'' Ta'li'n said quickly. ''But it is but for a short while, and will be returned to you as soon as—'' he groped for a convincing falsehood ''—as soon as we are able,'' he concluded lamely.

''But what of those in need of it?'' the healer asked, nodding toward outside, toward the waiting line of ill and injured. ''How long must they suffer?''

Ta'li'n was growing more frustrated and impatient. Damn the old man for his stubbornness. ''It is not our intent that *anyone* suffer,'' he said, taking a step forward, raising his voice, ''but we *must* have the stone. You are directed to give it to me, in the name of—''

The old man took a step forward, raising his hand in a placating gesture before the priest could invoke any deities. ''High One—please,'' he said quietly. ''I know why you need it. You need not dissemble.''

Ta'li'n bristled at the old man's impiety, accurate though it was. ''How dare you suggest that I—''

''You are not the only one,'' Ch'at'l said simply, ''to whom the peyote sings its sad chorale.''

Ta'li'n started. The healer moved slowly to a table crowded with urns and bottles, all filled with various herbs and roots; he took the lid off one jade bottle, drawing out a small white mescal cap. Ta'li'n stared at it, in disbelief. The old man hobbled toward him, the tiny white cap held aloft on the tip of one small, bony finger. He smiled.

''Teotihuacán,'' he said, and the priest flinched, as though at an insect's bite. ''That is what they will call us, in the time to come, is it not?''

The priest nodded, dully, taken completely off guard. The healer smiled again, but there was no trace of mockery in it, just a gentle reassurance. ''I know what is to come,'' he said, ''and I know what you are trying to do. And when the time is right, I shall give you the stone. But in the meantime, there are many ailments to be seen to, and many sufferings to be eased.''

Ta'li'n frowned ruefully. ''Only to die,'' he said, in a low voice, ''along with the City.''

''Not all of them,'' Ch'at'l said. ''The City will die, but many will escape. Who can say that a fractured bone I repair today will not carry a man out of the City? With perhaps a woman, or a child, in his arms?''

Ta'li'n hesitated, but the healer put a hand reassuringly on his arm. ''When the time comes,'' he said again, ''it will be yours. I promise.'' A hint of mischief gleamed in Ch'at'l's eyes. ''Or don't you trust me?''

The priest smiled, for perhaps the first time in days. ''After sixty years,'' he sighed, bemusedly, ''who am I to begin to doubt?''

The old man laughed, then hobbled over to draw back the curtain and admit his next patient.

* * *

The wife of the deputy commissioner of prisons had a malignant tumor in her left lung, and according to the latest magnetic resonance scan, the cancer had begun to metastasize to her right lung and upper colon. Despite his worries over the stone's spotty success in dealing with cancers, Jackie did his best, half out of concern for the woman—she was only forty-one but looked nearly sixty; drawn, haggard, wearing an obvious wig to hide the effects of chemo and radiation treatments—and half out of concern for himself, and Harry. If this worked, they would be beyond blackmail; if it failed, who was to say that the commissioner himself might not expose them, out of bitterness and disappointment? Jackie did his usual number, the stone covered in black cloth to hide the glow, did the laying on of hands, and, for the next three days, waited anxiously for the results of new tests from Cedars-Sinai.

On the morning of that Friday's taping, the word came in from Cedars: the growth of the tumor in the left lung had been arrested, and the cancer in the right lung and colon had similarly been halted. She wasn't cured, but she was in remission—and that was enough for her grateful husband. Within twenty-four hours, all traces of Faulk's and Thompson's criminal records—arrests, convictions, detentions—had been expunged, neatly, from the state computer system.

Jackie was surprised at the extent of relief he felt upon hearing the news; amazed at the sense of freedom it brought him. Even before Harry had told him about the extortion, a part of him had worried, every time he stepped onto that stage, that someone, anyone, everyone, would see through the neatly tailored suit and the salon-trimmed hair, to the frightened second-story man beneath. Now he went onstage and felt only confidence, and pride, when the crowd cheered at his entrance, or when he made a lame girl walk, or a deaf man hear. He was growing to like that sound, the applause and adulation, more and more—

And, conversely, coming to hate the awkward silence and unspoken disappointment when it *didn't* work—when the young man with MS *didn't* get up from his wheelchair and dance a little jig, when the AIDS victim's sores did not heal on the spot, and the emphysema sufferer failed to stop coughing and gasping for air. Jackie came to hate those moments, wanted less and less to hear that disillusioned silence and more and more the cheers and approbation.

So when Harry decided to allow no more AIDS victims on the broadcast, Jackie readily agreed. When Harry continued to front-load the program with simpler afflictions that made for more dramatic cures, Jackie no longer objected. And when Faulk began screening the supplicants more carefully, weeding out the cancer and leukemia sufferers—not because there was no chance at saving them, but because even if they were cured, it was impossible to see on the spot, because it didn't make for good *television*—Jackie kept his silence. They still took on the occasional private patient with cancer, of course, and when the results were positive, trumpeted them to the press; the failures were smoothed over with large monetary donations to the deceased's family. Tax-deductible.

The streamlined program was cut to ninety minutes but broadcast, via satellite now, four times a week instead of three; the net effect was approximately the same number of people healed, but an increase in profit margin. The Church of the Brotherhood quickly expanded to fill all five floors that Faulk had rented; donations increased by 55 percent over the next six months, bringing in an average of $115 million a year; competing evangelists chafed over the inroads the Church had made into their congregations, and at their inability to find any kind of sex or embezzlement scandals to discredit and dethrone the new king of tele-vangelism.

Harry was very careful not to give them any ammunition, either. Brother John's penthouse home was expensively, but not opulently, furnished; most of the luxuries in which Jackie indulged himself could reasonably be called deductible: state-of-the-art video and audio equipment, spa and gym facilities (how could Brother John be expected to heal others if he didn't take care of his own body?), and an abundance of foods Jackie had never had the money to even taste before (with Faulk always careful to donate a fraction of what they spent on food for themselves to some charity for the homeless and hungry). Compared to many evan-gelists' self-styled Disneylands, it all seemed positively modest.

As for women, Harry screened the supplicants very carefully for potential entertainment purposes: disfigured or crippled women were especially grateful when John's healing touch wiped away the scars that had made them feel like pariahs, or reawakened feeling in parts of their bodies long numb with paralysis. Such women were uncommonly thankful and loyal, and unlikely to sell their stories to the *Enquirer*—especially after being feted and gifted with jewelry, clothes, and cars.

Jackie no longer asked why they needed to make so much money. Jackie no longer asked any questions, to speak of. He was content to revel in the love and applause of the audience, and in the comforts which that love provided. He was still doing good, after all—wasn't he? And wasn't that what mattered, in the end?

They were going over last-minute scheduling details for that evening's telecast when the intercom in Jackie's inner office buzzed. "Brother John?" came his secretary's voice, rich and mellow. "There's someone here to see you. He doesn't have an appointment, but he says his name is—Joseph Rubello?"

Jackie exchanged a quick, startled look with Harry.

"Son of a bitch," said Faulk, a nasty smile coming to him, slowly. "You going to see him?"

Jackie considered a moment, then smiled back.

"Why not?" he allowed generously. But when his finger toggled the intercom, there were the beginnings of a satisfied, and not altogether pleasant, smile on his lips. "Send him in, Bobbi," he said, settling in behind his wide teakwood desk; Harry perched on the arm of a sofa across the room, looking like an owl about to watch a kill from the safety of a tree limb.

Bobbi ushered Rubello into the inner office, then discreetly shut the door behind her; Jackie rose from his seat and extended a hand to the visitor. Twenty years ago, in his prime, Joseph Rubello was a physically powerful man, broad, square-shouldered, barrel-chested; even now, in his late fifties, with more fat than muscle, his was still a commanding presence, though one tempered by age, infirmity, and . . . something else. Something that Jackie had never seen in him before; something like fear.

"Jackie," he said with a near-genuine heartiness; his grip was weaker than Jackie remembered it—not that Rubello had ever had much call to shake Jackie's hands before. "Good to see you. *Really* good . . ."

"Been a while, hasn't it, Joe," Jackie agreed. He had never called him "Joe" before; if the old man was affronted, he didn't show it.

"Yeah, must be, what, five, six years . . . ?"

"Eleven," Jackie said evenly. "Last I heard from you, your thugs put me in the hospital for botching a delivery for you. You sent flowers and a card. Thoughtful as hell."

Rubello paled, then laughed nervously.

"Hey . . . Jackie. That's history. I mean, c'mon, eleven years; you're not gonna hold that against me, are you?"

"John," said the younger man, suddenly.

"What?"

"It's John. My name is John now. Not Jackie."

"Oh. Sure. John." Rubello glanced appreciatively around Jackie's office. "Sweet little place you've got here."

He wasn't here for blackmail, that much Jackie was certain of; his demeanor would be entirely different. And surely, with his contacts, Rubello knew that digging up evidence for extortion would be nearly impossible now. That left only one possible reason for this visit.

"Something I can . . . do . . . for you, Joe?" Jackie asked quietly.

Rubello looked him square in the eye, and Jackie saw not just that glimmer of fear again, but the sweet complement of desperation, and need. "You . . . you really can do what they say?" he said. "It's not some kind of scam?"

Jackie smiled. He nodded.

"I can do it," he said. Then, with a trace of amusement in his voice: "What is it, Joe? Cancer? All those Honduran cigars catching up with you?"

Rubello hesitated—Jackie could almost see the struggle inside him, his dignity warring with his desperation—then took a short breath and shook his head. "Atherosclerosis," he said. "I had quadruple bypass surgery last year, cleared out two of the arteries, but I—" He winced slightly. "I had another heart attack, six months ago. Nearly died. Just a matter of time till the next one."

"All that high living and rich food, eh, Joe?" Faulk said speaking for the first time. Rubello glanced at him, a flicker of disgust crossing his face, then quickly gone as he nodded tightly. "Yeah," he said, swallowing his pride. "I guess so."

Jackie breathed a silent sigh of relief. Just an excess of fat cells clogging his arteries and blood vessels; a nutritional disease, not a viral one, nothing the stone couldn't tackle handily. Rubello turned from Faulk, looked pleadingly at Jackie.

"Ja—John," he said quietly. "Please. Anything you want, just name it. A blank check. Hundred, two hundred thousand dollars . . . whatever it takes, it's yours."

But Jackie stood his ground, voice flat, gaze cold as he stared at the older man.

"You treated me like shit, Joe. Like you treated all your runners. Like you treat everybody. And now you want me to cure you . . . give you another ten, twenty years to go *on* treating people like shit?" Jackie shook his head, started out from behind his desk with a quick nod to Faulk. "C'mon, Harry. We tape in another couple of—"

Rubello blocked his path, as Jackie knew he would. His lower lip trembled with rage and fear; his voice was disdainful and imploring at the same time. "What do you want me to do, Jackie? 'Scuse me—*John.* You want me to beg?"

Jackie gave him a chill smile. "That'd be nice."

There was a long pause, then Rubello nodded once and said, "Okay. Revenge. I can understand that. Maybe I'd do the same thing. Maybe I deserve it. Okay, Jackie—I'm *begging* you. Help me. You want me to get down on my knees? I'll do it. I don't care. I want to *live.*"

Jackie considered a long moment, then nodded with satisfaction.

"Okay, Joe," he said offhandedly. "That's fine. That, and, say, one million, ought to do it."

Rubello paled. "One *million?* Are you out of your—"

"Price just went up. One million five."

"Jackie, for God's sake—"

"Two million. I've got overhead, Joe, serious overhead."

At that, finally, Rubello caved in; the resistance seemed to leave him in a rush, like air from a slashed tire. "All right," he said, hoarsely. "Two million. Just *do* it, goddammit. *Do it!*"

Jackie smiled with satisfaction. "Sit down," he said, nodding toward the chair opposite Jackie's desk; while Rubello's face was turned, Jackie palmed the stone, wrapped in its black velvet cocoon, then went to Rubello, put his other hand over the old man's heart, and closed his eyes.

The stone became warm in Jackie's hand—but not very. Something was wrong; it was far cooler than it should have been, cooler than Jackie had yet felt it. The last several weeks, he'd noticed, the stone's heat had been gradually lessening, but he'd attributed that to overuse—had deliberately skipped the taping before tonight's, in fact, to give it a rest. But now he saw that it had not helped. It felt about as warm as a cup of tea, rapidly cooling to room temperature.

He didn't tell Rubello this, of course; and a day later, when Rubello called, joyously, to tell him that the latest blood tests showed an actual *decrease* in the number of fat cells in his system, he graciously accepted the mobster's thanks, as well as the two-million-dollar "love offering" that was messengered over that afternoon.

But all through the taping the night before, Jackie had felt the stone growing less and less warm . . . until, halfway through the program, he surreptitiously ditched the velvet cloak, thinking that perhaps that was inhibiting the stone's powers, and risked using it in his bare hand, risked exposing that glow. But there *was* no glow, to speak of; only a faint glimmer of light that people onstage could easily have mistaken for stage lights, and which was too dim to be picked up by the TV cameras.

Two weeks later, Jackie opened his morning paper to find a grainy photo of Joseph Rubello staring up at him beneath a twenty-point headline reading *Reputed Mafia Chieftain Dead of Heart Attack.*

One day later, a pale and shaken Harry Faulk entered Jackie's inner office and announced, shakily, that the wife of the deputy commissioner of prisons had died the night before, of lung cancer.

The end, when it came, came quicker than Ta'li'n could have imagined; for all his prescience, it caught him unawares, and threatened to unravel his carefully woven plans.

He had known the final conflagration would occur sometime that spring, but had not guessed that it would arrive on the very first day, in the very middle of the Rites of Renewal. He himself stood on the main ceremonial platform in the middle of the Avenue of the Dead; he himself wore the cloak of Ya'n'l and spoke the sacred words of celebration and rebirth, all the while gazing out at the parched and blistered valley of Tenan, his own voice ringing hollow in his ears. He did not notice until he looked down that a fight had erupted in the crowded street; he watched with horror as combatant pushed combatant, as attackers jostled onlookers, drawing them into the melee—as the violence rippled across the face of the crowd until the congregation had become a mob, and the ceremony a riot. Ta'li'n tried to continue, tried to shout the ritual words over the din of battle, but from deep inside the fray came a chant that drowned him out: *The old gods are dead. The old gods are dead!* The Priests' Guards were pushing into the crowd, shields and atlatls raised, trying to separate the combatants, but succeeding only in being forced into the fight themselves as daggers, spears, and knives were thrust at them.

"*Stop it,*" Ta'li'n shouted, trying to make himself heard above the din, "*stop—*"

Suddenly one of the fighters—a boy of no more than nineteen—launched himself at the ceremonial platform, scrambling up its wooden foundation, screaming obscenities at the priest. Another young man joined him; they hoisted themselves up onto the platform, blood in their eyes, the priest the object of their imminent violence—

But a contingent of Guards had already surrounded Ta'li'n and was hurrying him down the steps to safety, even as other Guards battled the rebels who had desecrated the platform. The phalanx of soldiers surrounding Ta'li'n pushed their way through the crowd, rectangular shields warding off the thrust of daggers and knives, forging safe passage; dazed, stunned, and despairing, the priest saw that nearly everyone in the crowd was now armed—daggers, obsidian blades, atlatls—and in the distance he could see the first awful flicker of torches being lit . . .

The Guards were steering him toward what they believed to be the sanctuary of the temple atop the Pyramid of the Sun, but the priest commanded them otherwise: "Not the temple. Take me to Ch'at'l. Take me now!"

They protested, but he insisted; and soon he found himself back at Ch'at'l's apartment compound, only this time no doorkeeper greeted him, and inside, in the central court, the laughter of children had been replaced with the moans of the injured, or dying: dozens of wounded lay bleeding on the tile floor, or sat hunched in corners, holding themselves and whispering soft prayers. Ta'li'n had not fully comprehended the extent of the riot, the depth of its violence, until this moment; the injured looked up at his entrance, reaching out to him as though the gods' power would pass from him into them, healing their wounds—but aside from the priest's murmured prayers and words of comfort for them, the only significant mark of his passage through the atrium was the bloody streaks staining his stark white robes. He was helpless to aid them; and now, he knew, he was about to take away the one thing that *might* . . .

He entered the healer's quarters and drew a short breath of surprise: it, too, was crowded with injured people. Ch'at'l was at the far end of the room, kneeling beside a semiconscious young woman; he was force-feeding her a liquid Ta'li'n recognized as an herbal remedy for concussion. Cries of pain were a constant background noise, but even the quiet rustling of the curtains caught Ch'at'l's attention; he looked over, saw the priest standing awkwardly in the middle of the room, and without hesitation, nodded toward a young man with a bleeding wound in the chest. "Tend to him," he said, pressing the priest into service. "I must keep this woman conscious, but his wounds are just as severe."

"How—?" Ta'li'n began—and was startled when the healer pressed the green marble stone into his palm, then half pushed the priest toward the injured man.

"You have used it before," Ch'at'l said, returning to the young woman.

"Yes," Ta'li'n said, albeit uncertainly. When first initiated into the holy order, Ta'li'n had learned how to use all the charms and talismans of the gods—but as he'd risen into the ranks of the priest-rulers, such practice grew less and less frequent. He prayed to X'l'o that he still remembered how. He knelt beside the young man, grasping the stone in one hand, placing his other on the gaping chest wound—

And recognized the injured man—*boy*—as one of the rebels who had incited today's riot . . . one of the proponents of the New, the one who had tried, dagger in hand, to climb the ceremonial platform and attack Ta'li'n. The priest paled, trying to ignore the tangle of conflicting emotions he felt, and shut his eyes. He concentrated on healing the wound, on stanching the flow of blood; he tried to visualize arteries mending, blood vessels closing, slashed flesh knitting together—

But the stone was not getting warmer, as he knew it should have been. He redoubled his efforts, but the stone remained cold in his fist. *Fist.* Yes. That was the problem, wasn't it? He opened his eyes and saw that the young man's wound was still bleeding profusely; he had had no effect on it whatsoever. And then he felt someone brushing him aside, prying the stone from his stiff fingers.

Ch'at'l took the stone from the priest, placed his hand on the young man's chest, and shook his head. "The eye cannot heal," the old man said, without apparent rancor, "what the heart cannot see."

Ta'li'n watched as the stone began to glow white-hot in the healer's hands. He lowered his gaze. "Were I truly the holy man I profess to be," the priest said, ashamed, "I would be able to care for my enemies as I do for my fellows."

But Ch'at'l merely shook his head. "You are a man," he said, with no recrimination. "All men have their limits." He took his hand away from the rebel's chest, and Ta'li'n saw that the blood had stopped and the wound had begun to heal. But the healer did not seem particularly happy; he looked around the crowded room, at the suffering and the injured, with great sad eyes. "Even as I," he said softly, "have *my* limits . . ."

"No one can heal an entire city," Ta'li'n said gently, "dying like a frightened beast in the night."

The old man looked up at him, his eyes now veiled. "The time has come?"

Ta'li'n nodded, silently.

The healer hesitated only a moment, then, with a quick nod, put the stone back into the priest's hand—standing up as he did. "Go," he said, returning to the young woman and her herbal medicine. "Save what you can . . . while I save what *I* can."

Ta'li'n turned and left, his guards enclosing him as they left the compound. In the street people chased and stoned one another, fought one another with sling and dagger and atlatl; they bellowed with rage, cried out in mortal pain, giggled with manic laughter. In the east, Ta'li'n saw the first hot lick of flame appear from behind the Butterfly Palace. He told his guards to hurry, praying that there was still time—praying to gods who seemed no longer to be listening.

Jackie could feel the stone growing colder and colder with each successive use. Harry was now weeding out all but the simplest, most easily cured ailments from the program: they were reduced to mending broken arms and compressed disks, torn tendons and sprained ankles. And as the more serious and more dramatic cases were shunted off the air, revenues began to dip—not much, at first, but by the end of the week, contributions had dropped by 15 percent.

At the same time, people whom Jackie had "healed" within the last few months began to appear, their injuries and illnesses abruptly returned, at the Church of the Brotherhood's Hollywood headquarters. Some were desperate, some were pleading; most became angry, and indignant, when staffers turned them away and told them there was nothing Brother John could do for them. Hurt, betrayed, they took their complaints to the press. Among these were several women whom either Jackie or Faulk had slept with after being "cured"—and who, their ailments or injuries returned, were eagerly selling their exclusive stories to the *Star* or the *Enquirer.*

Donations plunged by another 35 percent.

The first hard news story about Brother John's and Brother Faulk's prison records broke in the L.A. *Times* a few days later. The reporter, Marnie Eilers, detailed in depth Jackie's history as a second-story man, his conviction for burglary, and Harry's multiple convictions for mail fraud and passing counterfeit money. Apparently the deputy commissioner of prisons had had the presence of mind to retain a copy of the data when he had wiped the state's mainframe clean—though he'd covered his tracks well enough not to have been caught doing it. One minute the information wasn't there; the next, it was. As quickly as it had been initially expunged.

"Love offerings" bottomed out to nothing.

Harry laid off most of the Church staff and was scrambling to liquidate whatever assets he could—Rubello's "family" was demanding restitution of their two million dollars, alternately payable in blood—when the bunco squad sought and obtained a court injunction freezing the Church's bank account pending investigation of "improprieties." The time had come, Faulk decided, to pack up, cut their losses, and get the hell out of the country before either the IRS or their moral counterpart, the mob, got to them.

Jackie, leaving the building on Sunset for the last time, had to push his way through a crowd of ill and injured, people whose faces he vaguely recalled but for whom he felt nothing; all he felt was fear and disbelief, stunned astonishment that it had all fallen apart so quickly, so completely. Harry was a few steps ahead, trying to clear a path. "Please—let us through, just let us—"

"Brother John—please—"

"Brother—help me—"

"—you son of a bitch, you *promised,* you—"

"Oh God, Brother, help my boy, you helped him once—"

Jackie looked up and saw a mother, arms wrapped protectively around an eight-year-old boy. He recognized the boy, dimly, as a mute he'd given voice to, only—what? Two months ago? The last of those whom Jackie had truly, even in part, cared about . . . or the first of those for whom he had not. He felt a stab of guilt, of shame—

The mother stepped in front of him, blocking his path. "Brother John—please—"

"I *can't help* you!" he cried out, in anger and frustration. "Leave me *alone!*" He pushed her aside, her and the child both, away from him and into the crowd—

And with the next step he took, he felt a sudden, jolting stab of pain in his abdomen—so intense that he doubled over, crying out in inexplicable agony, hands going to his stomach—

His hands came away smeared with blood.

His blood.

He screamed. With an effort, he straightened, looked down at himself: blood was soaking through his shirt, his once immaculate white suit, a bright red stain growing larger and larger, product of what Jackie knew, instantly, was an open wound.

Those in the crowd closest to him saw the blood and jumped to an understandable—and, in a way, accurate—conclusion: "Oh Jesus," someone shouted, "he's been shot! Somebody's shot him!"

The crowd disintegrated into chaos as the former supplicants scattered, rushing to avoid becoming the unseen gunman's next victim; Jackie staggered forward, arm outstretched, imploringly: "No," he managed to choke out, "please—somebody, you've got to help me—"

But no one listened to his pleas; within moments the only person within twenty feet was Harry, who caught Jackie as he began to fall, lowering him onto the sidewalk as the blood continued to gush—staining his pants now, a long red finger running down the inseam to the cuff. "Jackie! What in *hell*—"

Jackie groped in his pocket for the stone, not finding it at first, fighting back a wave of terror until he felt it in his other pocket. He clenched the stone in his right hand, as he had in a deserted alley many months ago; now as then, he placed his left hand over the wound and closed his eyes. *Oh God,* he thought, *oh Jesus, I'm sorry, please* help *me* . . . He concentrated on healing, concentrated with all the failing strength and faltering will he could muster—

But when he opened his eyes, he saw the blood flowing from between the fingers of his left hand, and he knew instinctively that this time—this time it wasn't going to work . . .

He forced the stone into Harry's hand. "You've got to do it," he said, voice a hoarse whisper. "Please, Harry, you've got to do it!" He grabbed Faulk's other hand, put it on the bleeding wound—

Harry recoiled, drawing, back his hand in horror and disgust. "Jackie—I can't—"

"Harry, you *have* to!"

"I—" Harry clenched the stone in one hand, working up the nerve to put his hand near the wound again; he was perspiring, clearly terrified. "I don't know *how,* Jackie, I don't—" He suddenly tore his hand away, bolted to his feet, and dropped the stone on the sidewalk beside the injured man. "I *can't,* Jackie!" he cried out, backing away into the building. "I just can't!"

Jackie stared at him, disbelievingly, as though seeing him for the first time. *"Harry . . . ?"*

"I'll call an ambulance," Harry promised, and then he was gone, swallowed up in the revolving glass doors to the lobby. Jackie called after, weakly, but to no avail: Harry was gone.

Jackie closed his eyes. An ambulance, he knew, would arrive far too late. He fought back his terror, trying to come to terms with what was happening to him; trying to come to terms with death. Because he *was* going to die this time. He'd been given a second chance and he'd blown it, pissed it all away—allowed himself to be corrupted, by Harry, by the money, by the applause and the approbation. All right. He blew it. Time to pay the piper; time to accept his due. But God, he was frightened. Suddenly he felt like he was falling into a deep black well, enclosed by a solid darkness with a definite shape, like a tunnel; but far from the white light he'd heard people saw at the moment of death, he saw only the blackness above him, and below him, a fevered babble of voices— the damned, perhaps, crying out in pain, giggling with crazed glee, calling out to greet him, to welcome him to their ranks—yes, he could even feel himself growing warmer, felt a fire growing inside him. He was going to hell, no two ways about that, and he was—he was—

He was no longer falling. He'd stopped, somehow, though the fire inside him continued to grow hotter. And then—abruptly, inexplicably— he felt almost as though he were *rising* again, carried aloft on a hot gust of wind, ascending as quickly as he'd been dropping, moments before—

He opened his eyes.

An eight-year-old boy—the mute boy he'd pushed aside, along with his mother, lifetimes ago—was squatting beside him, eyes closed, left hand on Jackie's stomach, right hand pulsing with a hot white luminescence. His mother stood behind him, looking first anxious, then relieved as Jackie regained consciousness and began to stir.

He saw, Jackie thought dazedly. He saw what Harry tried to do—what Harry couldn't do—and he—

The boy kept his eyes closed until the light ceased to issue from his hand—until the stone cooled—then opened them. Jackie reached down, unbuttoned his shirt . . .

. . . to reveal smooth, unbroken skin, and no blood save for that which stained his clothes.

The boy smiled triumphantly, exchanging a silent grin of victory with his mother. And in that moment, Jackie understood. Why the stone had stopped working; where it had all gone wrong. Where *he* had gone wrong. Without even thinking about it, Jackie gently took the stone from the boy . . . held it tight in one hand . . . then cupped his other hand around the boy's throat, covering his larynx. Jackie closed his eyes, concentrated, and felt the stone growing warm in his hand . . . a warmth he hadn't felt this intensely in months. He'd forgotten how good that warmth could feel. After thirty seconds, it began to cool again; Jackie opened his eyes, took his hand away from the boy's throat.

Jackie remembered, now, the look on the boy's face when he had cured him the first time; remembered the smile that came to him, the raspy, inchoate sounds he had made with his newfound voice. Now that same smile lit up his face, but though his voice was at first raspy from disuse, he had apparently learned something of how to use it in the few short months he had been able to speak.

He looked up at Jackie and said, very slowly and carefully, "Thank you, Brother John," his grin growing broader with the completion of the sentence.

The man in the bloodstained suit tousled the boy's hair and smiled back. "No . . . thank *you,*" he said softly. "And please . . . call me Jackie."

He looked up and saw one or two members of the once and former crowd lingering at the end of the block: an old man, Jackie recalled, with severe rheumatitis, and a young black man with an ulcerated colon. Jackie motioned them to come closer. "Don't be afraid," he said gently. "Come on." He stood, started toward them even as they began to move hesitantly toward him; even as, to Jackie's right, Harry Faulk stepped out of the building, looking absolutely stunned.

"Jackie! Jackie, are you—"

Jackie paid him no mind, walking past him as though he no longer existed—all his attention on the two injured men who needed his help.

He took the old man's gnarled, rheumatic hands in his, and he thought: No; not attention—concern. That was the secret—wasn't it?

From atop the Pyramid of the Sun, Ta'li'n could see the last of the five young priests to whom he had entrusted the sacred talismans making his way up the terraced slopes of the valley of Tenan—far from the flames that were consuming the City, a wall of fire marching down what was now, truly, the Avenue of the Dead. Seared, charred bodies lay strewn in its wake; just ahead of it, onetime rioters fled, sparks blown before them on the hot, dry wind, igniting their clothes, turning the fleeing figures into living torches who ran and stumbled a few feet, a few yards, before falling before the oncoming flames. The Pyramid of the Moon and the Butterfly Palace—the first to feel the torch of the rebels—were no longer temples, but furnaces. Up and down the length of the City, pillars of black smoke rose to touch an uncaring sky; directly below, the heat from the oncoming sheet of flame was peeling the bright red and gold from the plaster facade of the Pyramid. Soon it, too, would be engulfed; only Ta'li'n remained in the temple, all others either murdered, immolated, or escaped.

The priest turned away from the open gateway, already feeling the intense heat rising up from below; he retreated to his meditation room, sat, took a last mescal cap from its jar, and ate it, waiting for the peyote to carry him away, even as his five young priests had been carried away— they to safety, and Ta'li'n to a different sort of refuge.

Ta'li'n had chosen them well: young enough not to have become involved in the internecine political warfare among the priest-rulers, yet old enough to be expert at the use of the talismans, and able to pass that expertise on to succeeding generations. Why that was important to him, the priest only dimly understood; he knew, from his visions of time to come, that no memory of him or his people would remain—their names, their language, their grand accomplishments, their greatest failures, all would be but blank parchment to they-who-would-follow. Why, then, even bother to preserve the talismans? Why bother to save these relics of a religion that would itself be nothing but a mystery, years from now?

Perhaps simply to remind the future . . . that the past was once the present. That for a time—a brief, golden march of centuries—the gods had made their home here; had blessed the City with their love and power, their only remembrance in the form of two jade and gold figurines, a long, leathery cloak, an amulet of small obsidian chips on a golden strand, and a green marbled stone polished by the sweat of countless hands and countless healers. Even if no one remembered the rites, the divinations, the sacred words, these small enchantments would serve to remind that once, for a time, the gods had lingered here . . . in this place, in this City . . . before moving on.

The smell of smoke now filled the temple, intruding even into Ta'li'n's meditation room; once it filled with the noxious black fumes, he would die very quickly. Now he cast out with his mind one last time, his soul riding the crest of the peyote, searching—longing—for some glimpse of the talismans in the days to come, some affirmation that his actions had had meaning. Eyes closed, images raced through his mind: the City, bleached of color and life; a woman—Mayan, perhaps—the necklace of Pe'x'r round her neck, life stirring in her womb; a park—

A park surrounded by tall structures—taller than even the tallest pyramid, roadways of some smooth black material ringing the island of grass and trees—

And a man. Dark hair, dark eyes, dressed in what looked like holy white—but a white streaked, oddly, with red; with blood. Like Ta'li'n's own robes. The thin, wiry young man knelt beside an older, injured man—an indigent of some sort—one hand on the man's chest, the other glowing with a pulsing white light that made Ta'li'n nod in recognition. The image, the glimpse, was gone within seconds—but as the air grew hotter around him, and the first gray fingers of smoke slipped beneath the door to the room, the priest smiled, content in the affirmation that his legacy had/would/did survive; secure in the knowledge that this small part of it, at least, was, somehow, in good hands.

NIGHTCRAWLERS
Robert R. McCammon

TELEPLAY BY PHILIP DEGUERE

AIRED OCTOBER 18, 1985

STARRING SCOTT PAULIN, JAMES WHITMORE, JR.,

EXENE CERVENKA, ROBERT SWAN

One

"HARD RAIN COMING DOWN," CHERYL SAID, AND I NOD-
ded in agreement.

Through the diner's plate-glass windows, a dense curtain of rain flapped
across the Gulf gas pumps and continued across the parking lot. It hit
Big Bob's with a force that made the glass rattle like uneasy bones. The
red neon sign that said BIG BOB'S! DIESEL FUEL! EATS! sat on top of a
high steel pole above the diner so the truckers on the interstate could see
it. Out in the night, the red-tinted rain thrashed in torrents across my old
pickup truck and Cheryl's baby-blue Volkswagen.

"Well," I said, "I suppose that storm'll either wash some folks in off
the interstate or we can just about hang it up." The curtain of rain parted
for an instant, and I could see the treetops whipping back and forth in
the woods on the other side of Highway 47. Wind whined around the
front door like an animal trying to claw its way in. I glanced at the
electric clock on the wall behind the counter. Twenty minutes before
nine. We usually closed up at ten, but tonight—with tornado warnings
in the weather forecast—I was tempted to turn the lock a little early.
"Tell you what," I said. "If we're empty at nine, we skedaddle. 'Kay?"

"No argument here," she said. She watched the storm for a moment
longer, then continued putting newly washed coffee cups, saucers and
plates away on the stainless steel shelves.

Lightning flared from west to east like the strike of a burning bullwhip.
The diner's lights flickered, then came back to normal. A shudder of
thunder seemed to come right up through my shoes. Late March is the
beginning of tornado season in south Alabama, and we've had some
whoppers spin past here in the last few years. I knew that Alma was at
home, and she understood to get into the root cellar right quick if she
spotted a twister, like that one we saw in '82 dancing through the woods
about two miles from our farm.

"You got any love-ins planned this weekend, hippie?" I asked Cheryl,
mostly to get my mind off the storm and to rib her, too.

She was in her late thirties, but I swear that when she grinned, she
could've passed for a kid. "Wouldn't *you* like to know, redneck?" she
answered; she replied the same way to all my digs at her. Cheryl Love-
song—and I *know* that couldn't have been her real name—was a mighty
able waitress, and she had hands that were no strangers to hard work.

64

But I didn't care that she wore her long silvery-blond hair in Indian braids with hippie headbands, or came to work in tie-dyed overalls. She was the best waitress who'd ever worked for me, and she got along with everybody just fine—even us rednecks. That's what I am, and proud of it: I drink Rebel Yell whiskey straight, and my favorite songs are about women gone bad and trains on the long track to nowhere. I keep my wife happy. I've raised my two boys to pray to God and to salute the flag, and if anybody don't like it, he can go a few rounds with Big Bob Clayton.

Cheryl would come right out and tell you she used to live in San Francisco in the late sixties and that she went to love-ins and peace marches and all that stuff. When I reminded her it was 1984 and Ronnie Reagan was president, she'd look at me like I was walking cow-flop. I always figured she'd start thinking straight when all that hippie-dust blew out of her head.

Alma said my tail was going to get burnt if I ever took a shine to Cheryl, but I'm a fifty-five-year-old redneck who stopped sowing his wild seed when he met the woman he married, more than thirty years ago.

Lightning crisscrossed the turbulent sky, followed by a boom of thunder. Cheryl said, "Wow! Look at that light show!"

"Light show, my ass," I muttered. The diner was as solid as the Good Book, so I wasn't too worried about the storm. But on a wild night like this, stuck out in the countryside like Big Bob's was, you had a feeling of being a long way off from civilization—though Mobile was only twenty-seven miles south. On a wild night like this, you had a feeling that anything could happen, as quick as a streak of lightning out of the darkness. I picked up a copy of the Mobile *Press-Register* that the last customer—a trucker on his way to Texas—had left on the counter a half hour before, and I started plowing through the news, most of it bad: those Arab countries were still squabbling like Hatfields and McCoys in white robes; two men had robbed a Qwik-Mart in Mobile and had been killed by the police in a shootout; cops were investigating a massacre at a motel near Daytona Beach; an infant had been stolen from a maternity ward in Birmingham. The only good things on the front page were stories that said the economy was up and that Reagan swore we'd show the Commies who was boss in El Salvador and Lebanon.

The diner shook under a blast of thunder, and I looked up from the paper as a pair of headlights emerged from the rain into my parking lot.

Two

The headlights were attached to an Alabama State Trooper car.

"Half alive, hold the onion, extra brown the buns." Cheryl was already writing on her pad in expectation of the order. I pushed the paper aside and went to the fridge for the hamburger meat.

When the door opened a windblown spray of rain swept in and stung like buckshot. "Howdy, folks!" Dennis Wells peeled off his gray rain slicker and hung it on the rack next to the door. Over his Smokey the Bear trooper hat was a protective plastic covering, beaded with rain-drops. He took off his hat, exposing the thinning blond hair on his pale scalp, as he approached the counter and sat on his usual stool, right next to the cash register. "Cup of black coffee and a rare—" Cheryl was already sliding the coffee in front of him, and the burger sizzled on the griddle. "Y'all are on the ball tonight!" Dennis said; he said the same thing when he came in, which was almost every night. Funny the kind of habits you fall into, without realizing it.

"Kinda wild out there, ain't it?" I asked as I flipped the burger over.

"Lordy, yes! Wind just about flipped my car over three, four miles down the interstate. Thought I was gonna be eatin' a little pavement tonight." Dennis was a husky young man in his early thirties with thick blond brows over deep-set, light brown eyes. He had a wife and three kids, and he was fast to flash a walletful of their pictures. "Don't reckon I'll be chasin' any speeders tonight, but there'll probably be a load of accidents. Cheryl, you sure look pretty this evenin'."

"Still the same old me." Cheryl never wore a speck of makeup, though one day she'd come to work with glitter on her cheeks. She had a place a few miles away, and I guessed she was farming that funny weed up there. "Any trucks moving?"

"Seen a few, but not many. Truckers ain't fools. Gonna get worse before it gets better, the radio says." He sipped at his coffee and grimaced. "Lordy, that's strong enough to jump out of the cup and dance a jig, darlin'!"

I fixed the burger the way Dennis liked it, put it on a platter with some fries and served it. "Bobby, how's the wife treatin' you?" he asked.

"No complaints."

"Good to hear. I'll tell you, a fine woman is worth her weight in gold. Hey, Cheryl! How'd you like a handsome young man for a husband?"

Cheryl smiled, knowing what was coming. "The man I'm looking for hasn't been made yet."

"Yeah, but you ain't met *Cecil* yet, either! He asks me about you every time I see him, and I keep tellin' him I'm doin' everything I can to get you two together." Cecil was Dennis's brother-in-law and owned a Chevy dealership in Bay Minette. Dennis had been ribbing Cheryl about going on a date with Cecil for the past four months. "You'd like him," Dennis promised. "He's got a lot of my qualities."

"Well, that's different. In that case, I'm *certain* I don't want to meet him."

Dennis winced. "Oh, you're a cruel woman! That's what smokin'

banana peels does to you—turn you mean. Anybody readin' this rag?''
He reached over for the newspaper.

"Waitin' here just for you," I said. Thunder rumbled, closer to the
diner. The lights flickered briefly once . . . then again before they returned to normal. Cheryl busied herself by fixing a fresh pot of coffee,
and I watched the rain whipping against the windows. When the lightning
flashed, I could see the trees swaying so hard, they looked about to snap.

Dennis read and ate his hamburger. "Boy," he said after a few minutes, "the world's in some shape, huh? Those A-rab pig-stickers are
itchin' for war. Mobile metro boys had a little gunplay last night. Good
for them." He paused and frowned, then tapped the paper with one thick
finger. "This I can't figure."

"What's that?"

"Thing in Florida couple of nights ago. Six people killed at the Pines
Haven Motor Inn, near Daytona Beach. Motel was set off in the woods.
Only a couple of cinder-block houses in the area, and nobody heard any
gunshots. Says here one old man saw what he thought was a bright white
star falling over the motel, and that was it. Funny, huh?"

"A UFO," Cheryl offered. "Maybe he saw a UFO."

"Yeah, and I'm a little green man from Mars," Dennis scoffed. "I'm
serious. This is weird. The motel was so blown full of holes, it looked
like a war had been going on. Everybody was dead—even a dog and a
canary that belonged to the manager. The cars out in front of the rooms
were blasted to pieces. The sound of one of them explodin' was what
woke up the people in those houses, I reckon." He skimmed the story
again. "Two bodies were out in the parkin' lot, one was holed up in a
bathroom, one had crawled under a bed, and two had dragged every
piece of furniture in the room over to block the door. Didn't seem to
help 'em any, though."

I grunted. "Guess not."

"No motive, no witnesses. You better believe those Florida cops are
shakin' the bushes for some kind of dangerous maniac—or maybe more
than one, it says here." He shoved the paper away and patted the service
revolver holstered at his hip. "If I ever got hold of him—or them—he'd
find out not to mess with a 'Bama trooper." He glanced quickly over at
Cheryl and smiled mischievously. "Probably some crazy hippie who'd
been smokin' his tennis shoes."

"Don't knock it," she said sweetly, "until you've tried it." She looked
past him, out the window into the storm. "Car's pullin' in, Bobby."

Headlights glared briefly off the wet windows. It was a station wagon
with wood-grained panels on the sides; it veered around the gas pumps
and parked next to Dennis's trooper car. On the front bumper was a
personalized license plate that said: *Ray & Lindy.* The headlights died,
and all the doors opened at once. Out of the wagon came a whole family:

a man and woman, a little girl and boy about eight or nine. Dennis got up and opened the diner door as they hurried inside from the rain.

All of them had got pretty well soaked between the station wagon and the diner, and they wore the dazed expressions of people who'd been on the road a long time. The man wore glasses and had curly gray hair, the woman was slim and dark-haired and pretty. The kids were sleepy-eyed. All of them were well dressed, the man in a yellow sweater with one of those alligators on the chest. They had vacation tans, and I figured they were tourists heading north from the beach after spring break.

"Come on in and take a seat," I said.

"Thank you," the man said. They squeezed into one of the booths near the windows. "We saw your sign from the interstate."

"Bad night to be on the highway," Dennis told them. "Tornado warnings are out all over the place."

"We heard it on the radio," the woman—Lindy, if the license was right—said. "We're on our way to Birmingham, and we thought we could drive right through the storm. We should've stopped at the Holiday Inn we passed about fifteen miles ago."

"That would've been smart," Dennis agreed. "No sense in pushin' your luck." He returned to his stool.

The new arrivals ordered hamburgers, fries and Cokes. Cheryl and I went to work. Lightning made the diner's lights flicker again, and the sound of thunder caused the kids to jump. When the food was ready and Cheryl served them, Dennis said, "Tell you what. You folks finish your dinners and I'll escort you back to the Holiday Inn. Then you can head out in the morning. How about that?"

"Fine," Ray said gratefully. "I don't think we could've got very much further, anyway." He turned his attention to his food.

"Well," Cheryl said quietly, standing beside me, "I don't guess we get home early, do we?"

"I guess not. Sorry."

She shrugged. "Goes with the job, right? Anyway, I can think of worse places to be stuck."

I figured that Alma might be worried about me, so I went over to the pay phone to call her. I dropped a quarter in—and the dial tone sounded like a cat being stepped on. I hung up and tried again. The cat-scream continued. "Damn!" I muttered. "Lines must be screwed up."

"Ought to get yourself a place closer to town, Bobby," Dennis said. "Never could figure out why you wanted a joint in the sticks. At least you'd get better phone service and good lights if you were nearer to Mo—"

He was interrupted by the sound of shrieking brakes, and he swiveled around on his stool.

I looked up as a car hurtled into the parking lot, the tires swerving, throwing up plumes of water. For a few seconds I thought it was going to keep coming, right through the window into the diner—but then the brakes caught and the car almost grazed the side of my pickup as it jerked to a stop. In the neon's red glow I could tell it was a beat-up old Ford Fairlane, either gray or a dingy beige. Steam was rising off the crumpled hood. The headlights stayed on for perhaps a minute before they winked off. A figure got out of the car and walked slowly—with a limp—toward the diner.

We watched the figure approach. Dennis's body looked like a coiled spring, ready to be triggered. "We got us a live one, Bobby boy," he said.

The door opened, and in a stinging gust of wind and rain, a man who looked like walking death stepped into my diner.

Three

He was so wet, he might well have been driving with his windows down. He was a skinny guy, maybe weighed all of a hundred and twenty pounds, even soaking wet. His unruly dark hair was plastered to his head, and he had gone a week or more without a shave. In his gaunt, pallid face his eyes were startlingly blue; his gaze flickered around the diner, lingered for a few seconds on Dennis. Then he limped on down to the far end of the counter and took a seat. He wiped the rain out of his eyes as Cheryl took a menu to him.

Dennis stared at the man. When he spoke, his voice bristled with authority. "Hey, fella." The man didn't look up from the menu. "Hey, I'm talkin' to *you.*"

The man pushed the menu away and pulled a damp packet of Kools out of the breast pocket of his patched army fatigue jacket. "I can hear you," he said; his voice was deep and husky, and didn't go with his less-than-robust physical appearance.

"Drivin' kinda fast in this weather, don't you think?"

The man flicked a cigarette lighter a few times before he got a flame, then he lit one of his smokes and inhaled deeply. "Yeah," he replied. "I was. Sorry. I saw the sign, and I was in a hurry to get here. Miss? I'd just like a cup of coffee, please. Hot and *real* strong, okay?"

Cheryl nodded and turned away from him, almost bumping into me as I strolled down behind the counter to check him out.

"That kind of hurry'll get you killed," Dennis cautioned.

"Right. Sorry." He shivered and pushed the tangled hair back from his forehead with one hand. Up close, I could see deep cracks around his mouth and the corners of his eyes, and I figured him to be in his late thirties or early forties. His wrists were as thin as a woman's; he looked like he hadn't eaten a good meal for more than a month. He stared at his hands through bloodshot eyes. Probably on drugs, I thought. The fella gave me the creeps. Then he looked at me with those eyes—so pale blue they were almost white—and I felt like I'd been nailed to the floor. "Something wrong?" he asked—not rudely, just curiously.

"Nope." I shook my head. Cheryl gave him his coffee and then went over to give Ray and Lindy their check.

The man didn't use either cream or sugar. The coffee was steaming, but he drank half of it down like mother's milk. "That's good," he said. "Keep me awake, won't it?"

"More than likely." Over the breast pocket of his jacket was the faint outline of the name that had been sewn there once. I think it was *Price,* but I could've been wrong.

"That's what I want. To stay awake, as long as I can." He finished the coffee. "Can I have another cup, please."

I poured it for him. He drank that one down just as fast, then he rubbed his eyes wearily.

"Been on the road a long time, huh?"

Price nodded. "Day and night. I don't know which is more tired, my mind or my butt." He lifted his gaze to me again. "Have you got anything else to drink? How about beer?"

"No, sorry. Couldn't get a liquor license."

He sighed. "Just as well. It might make me sleepy. But I sure could go for a beer right now. One sip, to clean my mouth out."

He picked up his coffee cup, and I smiled and started to turn away.

But then he wasn't holding a cup. He was holding a Budweiser can, and for an instant I could smell the tang of a newly popped beer.

The mirage was only there for maybe two seconds, I blinked, and Price was holding a cup again. "Just as well," he said, and put it down.

I glanced over at Cheryl, then at Dennis. Neither one was paying attention. Damn! I thought. I'm too young to be either losin' my eyesight or my senses. "Uh . . ." I said, or some other stupid noise.

"One more cup?" Price asked. "Then I'd better hit the road again."

My hand was shaking as I picked it up, but if Price noticed, he didn't say anything.

"Want anything to eat?" Cheryl asked him. "How about a bowl of beef stew?"

He shook his head. "No, thanks. The sooner I get back on the road, the better it'll be."

Suddenly Dennis swiveled toward him, giving him a cold stare that only cops and drill sergeants can muster. "Back on the *road?*" He snorted. "Fella, you ever been in a tornado before? I'm gonna escort those nice people to the Holiday Inn about fifteen miles back. If you're smart, that's where you'll spend the night, too. No use in tryin' to—"

"*No.*" Price's voice was rock-steady. "I'll be spending the night behind the wheel."

Dennis's eyes narrowed. "How come you're in such a hurry? Not runnin' from anybody, are you?"

"Nightcrawlers," Cheryl said.

Price turned toward her like he'd been slapped across the face, and I saw what might've been a spark of fear in his eyes.

Cheryl motioned toward the lighter Price had laid on the counter, beside the pack of Kools. It was a beat-up silver Zippo, and inscribed across it was *Nightcrawlers,* with the symbol of two crossed rifles beneath it. "Sorry," she said. "I just noticed that, and I wondered what it was."

Price put the lighter away. "I was in 'Nam," he told her. "Everybody in my unit got one."

"Hey." There was suddenly new respect in Dennis's voice. "You a *vet?*"

Price paused so long, I didn't think he was going to answer. In the quiet, I heard the little girl tell her mother that the fries were "ucky." Price said, "Yes."

"How about that! Hey, I wanted to go myself, but I got a high number and things were windin' down about that time, anyway. Did you see any action?"

A faint, bitter smiled passed over Price's mouth. "Too much."

"What? Infantry? Marines? Rangers?"

Price picked up his third cup of coffee, swallowed some and put it down. He closed his eyes for a few seconds, and when they opened, they were vacant and fixed on nothing. "Nightcrawlers," he said quietly. "Special unit. Deployed to recon Charlie positions in questionable villages." He said it like he was reciting from a manual. "We did a lot of crawling through rice paddies and jungles in the dark."

"Bet you laid a few of them Vietcong out, didn't you?" Dennis got up and came over to sit a few places away from the man. "Man, I was behind you guys all the way. I wanted you to stay in there and fight it out!"

Price was silent. Thunder echoed over the diner. The lights weakened for a few seconds; when they came back on, they seemed to have lost some of their wattage. The place was dimmer than before. Price's head slowly turned toward Dennis, with the inexorable motion of a machine. I was thankful I didn't have to take the full force of Price's dead blue eyes, and I saw Dennis wince. "I *should've* stayed," he said. "I should be there right now, buried in the mud of a rice paddy with the eight other men in my patrol."

"Oh." Dennis blinked. "Sorry. I didn't mean to—"

"I came home," Price continued calmly, "by stepping on the bodies of my friends. Do you want to know what that's like, Mr. Trooper?"

"The war's over," I told him. "No need to bring it back."

Price smiled grimly, but his gaze remained fixed on Dennis. "Some say it's over. I say it came back with the men who were there. Like me. *Especially* like me.'' Price paused. The wind howled around the door, and the lightning illuminated for an instant the thrashing woods across the highway. ''The mud was up to our knees, Mr. Trooper,'' he said. ''We were moving across a rice paddy in the dark, being real careful not to step on the bamboo stakes we figured were planted there. Then the first shots started: *pop pop pop*—like firecrackers going off. One of the Nightcrawlers fired off a flare and we saw the Cong ringing us. We'd walked right into hell, Mr. Trooper. Somebody shouted, 'Charlie's in the light!' and we started firing, trying to punch a hole through them. But they were everywhere. As soon as one went down, three more took his place. Grenades were going off, and more flares, and people were screaming as they got hit. I took a bullet in the thigh and another through the hand. I lost my rifle, and somebody fell on top of me with half his head missing.''

''Uh . . . listen,'' I said. ''You don't have to—''

''I *want* to, friend.'' He glanced quickly at me, then back to Dennis. I think I cringed when his gaze pierced me. ''I want to tell it all. They were fighting and screaming and dying all around me, and I felt the bullets tug at my clothes as they passed through. I know I was screaming, too, but what was coming out of my mouth sounded bestial. I ran. The only way I could save my own life was to step on their bodies and drive them down into the mud. I heard some of them choke and blubber as I put my boot on their faces. I knew all those guys like brothers . . . but at that moment they were only pieces of meat. I ran. A gunship chopper came over the paddy and laid down some fire, and that's how I got out. Alone.'' He bent his face closer toward the other man's. ''And you'd better believe I'm in that rice paddy in 'Nam every time I close my eyes. You'd better believe the men I left back there don't rest easy. So you keep your opinions about 'Nam and being 'behind you guys' to yourself, Mr. Trooper. I don't want to hear that bullshit. Got it?''

Dennis sat very still. He wasn't used to being talked to like that, not even from a 'Nam vet, and I saw the shadow of anger pass over his face.

Price's hands were trembling as he brought a little bottle out of his jeans pocket. He shook two blue-and-orange capsules out onto the counter, took them both with a swallow of coffee and then recapped the bottle and put it away. The flesh of his face looked almost ashen in the dim light.

''I know you boys had a rough time,'' Dennis said, ''but that's no call to show disrespect to the law.''

''The law,'' Price repeated. ''Yeah. Right. Bull*shit.*''

''There are women and children present,'' I reminded him. ''Watch your language.''

Price rose from his seat. He looked like a skeleton with just a little extra skin on the bones. ''Mister, I haven't slept for more than thirty-six hours. My nerves are shot. I don't mean to cause trouble, but when some fool says he *understands,* I feel like kicking his teeth down his throat—because no one who wasn't there can pretend to understand.'' He glanced at Ray, Lindy and the kids. ''Sorry, folks. Don't mean to disturb you. Friend, how much do I owe?'' he started digging for his wallet.

Dennis slid slowly from his seat and stood with his hands on his hips. ''Hold it.'' He used his trooper's voice again. ''If you think I'm lettin' you walk out of here high on pills and needin' sleep, you're crazy. I don't want to be scrapin' you off the highway.''

Price paid him no attention. He took a couple of dollars from his wallet and put them on the counter. I didn't touch them. ''Those pills will help keep me awake,'' Price said. ''Once I get on the road, I'll be fine.''

''Fella, I wouldn't let you go if it was high noon and not a cloud in the sky. I sure as hell don't want to clean up after the accident you're gonna have. Now, why don't you come along to the Holiday Inn and—''

Price laughed grimly. ''Mr. Trooper, the last place you want me staying is at a motel.'' He cocked his head to one side. ''I was in a motel in Florida a couple of nights ago, and I think I left my room a little untidy. Step aside and let me pass.''

''A motel in Florida?'' Dennis nervously licked his lower lip. ''What the hell you talkin' about?''

''Nightmares and reality, Mr. Trooper. The point where they cross. A couple of nights ago, they crossed at a motel. I wasn't going to let myself sleep. I was just going to rest for a little while, but I didn't know they'd come so *fast.*'' A mocking smile played at the edges of his mouth, but his eyes were tortured. ''You don't want me staying at that Holiday Inn, Mr. Trooper. You really don't. Now, step aside.''

I saw Dennis's hand settle on the butt of his revolver. His fingers unsnapped the fold of leather that secured the gun in the holster. I stared at him numbly. My God, I thought. What's goin' on? My heart had started pounding so hard, I was sure everybody could hear it. Ray and Lindy were watching, and Cheryl was backing away behind the counter.

Price and Dennis faced each other for a moment, as the rain whipped against the windows and thunder boomed like shellfire. Then Price sighed, as if resigning himself to something. He said, ''I think I want a T-bone steak. Extra-rare. How 'bout it?'' He looked at me.

''A steak?'' My voice was shaking. ''We don't have any T-bone—''

Price's gaze shifted to the counter right in front of me. I heard a sizzle. The aroma of cooking meat drifted up to me.

''Oh . . . wow,'' Cheryl whispered.

A large T-bone steak lay on the countertop, pink and oozing blood. You could've fanned a menu in my face and I would've keeled over. Wisps of smoke were rising from the steak.

The steak began to fade, until it was only an outline on the counter. The lines of oozing blood vanished. After the mirage was gone, I could still smell the meat—and that's how I knew I wasn't crazy.

Dennis's mouth hung open. Ray had stood up from the booth to look, and his wife's face was the color of spoiled milk. The whole world seemed to be balanced on a point of silence—until the wail of the wind jarred me back to my senses.

"I'm getting good at it," Price said softly. "I'm getting very, very good. Didn't start happening to me until about a year ago. I've found four other 'Nam vets who can do the same thing. What's in your head comes true—as simple as that. Of course, the images only last for a few seconds—as long as I'm awake, I mean. I've found out that those other men were drenched by a chemical spray we called Howdy Doody—because it made you stiffen up and jerk like you were hanging on strings. I got hit with it near Khe Sahn. That shit almost suffocated me. It fell like black tar, and it burned the land down to a paved parking lot." He stared at Dennis. "You don't want me around here, Mr. Trooper. Not with the body count I've still got in *my* head."

"You . . . were at . . . that motel, near Daytona Beach?"

Price closed his eyes. A vein had begun beating at his right temple, royal blue against the pale of his flesh. "Oh Jesus," he whispered. "I fell asleep, and I couldn't wake myself up. I was having the nightmare. The same one. I was locked in it, and I was trying to scream myself awake." He shuddered, and two tears ran slowly down his cheeks. *"Oh,"* he said, and flinched as if remembering something horrible. "They . . . they were coming through the door when I woke up. Tearing the door right off its hinges. I woke up . . . just as one of them was pointing his rifle at me. And I saw his face. I saw his muddy, misshapen face." His eyes suddenly jerked open. "I didn't know they'd come so fast."

"Who?" I asked him. *"Who* came so fast?"

"The Nightcrawlers," Price said, his face void of expression, masklike. "Dear God . . . maybe if I'd stayed asleep a second more. But I ran again, and I left those people dead in that motel."

"You're gonna come with me," Dennis started pulling his gun from his holster. Price's head snapped toward him. "I don't know what kinda fool game you're—"

He stopped, staring at the gun he held.

It wasn't a gun anymore. It was an oozing mass of hot rubber. Dennis cried out and slung the thing from his hand. The molten mess hit the floor with a pulpy *splat.*

"I'm leaving now," Price's voice was calm. "Thank you for the coffee." He walked past Dennis, toward the door.

Dennis grasped a bottle of ketchup from the counter. Cheryl cried out, *"Don't!"* but it was too late. Dennis was already swinging the bottle. It hit the back of Price's skull and burst open, spewing ketchup everywhere.

Price staggered forward, his knees buckling. When he went down, his skull hit the floor with a noise like a watermelon being dropped. His body began jerking involuntarily.

"Got him!" Dennis shouted triumphantly. "Got that crazy bastard, didn't I?"

Lindy was holding the little girl in her arms. The boy craned his neck to see. Ray said nervously, "You didn't kill him, did you?"

"He's not dead," I told him. I looked over at the gun; it was solid again. Dennis scooped it up and aimed it at Price, whose body continued to jerk. Just like Howdy Doody, I thought. Then Price stopped moving. "He's dead!" Cheryl's voice was near frantic. "Oh God, you killed him, Dennis!"

Dennis prodded the body with the toe of his boot, then bent down. "Naw. His eyes are movin' back and forth behind the lids." Dennis touched his wrist to check the pulse, then abruptly pulled his own hand away. "Jesus Christ! He's as cold as a meat locker!" He took Price's pulse and whistled. "Goin' like a racehorse at the Derby."

I touched the place on the counter where the mirage-steak had been. My fingers came away slightly greasy, and I could smell the cooked meat on them. At that instant, Price twitched. Dennis scuttled away from him like a crab. Price made a gasping, choking noise.

"What'd he say?" Cheryl asked. "He said something!"

"No he didn't." Dennis stuck him in the ribs with his pistol. "Come on. Get up."

"Get him out of here," I said. "I don't want him—"

Cheryl shushed me. "Listen. Can you hear that?"

I heard only the roar and crash of the storm.

"Don't you *hear* it?" she asked me. Her eyes were getting scared and glassy.

"Yes!" Ray said. "Yes! Listen!"

Then I did hear something, over the noise of the keening wind. It was a distant *chuk-chuk-chuk,* steadily growing louder and closer. The wind covered the noise for a minute, then it came back: CHUK-CHUK-CHUK, almost overhead.

"It's a helicopter!" Ray peered through the window. "Somebody's got a helicopter out there!"

"Ain't nobody can fly a chopper in a storm!" Dennis told him. The noise of rotors swelled and faded, swelled and faded . . . and stopped.

On the floor, Price shivered and began to contort into a fetal position. His mouth opened, his face twisted in what appeared to be agony.

Thunder spoke. A red fireball rose up from the woods across the road and hung lazily in the sky for a few seconds before it descended toward the diner. As it fell, the fire ball exploded soundlessly into a white, glaring eye of light that almost blinded me.

Price said something in a garbled, panicked voice. His eyes were tightly closed, and he had squeezed up with his arms around his knees.

Dennis rose to his feet; he squinted as the eye of light fell toward the parking lot and winked out in a puddle of water. Another fireball floated up from the woods, and again blossomed into painful glare.

Dennis turned toward me. "I heard him." His voice was raspy. "He said . . . 'Charlie's in the light.' "

As the second flare fell to the ground and illuminated the parking lot, I thought I saw figures crossing the road. They walked stiff-legged, in an eerie cadence. The flare went out.

"Wake him up," I heard myself whisper. "Dennis . . . dear God . . . *wake him up.*"

Four

Dennis stared stupidly at me, and I started to jump across the counter to get to Price myself.

A gout of flame leapt in the parking lot. Sparks marched across the concrete. I shouted, "Get down!" and twisted around to push Cheryl back behind the shelter of the counter.

"What the *hell—*" Dennis said.

He didn't finish. There was the metallic thumping of bullets hitting the gas pumps and the cars. I knew if that gas blew, we were all dead. My truck shuddered with the impact of slugs, and I saw the whole thing explode as I ducked behind the counter. Then the windows blew inward with a god-awful crash, and the diner was full of flying glass, swirling wind and sheets of rain. I heard Lindy scream, and both the kids were crying and I think I was shouting something myself.

The lights had gone out, and the only illumination was the reflection of red neon off the concrete and the glow of the fluorescents over the gas pumps. Bullets whacked into the wall, and crockery shattered as if it had been hit with a hammer. Napkins and sugar packets were flying everywhere.

Cheryl was holding on to me as if her fingers were nails sunk to my bones. Her eyes were wide and dazed, and she kept trying to speak. Her mouth was working, but nothing came out.

There was another explosion as one of the other cars blew. The whole place shook, and I almost puked with fear.

Another hail of bullets hit the wall. They were tracers, and they jumped and ricocheted like white-hot cigarette butts. One of them sang off the edge of a shelf and fell to the floor about three feet away from me. The glowing slug began to fade, like the beer can and the mirage-steak. I put my hand out to find it, but all I felt was splinters of glass and crockery.

A phantom bullet, I thought. Real enough to cause damage and death—
and then gone.

You don't want me around here, Mr. Trooper, Price had warned. *Not
with the body count I've got in my head.*

The firing stopped. I got free of Cheryl and said, "You stay right
here." Then I looked up over the counter and saw my truck and the
station wagon on fire, the flames being whipped by the wind. Rain
slapped me across the face as it swept in where the window-glass used
to be. I saw Price lying still huddled on the floor, with pieces of glass
all around him. His hands were clawing the air, and in the flickering red
neon, his face was contorted, his eyes still closed. The pool of ketchup
around his head made him look like his skull had been split open. He
was peering into hell, and I averted my eyes before I lost my own mind.

Ray and Lindy and the two children had huddled under the table of
their booth. The woman was sobbing brokenly. I looked at Dennis, lying
a few feet from Price: he was sprawled on his face, and there were four
holes punched through his back. It was not ketchup that ran in rivulets
around Dennis's body. His right arm was outflung, and the fingers
twitched around the gun he gripped.

Another flare sailed up from the woods like a Fourth of July sparkler.

When the light brightened, I saw them: at least five figures, maybe
more. They were crouched over, coming across the parking lot—but
slowly, the speed of nightmares. Their clothes flapped and hung around
them, and the flare's light glanced off their helmets. They were carrying
weapons—rifles, I guessed. I couldn't see their faces, and that was for
the best.

On the floor, Price moaned. I head him say, "light . . . in the light . . ."

The flare hung right over the diner. And then I knew what was going
on. *We* were in the light. We were all caught in Price's nightmare, and
the Nightcrawlers that Price had left in the mud were fighting the battle
again—the same way it had been fought at the Pines Haven Motor Inn.
The Nightcrawlers had come back to life, powered by Price's guilt and
whatever that Howdy Doody shit had done to him.

And we were in the light, where Charlie had been out in that rice
paddy.

There was a noise like castanets clicking. Dots of fire arced through
the broken windows and thudded into the corner. The stools squealed as
they were hit and spun. The cash register rang and the drawer popped
open, and then the entire register blew apart and bills and coins scattered. I ducked my head, but a wasp of fire—I don't know what, a bit of
metal or glass maybe—sliced my left cheek open from ear to upper lip.
I fell to the floor behind the counter with blood running down my face.

A blast shook the rest of the cups, saucers, plates and glasses off the
shelves. The whole roof buckled inward, throwing loose ceiling tiles,
light fixtures and pieces of metal framework.

We were all going to die. I knew it, right then. Those things were going to destroy us. But I thought of the pistol in Dennis's hand, and of Price lying near the door. If we were caught in Price's nightmare and the blow from the ketchup bottle had broken something in his skull, then the only way to stop his dream was to kill him.

I'm no hero. I was about to piss in my pants, but I knew I was the only one who could move. I jumped up and scrambled over the counter, falling beside Dennis and wrenching at that pistol. Even in death, Dennis had a strong grip. Another blast came, along the wall to my right. The heat of it scorched me, and the shock wave skidded me across the floor through glass and rain and blood.

But I had that pistol in my hand.

I heard Ray shout, "Look out!"

In the doorway, silhouetted by flames, was a skeletal thing wearing muddy green rags. It wore a dented-in helmet and carried a corroded, slime-covered rifle. Its face was gaunt and shadowy, the features hidden behind a scum of rice-paddy muck. It began to lift the rifle to fire at me—slowly, slowly . .

I got the safety off the pistol and fired twice, without aiming. A spark leapt off the helmet as one of the bullets was deflected, but the figure staggered backward and into the conflagration of the station wagon, where it seemed to melt into ooze before it vanished.

More tracers were coming in. Cheryl's Volkswagen shuddered, the tires blowing out almost in unison. The state trooper car was already bullet-riddled and sitting on flats.

Another Nightcrawler, this one without a helmet and with slime covering the skull where the hair had been, rose up beyond the window and fired its rifle. I heard the bullet whine past my ear, and as I took aim, I saw its bony finger tightening on the trigger again.

A skillet flew over my head and hit the thing's shoulder, spoiling its aim. For an instant the skillet stuck in the Nightcrawler's body, as if the figure itself was made out of mud. I fired once . . . twice . . . and saw pieces of matter fly from the thing's chest. What might've been a mouth opened in a soundless scream, and the thing slithered out of sight.

I looked around. Cheryl was standing behind the counter, weaving on her feet, her face white with shock. "Get down!" I shouted, and she ducked for cover.

I crawled to Price, shook him hard. His eyes would not open. "Wake up!" I begged him. "Wake up, damn you!" And then I pressed the barrel of the pistol against Price's head. Dear God, I didn't want to kill anybody, but I knew I was going to have to blow the Nightcrawlers right out of his brain. I hesitated—too long.

Something smashed into my left collarbone. I heard the bone snap like a broomstick being broken. The force of the shot slid me back against the counter and jammed me between two bullet-pocked stools. I lost the gun, and there was a roaring in my head that deafened me.

I don't know how long I was out. My left arm felt like dead meat. All the cars in the lot were burning, and there was a hole in the diner's roof that a tractor-trailer could've dropped through. Rain was sweeping into my face, and when I wiped my eyes clear, I saw them, standing over Price.

There were eight of them. The two I thought I'd killed were back. They trailed weeds, and their boots and ragged clothes were covered with mud. They stood in silence, staring down at their living comrade.

I was too tired to scream. I couldn't even whimper. I just watched.

Price's hands lifted into the air. He reached for the Nightcrawlers, and then his eyes opened. His pupils were dead white, surrounded by scarlet. "End it," he whispered. "End it . . ."

One of the Nightcrawlers aimed its rifle and fired. Price jerked. Another Nightcrawler fired, and then they were all firing, point-blank into Price's body. Price thrashed and clutched at his head, but there was no blood; the phantom bullets weren't hitting him.

The Nightcrawlers began to ripple and fade. I saw the flames of the burning cars through their bodies. The figures became transparent, floating in vague outlines. Price had awakened too fast at the Pines Haven Motor Inn, I realized; if he had remained asleep, the creatures of his nightmares would've ended it there, at that Florida motel. They were killing him in front of me—or he was allowing them to end it, and I think that's what he must've wanted for a long, long time.

He shuddered, his mouth releasing a half moan, half sigh.

It sounded almost like relief.

The Nightcrawlers vanished. Price didn't move anymore.

I saw his face. His eyes were closed, and I think he must've found peace at last.

Five

A trucker hauling lumber from Mobile to Birmingham saw the burning cars. I don't even remember what he looked like.

Ray was cut up by glass, but his wife and the kids were okay. Physically, I mean. Mentally, I couldn't say.

Cheryl went into the hospital for a while. I got a postcard from her with the Golden Gate Bridge on the front. She promised she'd write and let me know how she was doing, but I doubt if I'll ever hear from her. She was the best waitress I ever had, and I wish her luck.

The police asked me a thousand questions, and I told the story the same way every time. I found out later that no bullets or shrapnel were ever dug out of the walls or the cars or Dennis's body—just like in the case of that motel massacre. There was no bullet in me, though my collarbone was snapped clean in two.

Price had died of a massive brain hemorrhage. It looked, the police told me, as if it had exploded in his skull.

I closed the diner. Farm life is fine. Alma understands, and we don't talk about it.

But I never showed the police what I found, and I don't know exactly why not.

I picked up Price's wallet in the mess. Behind a picture of a smiling young woman holding a baby, there was a folded piece of paper. On that paper were the names of four men.

Beside one name, Price had written DANGEROUS.

I've found four other 'Nam vets who can do the same thing, Price had said.

I sit up at night a lot, thinking about that and looking at those names. Those men had gotten a dose of that Howdy Doody shit in a foreign place they hadn't wanted to be, fighting a war that turned out to be one of those crossroads of nightmare and reality. I've changed my mind about 'Nam, because I understand now that the worst of the fighting is still going on, in the battlefields of memory.

A Yankee who called himself Tompkins came to my house one May morning and flashed me an ID that said he worked for a veterans' association. He was very soft-spoken and polite, but he had deep-set eyes that were almost black, and he never blinked. He asked me all about Price, seemed real interested in picking my brain of every detail. I told him the police had the story, and I couldn't add any more to it. Then I turned the tables and asked him about Howdy Doody. He smiled in a puzzled kind of way and said he'd never heard of any chemical defoliant called that. No such thing, he said. Like I say, he was very polite.

But I know the shape of a gun tucked into a shoulder-holster. Tompkins was wearing one, under his seersucker coat. I never could find any veterans' association that knew anything about him, either.

Maybe I should give that list of names to the police. Maybe I will. Or maybe I'll try to find those four men myself, and try to make some sense out of what's being hidden.

I don't think Price was evil. No. He was just scared, and who can blame a man for running from his own nightmares? I like to believe that, in the end, Price had the courage to face the Nightcrawlers, and in committing suicide, he saved our lives.

The newspapers, of course, never got the real story. They called Price a 'Nam vet who'd gone crazy, killed six people in a Florida motel and then killed a state trooper in a shootout at Big Bob's diner and gas stop.

But I know where Price is buried. They sell little American flags at the five-and-dime in Mobile. I'm alive, and I can spare the change.

And then I've got to find out how much courage *I* have.

EXAMINATION DAY
Henry Slesar

Teleplay by Philip DeGuere

Aired November 1, 1985

Starring David Mendenhall, Christopher Allport,

Elizabeth Normant

THE JORDANS NEVER SPOKE OF THE EXAM, NOT UNTIL their son, Dickie, was twelve years old. It was on his birthday that Mrs. Jordan first mentioned the subject in his presence, and the anxious manner of her speech caused her husband to answer sharply.

"Forget about it," he said. "He'll do all right."

They were at the breakfast table, and the boy looked up from his plate curiously. He was an alert-eyed youngster, with flat blond hair and a quick, nervous manner. He didn't understand what the sudden tension was about, but he did know that today was his birthday, and he wanted harmony above all. Somewhere in the little apartment there were wrapped, beribboned packages waiting to be opened, and in the tiny wall-kitchen, something warm and sweet was being prepared in the automatic stove. He wanted the day to be happy, and the moistness of his mother's eyes, the scowl on his father's face, spoiled the mood of fluttering expectation with which he had greeted the morning.

"What exam?" he asked.

His mother looked at the tablecloth. "It's just a sort of Government intelligence test they give children at the age of twelve. You'll be getting it next week. It's nothing to worry about."

"You mean a test like in school?"

"Something like that," his father said, getting up from the table. "Go read your comic books, Dickie."

The boy rose and wandered toward that part of the living room which had been "his" corner since infancy. He fingered the topmost comic of the stack, but seemed uninterested in the colorful squares of fast-paced action. He wandered toward the window, and peered gloomily at the veil of mist that shrouded the glass.

"Why did it have to rain *today?*" he said. "Why couldn't it rain tomorrow?"

His father, now slumped into an armchair with the Government newspaper, rattled the sheets in vexation. "Because it just did, that's all. Rain makes the grass grow."

"Why, Dad?"

"Because it does, that's all."

Dickie puckered his brow. "What makes it green, though? The grass?"

"Nobody knows," his father snapped, then immediately regretted his abruptness.

Later in the day, it was birthday time again. His mother beamed as

she handed over the gaily colored packages, and even his father managed
a grin and a rumple-of-the-hair. He kissed his mother and shook hands
gravely with his father. Then the birthday cake was brought forth, and
the ceremonies concluded.

An hour later, seated by the window, he watched the sun force its way
between the clouds.

"Dad," he said, "how far away is the sun?"

"Five thousand miles," his father said.

Dickie sat at the breakfast table and again saw moisture in his mother's
eyes. He didn't connect her tears with the exam until his father suddenly
brought the subject to light again.

"Well, Dickie," he said, with a manly frown, "you've got an appointment today."

"I know, Dad. I hope—"

"Now, it's nothing to worry about. Thousands of children take this
test every day. The Government wants to know how smart you are,
Dickie. That's all there is to it."

"I get good marks in school," he said hesitantly.

"This is different. This is a—special kind of test. They give you this
stuff to drink, you see, and then you go into a room where there's a sort
of machine—"

"What stuff to drink?" Dickie said.

"It's nothing. It tastes like peppermint. It's just to make sure you
answer the questions truthfully. Not that the Government thinks you won't
tell the truth, but this stuff makes *sure.*"

Dickie's face showed puzzlement, and a touch of fright. He looked at
his mother, and she composed her face into a misty smile.

"Everything will be all right," she said.

"Of course it will," his father agreed. "You're a good boy, Dickie;
you'll make out fine. Then we'll come home and celebrate. All right?"

"Yes, sir," Dickie said.

They entered the Government Educational Building fifteen minutes
before the appointed hour. They crossed the marble floors of the great
pillared lobby, passed beneath an archway and entered an automatic elevator that brought them to the fourth floor.

There was a young man wearing an insignialess tunic, seated at a
polished desk in front of Room 404. He held a clipboard in his hand,
and he checked the list down to the Js and permitted the Jordans to enter.

The room was as cold and official as a courtroom, with long benches
flanking metal tables. There were several fathers and sons already there,
and a thin-lipped woman with cropped black hair was passing out sheets
of paper.

Mr. Jordan filled out the form, and returned it to the clerk. Then he told Dickie: "It won't be long now. When they call your name, you just go through the doorway at that end of the room." He indicated the portal with his finger.

A concealed loudspeaker crackled and called off the first name. Dickie saw a boy leave his father's side reluctantly and walk slowly toward the door.

At five minutes of eleven, they called the name of Jordan.

"Good luck, son," his father said, without looking at him. "I'll call for you when the test is over."

Dickie walked to the door and turned the knob. The room inside was dim, and he could barely make out the features of the gray-tunicked attendant who greeted him.

"Sit down," the man said softly. He indicated a high stool beside his desk. "Your name's Richard Jordan?"

"Yes, sir."

"Your classification number is 600-115. Drink this, Richard."

He lifted a plastic cup from the desk and handed it to the boy. The liquid inside had the consistency of buttermilk, tasted only vaguely of the promised peppermint. Dickie downed it, and handed the man the empty cup.

He sat in silence, feeling drowsy, while the man wrote busily on a sheet of paper. Then the attendant looked at his watch, and rose to stand only inches from Dickie's face. He unclipped a penlike object from the pocket of his tunic, and flashed a tiny light into the boy's eyes.

"All right," he said. "Come with me, Richard."

He led Dickie to the end of the room, where a single wooden armchair faced a multidialed computing machine. There was a microphone on the left arm of the chair, and when the boy sat down, he found its pinpoint head conveniently at his mouth.

"Now just relax, Richard. You'll be asked some questions, and you think them over carefully. Then give your answers into the microphone. The machine will take care of the rest."

"Yes, sir."

"I'll leave you alone now. Whenever you want to start, just say 'ready' into the microphone."

"Yes, sir."

The man squeezed his shoulder, and left.

Dickie said, "Ready."

Lights appeared on the machine, and a mechanism whirred. A voice said:

"Complete this sequence. One, four, seven, ten . . ."

Mr. and Mrs. Jordan were in the living room, not speaking, not even speculating.

It was almost four o'clock when the telephone rang. The woman tried to reach it first, but her husband was quicker.

"Mr. Jordan?"

The voice was clipped; a brisk, official voice.

"Yes, speaking."

"This is the Government Educational Services. Your son, Richard M. Jordan, Classification 600-115 has completed the Government examination. We regret to inform you that his intelligence quotient has exceeded the Government regulation, according to Rule 84, Section 5, of the New Code."

Across the room, the woman cried out, knowing nothing except the emotion she read on her husband's face.

"You may specify by telephone," the voice droned on, "whether you wish his body interred by the Government, or would you prefer a private burial place? The fee for Government burial is ten dollars."

A MESSAGE FROM CHARITY

CHARITY

William M. Lee

Teleplay by Alan Brennert

Aired November 1, 1985

Starring Kerry Noonan, Duncan McNeil, Gerald Hiken, James Cromwell

THAT SUMMER OF THE YEAR 1700 WAS THE HOTTEST IN the memory of the very oldest inhabitants. Because the year ushered in a new century, some held that the events were related and that for a whole hundred years Bay Colony would be as torrid and steamy as the Indies themselves.

There was a good deal of illness in Annes Towne, and a score had died before the weather broke at last in late September. For the great part they were oldsters who succumbed, but some of the young were sick too, and Charity Payne as sick as any.

Charity had turned eleven in the spring and had still the figure and many of the ways of thinking of a child, but she was tall and strong and tanned by the New England sun, for she spent many hours helping her father in the fields and trying to keep some sort of order in the dooryard and garden.

During the weeks when she lay bedridden and, for a time, burning up with fever, Thomas Carter and his good wife Beulah came as neighbors should to lend a hand, for Charity's mother had died abirthing and Obie Payne could not cope all alone.

Charity lay on a pallet covered by a straw-filled mattress which her father, frantic to be doing something for her and finding little enough to do beyond the saying of short, fervent prayers, refilled with fresh straw as often as Beulah would allow. A few miles down Harmon Brook was a famous beaver pond where in winter the Annes Towne people cut ice to be stored under layers of bark and chips. It had been used heavily early in the summer, and there was not very much ice left, but those families with sickness in the home might draw upon it for the patient's comfort. So Charity had bits of ice folded into a woolen cloth to lay on her forehead when the fever was bad.

William Trowbridge, who had apprenticed in medicine down in Philadelphia, attended the girl, and pronounced her illness a sort of summer cholera which was claiming victims all up and down the brook. Trowbridge was only moderately esteemed in Annes Towne, being better, it was said, at delivering lambs and foals than at treating human maladies. He was a gruff and notional man, and he was prone to state his views on a subject and then walk away instead of waiting to argue and perhaps be refuted. Not easy to get along with.

For Charity he prescribed a diet of beef tea with barley and another tea, very unpleasant to the taste, made from pounded willow bark. What was more, all her drinking water was to be boiled. Since there was no other advice to be had, they followed it, and in due course Charity got well.

She ran a great fever for five days, and it was midway in this period when the strange dreams began. Not dreams really, for she was awake, though often out of her senses, knowing her father now and then, other times seeing him as a gaunt and frightening stranger. When she was better, still weak but wholly rational, she tried to tell her visitors about these dreams.

"Some person was talking and talking," she recalled. "A man or perchance a lad. He talked not to me, but I could hear or understand all that he said. 'Twas strange talk indeed, a porridge of the King's English and other words of no sense at all. And with the talk I did see some fearful sights."

"La, now, don't even think of it," said Dame Beulah.

"But I would fen both think and talk of it, for I am no longer afeared. Such things I saw in bits and flashes, as 'twere seen by a strike of lightning."

"Talk and ye be so minded, then. There's naught impious in y'r conceits. Tell me again about the carriages which traneled along with nary horse."

Annes Towne survived the Revolution and the War of 1812, and for a time seemed likely to become a larger, if not an important, community. But when its farms became less productive and the last virgin timber disappeared from the area, Annes Towne began to disappear too, dwindling from two score of homes to a handful, then to none; and the last foundation had crumbled to rubble and been scattered a hundred years before it could have been nominated a historic site.

In time dirt tracks became stone roads, which gave way to black meanderings of macadam, and these in their turn were displaced by never-ending bands of concrete. The crossroads site of Annes Towne was presently cleared of brambles, sumac and red cedar, and overnight it was a shopping center. Now, for mile on spreading mile, the New England hills were dotted with ranch houses, salt boxes and split-level colonial homes.

During four decades Harmon Brook had been fouled and poisoned by a textile bleach and dye works. Rising labor costs had at last driven the small company to extinction. With that event and increasingly rigorous legislation, the stream had come back to the extent that it could now be bordered by some of these prosperous homes and by the golf course of the Anniston Country Club.

With aquatic plants and bullfrogs and a few fish inhabiting its waters, it was not obvious to implicate the Harmon for the small outbreak of typhoid which occurred in the hot, dry summer of 1965. No one was dependent on it for drinking water. To the discomfort of a local milk distributor, who was entirely blameless, indictment of the stream was delayed and obscured by the fact that the organisms involved were not a typical strain of *Salmonella typhosa*. Indeed they ultimately found a place in the American Type Culture Collection, under a new number.

Young Peter Wood, whose home was one of those pleasantly situated along the stream, was the most seriously ill of all the cases, partly because he was the first, mostly because his symptoms went unremarked for a time. Peter was sixteen and not highly communicative to either parents or friends. The Wood Seniors both taught, at Harvard and Wellesley respectively. They were intelligent and well-intentioned parents, but sometimes a little offhand, and like many of their friends, they raised their son to be a miniature adult in as many ways as possible. His sports, tennis, and golf, were adult sports. His reading tastes were catholic, ranging from Camus to Al Capp to science fiction. He had been carefully held back in his progress through the lower grades so that he would not enter college more than a year or so ahead of his age. He had an adequate number of friends and sufficient areas of congeniality with them. He had gotten a driver's license shortly after his sixteenth birthday and drove seriously and well enough to be allowed nearly unrestricted use of the second car.

So Peter Wood was not the sort of boy to complain to his family about headache, mild nausea and other symptoms. Instead, after they had persisted for forty-eight hours, he telephoned for an appointment on his own initiative and visited the family doctor. Suddenly, in the waiting room, he became much worse, and was given a cot in an examining room until Dr. Maxwell was free to drive him home. The doctor did not seriously suspect typhoid, though it was among several possibilities which he counted as less likely.

Peter's temperature rose from 104 degrees to over 105 degrees that night. No nurse was to be had until morning, and his parents alternated in attendance in his bedroom. There was no cause for alarm, since the patient was full of wide-spectrum antibiotic. But he slept only fitfully, with intervals of waking delirium. He slapped at the sheet, tossed around on the bed and muttered or spoke now and then. Some of the talk was understandable.

"There's a forest," he said.

"What?" asked his father.

"There's a forest the other side of the stream."

"Oh."

"Can you see it?"

"No, I'm sitting inside here with you. Take it easy, son."

"Some deer are coming down to drink, along the edge of Weller's pasture."

"Is that so?"

"Last year a mountain lion killed two of them, right where they drank. Is it raining?"

"No, it isn't. It would be fine if we could have some."

"It's raining. I can hear it on the roof." A pause. "It drips down the chimney."

Peter turned his head to look at his father, momentarily clear-eyed.

"How long since there's been a forest across the stream?"

Dr. Wood reflected on the usual difficulty of answering explicit questions and on his own ignorance of history.

"A long time. I expect this valley has been farmland since colonial days."

"Funny," Peter said. "I shut my eyes and I can see a forest. Really big trees. On our side of the stream there's a kind of garden and an apple tree, and a path goes down to the water."

"It sounds pleasant."

"Yeah."

"Why don't you try going to sleep?"

"Okay."

The antibiotic accomplished much less than it should have done in Peter's case, and he stayed very sick for several days. Even after diagnosis, there appeared no good reason to move him from home. A trained nurse was on duty after that first night, and tranquilizers and sedatives reduced her job to no more than keeping a watch. There were only a few sleepy communications from her young patient. It was on the fourth night, the last one when he had any significant fever, that he asked,

"Were you ever a girl?"

"Well, thanks a lot. I'm not as old as all that."

"I mean, were you ever inside a girl?"

"I think you'd better go back to sleep, young man."

He uttered no oddities thereafter, at least when there was anyone within hearing. During the days of his recovery and convalescence, abed and later stretched out on a chaise longue on the terrace looking down toward Harmon Brook, he took to whispering. He moved his lips hardly at all, but vocalized each word, or if he fell short of this, at least put each thought into carefully chosen words and sentences.

The idea that he might be in mental communication with another person was not, to him, very startling. Steeped in the lore of science fiction whose heroes were, as like as not, adepts at telepathy, the event seemed almost an expected outcome of his wishes. Many nights he had lain awake sending out (he hoped) a mental probe, trying and trying to find the trick, for surely there must be one, of making a contact.

Now that such a contact was established, he sought, just as vainly, for some means to prove it. How do you know you're not dreaming? he asked himself. How do you know you're not still delirious?

The difficulty was that his communication with Charity Payne could be by mental route only. Had there been any possibility for Peter to reach the girl by mail, by telephone, by travel and a personal visit, their rapport on a mental level might have been confirmed, and their messages cross-checked.

During their respective periods of illness, Peter and Charity achieved a communion of a sort which consisted at first of brief glimpses, each of the other's environment. They were not—then—seeing through one another's eyes, so much as tapping one another's visual recollections. While Peter stared at a smoothly plastered ceiling, charity looked at rough-hewn beams. He, when his aching head permitted, could turn on one side and watch a television program. She, by the same movement, could see a small, smoky fire in the monstrous stone fireplace, where water was heated and her beef and barley broth kept steaming.

Instead of these current images, current for each of them in their different times, they saw stored-up pictures, not perfect, for neither of them was remembering perfectly: rather like pictures viewed through a badly ground lens, with only the objects of principal interest in clear detail.

Charity saw her fearful sights with no basis for comprehension—a section of dual highway animated by hurtling cars and trucks and not a person, recognizable as a person, in sight; a tennis court, and what on earth could it be; a jet plane crossing the sky; a vast and many-storied building which glinted with glass and the silvery tracings of untarnished steel.

At the start she was terrified nearly out of her wits. It's all very well to dream, and a nightmare is only a bad dream after you waken, but a nightmare is assembled from familiar props. You could reasonably be chased by a dragon (like the one in the picture that St. George had to fight) or be lost in a cave (like the one on Parish Hill, only bigger and darker). To dream of things that have no meaning at all is worse.

She was spared prolongation of her terror by Peter's comprehension of their situation and his intuitive realization of what the experience, assuming a two-way channel, might be doing to her. The vignettes of her life which he was seeing were in no way disturbing. Everything he saw through her mind was within his framework of reference. Horses and cattle, fields and forest, rutted lanes and narrow wooden bridges were things he knew, even if he did not live among them. He recognized Harmon Brook because, directly below their home, there was an immense granite boulder parting the flow, shaped like a great bearlike animal with its head down, drinking. It was strange that the stream, in all those years, had neither silted up nor eroded away to hide or change the seeming of the rock, but so it was. He saw it through Charity's eyes and knew the place in spite of the forest on the far hill.

When he first saw this partly familiar, partly strange scene, he heard from somewhere within his mind the frightened cry of a little girl. His thinking at that time was fever-distorted and incoherent. It was two days later after a period of several hours of normal temperature when he conceived the idea—with sudden virtual certainty—these pastoral scenes he had been dreaming were truly something seen with other eyes. There were subtle perceptual differences between those pictures and his own seeing.

To his mother, writing at a table near the windows, he said, "I think I'm feeling better. How about a glass of orange juice?"

She considered. "The doctor should be here in an hour or so. In the meantime you can make do with a little more ice water. I'll get it. Drink it slowly, remember."

Two hundred sixty-five years away, Charity Payne thought suddenly, "How about a glass of orange juice?" She had been drowsing, but her eyes popped wide open. "Mercy," she said aloud. Dame Beulah bent over the pallet.

"What is it, child?"

"How about a glass of orange juice?" Charity repeated.

"La, 'tis gibberish." A cool hand was laid on her forehead. "Would ye like a bit of ice to bite on?"

Orange juice, whatever that might be, was forgotten.

Over the next several days Peter Wood tried time and again to address the stranger directly, and repeatedly failed. Some of what he said to others reached her in fragments and further confused her state of mind. What she had to say, on the other hand, was coming through to him with increasing frequency. Often it was only a word or a phrase with a quaint twist like a historical novel, and he would lie puzzling over it, trying to place the person on the other end of their erratic line of communication. His recognition of Bear Rock, which he had seen once again through her eyes, was disturbing. His science fiction conditioning led him naturally to speculate about the parallel-worlds concept, but that seemed not to fit the facts as he saw them.

Peter reached the stage of convalescence when he could spend all day on the terrace and look down, when he wished, at the actual rock. There for the hundredth time he formed the syllables "Hello, who are you?" and for the first time received a response. It was a silence, but a silence reverberating with shock, totally different in quality from the blankness that had met him before.

"My name is Peter Wood."

There was a long pause before the answer came, softly and timidly.

"My name is Charity Payne. Where are you? What is happening to me?"

The following days of enforced physical idleness were filled with exploration and discovery. Peter found out almost at once that, while they were probably no more than a few feet apart in their respective worlds, a gulf of more than a quarter of a thousand years stretched between them. Such a contact through time was a greater departure from known physical laws, certainly, than the mere fact of telepathic communication. Peter reveled in his growing ability.

In another way the situation was heartbreaking. No matter how well they came to know one another, he realized, they could never meet, and after no more than a few hours of acquaintance, he found that he was regarding this naive child of another time with esteem and a sort of affection.

They arrived shortly at a set of rules that seemed to govern and limit their communications. Each came to be able to hear the other speak, whether aloud or subvocally. Each learned to perceive through the other's senses, up to a point. Visual perception became better and better, especially for direct seeing, while, as they grew more skillful, the remembered scene became less clear. Tastes and odors could be transmitted, if not accurately, at least with the expected response. Tactile sensations could not be perceived in the slightest degree.

There was little that Peter Wood could learn from Charity. He came to recognize her immediate associates and liked them, particularly her gaunt, weather-beaten father. He formed a picture of Puritanism which, as an ethic, he had to respect, while the supporting dogma evoked nothing but impatience. At first he exposed her to the somewhat scholarly agnosticism that prevailed in his own home, but soon found that it distressed her deeply and he left off. There was so much he could report from the vantage of 1965, so many things he would show her that did not conflict with her tenets and faith.

He discovered that Charity's ability to read was remarkable, though what she had read was naturally limited—the Bible from cover to cover, *Pilgrim's Progress,* several essays and two of Shakespeare's plays. Encouraged by a schoolmaster who must have been an able and dedicated man, she had read and reread everything permitted to her. Her quite respectable vocabulary was gleaned from these sources and may have equaled Peter's own in size. In addition she possessed an uncanny word sense which helped her greatly in understanding Peter's jargon.

She learned the taste of bananas and frankfurters, chocolate ice cream and Coke, and displayed such an addiction to these delicacies that Peter rapidly put on some of the pounds he had lost. One day she asked him what he looked like.

"Well, I told you I am sixteen, and I'm sort of thin."

"Does thee possess a mirror?" she asked.

"Yes, of course."

At her urging and with some embarrassment, he went and stood before a mirrored door in his mother's bedroom.

"Marry," she said after a dubious pause, "I doubt not thee is comely. But folk have changed."

"Now let me look at you," he demanded.

"Nay, we have no mirror."

"Then go and look in the brook. There's a quiet spot below the rock where the water is dark."

He was delighted with her appearance, having remembered Hogarth's unkind representations of a not much later period and being prepared for disappointment. She was, in fact, very much prettier by Peter's standards than by those of her own time, which favored plumpness and smaller mouths. He told her she was a beauty, and her tentative fondness for him turned instantly to adulation.

Previously Peter had had fleeting glimpses of her slim, smoothly muscled body, as she had bathed or dressed. Now, having seen each other face to face, they were overcome by embarrassment and both of them, when not fully clothed, stared resolutely into the corners of the room.

For a time Charity believed that Peter was a dreadful liar. The sight and sound of planes in the sky were not enough to convince her of the fact of flying, so he persuaded his father to take him along on a business flight to Washington. After she had recovered from the marvels of airplane travel, he took her on a walking tour of the Capitol. Now she would believe anything, even that the American Revolution had been a success. They joined his father for lunch at an elegant French restaurant and she experienced, vicariously, the pleasures of half of a half bottle of white wine and a chocolate eclair. Charity was by way of getting spoiled.

Fully recovered and with school only a week away, Peter decided to brush up his tennis. When reading or doing nothing in particular, he was always dimly aware of Charity and her immediate surroundings, and by sharpening his attention, he could bring her clearly to the forefront of his mind. Tennis displaced her completely, and for an hour or two each day, he was unaware of her doings.

Had he been a few years older and a little more knowledgeable and realistic about the world, he might have guessed the peril into which he was leading her. Fictional villainy abounded, of course, and many items in the news didn't bear thinking about, but by his own firsthand experience, people were well intentioned and kindly, and for the most part they reacted to events with reasonable intelligence. It was what he expected instinctively.

A first hint of possible consequences reached him as he walked home from one of his tennis sessions.

"Ursula Miller said an ill thing to me today."

"Oh?" His answer was abstracted since, in all truth, he was beginning to run out of interest in the village gossip which was all the news she had to offer.

"Yesterday she said it was an untruth about the thirteen states. Today she avowed that I was devil-ridden. And Ursula has been my best friend."

"I warned you that people wouldn't believe you, and you might get yourself laughed at," he said. Then suddenly he caught up in his thinking. "Good Lord—Salem."

"Please, Peter, thee must stop taking thy Maker's name."

"I'll try to remember. Listen, Charity, how many people have you been talking to about our—about what's been happening?"

"As I have said. At first to Father and Aunt Beulah. They did believe I was still addled from the fever."

"And to Ursula."

"Aye, but she vowed to keep it secret."

"Do you believe she will, now that she's started name-calling?"

A lengthy pause.

"I fear she may have told the lad who keeps her company."

"I should have warned you. Damn it, I should have laid it on the line."

"Peter!"

"Sorry. Charity, not another word to anybody. Tell Ursula you've been fooling—telling stories to amuse her."

" 'Twould not be right."

"So what. Charity, don't be scared, but listen. People might get to thinking you're a witch."

"Oh, they couldn't."

"Why not?"

"Because I am not one. Witches are—oh, no, Peter."

He could sense her growing alarm.

"Go tell Ursula it was a pack of lies. Do it now."

"I must milk the cow."

"Do it now."

"Nay, the cow must be milked."

"Then milk her faster than she's ever been milked before."

On the Sabbath, three little boys threw stones at Charity as she and her father left the church. Obadiah Payne caught one of them and caned him, and then would have had to fight the lad's father save that the pastor intervened.

It was on the Wednesday that calamity befell. Two tight-lipped men approached Obadiah in the fields.

"Squire wants to see thy daughter Charity."

"Squire?"

"Aye. Squire Hacker. He would talk with her at once."

"Squire can talk to me if so be he would have her reprimanded. What has she been up to?"

"Witchcraft, that's what," said the second man, sounding as if he were savoring the dread news. "Croft's old ewe delivered a monstrous lamb. Pointy pinched-up face and an extra eye." He crossed himself.

"Great God!"

" 'Twill do ye no good to blaspheme, Obadiah. She's to come with us now."

"I'll not have it. Charity's no witch, as ye well know, and I'll not have her converse with Squire. Ye mind the Squire's lecherous ways."

"That's not here nor there. Witchcraft is afoot again and all are saying 'tis your Charity at bottom of it."

"She shall not go."

First one, then the other displayed the stout truncheons they had held concealed behind their backs.

" 'Twas of our own good will we told thee first. Come now and instruct thy daughter to go with us featly. Else take a clout on the head and sleep tonight in the gaol house."

They left Obie Payne gripping a broken wrist and staring in numbed bewilderment from his door stoop, and escorted Charity, not touching her, walking at a cautious distance to either side, to Squire Hacker's big house on the hill. In the village proper, little groups of people watched from doorways, and though some had always been her good friends, none had the courage now to speak a word of comfort.

Peter went with her each reluctant step of the way, counting himself responsible for her plight and helpless to do the least thing about it. He sat alone in the living room of his home, eyes closed to sharpen his reading of her surroundings. She offered no response to his whispered reassurances and perhaps did not hear them.

At the door her guards halted and stood aside, leaving her face to face with the grim-visaged squire. He moved backward step by step, and she followed him, as if hypnotized, into the shadowed room.

The squire lowered himself into a high-backed chair. "Look at me."

Unwillingly she raised her head and stared into his face.

Squire Hacker was a man of medium height, very broad in the shoulder and heavily muscled. His face was disfigured by deep pockmarks and the scar of a knife cut across the jaw, souvenirs of his earlier years in the Carib Islands. From the Islands he had also brought some wealth which he had since increased manyfold by the buying of land, sharecropping and moneylending.

"Charity Payne," he said sternly, "take off thy frock."

"No. No, please."

"I command it. Take off thy garments, for I must search thee for witch marks."

He leaned forward, seized her arm and pulled her to him. "If thee would avoid public trial and condemnation, thee will do as I say." His hands began to explore her body.

Even by the standards of the time, Charity regularly spent extraordinary hours at hard physical labor and she possessed a strength that would have done credit to many young men. Squire Hacker should have been more cautious.

"Nay," she shouted, and drawing back her arm, hit him in the nose with all the force she could muster. He released her with a roar of rage, then, while he was mopping away blood and tears with the sleeve of his ruffled shirt and shouting imprecations, she turned and shot out the door. The guards, converging, nearly grabbed her as she passed, but once she was away, they stood no chance of catching her, and for a wonder none of the villagers took up the chase.

She was well on the way home and covering the empty road at a fast trot before Peter was able to gain her attention.

"Charity," he said. "Charity, you mustn't go home. If that SOB of a squire has any influence with the court, you just fixed yourself."

She was beginning to think again and could even translate Peter's strange language.

"Influence!" she said. "Marry, he is the court. He is the judge."

"Ouch!"

"I wot well I must not be found at home. I am trying to think where to hide. I might have had trial by water. Now they will burn me for surety. I do remember what folk said about the last witch trials."

"Could you make your way to Boston and then maybe to New York— New Amsterdam?"

"Leave my home forever! Nay. And I would not dare the trip."

"Then take to the woods. Where can you go?"

"Take to—? Oh. To the cave, mayhap."

"Don't too many people know about it?"

"Aye. But there is another across the brook and beyond Tom Carter's freehold. I do believe none know of it but me. 'Tis very small. We must ford the brook just yonder, then walk that fallen tree. There is a trail which at sundown will be tromped by a herd of deer."

"You're thinking about dogs?"

"Aye, on the morrow. There is no good pack in Annes Towne."

"You live in a savage age. Charity."

"Aye," she said wryly. " 'Tis fortunate we have not invented the bomb."

"Damn it," Peter said, "I wish we'd never met. I wish I hadn't taken you on the plane trip. I wish I'd warned you to keep quiet about it."

"Ye could not guess I would be so foolish."

"What can you do out here without food?"

"I'd liefer starve than be in the stocks, but there is food to be had in the forest, some sorts of roots and toadstools and autumn berries. I shall hide myself for three days, I think, then seek out my father by night and do as he tells me."

When she was safely hidden in the cave, which was small indeed but well concealed by a thicket of young sassafras, she said:

"Now we can think. First, I would have an answer from thy superior wisdom. Can one be truly a witch and have no knowledge of it?"

"Don't be foolish. There's no such thing as a witch."

"Ah well, 'tis a matter for debate by scholars. I do feel in my heart that I am not a witch, if there be such creatures. That book, Peter, of which ye told me, which recounts the history of these colonies.''

"Yes?''

"Will ye look in it and learn if I came to trial and what befell me?''

"There'd be nothing about it. It's just a small book. But—''

To his parents' puzzlement, Peter spent the following morning at the Boston Public Library. In the afternoon he shifted his operations to the Historical Society. He found at last a listing of the names of women known to have been tried for witchcraft between the years 1692 and 1697. Thereafter he could locate only an occasional individual name. There was no record of any Charity Payne in 1700 or later.

He started again when the reading room opened next day, interrupting the task only momentarily for brief exchanges with Charity. His lack of success was cheering to her, for she overestimated the completeness of the records.

At close to noon he was scanning the pages of a photostated doctoral thesis when his eye caught a familiar name.

Jonas Hacker, born Liverpool, England, date uncertain, perhaps 1659, was the principal figure in a curious action of law which has not become a recognized legal precedent in English courts.

Squire Hacker, a resident of Annes Towne (cf. Anniston), was tried and convicted of willful murder and larceny. The trial was posthumous, several months after his decease from natural causes in 1704. The sentence pronounced was death by hanging, which, since it could not be imposed, was commuted to forfeiture of his considerable estate. His land and other possessions reverted to the Crown and were henceforward administered by the Governor of Bay Colony.

While the motivation and procedure of the court may have been open to question, evidence of Hacker's guilt was clear-cut. The details are these . . .

"Hey, Charity,'' Peter rumbled in his throat.

"Aye?''

"Look at this page. Let me flatten it out.''

"Read it please, Peter. Is it bad news?''

"No. Good, I think.'' He read the paragraphs on Jonas Hacker.

"Oh, Peter, can it be true?''

"It has to be. Can you remember any details?''

"Marry, I remember well when they disappeared, the ship's captain and a common sailor. They were said to have a great sack of gold for some matter of business with Squire. But it could not be, for they never reached his house.''

"That's what Hacker said, but the evidence showed that they got there—got there and never got away. Now, here's what you must do. Late tonight, go home.''

''I would fen do so, for I am terrible athirst.''

''No, wait. What's your parson's name?''

''John Hix.''

''Can you reach his house tonight without being seen?''

''Aye. It backs on a glen.''

''Go there. He can protect you better than your father can until your trial.''

''Must I be tried?''

''Of course. We want to clear your name. Now let's do some planning.''

The town hall could seat no more than a score of people, and the day was fair; so it was decided that the trial should be held on the common, in discomforting proximity to the stocks.

Visitors came from as far as twenty miles away, afoot or in carts, and nearly filled the common itself. Squire Hacker's own armchair was the only seat provided. Others stood or sat on the patchy grass.

The squire came out of the inn presently, fortified with rum, and took his place. He wore a brocaded coat and a wide-brimmed hat and would have been more impressive if it had not been for his still swollen nose, now permanently askew.

A way was made through the crowd then, and Charity, flanked on one side by John Hix, on the other by his tall son, walked to the place where she was to stand. Voices were suddenly stilled. Squire Hacker did not condescend to look directly at the prisoner, but fixed a cold stare on the minister: a warning that his protection of the girl would not be forgiven. He cleared his throat.

''Charity Payne, is thee willing to swear upon the Book?''

''Aye.''

''No mind. We may forgo the swearing. All can see that ye are fearful.''

''Nay,'' John Hix interrupted. ''She shall have the opportunity to swear to her word. 'Twould not be legal otherwise.'' He extended a Bible to Charity, who placed her fingers on it and said, ''I do swear to speak naught but the truth.''

Squire Hacker glowered and lost no time coming to the attack. ''Charity Payne, do ye deny being a witch?''

''I do.''

''Ye do be one?''

''Nay, I do deny it.''

''Speak what ye mean. What have ye to say of the monstrous lamb born of Master Croft's ewe?''

''I know naught of it.''

''Was't the work of Satan?''

"I know not."

"Was't then the work of God?"

"I know not."

"Thee holds then that He might create such a monster?'"

"I know naught about it."

"In thy own behalf will thee deny saying that this colony and its neighbors will in due course make wars against our King?"

"Nay, I do not deny that."

There was a stir in the crowd and some angry muttering.

"Did ye tell Mistress Ursula Miller that ye had flown a great journey through the air?"

"Nay."

"Mistress Ursula will confound thee in that lie."

"I did tell Ursula that someday folk would travel in that wise. I did tell her that I had seen such travel through eyes other than my own."

Squire Hacker leaned forward. He could not have hoped for a more damning statement. John Hix's head bowed in prayer.

"Continue."

"Aye. I am blessed with a sort of second sight."

"Blessed or cursed?"

"God permits it. It cannot be accursed."

"Continue. What evil things do ye see by this second sight?"

"Most oftentimes I see the world as it will one day be. Thee said evil. Such sights are no more and no less evil than we see around us.'

Hacker pondered. There was an uncomfortable wrongness about this child's testimony. She should have been gibbering with fear, when in fact she seemed self-possessed. He wondered if by some strange chance she really had assistance from the devil's minions.

"Charity Payne, thee has confessed to owning second sight. Does thee use this devilish power to spy on thy neighbors?"

It was a telling point. Some among the spectators exchanged discomfited glances.

"Nay, 'tis not devilish, and I cannot see into the doings of my neighbors—except—"

"Speak up, girl. Except what?"

"Once I did perceive by my seeing a most foul murder."

"Murder!" The squire's voice was harsh. A few in the crowd made the sign of the cross.

"Aye. To tell true, two murders. Men whose corpses do now lie buried unshriven in a dark cellar close onto this spot. 'Tween them lies a satchel of golden guineas."

It took a minute for the squire to find his voice.

"A cellar?" he croaked.

"Aye, a root cellar, belike the place one would keep winter apples."

She lifted her head and stared straight into the squire's eyes, challenging him to inquire further.

The silence was ponderous as he strove to straighten out his thoughts. To this moment he was safe, for her words described every cellar in and about the village. But she knew. Beyond any question, she knew. Her gaze, seeming to penetrate the darkest corners of his mind, told him that, even more clearly than her words.

Squire Hacker believed in witches and considered them evil and deserving of being destroyed. He had seen and shuddered at the horrible travesty of a lamb in farmer Croft's stable yard, but he had seen like deformities in the Caribbee and did not hold the event an evidence of witchcraft. Not for a minute had he thought Charity a witch, for she showed none of the signs. Her wild talk and the growing rumors had simply seemed to provide the opportunity for some dalliance with a pretty young girl and possibly, in exchange for an acquittal, a lien upon her father's land.

Now he was unsure. She must indeed have second sight to have penetrated his secret, for it had been stormy that night five years ago, and none had seen the missing sailors near to his house. Of that he was confident. Further, shockingly, she knew how and where they lay buried. Another question and answer could not be risked.

He moved his head slowly and looked right and left at the silent throng.

"Charity Payne," he said, picking his words with greatest care, "has put her hand on the Book and sworn to tell true, an act, I opine, she could scarce perform, were she a witch. Does any person differ with me?"

John Hix looked up in startled hopefulness.

"Very well. The lambing at Master Croft's did have the taint of witchcraft, but Master Trowbridge has stated his belief that some noxious plant is growing in Croft's pasture, and 'tis at the least possible. Besides, the ewe is old and she has thrown runty lambs before.

"To quote Master Trowbridge again, he holds that the cholera which has afflicted us so sorely comes from naught but the drinking of bad water. He advises boiling it. I prefer adding a little rum."

He got the laughter he sought. There was a lessening of tension.

"As to second sight." Again he swept the crowd with his gaze. "Charity had laid claim to it, and I called it a devilish gift to test her, but second sight is not witchcraft, as ye well know. My own grandmother had it, and a better women ne'er lived. I hold it to be a gift of God. Would any challenge me?

"Very well. I would warn Charity to be cautious in what she sees and tells, for second sight can lead to grievous disputations. I do not hold with her story of two murdered men, although I think that in her own sight she is telling true. If any have aught of knowledge of so dire a crime, I adjure him to step forth and speak."

He waited. "Nobody? Then, by the authority conferred on me by his Excellency the Governor, I declare that Charity Payne is innocent of the charges brought. She may be released."

This was not at all the eventuality that a few of Squire Hacker's cronies had foretold. The crowd had clearly expected a daylong inquisition climaxed by a prisoner to bedevil in the stocks. The squire's about-face and his abrupt ending of the trial surprised them and angered a few. They stood uncertain.

Then someone shouted hurrah and someone else called for three cheers for Squire Hacker, and all in a minute the gathering had lost its hate and was taking on the look of a picnic. Men headed for the tavern. Parson Hix said a long prayer to which few listened, and everybody gathered around to wring Obie Payne's good hand and to give his daughter a squeeze.

At intervals through the afternoon and evening Peter touched lightly on Charity's mind, finding her carefree and happily occupied with visitors. He chose not to obtrude himself until she called.

Late that night she lay on her mattress and stared into the dark.

"Peter," she whispered.

"Yes, Charity."

"Oh, thank you again."

"Forget it. I got you into the mess. Now you're out of it. Anyway, I didn't really help. It all had to work out the way it did, because that's the way it had happened. You see?"

"No, not truly. How do we know that Squire won't dig up those old bones and burn them?"

"Because he didn't. Four years from now somebody will find them."

"No, Peter, I do not understand, and I am afeared again."

"Why, Charity?"

"It must be wrong, thee and me talking together like this and knowing what is to be and what is not."

"But what could be wrong about it?"

"That I do not know, but I think 'twere better you should stay in your time and me in mine. Good-bye, Peter."

"Charity!"

"And God bless you."

Abruptly she was gone and in Peter's mind there was an emptiness and a knowledge of being alone. He had not known that she could close him out like this.

With the passing of days he became skeptical and in time he might have disbelieved entirely. But Charity visited him again. It was October. He was alone and studying, without much interest.

"Peter."

"Charity, it's you."

"Yes. For a minute, please, Peter, for only a minute, but I had to tell you. I—" She seemed somehow embarrassed. "There is a message."

"A what?"

"Look at Bear Rock, Peter, under the bear's jaw on the left side."

With that, she was gone.

The cold water swirled around his legs as he traced with one finger the painstakingly chiseled message she had left: a little-girl message in a symbol far older than either of them.

PALADIN OF THE LOST HOUR*

Harlan Ellison

TELEPLAY BY HARLAN ELLISON

AIRED NOVEMBER 8, 1985

STARRING DANNY KAYE, GLYNN TURMAN

*The author gratefully acknowledges the importance of a discussion with Ms. Ellie Grossman in the creation of this work of fiction.

THIS WAS AN OLD MAN. NOT AN INCREDIBLY OLD MAN; obsolete, spavined; not as worn as the sway-backed stone steps ascending the Pyramid of the Sun to an ancient temple; not yet a relic. But even so, a *very* old man, this old man perched on an antique shooting stick, its handles open to form a seat, its spike thrust at an angle into the soft ground and trimmed grass of the cemetery. Gray, thin rain misted down at almost the same angle as that at which the spike pierced the ground. The winter-barren trees lay flat and black against an aluminum sky, unmoving in the chill wind. An old man sitting at the foot of a grave mound whose headstone had tilted slightly when the earth had settled; sitting in the rain and speaking to someone below.

"They tore it down, Minna.

"I tell you, they must have bought off a councilman.

"Came in with bulldozers at six o'clock in the morning, and you *know* that's not legal. There's a Municipal Code. Supposed to hold off till at least seven on weekdays, eight on the weekend; but there they were at six, even *before* six, barely light, for godsakes. Thought they'd sneak in and do it before the neighborhood got wind of it and call the landmarks committee. Sneaks: they come on *holidays,* can you imagine!

"But I was out there waiting for them, and I told them, 'You can't do it, that's Code number 91.03002, subsection E,' and they lied and said they had special permission, so I said to the big muckymuck in charge, 'Let's see your waiver permit,' and he said the Code didn't apply in this case because it was supposed to be only for grading, and since they were demolishing and not grading, they could start whenever they felt like it. So I told him I'd call the police, then, because it came under the heading of Disturbing the Peace, and he said . . . well, I know you hate that kind of language, old girl, so I won't tell you what he said, but you can imagine.

"So I called the police, and gave them my name, and of course they didn't get there till almost quarter after seven (which is what makes me think they bought off a councilman), and by then those 'dozers had leveled most of it. Doesn't take long, you know that.

"And I don't suppose it's as great a loss as, maybe, say, the Great Library of Alexandria, but it was the last of the authentic Deco-design drive-ins, and the carhops still served you on roller skates, and it was a landmark, and just about the only place left in the city where you could still get a decent grilled cheese sandwich pressed very flat on the grill by one of those weights they used to use, made with real cheese and not that rancid plastic they cut into squares and call it 'cheese food.'

"Gone, old dear, gone and mourned. And I understand they plan to put up another one of those mini-malls on the site, just ten blocks away from one that's already there, and you know what's going to happen: this new one will drain off the traffic from the older one, and then that one will fail the way they all do when the next one gets built, you'd think they'd see some history in it; but no, they never learn. And you should have seen the crowd by seven-thirty. All ages, even some of those kids painted like aborigines, with torn leather clothing. Even they came to protest. Terrible language, but at least they were concerned. And nothing could stop it. They just whammed it, and down it went.

"I do so miss you today, Minna. No more good grilled cheese." Said the *very* old man to the ground. And now he was crying softly, and now the wind rose, and the mist rain stippled his overcoat.

Nearby, yet at a distance, Billy Kinetta stared down at another grave. He could see the old man over there off to his left, but he took no further notice. The wind whipped the vent of his trenchcoat. His collar was up but rain trickled down his neck. This was a younger man, not yet thirty-five. Unlike the old man, Billy Kinetta neither cried nor spoke to memories of someone who had once listened. He might have been a geomancer, so silently did he stand, eyes toward the ground.

One of these men was black; the other was white.

Beyond the high, spiked-iron fence surrounding the cemetery, two boys crouched, staring through the bars, through the rain; at the men absorbed by grave matters, by matters of graves. These were not really boys. They were legally young men. One was nineteen, the other two months beyond twenty. Both were legally old enough to vote, to drink alcoholic beverages, to drive a car. Neither would reach the age of Billy Kinetta.

One of them said, "Let's take the old man."

The other responded, "You think the guy in the trenchcoat'll get in the way?"

The first one smiled; and a mean little laugh. "I sure as shit hope so." He wore, on his right hand, a leather carnaby glove with the fingers cut off, small round metal studs in a pattern along the line of his knuckles. He made a fist, flexed, did it again.

They went under the spiked fence at a point where erosion had created a shallow gully. "Son of a bitch!" one of them said, as he slid through on his stomach. It was muddy. The front of his sateen roadie jacket was filthy. "Son of a bitch!" He was speaking in general of the fence, the sliding under, the muddy ground, the universe in total. And the old man, who would now *really* get the crap kicked out of him for making this fine sateen roadie jacket filthy.

They sneaked up on him from the left, as far from the young guy in the trenchcoat as they could. The first one kicked out the shooting stick with a short, sharp, downward movement he had learned in his tae kwon do class. It was called the *yup-chagi*. The old man went over backward.

Then they were on him, the one with the filthy son of a bitch sateen roadie jacket punching at the old man's neck and the side of his face as he dragged him around by the collar of the overcoat. The other one began ransacking the coat pockets, ripping the fabric to get his hand inside.

The old man commenced to scream. "Protect me! You've got to protect me . . . it's necessary to protect me!"

The one pillaging pockets froze momentarily. What the hell kind of thing is that for this old fucker to be saying? Who the hell does he think'll protect him? Is he asking *us* to protect him? I'll protect you, scumbag! I'll kick in your fuckin' lung! "Shut 'im up!" he whispered urgently to his friend. "Stick a fist in his mouth!" Then his hand, wedged in an inside jacket pocket, closed over something. He tried to get his hand loose, but the jacket and coat and the old man's body had wound around his wrist. "C'mon loose, motherfuckah!" he said to the very old man, who was still screaming for protection. The other young man was making huffing sounds, as dark as mud, as he slapped at the rain-soaked hair of his victim. "I can't . . . he's all twisted 'round . . . getcher hand outta there so's I can . . ." Screaming, the old man had doubled under, locking their hands on his person.

And then the pillager's fist came loose, and he was clutching—for an instant—a gorgeous pocket watch.

What used to be called a turnip watch.

The dial face was *cloisonné*, exquisite beyond the telling.

The case was of silver, so bright it seemed blue.

The hands, cast as arrows of time, were gold. They formed a shallow V at precisely eleven o'clock. This was happening at 3:45 in the afternoon, with rain and wind.

The timepiece made no sound, no sound at all.

Then: there was space all around the watch, and in that space in the palm of the hand, there was heat. Intense heat for just a moment, just long enough for the hand to open.

The watch glided out of the boy's palm and levitated.

"Help me! You *must* protect me!"

Billy Kinetta heard the shrieking, but did not see the pocket watch floating in the air above the astonished young man. It was silver, and it was end-on toward him, and the rain was silver and slanting; and he did not see the watch hanging free in the air, even when the furious young man disentangled himself and leaped for it. Billy did not see the watch rise just so much, out of reach of the mugger.

Billy Kinetta saw two boys, two young men of rat-pack age, beating someone much older; and he went for them. Pow, like that!

Thrashing his legs, the old man twisted around—over, under—as the boy holding him by the collar tried to land a punch to put him away. Who would have thought the old man to have had so much battle in him?

A flapping shape, screaming something unintelligible, hit the center of the group at full speed. The carnaby-gloved hand reaching for the watch grasped at empty air one moment, and the next was buried under its owner as the boy was struck a crackback block that threw him face-first into the soggy ground. He tried to rise, but something stomped him at the base of his spine; something kicked him twice in the kidneys; something rolled over him like a flash flood.

Twisting, twisting, the very old man put his thumb in the right eye of the boy clutching his collar.

The great trenchcoated maelstrom that was Billy Kinetta whirled into the boy as he let loose of the old man on the ground and, howling, slapped a palm against his stinging eye. Billy locked his fingers and delivered a roundhouse wallop that sent the boy reeling backward to fall over Minna's tilted headstone.

Billy's back was to the old man. He did not see the miraculous pocket watch smoothly descend through rain that did not touch it, to hover in front of the old man. He did not see the old man reach up, did not see the timepiece snuggle into an arthritic hand, did not see the old man return the turnip to an inside jacket pocket.

Wind, rain and Billy Kinetta pummeled two young men of a legal age that made them accountable for their actions. There was no thought of the knife stuck down in one boot, no chance to reach it, no moment when the wild thing let them rise. So they crawled. They scrabbled across the muddy ground, the slippery grass, over graves and out of his reach. They ran; falling, rising, falling again; away, without looking back.

Billy Kinetta, breathing heavily, knees trembling, turned to help the old man to his feet; and found him standing, brushing dirt from his overcoat, snorting in anger and mumbling to himself.

"Are you all right?"

For a moment the old man's recitation of annoyance continued, then he snapped his chin down sharply as if marking end to the situation, and looked at his cavalry to the rescue. "That was very good, young fella. Considerable style you've got there."

Billy Kinetta stared at him wide-eyed. "Are you sure you're okay?" He reached over and flicked several blades of wet grass from the shoulder of the old man's overcoat.

"I'm fine. I'm fine, but I'm wet and I'm cranky. Let's go somewhere and have a nice cup of Earl Grey."

There had been a look on Billy Kinetta's face as he stood with lowered eyes, staring at the grave he had come to visit. The emergency had removed that look. Now it returned.

"No, thanks. If you're okay, I've got to do some things."

The old man felt himself all over, meticulously, as he replied, "I'm only superficially bruised. Now, if I were an old woman, instead of a spunky old man, same age though, I'd have lost considerable of the calcium in my bones, and those two would have done me some mischief. Did you know that women lose a considerable part of their calcium when they reach my age? I read a report.'' Then he paused, and said shyly, ''Come on, why don't you and I sit and chew the fat over a nice cup of tea?''

Billy shook his head with bemusement, smiling despite himself. ''You're something else, Dad. I don't even know you.''

''I like that.''

''What: that I don't know you?''

''No, that you called me 'Dad' and not 'Pop.' I *hate* 'Pop.' Always makes me think the wise-apple wants to snap off my cap with a bottle opener. Now, *Dad* has a ring of respect to it. I like that right down to the ground. Yes, I believe we should find someplace warm and quiet to sit and get to know each other. After all, you saved my life. And you know what that means in the Orient.''

Billy was smiling continuously now. ''In the first place, I doubt very much I saved your life. Your wallet, maybe. And in the second place, I don't even know your name; what would we have to talk about?''

''Gaspar,'' he said, extending his hand. ''That's a first name. Gaspar. Know what it means?''

Billy shook his head.

''See, already we have something to talk about.''

So Billy, still smiling, began walking Gaspar out of the cemetery. ''Where do you live? I'll take you home.''

They were on the street, approaching Billy Kinetta's 1979 Cutlass. ''Where I live is too far for now. I'm beginning to feel a bit peaky. I'd like to lie down for a minute. We can just go on over to your place, if that doesn't bother you. For a few minutes. A cup of tea. Is that all right?''

He was standing beside the Cutlass, looking at Billy with an old man's expectant smile, waiting for him to unlock the door and hold it for him till he'd placed his still-calcium-rich but nonetheless old bones in the passenger seat. Billy stared at him, trying to figure out what was at risk if he unlocked that door. Then he snorted a tiny laugh, unlocked the door, held it for Gaspar as he seated himself, slammed it and went around to unlock the other side and get in. Gaspar reached across and thumbed up the door lock knob. And they drove off together in the rain.

Through all of this the timepiece made no sound, no sound at all.

Like Gaspar, Billy Kinetta was alone in the world.

His three-room apartment was the vacuum in which he existed. It was furnished, but if one stepped out into the hallway and, for all the money in all the numbered accounts in all the banks in Switzerland, one was asked to describe those furnishings, one would come away no richer than before. The apartment was charisma poor. It was a place to come when all other possibilities had been expended. Nothing green, nothing alive, existed in those boxes. No eyes looked back from the walls. Neither warmth nor chill marked those spaces. It was a place to wait.

Gaspar leaned his closed shooting stick, now a walking stick with handles, against the bookcase. He studied the titles of the paperbacks stacked haphazardly on the shelves.

From the kitchenette came the sound of water running into a metal pan. Then tin on cast iron. Then the hiss of gas and the flaring of a match as it was struck; and the pop of the gas being lit.

"Many years ago," Gaspar said, taking out a copy of Moravia's *The Adolescents* and thumbing it as he spoke, "I had a library of books, oh, thousands of books—never could bear to toss one out, not even the bad ones—and when folks would come to the house to visit, they'd look around at all the nooks and crannies stuffed with books; and if they were the sort of folks who don't snuggle with books, they'd always ask the same dumb question." He waited for a moment for a response and when none was forthcoming (the sound of china cups on sink tile), he said, "Guess what the question was."

From the kitchen, without much interest: "No idea."

"They'd always ask it with the kind of voice people use in the presence of large sculptures in museums. They'd ask me, 'Have you read all these books?' " He waited again, but Billy Kinetta was not playing the game. "Well, young fella, after a while the same dumb question gets asked a million times, you get sorta snappish about it. And it came to annoy me more than a little bit. Till I finally figured out the right answer.

"And you know what that answer was? Go ahead, take a guess."

Billy appeared in the kitchenette doorway. "I suppose you told them you'd read a lot of them but not all of them."

Gaspar waved the guess away with a flapping hand. "Now, what good would that have done? They wouldn't know they'd asked a dumb question, but I didn't want to insult them, either. So when they'd ask if I'd read all those books, I'd say, 'Hell, no. Who wants a library full of books you've already read?' "

Billy laughed despite himself. He scratched at his hair with idle pleasure, and shook his head at the old man's verve. "Gaspar, you are a wild old man. You retired?"

The old man walked carefully to the most comfortable chair in the room, an overstuffed Thirties-style lounger that had been reupholstered many times before Billy Kinetta had purchased it at the American Cancer Society Thrift Shop. He sank into it with a sigh. "No, sir, I am not by any means retired. Still very active."

"Doing what, if I'm not prying?"

"Doing ombudsman."

"You mean, like a consumer advocate? Like Ralph Nader?"

"Exactly. I watch out for things. I listen, I pay some attention; and if I do it right, sometimes I can even make a little difference. Yes, like Mr. Nader. A very fine man."

"And you were at the cemetery to see a relative?"

Gaspar's face settled into an expression of loss. "My dear old girl. My wife, Minna. She's been gone, well, it was twenty years in January." He sat silently staring inward for a while, then: "She was everything to me. The nice part was that I knew how important we were to each other; we discussed, well, just *everything*. I miss that the most, telling her what's going on.

"I go to see her every other day.

"I used to go every day. But. It. Hurt. Too much."

They had tea. Gaspar sipped and said it was very nice, but had Billy ever tried Earl Grey? Billy said he didn't know what that was, and Gaspar said he would bring him a tin, that it was splendid. And they chatted. Finally, Gaspar asked, "And who were you visiting?"

Billy pressed his lips together. "Just a friend." And would say no more. Then he sighed and said, "Well, listen, I have to go to work."

"Oh? What do you do?"

The answer came slowly. As if Billy Kinetta wanted to be able to say that he was in computers, or owned his own business, or held a position of import. "I'm night manager at a 7-Eleven."

"I'll bet you meet some fascinating people coming in late for milk or one of those slushies," Gaspar said gently. He seemed to understand.

Billy smiled. He took the kindness as it was intended. "Yeah, the cream of high society. That is, when they're not threatening to shoot me through the head if I don't open the safe."

"Let me ask you a favor," Gaspar said. "I'd like a little sanctuary, if you think it's all right. Just a little rest. I could lie down on the sofa for a bit. Would that be all right? You trust me to stay here while you're gone, young fella?"

Billy hesitated only a moment. The very old man seemed okay, not a crazy, certainly not a thief. And what was there to steal? Some tea that wasn't even Earl Grey?

"Sure. That'll be okay. But I won't be coming back till two A.M. So just close the door behind you when you go; it'll lock automatically."

They shook hands, Billy shrugged into his still wet trenchcoat, and he went to the door. He paused to look back at Gaspar sitting in the lengthening shadows as evening came on. "It was nice getting to know you, Gaspar."

"You can make that a mutual pleasure, Billy. You're a nice young fella."

And Billy went to work, alone as always.

* * *

When he came home at two, prepared to open a can of Hormel chili, he found the table set for dinner, with the scent of an elegant beef stew enriching the apartment. There were new potatoes and stir-fried carrots and zucchini that had been lightly battered to delicate crispness. And cupcakes. White cake with chocolate frosting. From a bakery.

And in that way, as gently as that, Gaspar insinuated himself into Billy Kinetta's apartment and his life.

As they sat with tea and cupcakes, Billy said, "You don't have any-place to go, do you?"

The old man smiled and made one of those deprecating movements of the head. "Well, I'm not the sort of fella who can bear to be homeless, but at the moment I'm what vaudevillians used to call 'at liberty.' "

"If you want to stay on a time, that would be okay," Billy said. "It's not very roomy here, but we seem to get on all right."

"That's strongly kind of you, Billy. Yes, I'd like to be your roommate for a while. Won't be too long, though. My doctor tells me I'm not long for this world." He paused, looked into the teacup, and said softly, "I have to confess . . . I'm a little frightened. To go. Having someone to talk to would be a great comfort."

And Billy said, without preparation, "I was visiting the grave of a man who was in my rifle company in Vietnam. I go there sometimes." But there was such pain in his words that Gaspar did not press him for details.

So the hours passed, as they will with or without permission, and when Gaspar asked Billy if they could watch television, to catch an early news-cast, and Billy tuned in the old set just in time to pick up dire reports of another aborted disarmament talk, and Billy shook his head and observed that it wasn't only Gaspar who was frightened of something like death, Gaspar chuckled, patted Billy on the knee and said, with unassailable assurance, "Take my word for it, Billy . . . it isn't going to happen. No nuclear holocaust. Trust me, when I tell you this: it'll never happen. Never, never, not ever."

Billy smiled wanly. "And why not? What makes *you* so sure . . . got some special inside information?"

And Gaspar pulled out the magnificent timepiece, which Billy was seeing for the first time, and he said, "It's not going to happen because it's only eleven o'clock."

Billy stared at the watch, which read 11:00 precisely. He consulted his wristwatch. "Hate to tell you this, but your watch has stopped. It's al-most five-thirty."

Gaspar smiled his own certain smile. "No, it's eleven."

And they made up the sofa for the very old man, who placed his pocket change and his fountain pen and the sumptuous turnip watch on the now silent television set, and they went to sleep.

* * *

One day Billy went off while Gaspar was washing the lunch dishes, and when he came back, he had a large paper bag from Toys R Us.

Gaspar came out of the kitchenette rubbing a plate with a souvenir dish towel from Niagara Falls, New York. He stared at Billy and the bag. ''What's in the bag?'' Billy inclined his head, and indicated the very old man should join him in the middle of the room. Then he sat down cross-legged on the floor, and dumped the contents of the bag. Gaspar stared with startlement, and sat down beside him.

So for two hours they played with tiny cars that turned into robots when the sections were unfolded.

Gaspar was excellent at figuring out all the permutations of the Trans-formers, Starriors and GoBots. He played well.

And they went for a walk. ''I'll treat you to a matinee,'' Gaspar said. ''But no films with Karen Black, Sandy Dennis or Meryl Streep. They're always crying. Their noses are always red. I can't stand that.''

They started to cross the avenue. Stopped at the light was this year's Cadillac Brougham, vanity license plates, ten coats of acrylic lacquer and two coats of clear (with a little retarder in the final ''color coat'' for a slow dry) of magenta hue so rich that it approximated the shade of light shining through a decanter filled with Château Lafite-Rothschild 1945.

The man driving the Cadillac had no neck. His head sat thumped down hard on the shoulders. He stared straight ahead, took one last deep pull on the cigar, and threw it out the window. The still-smoking butt landed directly in front of Gaspar as he passed the car. The old man stopped, stared down at this coprolitic metaphor, and then stared at the driver. The eyes behind the wheel, the eyes of a macaque, did not waver from the stoplight's red circle. Just outside the window, someone was looking in, but the eyes of the rhesus were on the red circle.

A line of cars stopped behind the Brougham.

Gaspar continued to stare at the man in the Cadillac for a moment, and then, with creaking difficulty, he bent and picked up the smoldering butt of stogie.

The old man walked the two steps to the car—as Billy watched in confusion—thrust his face forward till it was mere inches from the driv-er's profile, and said with extreme sweetness, ''I think you dropped this in our living room.''

And as the glazed simian eyes turned to stare directly into the pedes-trian's face, nearly nose to nose, Gaspar casually flipped the butt, with its red glowing tip, into the back seat of the Cadillac, where it began to burn a hole in the fine Corinthian leather.

Three things happened simultaneously:

The driver let out a howl, tried to see the butt in his rearview mirror, could not get the angle, tried to look over his shoulder into the back seat but without a neck could not perform that feat of agility, put the car into neutral, opened his door and stormed into the street trying to grab Gaspar. "You fuckin' bastid, whaddaya think you're doin' tuh my car you asshole bastid, I'll kill ya . . ."

Billy's hair stood on end as he saw what Gaspar was doing; he rushed back the short distance in the crosswalk to grab the old man; Gaspar would not be dragged away, stood smiling with unconcealed pleasure at the mad bull rampaging and screaming of the hysterical driver. Billy yanked as hard as he could and Gaspar began to move away, around the front of the Cadillac, toward the far curb. Still grinning with octogeneric charm.

The light changed.

These three things happened in the space of five seconds, abetted by the impatient honking of the cars behind the Brougham; as the light turned green.

Screaming, dragging, honking, as the driver found he could not do three things at once: he could not go after Gaspar while the traffic was clanging at him; could not let go of the car door to crawl into the backseat from which now came the stench of charring leather that could not be rectified by an inexpensive Tijuana tuck-'n-roll; could not save his backseat and at the same time stave off the hostility of a dozen drivers cursing and honking. He trembled there, torn three ways, doing nothing.

Billy dragged Gaspar.

Out of the crosswalk. Out of the street. Onto the curb. Up the side street. Into the alley. Through a backyard. To the next street from the avenue.

Puffing with the exertion, Billy stopped at last, five houses up the street. Gaspar was still grinning, chuckling softly with unconcealed pleasure at his puckish ways. Billy turned on him with wild gesticulations and babble.

"You're *nuts!*"

"How about that?" the old man said, giving Billy an affectionate poke in the bicep.

"Nuts! Looney! That guy would've torn off your head! What the hell's wrong with you, old man? Are you out of your boots?"

"I'm not crazy. I'm responsible."

"Responsible!?! Re*spon*sible, fer chrissakes? For what? For all the butts every yotz throws into the street?"

The old man nodded. "For butts, and trash, and pollution, and toxic waste dumping in the dead of night; for bushes, and cactus, and the baobab tree; for pippin apples and even lima beans, which I despise. You show me someone who'll eat lima beans without being at gunpoint, I'll show you a pervert!"

Billy was screaming. "What the hell are you talking about?"

"I'm also responsible for dogs and cats and guppies and cockroaches and the President of the United States and Jonas Salk and your mother and the entire chorus line at the Sands Hotel in Las Vegas. Also their choreographer.''

"Who do you think you are? God?"

"Don't be sacrilegious. I'm too old to wash your mouth out with laundry soap. Of course I'm not God. I'm just an old man. *But I'm responsible.*"

Gaspar started to walk away, toward the corner and the avenue and a resumption of their route. Billy stood where the old man's words had pinned him.

"Come on, young fella," Gaspar said, walking backward to speak to him, "we'll miss the beginning of the movie. I hate that."

Billy had finished eating, and they were sitting in the dimness of the apartment, only the lamp in the corner lit. The old man had gone to the County Art Museum and had bought inexpensive prints—Max Ernst, Gérôme, Richard Dadd, a subtle Feininger—which he had mounted in Insta-Frames. They sat in silence for a time, relaxing; then murmuring trivialities in a pleasant undertone.

Finally, Gaspar said, "I've been thinking a lot about my dying. I like what Woody Allen said."

Billy slid to a more comfortable position in the lounger. "What was that?"

"He said: I don't mind dying, I just don't want to be there when it happens."

Billy snickered.

"I feel something like that, Billy. I'm not afraid to go, but I don't want to leave Minna entirely. The times I spend with her, talking to her, well, it gives me the feeling we're still in touch. When I go, that's the end of Minna. She'll be well and truly dead. We never had any children, almost everyone who knew us is gone, no relatives. And we never did anything important that anyone would put in a record book, so that's the end of us. For me, I don't mind; but I wish there was someone who knew about Minna . . . she was a remarkable person."

So Billy said, "Tell me. I'll remember for you."

Memories in no particular order. Some as strong as ropes that could pull the ocean ashore. Some that shimmered and swayed in the faintest breeze like spiderwebs. The entire person, all the little movements, that dimple that appeared when she was amused at something foolish he had said. Their youth together, their love, the procession of their days toward middle age. The small cheers and the pain of dreams never realized. So much about him, as he spoke of her. His voice soft and warm and filled with a longing so deep and true that he had to stop frequently because the words broke and would not come out till he had thought away some of the passion. He thought of her and was glad. He had gathered her together, all her dowry of love and taking care of him, her clothes and the way she wore them, her favorite knickknacks, a few clever remarks: and he packed it all up and delivered it to a new repository.

The very old man gave Minna to Billy Kinetta for safekeeping.

Dawn had come. The light filtering in through the blinds was saffron. "Thank you, Dad," Billy said. He could not name the feeling that had taken him hours earlier. But he said this: "I've never had to be responsible for anything, or anyone, in my whole life. I never belonged to anybody . . . I don't know why. It didn't bother me, because I didn't know any other way to be."

Then his position changed, there in the lounger. He sat up in a way that Gaspar thought was important. As if Billy were about to open the secret box buried at his center. And Billy spoke so softly, the old man had to strain to hear him.

"I didn't even know him.

"We were defending the airfield at Danang. Did I tell you we were 1st Battalion, 9th Marines? Charlie was massing for a big push out of Quang Ngai province, south of us. Looked as if they were going to try to take the provincial capital. My rifle company was assigned to protect the perimeter. They kept sending in patrols to bite us. Every day we'd lose some poor bastard who scratched his head when he shouldn't of. It was June, late in June, cold and a lot of rain. The foxholes were hip-deep in water.

"Flares first. Our howitzers started firing. Then the sky was full of tracers, and I started to turn toward the bushes when I heard something coming, and these two main-force regulars in dark blue uniforms came toward me. I could see them so clearly. Long black hair. All crouched over. And they started firing. And that goddam carbine seized up, wouldn't fire; and I pulled out the banana clip, tried to slap in another, but they saw me and just turned a couple of AK-47's on me . . . God, I remember everything slowed down . . . I looked at those things, seven-point-six-two-millimeter assault rifles, they were . . . I got crazy for a second, tried to figure out in my own mind if they were Russian-made, or Chinese, or Czech, or North Korean. And it was so bright from the flares, I could see them starting to squeeze off the rounds, and then from out of nowhere this lance corporal jumped out at them and yelled some-damnthing like, 'Hey, you VC fucks, looka here!' except it wasn't that . . . I never could recall what he said actually . . . and they turned to brace him . . . and they opened him up like a Baggie full of blood . . . and he was all over me, and the bushes, and oh God there was pieces of him floating on the water I was standing in . . ."

Billy was heaving breath with impossible weight. His hands moved in the air before his face without pattern or goal. He kept looking into far corners of the dawn-lit room as if special facts might present themselves to fill out the reasons behind what he was saying.

"Aw, Jeezus, he was *floating* on the water . . . aw, Christ, *he got in my boots!*" Then a wail of pain so loud it blotted out the sound of traffic beyond the apartment; and he began to moan, but not cry; and the moaning kept on; and Gaspar came from the sofa and held him and said such words as *it's all right,* but they might not have been those words, or *any* words.

And pressed against the old man's shoulder, Billy Kinetta ran on only half-sane: "He wasn't my friend, I never knew him, I'd never talked to him, but I'd seen him, he was just this guy, and there wasn't any reason to do that, he didn't know whether I was a good guy or a shit or anything, so why did he do that? He didn't need to do that. They wouldn't of seen him. He was dead before I killed them. He was gone already. I never got to say thank you or thank you or . . . *anything!*

"Now he's in that grave, so I came here to live, so I can go there, but I try and try to say thank you, and he's dead, and he can't hear me, he can't hear anything, he's just down there, down in the ground, and I can't say thank you . . . oh, Geezus, Geezus, why don't he hear me, I just want to say thanks . . ."

Billy Kinetta wanted to assume the responsibility for saying thanks, but that was possible only on a night that would never come again; and this was the day.

Gaspar took him to the bedroom and put him down to sleep in exactly the same way one would soothe an old, sick dog.

Then he went to his sofa, and because it was the only thing he could imagine saying, he murmured, "He'll be all right. Minna. Really he will."

When Billy left for the 7-Eleven the next evening, Gaspar was gone. It was an alternate day, and that meant he was out at the cemetery. Billy fretted that he shouldn't be there alone, but the old man had a way of taking care of himself. Billy was not smiling as he thought of his friend, and the word *friend* echoed as he realized that, yes, this was his friend, truly and really his friend. He wondered how old Gaspar was, and how soon Billy Kinetta would be once again what he had always been: alone.

When he returned to the apartment at two-thirty, Gaspar was asleep, cocooned in his blanket on the sofa. Billy went in and tried to sleep, but hours later, when sleep would not come, when thoughts of murky water and calcium night light on dark foliage kept him staring at the bedroom ceiling, he came out of the room for a drink of water. He wandered around the living room, not wanting to be by himself even if the only companionship in this sleepless night was breathing heavily, himself in sleep.

He stared out the window. Clouds lay in chiffon strips across the sky.
The squealing of tires from the street.

Sighing, idle in his movement around the room, he saw the old man's
pocket watch lying on the coffee table beside the sofa. He walked to the
table. If the watch was still stopped at eleven o'clock, perhaps he would
borrow it and have it repaired. It would be a nice thing to do for Gaspar.
He loved that beautiful timepiece.

Billy bent to pick it up.

The watch, stopped at the V of eleven precisely, levitated at an angle,
floating away from him.

Billy Kinetta felt a shiver travel down his back to burrow in at the base
of his spine. He reached for the watch hanging in air before him. It
floated away just enough that his fingers massaged empty space. He tried
to catch it. The watch eluded him, lazily turning away like an opponent
who knows he is in no danger of being struck from behind.

Then Billy realized Gaspar was awake. Turned away from the sofa,
nonetheless he knew the old man was observing him. And the blissful
floating watch.

He looked at Gaspar.

They did not speak for a long time.

Then: "I'm going back to sleep," Billy said. Quietly.

"I think you have some questions," Gaspar replied.

"Questions? No, of course not, Dad. Why in the world would I have
questions? I'm still asleep." But that was not the truth, because he had
not been asleep that night.

"Do you know what 'Gaspar' means? Do you remember the three
wise men of the Bible, the Magi?"

"I don't want any frankincense and myrrh. I'm going back to bed.
I'm going now. You see, I'm going right now."

" 'Gaspar' means master of the treasure, keeper of the secrets, paladin
of the palace." Billy was staring at him, not walking into the bedroom;
just staring at him. As the elegant timepiece floated to the old man, who
extended his hand palm-up to receive it. The watch nestled in his hand,
unmoving, and it made no sound, no sound at all.

"You go back to bed. But will you go out to the cemetery with me
tomorrow? It's important."

"Why?"

"Because I believe I'll be dying tomorrow."

It was a nice day, cool and clear. Not at all a day for dying, but neither
had been many such days in Southeast Asia, and death had not been
deterred.

They stood at Minna's gravesite, and Gaspar opened his shooting stick
to form a seat, and he thrust the spike into the ground, and he settled

onto it, and sighed, and said to Billy Kinetta, "I'm growing cold as that stone."

"Do you want my jacket?"

"No. I'm cold inside." He looked around at the sky, at the grass, at the rows of markers. "I've been responsible, for all of this, and more."

"You've said that before."

"Young fella, are you by any chance familiar, in your reading, with an old novel by James Hilton called *Lost Horizon?* Perhaps you saw the movie. It was a wonderful movie, actually much better than the book. Mr. Capra's greatest achievement. A human testament. Ronald Colman was superb. Do you know the story?"

"Yes."

"Do you remember the High Lama, played by Sam Jaffe? His name was Father Perrault?"

"Yes."

"Do you remember how he passed on the caretakership of that magical hidden world, Shangri-La, to Ronald Colman?"

"Yes, I remember that." Billy paused. "Then he died. He was very old, and he died."

Gaspar smiled up at Billy. "Very good, Billy. I knew you were a good boy. So now, if you remember all that, may I tell you a story? It's not a very long story."

Billy nodded, smiling at his friend.

"In 1582 Pope Gregory XIII decreed that the civilized world would no longer observe the Julian calendar. October 4th, 1582 was followed, the next day, by October 15th. Eleven days vanished from the world. One hundred and seventy years later, the British Parliament followed suit, and September 2nd, 1752 was followed the next day by September 14th. Why did he do that, the Pope?"

Billy was bewildered by the conversation. "Because he was bringing it into synch with the real world. The solstices and equinoxes. When to plant, when to harvest."

Gaspar waggled a finger at him with pleasure. "Excellent, young fella. And you're correct when you say Gregory abolished the Julian calendar because its error of one day in every one hundred and twenty-eight years had moved the vernal equinox to March 11th. That's what the history books say. It's what *every* history book says. But what if?"

"What if *what?* I don't know what you're talking about."

"What if: Pope Gregory had the knowledge revealed to him that he *must* readjust time in the minds of men? What if: the excess time in 1582 was eleven days and one hour? What if: he accounted for those eleven days, vanished those eleven days, but that one hour slipped free, was left loose to bounce through eternity? A very special hour . . . an hour that must *never* be used . . . an hour that must never toll. What if?"

Billy spread his hands. "What if, what if, what if! It's all just philosophy. It doesn't mean anything. Hours aren't real, time isn't something that you can bottle up. So what if there *is* an hour out there somewhere that . . .''

And he stopped.

He grew tense, and leaned down to the old man. "The watch. Your watch. It doesn't work. It's stopped.''

Gaspar nodded. "At eleven o'clock. My watch works; it keeps very special time, for one very special hour.''

Billy touched Gaspar's shoulder. Carefully he asked, "Who are you, Dad?''

The old man did not smile as he said, "Gaspar. Keeper. Paladin. Guardian.''

"Father Perrault was hundreds of years old.''

Gaspar shook his head with a wistful expression on his old face. "I'm eighty-six years old, Billy. You asked me if I thought I was God. Not God, not Father Perrault, not an immortal, just an old man who will die too soon. Are you Ronald Colman?''

Billy nervously touched his lower lip with a finger. He looked at Gaspar as long as he could, then turned away. He walked off a few paces, stared at the barren trees. It seemed suddenly much chillier here in this place of entombed remembrances. From a distance he said, "But it's only . . . what? A chronological convenience. Like daylight saving time; Spring forward, Fall back. We don't actually *lose* an hour; we get it back.''

Gaspar stared at Minna's grave. "At the end of April I lost an hour. If I die now, I'll die an hour short in my life. I'll have been cheated out of one hour I want, Billy.'' He swayed toward all he had left of Minna. "One last hour I could have with my old girl. That's what I'm afraid of, Billy. I have that hour in my possession. I'm afraid I'll use it, God help me, I want so much to use it.''

Billy came to him. Tense, and chilled, he said, "Why must that hour never toll?''

Gaspar drew a deep breath and tore his eyes away from the grave. His gaze locked with Billy's. And he told him.

The years, all the days and hours, exist. As solid and as real as mountains and oceans and men and women and the baobab tree. Look, he said, at the lines in my face and deny that time is real. Consider these dead weeds that were once alive and try to believe it's all just vapor or the mutual agreement of Popes and Caesars and young men like you.

"The lost hour must never come, Billy, for in that hour it all ends. The light, the wind, the stars, this magnificent open place we call the universe. It all ends, and in its place—waiting, always waiting—is eternal darkness. No new beginnings, no world without end, just the infinite emptiness.''

And he opened his hand, which had been lying in his lap, and there, in his palm, rested the watch, making no sound at all, and stopped dead at eleven o'clock. "Should it strike twelve, Billy, eternal night falls; from which there is no recall."

There he sat, this very old man, just a perfectly normal old man. The most recent in the endless chain of keepers of the lost hour, descended in possession from Caesar and Pope Gregory XIII, down through the centuries of men and women who had served as caretakers of the excellent timepiece. And now he was dying, and now he wanted to cling to life as every man and woman clings to life no matter how awful or painful or empty, even if it is for one more hour. The suicide, falling from the bridge, at the final instant, tries to fly, tries to climb back up the sky. This weary old man, who only wanted to stay one brief hour more with Minna. Who was afraid that his love would cost the universe.

He looked at Billy, and he extended his hand with the watch waiting for its next paladin. So softly Billy could barely hear him, knowing that he was denying himself what he most wanted at this last place in his life, he whispered, "If I die without passing it on . . . it will begin to tick."

"Not me," Billy said. "Why did you pick me? I'm no one special. I'm not someone like you. I run an all-night service mart. There's nothing special about me the way there is about you! I'm *not* Ronald Colman! I don't want to be responsible, I've *never* been responsible!"

Gaspar smiled gently. "You've been responsible for me."

Billy's rage vanished. He looked wounded.

"Look at us, Billy. Look at what color you are; and look at what color I am. You took me in as a friend. I think of you as worthy, Billy. Worthy."

They remained there that way, in silence, as the wind rose. And finally, in a timeless time, Billy nodded.

Then the young man said, "You won't be losing Minna, Dad. Now you'll go to the place where she's been waiting for you, just as she was when you first met her. There's a place where we find everything we've ever lost through the years."

"That's good, Billy, that you tell me that. I'd like to believe it, too. But I'm a pragmatist. I believe what exists . . . like rain and Minna's grave and the hours that pass that we can't see, but they *are*. I'm afraid, Billy. I'm afraid this will be the last time I can speak to her. So I ask a favor. As payment, in return for my life spent protecting the watch.

"I ask for one minute of the hour, Billy. One minute to call her back, so we can stand face-to-face and I can touch her and say good-bye. You'll be the new protector of this watch, Billy, so I ask you please, just let me steal one minute."

Billy could not speak. The look on Gaspar's face was without horizon, empty as tundra, bottomless. The child left alone in darkness; the pain of eternal waiting. He knew he could never deny this old man, no matter what he asked, and in the silence he heard a voice say: *"No!"* And it was his own.

He had spoken without conscious volition. Strong and determined, and without the slightest room for reversal. If a part of his heart had been swayed by compassion, that part had been instantly overridden. No. A final, unshakable no.

For an instant Gaspar looked crestfallen. His eyes clouded with tears; and Billy felt something twist and break within himself at the sight. He knew he had hurt the old man. Quickly, but softly, he said urgently, "You know that would be wrong, Dad. We mustn't . . ."

Gaspar said nothing. Then he reached out with his free hand and took Billy's. It was an affectionate touch. "That was the last test, young fella. Oh, you know I've been testing you, don't you? This important item couldn't go to just anyone.

"And you passed the test, my friend: my last, best friend. When I said I could bring her back from where she's gone, here in this place we've both come to so often, to talk to someone lost to us, I knew you would understand that *anyone* could be brought back in that stolen minute. I knew you wouldn't use it for yourself, no matter how much you wanted it; but I wasn't sure that as much as you like me, it might not sway you. But you wouldn't even give it to *me,* Billy."

He smiled up at him, his eyes now clear and steady.

"I'm content, Billy. You needn't have worried. Minna and I don't need that minute. But if you're to carry on for me, I think you *do* need it. You're in pain, and that's no good for someone who carries this watch. You've got to heal, Billy.

"So I give you something you would never take for yourself. I give you a going-away present . . ."

And he started the watch, whose ticking was as loud and as clear as a baby's first sound; and the sweep-second hand began to move away from eleven o'clock.

Then the wind rose, and the sky seemed to cloud over, and it grew colder, with a remarkable silver-blue mist that rolled across the cemetery; and though he did not see it emerge from that grave at a distance far to the right, Billy Kinetta saw a shape move toward him. A soldier in the uniform of a day past, and his rank was Lance Corporal. He came toward Billy Kinetta, and Billy went to meet him as Gaspar watched.

They stood together and Billy spoke to him. And the man whose name Billy had never known when he was alive, answered. And then he faded, as the seconds ticked away. Faded, and faded, and was gone. And the silver-blue mist rolled through them, and past them, and was gone; and the soldier was gone.

Billy stood alone.

When he turned back to look across the grounds to his friend, he saw that Gaspar had fallen from the shooting stick. He lay on the ground.

Billy rushed to him, and fell to his knees and lifted him onto his lap. Gaspar was still.

"Oh, god, Dad, you should have heard what he said. Oh, Geez, he let me go. He let me go so I didn't even have to say I was sorry. He told me he didn't even *see* me in that foxhole. He never knew he'd saved my life. I said thank you and he said no, thank *you*, that he hadn't died for nothing. Oh, please, Dad, please don't be dead yet. I want to tell you . . ."

And, as it sometimes happens, rarely but wonderfully, sometimes they come back for a moment, for an instant before they go, the old man, the very old man, opened his eyes, just before going on his way, and he looked through the dimming light at his friend, and he said, "May I remember you to my old girl, Billy?"

And his eyes closed again, after only a moment; and his caretakership was at an end; as his hand opened and the most excellent timepiece, now stopped again at one minute past eleven, floated from his palm and waited till Billy Kinetta extended his hand; and then it floated down and lay there silently, making no sound, no sound at all. Safe. Protected.

There in the place where all lost things returned, the young man sat on the cold ground, rocking the body of his friend. And he was in no hurry to leave. There was time.

A blessing of the 18th Egyptian Dynasty:

God be between you and harm in
all the empty places you walk.

THE BURNING MAN
Ray Bradbury

Teleplay by J. D. Feigelson

Aired November 15, 1985

Starring Piper Laurie, Roberts Blossom, Andre Gower, Danny Cooksey

THE RICKETY FORD CAME ALONG A ROAD THAT PLOWED
up dust in yellow plumes which took an hour to lie back down and move
no more in that special slumber that stuns the world in mid-July. Far
away, the lake waited, a cool-blue gem in a hot-green lake of grass, but
it was indeed still far away, and Neva and Doug were bucketing along
in their barrelful of red-hot bolts with lemonade slopping around in a
thermos on the backseat and deviled-ham sandwiches fermenting on
Doug's lap. Both boy and aunt sucked in hot air and talked out even
hotter.

"Fire-eater," said Douglas. "I'm eating fire. Heck, I can hardly *wait*
for that lake!"

Suddenly, up ahead, there was a man by the side of the road.

Shirt open to reveal his bronzed body to the waist, his hair ripened to
wheat color by July, the man's eyes burned fiery blue in a nest of sun
wrinkles. He waved, dying in the heat.

Neva tromped on the brake. Fierce dust clouds rose to make the man
vanish. When the golden dust sifted away, his hot yellow eyes glared
balefully, like a cat's, defying the weather and the burning wind.

He stared at Douglas.

Douglas glanced away, nervously.

For you could see where the man had come across a field high with
yellow grass baked and burnt by eight weeks of no rain. There was a
path where the man had broken the grass and cleaved a passage to the
road. The path went as far as one could see down to a dry swamp and
an empty creek bed with nothing but baked hot stones in it and fried
rock and melting sand.

"I'll be damned, you stopped!" cried the man, angrily.

"I'll be damned, I did," Neva yelled back. "Where you going?"

"I'll think of someplace." The man hopped up like a cat and swung
into the rumble seat. "Get going. It's *after* us! The sun, I mean, of
course!" He pointed straight up. "Git! Or we'll *all* go mad!"

Neva stomped on the gas. The car left gravel and glided on pure white-
hot dust, coming down only now and then to careen off a boulder or kiss
a stone. They cut the land in half with racket. Above it, the man shouted:

"Put 'er up to seventy, eighty, hell, why not ninety!"

Neva gave a quick, critical look at the lion, the intruder in the backseat, to see if she could shut his jaws with a glance. They shut.

And that, of course, is how Doug felt about the beast. Not a stranger, no, not hitchhiker, but intruder. In just two minutes of leaping into the red-hot car, with his jungle hair and jungle smell, he had managed to disingratiate himself with the climate, the automobile, Doug, and the honorable and perspiring aunt. Now she hunched over the wheel and nursed the car through further storms of heat and backlashes of gravel.

Meanwhile, the creature in the back, with his great lion ruff of hair and mint-fresh yellow eyes, licked his lips and looked straight on at Doug in the rearview mirror. He gave a wink. Douglas tried to wink back, but somehow the lid never came down.

"You ever try to figure—" yelled the man.

"What?" cried Neva.

"You ever try to figure," shouted the man, leaning forward between them "—whether or not the weather is driving you crazy, or you're crazy *already?*"

It was a surprise of a question, which suddenly cooled them on this blast-furnace day.

"I don't quite understand—" said Neva.

"Nor does anyone!" The man smelled like a lion house. His thin arms hung over and down between them, nervously tying and untying an invisible string. He moved as if there were nests of burning hair under each armpit. "Day like today, all hell breaks loose inside your head. Lucifer was born on a day like this, in a wilderness like this," said the man. "And everything so hot you can't touch it, and people not wanting to be touched," said the man.

He gave a nudge to her elbow, a nudge to the boy.

They jumped a mile.

"You see?" The man smiled. "Day like today, you get to thinking lots of things." He smiled. "Ain't this the summer when the seventeen-year locusts are supposed to come back like pure holocaust? Simple but multitudinous plagues?"

"Don't know!" Neva drove fast, staring ahead.

"This *is* the summer. Holocaust just around the bend. I'm thinking so swift, it hurts my eyeballs, cracks my head. I'm liable to explode in a fireball with just plain disconnected thought. Why—why—why—"

Neva swallowed hard. Doug held his breath.

Quite suddenly they were terrified. For the man simply idled on with his talk, looking at the shimmering green fire trees that burned by on both sides, sniffing the rich hot dust that flailed up around the tin car, his voice neither high nor low, but steady and calm now in describing his life:

"Yes, sir, there's more to the world than people appreciate. If there can be seventeen-year locusts, why not seventeen-year people? Ever *thought* of that?"

"Never did," said someone.

Probably me, thought Doug, for his mouth had moved like a mouse.

"Or how about twenty-four-year people, or fifty-seven-year people? I mean, we're all so used to people growing up, marrying, having kids, we never stop to think maybe there's other ways for people coming into the world, maybe like locusts, once in a while, who can tell, one hot day, middle of summer!"

"Who can tell?" There was the mouse again. Doug's lips trembled.

"And who's to say there ain't genetic evil in the world?" asked the man of the sun, glaring right up at it without blinking.

"*What* kind of evil?" asked Neva.

"Genetic, ma'am. In the blood, that is to say. People born evil, growed evil, died evil, no changes all the way down the line."

"Whew!" said Douglas. "You mean people who start out mean and stay *at* it?"

"You got the sum, boy. Why not? If there are people everyone thinks are angel-fine from their first sweet breath to their last pure declaration, why not sheer orneriness from January first to December, three hundred sixty-five days later?"

"I never thought of that," said the mouse.

"Think," said the man. *"Think."*

They thought for about five seconds.

"Now," said the man, squinting one eye at the cool lake five miles ahead, his other eye shut into darkness and ruminating on coal-bins of fact there, "listen. What if the intense heat, I mean the really hot hot heat of a month like this, week like this, day like today, just baked the Ornery Man right out of the river mud. Been there buried in the mud for forty-seven years, like a damn larva, waiting to be born. And he shook himself awake and looked around, full grown, and climbed out of the hot mud into the world and said, 'I think I'll eat me some summer.' "

"How's that again?"

"Eat me some summer, boy, summer, ma'am. Just devour it whole. Look at them trees, ain't they a whole dinner? Look at that field of wheat, ain't that a feast? Them sunflowers by the road, by golly, there's breakfast. Tarpaper on top that house, there's lunch. And the lake, way up ahead. Jehoshaphat, that's dinner wine, drink it all!"

"I'm thirsty, all right," said Doug.

"Thirsty, hell, boy, thirst don't begin to describe the state of a man, come to think about him, come to talk, who's been waiting in the hot mud thirty years and is born but to die in one day! Thirst! Ye Gods! Your ignorance is complete."

"Well," said Doug.

"Well," said the man. "Not only thirst but hunger. Hunger. Look around. Not only eat the trees and then the flowers blazing by the roads but then the white-hot panting dogs. There's one. There's another! And all the cats in the country. There's two, just passed three! And then just glutton-happy begin to why, why not, begin to get around to, let me tell you, how's this strike you, eat people? I mean—people! Fried, cooked, boiled, and parboiled people. Sunburnt beauties of people. Old men, young. Old ladies' hats and then old ladies under their hats and then young ladies' scarves and young ladies, and then young boys' swim-trunks, by God, and young boys, elbows, ankles, ears, toes, and eyebrows! Eyebrows, by God, men, women, boys, ladies, dogs, fill up the menu, sharpen your teeth, lick your lips, dinner's *on!*"

"Wait!" someone cried.

Not me, thought Doug. I said nothing.

"Hold on!" someone yelled.

It was Neva.

He saw her knee fly up as if by intuition and down as if by finalized gumption.

Stomp! went her heel on the floor.

The car braked. Neva had the door open, pointing, shouting, pointing, shouting, her mouth flapping, one hand seized out to grab the man's shirt and rip it.

"Out! Get out!"

"*Here,* ma'am?" The man was astonished.

"Here, here, here, out, out, out!"

"But, ma'am . . . !"

"Out, or you're finished, through!" cried Neva, wildly. "I got a load of Bibles in the back trunk, a pistol with a silver bullet here under the steering wheel. A box of crucifixes under the seat! A wooden stake taped to the axle, with a hammer. I got holy water in the carburetor, blessed before it boiled early this morning at three churches on the way: St. Matthew's Catholic, the Green Town Baptist, and the Zion City High Episcopal. The steam from that will get you alone. Following us, one mile behind, and due to arrive in one minute, is the Reverend Bishop Kelly from Chicago. Up at the lake is Father Rooney from Milwaukee, and Doug, why, Doug here has in his back pocket at this minute one sprig of wolfbane and two chunks of mandrake root. Out! out! out!"

"Why, ma'am," cried the man. "I *am!*"

And he was.

He landed and fell rolling in the road.

Neva banged the car into full flight.

Behind, the man picked himself up and yelled, "You must be nuts. You must be crazy. Nuts. Crazy."

"*I'm* nuts? *I'm* crazy?" said Neva, and hooted, "Boy!"

". . . nuts . . . crazy . . ." The voice faded.

Douglas looked back and saw the man shaking his fist, then ripping off his shirt and hurling it to the gravel and jumping big puffs of white-hot dust out of it with his bare feet.

The car exploded, rushed, raced, banged pell-mell ahead, his aunt ferociously glued to the hot wheel, until the little sweating figure of the talking man was lost in sun-drenched marshland and burning air. At last Doug exhaled:

"Neva, I never heard you talk like that before."

"And never will again, Doug."

"Was what you said *true?*"

"Not a word."

"You lied, I mean, you *lied?*"

"I lied." Neva blinked. "Do you think *he* was lying, too?"

"I don't know."

"All I know is sometimes it takes a lie to kill a lie, Doug. This time, anyway. Don't let it become customary."

"No, ma'am." He began to laugh. "Say the thing about mandrake root again. Say the thing about wolfbane in my pocket. Say it about a pistol with a silver bullet, say it."

She said it. They both began to laugh.

Whooping and shouting, they went away in their tin-bucket-junking car over the gravel ruts and humps, her saying, him listening, eyes squeezed shut, roaring, snickering, raving.

They didn't stop laughing until they hit the water in their bathing suits and came up all smiles.

The sun stood hot in the middle of the sky and they dog-paddled happily for five minutes before they began to really swim in the menthol-cool waves.

Only at dusk when the sun was suddenly gone and the shadows moved out from the trees did they remember that now they had to go *back* down that lonely road through all the dark places and past that empty swamp to get to town.

They stood by the car and looked down that long road. Doug swallowed hard.

"Nothing can happen to us going home."

"Nothing."

"Jump!"

They hit the seats and Neva kicked the starter like it was a dead dog and they were off.

They drove along under plum-colored trees and among velvet purple hills.

And nothing happened.

They drove along a wide raw gravel road that was turning the color of plums and smelled the warm-cool air that was like lilacs and looked at each other, waiting.

And nothing happened.

Neva began at last to hum under her breath.

The road was empty.

And then it was not empty.

Neva laughed. Douglas squinted and laughed with her.

For there was a small boy, nine years old maybe, dressed in a vanilla-white summer suit, with white shoes and a white tie and his face pink and scrubbed, waiting by the side of the road. He waved.

Neva braked the car.

"Going in to town?" called the boy, cheerily. "Got lost. Folks at a picnic, left without me. Sure glad you came along. It's *spooky* out here."

"Climb in!"

The boy climbed and they were off, the boy in the backseat, and Doug and Neva up front glancing at him, laughing, and then getting quiet.

The small boy kept silent for a long while behind them, sitting straight upright and clean and bright and fresh and new in his white suit.

And they drove along the empty road under a sky that was dark now with a few stars and a wind getting cool.

And at last the boy spoke and said something that Doug didn't hear but he saw Neva stiffen and her face grow as pale as the ice cream from which the small boy's suit was cut.

"What?" asked Doug, glancing back.

The small boy stared directly at him, not blinking, and his mouth moved all to itself as if it were separate from his face.

The car's engine missed fire and died.

They were slowing to a dead stop.

Doug saw Neva kicking and fiddling at the gas and the starter. But most of all he heard the small boy say, in the new and permanent silence:

"Have either of you ever wondered—"

The boy took a breath and finished:

"—if there is such a thing as genetic evil in the world?"

WONG'S LOST AND FOUND EMPORIUM

EMPORIUM

William F. Wu

TELEPLAY BY ALAN BRENNERT

AIRED NOVEMBER 22, 1985

STARRING BRIAN TOCHI, ANNA MARIA POON, CAROL BRUCE,

STACY KEACH, SR.

THE SHARP CLICKING OF HIGH HEELS ECHOED IN THE dark shop. The brisk footsteps on the unpolished wooden floor slowed and became irregular and uncertain as my new visitor saw some of the stuff on the shelves. They always did that.

I was on a different aisle. The shop was very big, though crammed, with all kinds of objects to the point where every shelf was crowded and overflowing. Most of the stuff was inanimate, or at least dead. However, many of the beasties still stirred when adequately provoked. The inanimate objects included everything from uncut diamonds to nail clippers to bunny bladders. Still more of the sealed crates and boxes and bottles contained critters, or other things, that might or might not be counted among the living. I had no idea and didn't care, either. For instance, whoever had hung big wooden crates from the ceiling—and there were plenty, up where they couldn't endanger anybody—must have had a good reason.

The edges of the shop were a little mysterious. I tried not to go too far down any of the aisles except the two big perpendicular corridors that ended in doors to the outside. They formed a cross in the center of the shop. The farther from the middle I went in any direction, the darker the place became, and colder. On a few occasions, I had had to go out to shelf space on the fringe that was mostly empty, and in almost complete darkness. All the edges were like that, except for the four doors at each end of those main corridors.

I didn't dare venture into the real darkness, where nothing was visible. Cold stale air seemed to be all it contained, but I wasn't going to investigate. I also had a suspicion that the shop kept growing of its own accord, outward into that nothingness. I had seen for myself that new stuff spontaneously appeared on all the shelves, but if the shop had been finite in size, it would have been absolutely crammed to the ceiling. Instead, I guessed, it simply extended its aisles and plain wooden shelves outward somehow, always providing just enough new empty space to avoid total chaos. The place was weird enough where I was; I didn't see any need to wander off the edge of the world or something.

I was seeking my destiny in this world, or at least I had been hoping to when I first came in here. My visitor was probably doing the same right now.

I came around the corner into one of the two main corridors, where the light was a little better. For a second, I thought I heard someone in one of the aisles, but that sort of thing happened all the time. Some of the live beings thumped and slithered in their containers occasionally.

My customer was a woman with snow-white hair, slender and well dressed with a good tan. She wore a peach-colored suit and four gold chains around her neck. One hand with long, peach-colored fingernails clutched a small handbag. She looked like a shriveled peach in a light snowfall.

"Oh—uh, I'm looking for Mr. Wong, I guess." She smiled cautiously.

"That's me," I said, walking forward briskly. After I had been here a while, I had put my signs on the four doors, saying "Wong's Lost and Found Emporium."

She looked me over in some surprise; they always seemed to expect a doddering old geezer with a wispy white beard and an opium pipe, muttering senilities to the spirit world. I wore a blue T-shirt, fading Levi's, and Adidas indoor track shoes. After all, I'd only been here a few months, though time was different in here than on the outside. This was that kind of place.

"Oh. I'm sorry." She smiled apologetically, fidgeting now with all ten peach fingernails scratching at her purse.

"The name is Wong," I said casually, "but you can call me Mr. Double-you for short."

She didn't get the joke—they never do.

"Thank you. I, uh, was told that . . . this is an unusual shop? Where one can find something . . . she lost?"

"If you lost it, I got it." Like most of the others, she needed more encouragement. I waited for her to ask.

"I mean . . . well, I suppose this will sound silly, but . . . I'm not looking for a thing, exactly, not a solid object. I don't suppose you have a . . . second chance?" She forced herself to laugh, a little, like it was a joke. "Well, no, I'm sorry. I really just need a rest room, and—"

"Of course I have it," I said. "If you lost a chance at something, it's here. Follow me."

I looked around on the floor and pointed to the little blue throw rug. "Have to watch out for this. It slips."

She smiled politely, but I could see her shaking with anticipation.

I glanced around the shelves, looking for the little spot of white. "What's your name?" It didn't matter, but asking made me sound official.

"I'm Mrs. Barbara Patricia Whitford and I live here in Boca. Um—I was born in New York in 1926. I grew up . . ."

I didn't care. A bit of white light was shining on a shoulder-high shelf across the main corridor from me. "This way," I said, signaling over my shoulder. She shut up and followed me.

As we walked, the light moved ahead of us toward the object she wanted to recover. I had no idea how it worked—I had figured it out by trial and error, or I might say by accident. I had come in here myself looking for something I had lost, but the place had had no one in it. Now, I was waiting for the proprietor, but everyone else who came in thought I was in charge. So I was.

"What kind of chance was it?" I asked over my shoulder, like it was a shoe size or something. It might be a long walk.

"Well," she said, just a little breathless behind me. "I always wanted to be an artist—a painter. I didn't get started until fifteen years ago, when I started taking lessons in acrylics. And even oils. I got pretty good, even if I do say so. Several of my paintings sold at art fairs and I was just getting a few exhibited, even. I got discouraged, though. It was so hard to keep going."

The white light turned down another aisle, more cramped and dimly lit than the last. Th light was brighter in these shadows, but she couldn't see it. Only I could. I had tested that on earlier customers. Unfortunately, I couldn't see my own.

A shadow shifted in the corner of my eye that was not mine or hers, but I ignored it. If something large was loose in here, it was apparently shy. It was nothing new.

"Six or seven years ago," she continued, "all of my friends were going back to school. It was easier than painting—I went for my master's, and since I was just going to go, I didn't really have to hurry, or worry about grades. It was the thing to do, and so much easier than painting. Only, I didn't care about it." Her voice caught, and she paused to swallow. "I do care about my painting. Now, well, I just would like to have the chance I missed, when my skills were still sharp and I had more time and business connections. It—I know it sounds small. But it's the only thing I've ever accomplished. And I don't have time to start over."

She started crying.

I nodded. The white light had come to a stop, playing across a big open wooden box on an upper shelf. "Just a moment. I'll get it. It's very important to get exactly the right one, because if you get the wrong object, you're still stuck with it."

She nodded, watching me start to climb up the wooden shelves.

"For instance, if I gave you someone else's lost chance to work a slow freighter to Sakhalin Island, why, it would just happen. You'd have to go."

"I would? . . . oh. Well, be careful." She sniffled. "No, uh, glove cleaner or anything like that. If you know what I mean."

The shelves were dusty and disgusting. My fingers caught cobwebs and brushed against small, feathery clumps that were unidentifiable in the shadowy aisle. Tiny feet scurried away from me on the shelves as I climbed, prodding aside old jars with my feet. Faint shuffling noises came from inside some of them.

I finally got my head up to the shelf with the little light. It was now sitting on a transparent cylindrical container inside the wooden box. Inside, ugly brown lumps swirled around in a thick, emerald-green solution.

The box had several similar containers and a lot of miscellaneous junk. I grabbed one of the smaller pieces at random and stuck it in my pants pocket. Then I tucked the swirling green cylinder under one arm and started down.

When I had reached the floor, I held it up. Her eyes grew wide when she saw the liquid spinning inside. "Okay," I said. "When you open this, the contents will evaporate very quickly. You have to breathe in the vapor before it disappears, or the chance is lost forever." I had done this before.

She took it from me, glowing like a half-lit wino.

"You can do it here if you want," I said, "but the light's better in the main corridors."

She nodded and followed me as close as one dog behind another.

We turned along the main corridor, and I walked at a good clip back toward my beat-up steel desk and battered piano stool. They were near the junction of the main corridors. This was her business.

Before I got there, I heard a slight gasp behind me and turned around. She had slipped on the throw rug, and as I turned, her slender legs were struggling for balance. Her arms reflexively made a sharp upward movement and her precious transparent cylinder was tossed out to one side.

The woman let out a wail as it sailed away and smashed on the hard floorboards. She clattered after it clumsily in her high heels. When she finally reached it, she bent over and started sniffing around like a bowser at a barbecue.

I got up stiffly and walked over.

"Did I get it? Did I get it?" she whimpered frantically.

"Doubt it," I said, sniffing around. If the stuff had lingered long enough for her to inhale it, I would have smelled some residual scent.

"Oh, *no*—I . . . uh . . . but, but—" She started to cry.

Criers bore me. I had a vague sense that I was expected to be sympathetic, but I had lost that ability. That's what I was here for, in fact.

"Wait a minute," I said, tapping her on the shoulder. I reached into my pocket for the other lost object I had taken from her box. It was a metal ring with four or five keys on it and a leather circle with "BPW" stamped in gold. The keys looked fairly new; I figured she had lost them some time in the last decade or so. "Here," I said. "You lost these, too."

"What?" She looked up between sobs.

I gave her the keys. "I'm glad you came. Have a nice day."

"What?" She stared at the keys. "It was the *only* thing I ever accomplished," she whimpered. "Ever." She turned away, in shock, her wide eyes fixed blankly on her old car keys. "It was my very last chance," she squeaked in a high, tiny voice.

"That way." I took her shoulders and aimed her down the corridor that led to a shopping mall in Florida.

She staggered away, snuffling.

I sat down disgustedly on a nearby stool. My time was almost up. I had to leave soon in order to get any sleep at home and then show up at work tomorrow. Without savings, I couldn't afford to leave my job, even for something as important as this. If the proprietor had been coming back, he, she, or it would probably have returned by now. The dual passages of time in here and outside meant that I had spent over two months here, and only spent one week of sick days and vacation days back in New York, on the other side of one of the doors.

I had even taken my job on a loading dock in Chinatown just to be near this shop. That was why I had moved to New York. When a friend had first told me about this establishment, she had warned me of the trickiest part—the doors could not always be located. Different people could find them at their own times, sometimes. The door in New York appeared, when it did, in the back hall of a small, second-story Chinatown restaurant. Most of the time, the hall ended in two rest room doors. For a select few, though, it occasionally had three, and now the mystic third door bore my sign.

I had checked the spot often, and when I had found the door, I had phoned in immediately for a week off, begging an emergency. It had taken some arguing, but I had managed. The presence of the restaurant had allowed me to stay so long, since I sneaked food out when night fell in New York. Naturally, the shop had a few misplaced refrigerators and other appliances; a few even worked.

Once I left this place, I might not find the door again for years—if ever.

I kicked in annoyance at a random bit of crud on the floor. It unfolded five legs and scurried away under a nearby shelf. Well, I had left a mark; the doors all bore my handmade signs, minor amusement though they were.

At least my stay had been eventful. My first customer after I had figured out how the place worked had been a tall, slender Chinese guy from the San Francisco corridor. The door there was in the back of a porno shop. He had been in his fifties and wore a suit that had been in style in 1961, when it was last pressed. Something about him suggested Taiwan.

He had come looking for the respect of his children, which he had, of course, lost. I found him a box with five frantic mice in it; what he had to do was pet them until they calmed down. However, while he was gingerly poking at them, a boa constrictor glided silently out of the shadows unnoticed. It ate all the mice and then quietly slithered away. The guy got hysterical. I almost pointed out that snakes have to eat, too, but actually I didn't care about the snake, either. I'm strictly neutral.

My youngest visitor had been a little boy, maybe about ten, who came in through the boarded-up gas station in Bosworth, Missouri. It was a one-stoplight town that didn't send me much company. The kid wore jeans and a blue Royals baseball cap. He was looking for a dog whistle he had lost. I found it for him. Nothing happened to him or it. That was okay with me, too.

I sighed and stood up. No one else would be coming in. As I rose, I saw a large shadow out of the corner of my eye and glanced toward it, expecting it to slide away among the shelves as usual. Instead, it stayed where it was. I was looking at a young woman of Asian descent, wrapped up in a long white crocheted shawl. She also wore a denim skirt and striped knee socks.

"You're sickening." She spoke with elegant disgust, in a New York accent.

I knew that, but I didn't like hearing it. "You've been here a while, haven't you?"

"I think about two days." She brushed back her hair with one hand. It was cut short and blunt. "You were asleep when I came in."

That was a relief. She didn't belong here any more than I did. On the other hand, she had apparently been watching me.

"Where've you been sleeping?" I asked out of curiosity. On my first day, I had spent several hours locating a sleeping bag.

"I found an air mattress," she said, still angrily. "I just meant to sleep until you woke up, but you had a—a client when I got up. After I saw the way you treated him—and all the rest of them—I decided not to approach you at all. Don't you have any feelings for them? When something goes wrong? You could at least try to help them."

"I don't sabotage anybody. Whatever happens, happens—good or bad or indifferent."

She tossed her short hair, probably less to move it than for the disdain it conveyed. "I can't stand it. Why are you so callous?"

I shrugged. "What do you care? Anyhow, some go away happy."

"What?" She looked astonished. "Can't you even understand simple—" She stopped and shook her head. "Maybe you'll understand selfishness. Suppose *I* want what I came for. I can't get any help from you if I have trouble."

"Well, I guess that's logi—"

I stopped when she reached for a big stoppered metal bottle, on the shelf next to her. She heaved it at me, and I only had time to spin around. It hit my shoulder blade, hard, and bounced unharmed to the floor.

I whirled back toward her, ready to grab it and throw it back at her, but she was already striding quickly toward me.

"What's *wrong* with you?" she demanded. "I want to know! Why are you so callous?'' She snatched up the metal container from the floor in front of me and held it wrapped in her shawl. "Tell me *now!*" she screamed, right in front of me.

I leaned forward and spoke, glaring into her eyes. "*I* came in here looking for my compassion. I lost it years ago, bit by bit. I lost it when I was eight, and other kids chased me around the playground for no visible reason—and they weren't playing. When I started junior high and got beat up in gym class because the rest of the school was white, like my grade school. When I ran for student congress and had my posters covered with swastikas and KKK symbols. And that was *before* I got out into the world on my own. You want to hear about my *adult* life?''

I paused to catch my breath. She backed away from me.

"I've lost more of my compassion every year of my life for every year I can remember, until I don't have any more. Well, it's here, but I can't find it.''

She stood speechless in front of me. Letting her have it all at once accomplished that much, at least.

"Maybe you were in the wrong town,'' she muttered.

"You think I *like* being like this? Hating the memories of my life and not caring what happens to anybody? I said I've lost my compassion, not my conscience.''

She walked back and put the metal bottle back in its place on the shelf. "I can find it,'' she said quietly.

"What?''

"I've been watching you. When you get something for someone, you follow the little white light that appears.''

"You can see that?''

"Of course I can—anybody can. You think you're special? We just can't see our own. *I* figured that out.''

"Well . . . so did I,'' I said lamely.

"So I could get your compassion for you.''

"Yeah?'' I didn't think she would, considering all she'd said.

"Only you have to get what I want, first.''

"You don't trust me, remember?''

She smiled smugly. It looked grotesque, as though she hadn't smiled in ages. "I can trust you. Because you know that if you don't give me what I want, I won't give you your compassion. Besides, if all goes well, your lack of compassion won't make any difference.''

"Well, yeah. I guess so.'' I hadn't considered a deal with another customer before. Until now, I had just been waiting for the no-show proprietor, and then given up even on that.

"Well?'' she demanded, still with that weird forced smile.

"Uh—yeah, okay.'' It was my last chance. I glanced around and found her spot of white light behind me on a lower shelf. "This way.''

She walked next to me, watching me carefully as the white light led us down the crowded aisle. A large porcelain vase emitted guttural mutterings on an upper shelf as we passed. Two small lizards from the Florida corridor and something resembling a T-bone steak with legs were drinking at a pool of shiny liquid in the middle of the floor. The viscous liquid was oozing slowly out of a cracked green bottle. We stepped over it and kept going.

The light finally stopped on the cork of a long-necked blue bottle at the back of a bottom shelf. I stopped and looked down at it, wondering if this deal had an angle I hadn't figured.

"Well?" She forced herself to smile again. It gave her a sort of tortured visage.

"What is it, anyway?" I tried to sound casual.

"You don't need to know. I know that, too."

"Suppose I don't get it till you tell me."

"I won't tell you. And you won't get what you want."

She couldn't have known I had to leave soon, but she was still my last chance. I would be getting home late as it was. Besides, she was the sort who might really want more compassion in the world.

"Hurry up," she said.

I knelt down and looked at the bottle. She might have guessed what I had focused on, but with all the other junk jammed around it, she couldn't be sure. Well, I knew she had compassion herself, already. She wouldn't want to regain any lost tendencies that were nasty, like cruelty or vengefulness, so I was not in personal danger.

I took the bottle by the long neck and stood up. "It's in here, whatever it is. If it's a material object, you just open the bottle and spill it out. If it's a chance, or a personal trait, you have to uncork the bottle and inhale the fumes as they come out."

She was already taking the bottle from me, carefully in both hands. I backed away as she sank her teeth into the cork and yanked it out with a pop. White vapor issued from the bottle. She started taking deep breaths in through her nose, with her eyes closed.

I backed away, smelling something like rotten lettuce mixed with wet gerbil fur.

She kept on breathing until the vapors ran out. Then she recorked the bottle and smiled at me, looking relaxed and natural. "Well! You're still sickening, but that was it, all right." She laughed gently. "Wow, that stuff stunk. Smelled like rotting cabbage and wet cat fur, didn't it?"

"Wha—?" I laughed, surprised at her sudden good humor. "It sure did."

"Okay, brown eyes. I see your little spot of light. Follow the swaying rear." She sashayed past me and walked casually down another dark aisle, humming to herself.

At one point, something on a shelf caught her eye and she stopped to giggle at it. It was a large brown and white snake, shoved into a jar of some kind of clear solution. She paused to make a face, imitating the snake's motionless expression. Here, of course, one never knew if a pickled snake was really a pickled snake or something else temporarily in that guise. Anyway, she made a funny face and then laughed delightedly. After that, we pushed on.

When she stopped again, she was looking up at a shelf just within her reach. "There it is." She chuckled, without moving to take anything.

"Yeah?" I was suddenly afraid of that laugh.

She looked at me and laughed again.

"What's so funny?"

She shook her head and reached up on tiptoe with both hands. When she came down, she was cradling four sealed containers in her arms. One was a short-necked brown bottle encrusted with dry sand. Two were sealed jars of smoky glass, and the last was a locked wooden box engraved with smile faces. She squatted on the floor Asian-style and set them down.

"One of these holds your lost compassion." She looked up and laughed. "Guess which one."

My stomach tightened. I could not be sure of getting my compassion back this way. After my general insensitivity to people here, I didn't think I would ever be allowed back in, either.

"We had a deal," I said weakly. "You were going to give it to me."

"I have; it's right here. Besides, you should talk. And remember—if you inhale someone else's lost chance to wrestle an alligator or something, you'll wrestle it." She clapped her hands and laughed.

I stared at her. Maybe I deserved it, but I couldn't figure out what had happened to her. She had been concerned and compassionate before I had given her the long-necked bottle, and she certainly didn't seem angry or self-righteous now. I wondered what she had regained.

"Well?" She giggled at me and stood up. "One of them is it. That's a better chance than you gave anyone."

I looked down at the containers. She had no more idea what was in three of them than I did. "I have no intention of opening any of these," I said.

She shrugged, still grinning. "Have it your way, brown eyes. I'm leaving." She started strolling away.

"Wait."

She turned and walked away backward, facing me. "What?"

"Uh—" I couldn't think of anything.

" 'Bye!"

"No—uh, hey, what *did* I give back to you, anyway?"

"Oh!" She laughed. "My sense of humor." She was still backpedaling.

"I'll do it! Wait a minute."

She stopped and folded her arms. "You'll really do it?"

"Come on. Come on back here while I do this." I wasn't sure why I wanted company, but I did.

She came back, grinning. "If you got the guts, brown eyes, you can open 'em all."

I smiled weakly. "They could all be good."

She smirked. "Sure—it's possible."

I looked down at the four containers. The wooden box seemed more likely to hold a tangible object than a lost quality. Though this place had few reliable rules, I decided to leave the box alone. The brown bottle with the short neck had such a heavy layer of sand that its contents were hidden. I knelt down and looked over the two smoky jars.

"Come on, sweetie." She started tapping her foot.

Quickly, before I could reconsider, I grabbed both jars, stood, and smashed them down on the floor. The glass shattered and two small billows of blue-gray smoke curled upward.

She stepped back.

I leaned forward, waited for the smoke to reach me, and inhaled. One strand smelled like charcoal-broiled Kansas City steak; the other, like the inside of a new car. I breathed both in, again and again, until the vapors were gone.

After a moment, I blinked and looked around. "I don't feel any different."

"Sure you do." She smiled. "Just go on as normal, and it'll come clear.

"Okay." I bent down and picked up the box and the bottle. "Where were these? I'll put them back. There's a broom—"

"You?" She laughed gaily. "Well, that's something. You mean you're actually going to straighten up this place?"

"No, I—well, I've been in charge; I suppose I should do something . . ." I replaced the items where she pointed.

"Integrity."

"What?"

"You've got your integrity back, for one."

"Oh, I don't know . . ." I looked at her for a moment and then gazed up the dark aisle toward the light from one of the main corridors. "I guess I did lose that, too . . . Otherwise, I couldn't have been so cruel to people, even without compassion. They trusted me." I started walking up the aisle.

She followed, watching me closely. "So what are you going to do?"

"I guess I'll stay and run the shop." It just came out naturally. I hadn't even realized I was going to say it. "The . . . other thing I got back is kind of minor. For a long time, I used to try to remember the details of a fishing trip in the mountains my family went on, back when

I was little. I knew I had a great time, but that was all. Now, all of a sudden, I can remember it completely.''

She cocked her head to one side. ''Was it still really wonderful?''

I considered my new memories a moment. ''Yeah.''

''Aw . . .'' She looked at me, smiling. ''I can't help it, brown eyes. I give in. It's in that brown thing, with the sand all over it.''

Excitement surged in my chest. *''Thanks!''* I reached up with trembling fingers and snatched it off the shelf.

''Careful—''

I fumbled it away. It hit my shoulder, bounced to the floor, and cracked. It rolled, and before I could bend down to grab it, it was under a bottom shelf. I dropped to the floor and slid my face under the shelf. The cracked bottle was hissing in the darkness as the special vapors escaped. I couldn't smell anything. It was too far from me.

I reached for it with one hand. It was wedged against something and stuck. I could touch it, but I couldn't get enough of a hold to pull it back.

I remained on the floor, inhaling frantically, motionless until the hissing stopped. Then, suddenly feeling heavy all over, I managed to stand up.

''What happened?'' She smiled hopefully.

''It's gone,'' I muttered. ''It . . . sure was over quick.'' I hesitated, then added, ''Thanks anyhow.'' Stunned, I eased past her and started walking. I could hear her follow me.

We came out into the main corridor. I picked up the little blue throw rug and hung it on a nearby hook. Then I turned, all the way around, surveying my shop. ''Maybe it was no accident.''

''You were nervous, that's all—''

''I don't mean that. I mean my finding the door to this place when I most needed it, and staying until . . . someone came in to find my stuff.''

''You think your new integrity adds up to something, it sounds like.''

''My destiny.''

She laughed, then tapered off when I looked at her calmly. ''You serious?''

I shrugged. ''This place is mine. I knew that, somehow, when I put my signs up. And now I owe this shop my best attention.''

''With integrity.''

I shrugged again. Taking care of the shop and its customers was important; the reasons I felt that way were not.

''I . . . think I got news for you, brown eyes.''

''I don't want any news.'' I was still in shock from disappointment. It was justice of a sort, but it wasn't pleasant.

''You have your compassion back. I'm sure of it. You can't help it.''

''But you said it was in that bottle I broke—''

"It was, as a separate quality. Only, I think your integrity comes with a little compassion in a package deal. Forces it on you."

I looked up at her, hopeful. "Really?"

"You could try it." She pointed down the Florida corridor.

Whatshername, the peach-colored former artist lady, had never made it out the door. She was sitting near it, slumped on the floor, an incongruous position for a woman of her age and dignity. The skirt of her suit was smudged and rumpled under her, exposing more of her legs than it was supposed to.

"This is your shop now," said my companion. She put a hand on my shoulder.

I didn't say anything.

"You can't just let a customer sit there, can you?"

"No—not anymore. A matter of . . . integrity."

"In this case, it's the same as compassion. I don't see how you can help her, but if you try—"

"I know how."

"Huh?"

"I lost one chance to help her." I smiled, suddenly understanding the true potential of this place. "If you'll go down the aisles and find it, we can fix up that customer after all."

She winked. "You got it, brown eyes."

ONE LIFE, FURNISHED IN EARLY POVERTY
EARLY POVERTY
Harlan Ellison

TELEPLAY BY ALAN BRENNERT

AIRED DECEMBER 6, 1985

STARRING PETER REIGERT, CHRIS HEBERT, JACK KEHOE

AND SO IT WAS—STRANGELY, STRANGELY—THAT I FOUND myself standing in the backyard of the house I had lived in when I was seven years old. At thirteen minutes till midnight on no special magical winter's night, in a town that had held me only till I was physically able to run away. In Ohio, in winter, near midnight—certain I could go back.

Back to a time when what was now . . . was then.

Not truly knowing *why* I even wanted to go back. But certain that I could. Without magic, without science, without alchemy, without supernatural assistance; just *go back*. Because I had to, I needed to . . . go back.

Back; thirty-five years and more. To find myself at the age of seven, before any of it had begun; before any of the directions had been taken; to find out what turning point in my life it had been that had wrenched me from the course all little boys took to adulthood; that had set me on the road of loneliness and success ending here, back where I'd begun, in a backyard at now twelve minutes to midnight.

At forty-two I had come to that point in my life toward which I'd struggled since I'd been a child: a place of security, importance, recognition. The only one from this town who had made it. The ones who had had the most promise in school were now milkmen, used-car salesmen, married to fat, stupid, *dead* women who had, themselves, been girls of exceeding promise in high school. *They* had been trapped in this little Ohio town, never to break free. To die there, unknown. I had broken free, had done all the wonderful things I'd said I would do.

Why should it all depress me now?

Perhaps it was because Christmas was nearing and I was alone, with bad marriages and lost friendships behind me.

I walked out of the studio, away from the wet-ink-new fifty-thousand-dollar contract, got in my car and drove to International Airport. It was a straight line made up of in flight meals and jet airliners and rental cars and hastily-purchased winter clothing. A straight line to a backyard I had not seen in over thirty years.

I had to find the dragoon to go back.

Crossing the rime-frosted grass that crackled like cellophane, I walked under the shadow of the lightning-blasted pear tree. I had climbed in that tree endlessly when I was seven years old. In summer, its branches hung far over and scraped the roof of the garage. I could shinny out across the limb and drop onto the garage roof. I had once pushed Johnny

148

Mummy off that garage roof . . . not out of meanness, but simply because I had jumped from it many times and I could not understand anyone's not finding it a wonderful thing to do. He had sprained his ankle, and his father, a fireman, had come looking for me. I'd hidden on the garage roof.

I walked around the side of the garage, and there was the barely visible path. To one side of the path I had always buried my toy soldiers. For no other reason than to bury them, know I had a secret place, and later dig them up again, as if finding treasure.

(It came to me that even now, as an adult, I did the same thing. Dining in a Japanese restaurant, I would hide small pieces of *pakkai* or pineapple or *teriyaki* in my rice bowl, and pretend to be delighted when, later in the meal, my chopsticks encountered the tiny treasures down in among the rice grains.)

I knew the spot, of course. I got down on my hands and knees and began digging with the silver penknife on my watch chain. It had been my father's penknife—almost the only thing he had left me when he'd died.

The ground was hard, but I dug with enthusiasm, and the moon gave me more than enough light. Down and down I dug, knowing eventually I would come to the dragoon.

He was there. The bright paint rusted off his body, the saber corroded and reduced to a stub. Lying there in the grave I had dug for him thirty-five years before. I scooped the little metal soldier out of the ground, and cleaned him off as best I could with my paisley dress handkerchief. He was faceless now and as sad as I felt.

I hunkered there, under the moon, and waited for midnight, only a minute away, knowing it was all going to come right for me. After so terribly long.

The house behind me was silent and dark. I had no idea who lived there now. It would have been unpleasant if the strangers who now lived here had been unable to sleep and, rising to get a glass of water, had idly looked into the backyard. *Their* backyard. I had played here, and built a world for myself here, from dreams and loneliness. Using talismans of comic books and radio programs and matinee movies, and potent charms like the sad little dragoon in my hand. But it was now *their* backyard.

My wristwatch said midnight, one hand laid straight on top of the other.

The moon faded. Slowly, it went gray and shadowy, till the glow was gone, and then even the gray after-image was gone.

The wind rose. Slowly it came from somewhere far away and built around me. I stood up, pulling the collar of my topcoat around my neck. The wind was neither warm nor cold, yet it rushed, without even ruffling my hair. I was not afraid.

The ground was settling. Slowly, it lowered me the tiniest fractions of inches. But steadily, as though the layers of tomorrows that had been built up were vanishing.

My thoughts were of myself: *I'm coming to save you. I'm coming, Gus. You won't hurt anymore . . . you'll never have hurt.*

The moon came back. It had been full; now it was new. The wind died. It had carried me where I'd needed to go. The ground settled. The years had been peeled off.

I was alone in the backyard of the house at 89 Harmon Drive. The snow was deeper. It was a different house, though it was the same. It was not recently painted. The Depression had not been long ago; money was still tight. It wasn't weatherbeaten, but in a year or two my father would have it painted. Light yellow.

There was a sumac tree growing below the window of the dinette. It was nourished by lima beans and soup and cabbage.

"You'll just sit there until you finish every drop of your dinner. We're not wasting food. There are children starving in Russia."

I put the dragoon in my topcoat pocket. He had worked more than hard enough. I walked around the side of the house. I smiled as I saw again the wooden milk box by the side door. In the morning, very early, the milkman would put three quarts of milk there, but before anyone could bring them in, this very cold winter morning in December, the cream would push its way up and the little cardboard cap would be an inch above the mouth of the bottle.

The gravel talked beneath my feet. The street was quiet and cold. I stood in the front yard, beside the big oak tree, and looked up and down.

It was the same. It was as though I'd never been away. I started to cry. Hello.

Gus was on one of the swings in the playground. I stood outside the fence of Lathrop Grade School and watched him standing on the seat, gripping the ropes, pumping his little legs. He was smaller than I'd remembered him. He wasn't smiling as he tried to swing higher. It was serious work to him.

Standing outside the hurricane fence, watching Gus, I was happy. I scratched at a rash on my right wrist, and smoked a cigarette, and was happy.

I didn't see them until they were out of the shadows of the bushes, almost upon him.

One of them rushed up and grabbed Gus's leg, and tried to pull him off the seat, just as he reached the bottom of his swing. Gus managed to hold on, but the chain-ropes twisted crazily, and when it went back up, it hit the metal leg of the framework.

Gus fell, rolled facedown in the dust of the playground, and tried to sit up. The boys pushed through between the swings, avoiding the one that clanged back and forth.

Gus managed to get up, and the boys formed a circle around him. Then Jack Wheeldon stepped out and faced him. I remembered Jack Wheeldon.

He was taller than Gus. They were *all* taller than Gus, but Wheeldon was beefier. I could see shadows surrounding him. Shadows of a boy who would grow into a man with a beer stomach and thick arms. But the eyes would always remain the same.

He shoved Gus in the face. Gus went back, dug in and charged him. Gus came at him low, head tucked under, fists tight at the ends of arms braced close to the body, extended forward. He hit him in the stomach and wrestled him around. They struggled together like inept club fighters, raising dust.

One of the boys in the circle took a step forward and hit Gus hard in the back of the head. Gus turned his face out of Wheeldon's stomach, and Wheeldon punched him in the mouth. Gus started to cry.

I'd been frozen, watching it happen; but he was crying—

I looked both ways down the fence and found the break far to my right. I threw the cigarette away as I dashed down the fence, trying to look behind me. Then through the break and I was running toward them the long distance from far right field of the baseball diamond, toward the swings and see-saws. They had Gus down now, and they were kicking him.

When they saw me coming, they started to run away. Jack Wheeldon paused to kick Gus once more in the side, then he, too, ran.

Gus was lying there, on his back, the dust smeared into mud on his face. I bent down and picked him up. He wasn't moving, but he wasn't really hurt. I held him very close and carried him toward the bushes that rose on a small incline at the side of the playground. The bushes were cool overhead and they canopied us; I laid him down and used my handkerchief to clean away the dirt. His eyes were very blue. I smoothed the straight brown hair off his forehead. He wore braces; one of the rubber bands hooked onto the pins of the braces, used to keep them tension-tight, had broken. I pulled it free.

He opened his eyes and started crying again.

Something hurt in my chest.

He started snuffling, unable to catch his breath. He tried to speak, but the words were only mangled sounds, huffed out with too much air and pain.

Then he forced himself to sit up and rubbed the back of his hand across his runny nose.

He stared at me. It was panic and fear and confusion and shame at being seen this way. "Th-they hit me from in back," he said, snuffling.

"I know. I saw."

"D'jou scare'm off?"

"Yes."

He didn't say thank you. It wasn't necessary. The backs of my thighs hurt from squatting. I sat down.

"My name is Gus," he said, trying to be polite.

I didn't know what name to give him. I was going to tell him the first name to come into my head, but I heard myself say, "My name is Mr. Rosenthal."

He looked startled. "That's *my* name, too. Gus Rosenthal!"

"Isn't that peculiar," I said. We grinned at each other, and he wiped his nose again.

I didn't want to see my mother or father. I had those memories. They were sufficient. It was little Gus I wanted to be with. But one night I crossed into the backyard at 89 Harmon Drive from the empty lots that would later be a housing development.

And I stood in the dark, watching them eat dinner. There was my father. I hadn't remembered him as being so handsome. My mother was saying something to him, and he nodded as he ate. They were in the dinette. Gus was playing with his food. *Don't mush your food around like that, Gus. Eat, or you can't stay up to hear Lux Presents Hollywood.*

But they're doing "Dawn Patrol."

Then don't mush your food.

"Momma," I murmured, standing in the cold, "Momma, there are children starving in Russia." And I added, thirty-five years late, "Name two, Momma."

I met Gus downtown at the newsstand.

"Hi."

"Oh. Hullo."

"Buying some comics?"

"Uh-huh."

"You ever read *Doll Man* and *Kid Eternity?*"

"Yeah, they're great. But I got them."

"Not the new issues."

"Sure do."

"Bet you've got *last* month's. He's just checking in the new comics right now."

So we waited while the newsstand owner used the heavy wire snips on the bundles, and checked off the magazines against the distributor's long white mimeographed sheet. And I bought Gus *Airboy* and *Jingle Jangle Comics* and *Blue Beetle* and *Whiz Comics* and *Doll Man* and *Kid Eternity.*

Then I took him to Isaly's for a hot fudge sundae. They served it in a tall tulip glass with the hot fudge in a little pitcher. When the waitress had gone to get the sundaes, little Gus looked at me. "Hey, how'd you know I only liked crushed nuts, an' not whipped cream or a cherry?"

I leaned back in the high-walled booth and smiled at him. "What do you want to be when you grow up, Gus?"

He shrugged. "I don't know."

Somebody put a nickel in the Wurlitzer in his booth, and Glenn Miller swung into "String of Pearls."

"Well, did you ever think about it?"

"No, huh-uh. I like cartooning; maybe I could draw comic books."

"That's pretty smart thinking, Gus. There's a lot of money to be made in art." I stared around the dairy store, at the Coca-Cola posters of pretty girls with page boy hairdos, drawn by an artist named Harold W. McCauley whose style would be known throughout the world, whose name would never be known.

He stared at me. "It's fun, too, isn't it?"

I was embarrassed. I'd thought first of money, he'd thought first of happiness. I'd reached him before he'd chosen his path. There was still time to make him a man who would think first of joy, all through his life.

"Mr. Rosenthal?"

I looked down and across, just as the waitress brought the sundaes. She set them down and I paid her. When she'd gone, Gus asked me, "Why did they call me a dirty Jewish elephant?"

"Who called you that, Gus?"

"The guys."

"The ones you were fighting that day?"

He nodded. "Why'd they say elephant?"

I spooned up some vanilla ice cream, thinking. My back ached, and the rash had spread up my right wrist onto my forearm. "Well, Jewish people are supposed to have big noses, Gus." I poured the hot fudge out of the little pitcher. It bulged with surface tension for a second, then spilled through its own dark brown film, covering the three scoops of real ice cream; not tastee whipee freezee gunk substitute; *real* ice cream. "I mean, that's what some people *believe*. So I suppose they thought it was smart to call you an elephant, because an elephant has a big nose . . . a trunk. Do you understand?"

"That's dumb. I don't have a big nose . . . do I?"

"I wouldn't say so, Gus. They most likely said it just to make you mad. Sometimes people do that."

"That's dumb."

We sat there for a while and talked. I went far down inside the tulip glass with the long-handled spoon, and finished the deep dark, almost black bittersweet hot fudge. They hadn't made hot fudge like that in many years. Gus got ice cream up the spoon handle, on his fingers, on his chin, on his T-shirt, on the top of his head. We talked about a great many things.

We talked about how difficult arithmetic was. (How I would still have to use my fingers sometimes even as an adult, when I did my checkbook.) How the guys never gave a short kid his "raps" when the sandlot ball games were in progress. (How I overcompensated with women from doubts about stature.) How different kinds of food were pretty bad-tasting. (How I still used ketchup on well-done steak.) How it was pretty lonely in the neighborhood with nobody for friends. (How I had erected a façade of charisma and glamour so no one could reach me deeply enough to hurt me.) How Leon always invited all the kids over to his house, but when Gus got there, they slammed the door and stood behind the screen laughing and jeering. (How even now, a slammed door raised the hair on my neck, and a phone receiver slammed down, cutting me off, sent me into a senseless rage.) How comic books were great. (How my scripts sold so easily because I had never learned to rein in my imagination.)

We talked about a great many things.

"I'd better get you home now," I said.

"Okay." We got up. "Hey, Mr. Rosenthal?"

"You'd better wipe the chocolate off your face."

He wiped. "Mr. Rosenthal . . . how'd you know I like crushed nuts, an' not whipped cream or a cherry?"

We spent a great deal of time together. I bought him a copy of a pulp magazine called *Startling Stories,* and read him a story about a space pirate who captures a man and his wife and offers the man the choice of opening one of two large boxes—in one is the man's wife, with twelve hours of air to breathe, in the other is a terrible alien fungus that will eat him alive. Little Gus sat on the edge of the big hole he'd dug, out in the empty lots, dangling his feet, and listening. His forehead was furrowed as he listened to the marvels of Jack Williamson's "Twelve Hours to Live," there on the edge of the "fort" he'd built.

We discussed the radio programs Gus heard every day: Tennessee Jed, Captain Midnight, Jack Armstrong, Superman, Don Winslow of the Navy. And the nighttime programs: *I Love a Mystery, Suspense, The Adventures of Sam Spade.* And the Sunday programs: *The Shadow, Quiet, Please, The Mollé Mystery Theater.*

We became good friends. He had told his mother and father about "Mr. Rosenthal," who was his friend, but they'd spanked him for the *Startling Stories,* because they thought he'd stolen it. So he stopped telling them about me. That was all right; it made the bond between us stronger.

One afternoon we went down behind the Colony Lumber Company, through the woods and the weeds to the old condemned pond. Gus told

me he used to go swimming there, and fishing sometimes, for a black
oily fish with whiskers. I told him it was a catfish. He liked that. Liked
to know the names of things. I told him *that* was called nomenclature,
and he laughed to know there was a name for knowing names.

We sat on the piled logs rotting beside the black mirror water, and
Gus asked me to tell him what it was like where I lived, and where I'd
been, and what I'd done, and everything.

"I ran away from home when I was thirteen, Gus."

"Wasn't you happy there?"

"Well, yes and no. They loved me, my mother and father. They really
did. They just didn't understand what I was all about."

There was a pain on my neck. I touched a fingertip to the place. It
was a boil beginning to grow. I hadn't had a boil in years, many years,
not since I was a . . .

"What's the matter, Mr. Rosenthal?"

"Nothing, Gus. Well, anyhow, I ran away, and joined a carny."

"Huh?"

"A carnival. The Tri-State Shows. We moved through Illinois, Ohio,
Pennsylvania, Missouri, even Kansas . . ."

"Boy! A carnival! Just like in TOBY TYLER, or *Ten Weeks with a Circus?*
I really cried when Toby Tyler's monkey got killed, that was the worst part
of it, did you do stuff like that when you were with the circus?"

"Carnival."

"Yeah. Uh-huh. Did'ja?"

"Something like that. I carried water for the animals sometimes, although we only had a few of those, and mostly in the freak show. But
usually what I did was clean up, and carry food to the performers in
their tops—"

"What's that?"

"That's where they sleep, in rigged tarpaulins. You know, tarps."

"Oh. Yeah, I know. Go on, huh."

The rash was all the way up to my shoulder now. It itched like hell,
and when I'd gone to the drugstore to get an aerosol spray to relieve it,
so it wouldn't spread, I had only to see those round wooden display tables
with their glass centers, under which were bottles of Teel tooth liquid,
Tangee Red-Red lipstick and nylons with a seam down the back, to know
the druggist wouldn't even know what I meant by Bactine or Liquid
Band-Aid.

"Well, along about K.C. the carny got busted because there were too
many moll dips and cannons and paperhangers in the tip . . ." I waited,
his eyes growing huge.

"What's all *thaaat* mean, Mr. Rosenthal?!?"

"Ah-ha! Fine carny stiff *you'd* make. You don't even know the lingo."

"Please, Mr. Rosenthal, please tell me!"

"Well, K.C. is Kansas City, Missouri . . . when it isn't Kansas City,

Kansas. Except, really, on the other side of the river is Weston. And busted means thrown in jail, and . . .''

''You were in *jail?*''

''Sure was, little Gus. But let me tell you now. Cannons are pickpockets, and moll dips are lady pickpockets, and paperhangers are fellows who write bad checks. And a tip is a group.''

''So what happened, what happened?''

''One of these bad guys, one of these cannons, you see, picked the pocket of an assistant district attorney, and we all got thrown in jail. And after a while everyone was released on bail, except me and the Geek. Me, because I wouldn't tell them who I was, because I didn't want to go home, and the Geek, because a carny can find a wet-brain in *any* town to play Geek.''

''What's a Geek, huh?''

The Geek was a sixty-year-old alcoholic. So sunk in his own endless drunkenness that he was almost a zombie . . . a wet-brain. He was billed as The Thing and he lived in a portable pit they carried around, and he bit the heads off snakes and ate live chickens and slept in his own dung. And all for a bottle of gin every day. They locked me in the drunk tank with him. The smell. The smell of sour liquor oozing with sweat out of his pores, it made me sick, it was a smell I could never forget. And the third day, he went crazy. They wouldn't fix him with gin, and he went crazy. He climbed the bars of the big free-standing drunk tank in the middle of the lockup, and he banged his head against the bars and ceiling where they met, till he fell back and lay there, breathing raggedly, stinking of that terrible smell, his face like a pound of raw meat.

The pain in my stomach was worse now. I took Gus back to Harmon Drive, and let him go home.

My weight had dropped to just over a hundred and ten. My clothes didn't fit. The acne and boils were worse. I smelled of witch hazel. Gus was getting more antisocial.

I realized what was happening.

I was alien in my own past. If I stayed much longer, God only knew what would happen to little Gus . . . but certainly I would waste away. Perhaps just vanish. Then . . . would Gus's future cease to exist, too? I had no way of knowing; but my choice was obvious. I had to return.

And couldn't! I was happier here than I'd ever been before. The bigotry and violence Gus had known before I came to him had ceased. They knew he was being watched over. But Gus was becoming more erratic. He was shoplifting toy soldiers and comic books from the Kresge's and constantly defying his parents. It was turning bad. I had to go back.

I told him on a Saturday. We had gone to see a Lash LaRue western and Val Lewton's *The Cat People* at the Lake Theater. When we came back, I parked the car on Mentor Avenue, and we went walking in the big, cool, dark woods that fronted Mentor where it met Harmon Drive.

"Mr. Rosenthal," Gus said. He looked upset.

"Yes, Gus?"

"I gotta problem, sir."

"What's that, Gus?" My head ached. It was a steady needle of pressure above the right eye.

"My mother's gonna send me to a military school."

I remembered. *Oh, God,* I thought. It had been terrible. Precisely the thing *not* to do to a child like Gus.

"They said it was 'cause I was rambunctious. They said they were gonna send me there for a *year* or two. Mr. Rosenthal . . . don't let'm send me there. I din't mean to be bad. I just wanted to be around you."

My heart slammed inside me. Again. Then again. "Gus, I have to go away."

He stared at me. I heard a soft whimper.

"Take me with you, Mr. Rosenthal. Please. I want to see Galveston. We can drive a dynamite truck in North Carolina. We can go to Matawatchan, Ontario, Canada, and work topping trees, we can sail on boats, Mr. Rosenthal!"

"Gus . . ."

"We can work the carny, Mr. Rosenthal. We can pick peanuts and oranges all across the country. We can hitchhike to San Francisco and ride the cable cars. We can ride the boxcars, Mr. Rosenthal . . . I promise I'll keep my legs inside an' not dangle 'em. I remember what you said about the doors slamming when they hook'm up. I'll keep my legs inside, honest I will . . ."

He was crying. My head ached hideously. But he was *crying!*

"I'll *have* to go, Gus!"

"You don't care!" He was shouting. "You don't care about me, you don't care what happens to me! You don't care if I die . . . you don't . . ."

He didn't have to say it: *you don't love me.*

"I do, Gus. I swear to God, I do!"

I looked up at him; he was supposed to be my friend. But he wasn't. He was going to let them send me off to that military school.

"I hope you die!"

Oh, dear God, Gus, I am! I turned and ran out of the woods as I watched him run out of the woods.

I drove away. The green Plymouth with the running boards and the heavy body; it was hard steering. The world swam around me. My eyesight blurred. I could feel myself withering away.

I thought I'd left myself behind, but little Gus had followed me out of the woods. Having done it, I now remembered: why had I remembered none of it before? As I drove off down Mentor Avenue, I came out of the woods and saw the big green car starting up, and I ran wildly forward, crouching low, wanting only to go with him, my friend, me. I threw in the clutch and dropped the stick into first, and pulled away from the curb as I reached the car and climbed onto the rear fender, pulling my legs up, hanging onto the trunk latch. I drove weaving, my eyes watering and things going first blue, then green, hanging on for dear life to the cold latch handle. Cars whipped around, honking madly, trying to tell me that I was on the rear of the car, but I didn't know what they were honking about, and scared their honking would tell me I was back there, hiding. After I'd gone almost a mile, a car pulled up alongside, and a woman sitting next to the driver looked down at me crouching there, and I made a *please don't tell* sign with my finger to my freezing lips, but the car pulled ahead and the woman rolled down her window and motioned to me. I rolled down my window and the woman yelled across through the rushing wind that I was back there on the rear fender. I pulled over and fear gripped me as the car stopped and I saw me getting out of the door, and I crawled off the car and started running away. But my legs were cramped and cold from having hung on back there, and I ran awkwardly; then coming out of the dark was a road sign, and I hit it, and it hit me in the side of the face, and I fell down, and I ran toward myself, lying there, crying, and I got to him just as I got up and ran off into the gravel yard surrounding the Colony Lumber Company.

Little Gus was bleeding from the forehead where he'd struck the metal sign. He ran into the darkness, and I knew where he was running . . . I had to catch him, to tell him, to make him understand why I had to go away.

I came to the hurricane fence, and ran and ran till I found the place where I'd dug out under it, and I slipped down and pulled myself under and got my clothes all dirty, but I got up and ran back behind the Colony Lumber Company, into the sumac and the weeds, till I came to the condemned pond back there. Then I sat down and looked out over the black water. I was crying.

I followed the trail down to the pond. It took me longer to climb over the fence than it had taken him to crawl under it. When I came down to the pond, he was sitting there with a long blade of saw-grass in his mouth, crying softly.

I heard him coming, but I didn't turn around.

I came down to him, and crouched down behind him. "Hey," I said quietly. "Hey, little Gus."

I wouldn't turn around. I wouldn't.

I spoke his name again, and touched him on the shoulder, and in an instant he was turned to me, hugging me around the chest, crying into my jacket, mumbling over and over, "Don't go, please don't go, please take me with you, please don't leave me here alone . . ."

And I was crying, too. I hugged little Gus, and touched his hair, and felt him holding on to me with all his might, stronger than a seven-year-old should be able to hold on, and I tried to tell him how it was, how it would be: "Gus . . . hey, hey, little Gus, listen to me . . . I *want* to stay, you *know* I want to stay . . . but I can't."

I looked up at him; he was crying, too. It seemed so strange for a grown-up to be crying like that, and I said, "If you leave me, *I'll* die. I will!"

I knew it wouldn't do any good to try explaining. He was too young. He wouldn't be able to understand.

He pulled my arms from around him, and he folded my hands in my lap, and he stood up, and I looked at him. He was gonna leave me. I knew he was. I stopped crying. I wouldn't let him see me cry.

I looked down at him. The moonlight held his face in a pale photograph. I wasn't fooling myself. He'd understand. He'd know. Kids *always* know. I turned and started back up the path. Little Gus didn't follow. He sat there looking back at me. I only turned once to look at him. He was still sitting there like that.

He was watching me. Staring up at me from the pond side. And I knew what instant it had been that had formed me. It hadn't been all the people who'd called me a wild kid, or a strange kid, or any of it. It wasn't being poor, or being lonely.

I watched him go away. He was my friend. But he didn't have no guts. He didn't. But I'd show him! I'd really show him! I was gonna get out of here, go away, be a big person and do a lot of things, and someday I'd run into him someplace and see him and he'd come up and shake my hand and I'd spit on him. Then I'd beat him up.

He walked up the path and went away. I sat there for a long time, by the pond. Till it got real cold.

I got back in the car, and went to find the way back to the future; where I belonged. It wasn't much, but it was all I had. I would find it . . . I still had the dragoon . . . and there were many stops I'd made on the way to becoming me. Perhaps Kansas City; perhaps Matawatchan, Ontario, Canada; perhaps Galveston; perhaps Shelby, North Carolina.

And crying, I drove. Not for myself, but for myself, for little Gus, for what I'd done to him, forced him to become. Gus . . . Gus!

But . . . oh, God . . . what if I came back again . . . and again? Suddenly, the road did not look familiar.

I OF NEWTON
Joe Haldeman

TELEPLAY BY ALAN BRENNERT

AIRED DECEMBER 13, 1985

STARRING SHERMAN HEMSLEY, RON GLASS

SAMUEL INGARD GLARED SULLENLY AT THE BURBLING coffeepot and felt his stomach pucker in revulsion. Eighty hours he had been up; eighty hours on coffee and amphetamine, 3.333 days of weaving a beautiful tapestry of mathematical logic, only to find that a skipped stitch in the beginning was causing the whole thing to unravel. But he would patch it yet.

"The integral, the integral," he said to no one in particular. "Who's got the integral?" He had first caught himself mumbling out loud about twenty hours ago. By now he'd stopped catching himself.

He opened a thick book provocatively titled *Two Thousand Integrals,* closed it in disgust, and leaned back, rubbing his nicotine-stained eyeballs.

"The integral of dx over the cosine to the n of x," he intoned portentously, "is sine x over n-1 times the cosine to the n-1 of x plus n-1—no, godammit—n-2 over n-1 times the integral of . . ."

Sam smelled something vaguely reminiscent of freshman chemistry and opened his eyes. Seated Yoga-style on his desk, stripping pages from his flaming table of integrals and eating them with great relish, was a red-complected creature with ivory horns, hooves, and a black, scaly tail twitching with pleasure. He was all of three feet tall.

This was even better than yesterday—or was it the day before?—when he had looked in a table of random numbers and thought he saw a pattern! And the head of the department said he lacked imagination.

The apparition cleared its throat—a sound somewhere between a buzz saw and a double bassoon warming up—and said in a gravelly monotone, "I really wish I didn't have to inform you of this. It would make my job a lot simpler, and less time-consuming, if I could just leave you to your own devices. But I am required to give you an explanation; required by an Authority—" he glanced upward with mild distaste "—whose nature you could never hope to comprehend." The creature took a deep breath, disappeared for a moment, then reappeared in the form of an elderly gentleman wearing gold-rimmed spectacles and a rumpled double-breasted suit. He climbed gingerly off the desk and brushed chalk dust from his coat with an age-spotted hand.

"Bring on the parchment, the sterilized pin!" Sam resolved to play out this hallucination for all it was worth, then get a couple of days' sleep. "That's the way the game is played, isn't it? My soul for the answer to

162

this problem?'' He gestured grandly at the reams of hieroglyphics cluttering his desk, spilling onto the floor.

"I'm afraid you've been rather misled by your folklore and literature." The professor-demon flicked at a dust mote on his broad lapel, causing a shower of blue sparks. "I don't *trade* anything. That is what I am unfortunately required to explain. We go through a silly little ritual, and then I *take*. Your soul was forfeit the moment you summoned me."

"Summoned . . . ?"

"Hush!" The professor dissolved into an even more ancient schoolmarm, then to a bushy-haired-and-faced undergraduate (obviously mathematics), who pointed a skewering forefinger at him, "Or you'll regret it! That garbage you were mumbling." He made an imperious gesture and Sam heard his own voice saying,

". . . of x plus n-1—no, godammit—n-2 over n-1 . . ."

"That garbage had the right phonetic and semantic structure to be a curse, especially since a neat little god-denial was woven into it. A nice, omnidirectional curse; easy to home in on while the supporting mood still exists."

Sam thought of his colleagues over the years who had disappeared or died in their prime. He grew a little pale.

"Yes, Samuel Ingard, you *do* have a soul, though it be a withered-up little kernel that will probably give me acute indigestion. Enjoy it while you can.

"But, quickly, to the business at hand. You are allowed to ask me three questions pertaining to my abilities. Then you will ask me another question, which I will attempt to answer, or set a task for me, which I will attempt to perform.

"In the past, mathematicians have asked me to prove Fermat's Theorem, which I can prove to be false." He gestured and a blackboard full of scribblings appeared. Sam, a man who reads the last page of a mystery first, as well as being a mathematician, managed to jot down the last three equations before the board evaporated.

"They have asked me to square the circle, which is trivial, find the ultimate prime, which is only a little harder, or other such banalities. I hope you can come up with something more original.

"If I fail to resolve your problem, I will be gone." The undergraduate-demon smiled a little smile.

"And if you succeed?" Sam tried to sound casual and failed.

"Ah! First question!"

"No!"

"Sorry, I'm playing by the rules, and I expect you to as well. If I should succeed, as I have in every encounter since 1930, I shall consume your soul; a relatively painless process. I *am* a soul-eater. Unfortunately, the loss of your soul will drop your intelligence to that of a vegetable."

A long yellow tusk grew out of the center of his mouth; he watched it with an eye on a stalk until it reached his chin.

"I am also a vegetarian."

Sam was strangely calm as he worded his first—no, second—question. He had the germ of an idea. "Aside from the, uh, divine restriction you mentioned at the outset, which you complied with by telling me where I stand, are there any physical or temporal limitations to your abilities?"

"None." The Ollie-the-dragonesque demon scratched his tusk idly and added complacently, "Don't try to take refuge in your own parochial view of the universe. I can go faster than the speed of light or make two electrons in an atom occupy the same quantum state as easily as you can blow your nose." He peered intently at Sam's nose. "More easily. Next question."

"My next question affirms a corollary to the first. Is there anyplace in the universe, in all of . . . being . . . where you could go and not be able to find your way back here?"

The demon licked his tusk with a bilious green tongue. "No. I could go to the Andromeda Galaxy and back in a microsecond. In the same manner I could go to, say, what would be Berlin if the Nazis had won the war, or Atlanta if the South had, or twentieth-century Rome if Alexander had lived to a ripe old age." While saying this, the demon danced an Irish jig and his hair turned into a writhing mass of coral snakes, who arranged themselves into a pompadour.

"Now, finally, ask me a question I can't answer; or a task I can't perform."

Sam looked coolly at the demon, who was now a quivering lump of yellow protoplasm hanging in midair, covered with obscene black stubble, bisected by a scarlet orifice filled with hundreds of tiny pointed teeth grinding together with a sandpapery sound. "The question," it growled.

"Not a question," said Sam, enjoying the creature's agony, ". . . a command!"

"Out with it!"

Sam smiled, a little sadly. "Get lost."

The demon resumed his original shape, but ten feet tall and all black cape and brimstone. He cursed and clutched impotently at the smiling mathematician and started to shrink. At five feet tall, he stood still and wrung his tail nervously. One foot tall, he started to stamp up and down in inarticulate rage. The size of a thimble, he whined in a piteously shrill voice, "You and Ernest Hemingway!" and disappeared.

Sam walked over and opened a window to let out the sulfur dioxide. Then he sat down at his desk, shoved all the papers on the floor, and started to play algebraic games with the Fermat Theorem fragment he had filched from the demon. As he worked, he mumbled and chortled to himself. Perhaps one day he would summon the poor thing again, and trick him into squaring the circle.

But he had only been a demon, and a little one at that.

He had a supervisor, who was to him as he was to Sam. The supervisor was a hundred billion light years away now, doing something unspeakable, on a scale that would make Genghis Khan look like a two-bit hood.

But in a way that is His alone, He was also in that room, standing behind Sam.

Watching his language.

THE STAR
Arthur C. Clarke

TELEPLAY BY ALAN BRENNERT

AIRED DECEMBER 20, 1985

STARRING FRITZ WEAVER, DONALD MOFFAT, ELIZABETH HUDDLE

IT IS THREE THOUSAND LIGHT-YEARS TO THE VATICAN. Once, I believed that space could have no power over faith, just as I believed that the heavens declared the glory of God's handiwork. Now I have seen that handiwork, and my faith is sorely troubled. I stare at the crucifix that hangs on the cabin wall above the Mark VI Computer, and for the first time in my life I wonder if it is not more than an empty symbol.

I have told no one yet, but the truth cannot be concealed. The facts are there for all to read, recorded on the countless miles of magnetic tape and the thousands of photographs we are carrying back to Earth. Other scientists can interpret them as easily as I can, and I am not one who would condone that tampering with the truth which often gave my order a bad name in the olden days.

The crew were already sufficiently depressed: I wonder how they will take this ultimate irony. Few of them have any religious faith, yet they will not relish using this final weapon in their campaign against me— that private, good-natured, but fundamentally serious war which lasted all the way from Earth. It amused them to have a Jesuit as chief astrophysicist: Dr. Chandler, for instance, could never get over it. (Why are medical men such notorious atheists?) Sometimes he would meet me on the observation deck, where the lights are always low so that the stars shine with undiminished glory. He would come up to me in the gloom and stand staring out of the great oval port, while the heavens crawled slowly around us as the ship turned end over end with the residual spin we had never bothered to correct.

"Well, Father," he would say at last, "it goes on forever and forever, and perhaps *Something* made it. But how you can believe that Something has a special interest in us and our miserable little world—that just beats me." Then the argument would start, while the stars and nebulae would swing around us in silent, endless arcs beyond the flawlessly clear plastic of the observation port.

It was, I think, the apparent incongruity of my position that caused most amusement to the crew. In vain I would point to my three papers in the *Astrophysical Journal,* my five in the *Monthly Notices of the Royal Astronomical Society.* I would remind them that my order has long been famous for its scientific works. We may be few now, but ever since the eighteenth century, we have made contributions to astronomy and geophysics out of all proportion to our numbers. Will my report on the

Phoenix Nebula end our thousand years of history? It will end, I fear, much more than that.

I do not know who gave the nebula its name, which seems to me a very bad one. If it contains a prophecy, it is one that cannot be verified for several billion years. Even the word "nebula" is misleading; this is a far smaller object than those stupendous clouds of mist—the stuff of unborn stars—that are scattered throughout the length of the Milky Way. On the cosmic scale, indeed, the Phoenix Nebula is a tiny thing—a tenuous shell of gas surrounding a single star.

Or what is left of a star . . .

The Rubens engraving of Loyola seems to mock me as it hangs there above the spectrophotometer tracings. What would *you*, Father, have made of this knowledge that has come into my keeping, so far from the little world that was all the Universe you knew? Would your faith have risen to the challenge, as mine has failed to do?

You gaze into the distance, Father, but I have traveled a distance beyond any that you could have imagined when you founded our order a thousand years ago. No other survey ship has been so far from Earth: we are at the very frontiers of the explored universe. We set out to reach the Phoenix Nebula, we succeeded, and we are homeward bound with our burden of knowledge. I wish I could lift that burden from my shoulders, but I call to you in vain across the centuries and the light-years that lie between us.

On the book you are holding, the words are plain to read. AD MAIOREM DEI GLORIAM, the message runs, but it is a message I can no longer believe. Would you still believe it, if you could see what we have found?

We knew, of course, what the Phoenix Nebula was. Every year, in our Galaxy alone, more than a hundred stars explode, blazing for a few hours or days with thousands of times their normal brilliance before they sink back into death and obscurity. Such are the ordinary novae—the commonplace disasters of the universe. I have recorded the spectrograms and light curves of dozens since I started working at the Lunar Observatory.

But three or four times in every thousand years occurs something beside which even a nova pales into total insignificance.

When a star becomes a *supernova*, it may for a little while outshine all the massed suns of the galaxy. The Chinese astronomers watched this happen A.D. 1054, not knowing what it was they saw. Five centuries later, in 1572, a supernova blazed in Cassiopeia so brilliantly that it was visible in the daylight sky. There have been three more in the thousand years that have passed since then.

Our mission was to visit the remnants of such a catastrophe, to reconstruct the events that led up to it, and, if possible, to learn its cause. We came slowly in through the concentric shells of gas that had been blasted out six thousand years before, yet were expanding still. They were immensely hot, radiating even now with a fierce violet light, but were far too tenuous to do us any damage. When the star had exploded, its outer layers had been driven upward with such speed that they had escaped completely from its gravitational field. Now they formed a hollow shell large enough to engulf a thousand solar systems, and at its center burned the tiny, fantastic object which the star had now become—a white dwarf, smaller than the Earth, yet weighing a million times as much.

The glowing gas shells were all around us, banishing the normal night of interstellar space. We were flying into the center of the cosmic bomb that had detonated millennia ago and whose incandescent fragments were still hurtling apart. The immense scale of the explosion, and the fact that the debris already covered a volume of space many billions of miles across, robbed the scene of any visible movement. It would take decades before the unaided eye could detect any motion in these tortured wisps and eddies of gas, yet the sense of turbulent expansion was overwhelming.

We had checked our primary drive hours before, and were drifting slowly toward the fierce little star ahead. Once it had been a sun like our own, but it had squandered in a few hours the energy that should have kept it shining for a million years. Now it was a shrunken miser, hoarding its resources as if trying to make amends for its prodigal youth.

No one seriously expected to find planets. If there had been any before the explosion, they would have been boiled into puffs of vapor, and their substance lost in the greater wreckage of the star itself. But we made the automatic search, as we always do when approaching an unknown sun, and presently we found a single small world circling the star at an immense distance. It must have been the Pluto of this vanished solar system, orbiting on the frontiers of the night. Too far from the central sun ever to have known life, its remoteness had saved it from the fate of all its lost companions.

The passing fires had seared its rocks and burned away the mantle of frozen gas that must have covered it in the days before the disaster. We landed, and we found the Vault.

Its builders had made sure that we should. The monolithic marker that stood above the entrance was now a fused stump, but even the first long-range photographs told us that here was the work of intelligence. A little later we detected the continent-wide pattern of radioactivity that had been buried in the rock. Even if the pylon above the Vault had been destroyed, this would have remained, an immovable and all but eternal beacon calling to the stars. Our ship fell toward this gigantic bull's-eye like an arrow into its target.

The pylon must have been a mile high when it was built, but now it looked like a candle that had melted down into a puddle of wax. It took us a week to drill through the fused rock, since we did not have the proper tools for a task like this. We were astronomers, not archaeologists, but we could improvise. Our original purpose was forgotten: This lonely monument, reared with such labor at the greatest possible distance from the doomed sun, could have only one meaning. A civilization that knew it was about to die had made its last bid for immortality.

It will take us generations to examine all the treasures that were placed in the Vault. They had plenty of time to prepare, for their sun must have given its first warnings many years before the final detonation. Everything that they wished to preserve, all the fruits of their genius, they brought here to this distant world in the days before the end, hoping that some other race would find it and that they would not be utterly forgotten. Would we have done as well, or would we have been too lost in our own misery to give thought to a future we could never see or share?

If only they had had a little more time! They could travel freely enough between the planets of their own sun, but they had not yet learned to cross the interstellar gulfs, and the nearest solar system was a hundred light-years away. Yet even had they possessed the secret of the Transfinite Drive, no more than a few millions could have been saved. Perhaps it was better thus.

Even if they had not been so disturbingly human as their sculpture shows, we could not have helped admiring them and grieving for their fate. They left thousands of visual records and the machines for projecting them, together with elaborate pictorial instructions from which it will not be difficult to learn their written language. We have examined many of these records, and brought to life for the first time in six thousand years the warmth and beauty of a civilization that in many ways must have been superior to our own. Perhaps they only showed us the best, and one can hardly blame them. But their worlds were very lovely, and their cities were built with a grace that matches anything of man's. We have watched them at work and play, and listened to their musical speech sounding across the centuries. One scene is still before my eyes—a group of children on a beach of strange blue sand, playing in the waves as children play on Earth. Curious whiplike trees line the shore, and some very large animal is wading in the shallows yet attracting no attention at all.

And sinking into the sea, still warm and friendly and life-giving, is the sun that will soon turn traitor and obliterate all this innocent happiness.

Perhaps if we had not been so far from home and so vulnerable to loneliness, we should not have been so deeply moved. Many of us had seen the ruins of ancient civilizations on other worlds, but they had never affected us so profoundly. This tragedy was unique. It is one thing for a race to fail and die, as nations and cultures have done on Earth. But to be destroyed so completely in the full flower of its achievement, leaving no survivors—how could that be reconciled with the mercy of God?

My colleagues have asked me that, and I have given what answers I can. Perhaps you could have done better, Father Loyola, but I have found nothing in the *Exercitia Spiritualia* that helps me here. They were not an evil people: I do not know what gods they worshiped, if indeed they worshiped any. But I have looked back at them across the centuries, and have watched while the loveliness they used their last strength to preserve was brought forth again into the light of their shrunken sun. They could have taught us much: why were they destroyed?

I know the answers that my colleagues will give when they get back to Earth. They will say that the universe has no purpose and no plan, that since a hundred suns explode every year in our galaxy, at this very moment some race is dying in the depths of space. Whether that race has done good or evil during its lifetime will make no difference in the end: there is no divine justice, for there is no God.

Yet, of course, what we have seen proves nothing of the sort. Anyone who argues thus is being swayed by emotion, not logic. God has no need to justify His actions to man. He who built the universe can destroy it when He chooses. It is arrogance—it is perilously near blasphemy—for us to say what He may or may not do.

This I could have accepted, hard though it is to look upon whole worlds and peoples thrown into the furnace. But there comes a point when even the deepest faith must falter, and now, as I look at the calculations lying before me, I know I have reached that point at last.

We could not tell, before we reached the nebula, how long ago the explosion took place. Now, from the astronomical evidence and the record in the rocks of that one surviving planet, I have been able to date it very exactly. I know in what year the light of this colossal conflagration reached our Earth. I know how brilliantly the supernova whose corpse now dwindles behind our speeding ship once shone in terrestrial skies. I know how it must have blazed low in the east before sunrise, like a beacon in that oriental dawn.

There can be no reasonable doubt: the ancient mystery is solved at last. Yet, oh God, there were so many stars you could have used. What was the need to give these people to the fire, that the symbol of their passing might shine above Bethlehem?

THE MISFORTUNE COOKIE
Charles E. Fritch

TELEPLAY BY STEVEN RAE

AIRED JANUARY 3, 1986

STARRING ELLIOT GOULD, BENNETT OHTA,

CAROLINE LAGERFELT

WITH AN EASE BORN OF LONG PRACTICE, HARRY FOLGER cracked open the Chinese cookie and pulled the slip of paper free. He smoothed it out on the table and read the message printed there:

YOU WILL MEET AN OLD FRIEND!

Harry chuckled to himself. It was inevitable that he would meet an old friend. He met them every day—on his way to work, at the office, in his apartment building—even in the various Chinese restaurants he frequented.

He bit into the cookie, crunched the remnants between his teeth, and washed them down with a swig of the now lukewarm tea. He enjoyed the fortune cookie as much as the fortune itself. But then, he enjoyed everything about the Chinese food that he always ate, without ever tiring of it—the chow mein, the chop suey, the chicken fried rice, the won ton, the egg foo yung, the—oh, why go on? Heaven, to Harry Folger, was eating in a Chinese restaurant.

And as he was leaving the place, he met an old friend.

Her name was Cynthia Peters, or had been until she'd married. She was not old in the chronological sense, however, but a young woman not yet in her thirties. Harry had fond memories of the tempestuous affair he had experienced with the lady when both were younger, and frequently his dreams were filled with such pleasant recollections.

"Cynthia!" he said, surprised but pleased.

"Harry!" she exclaimed, tears of sudden happiness welling in her hazel-green eyes.

And Harry knew that despite the fact they were both married, he was going to have an affair with her.

When he finally got around to thinking about it, Harry marveled at the coincidence of his meeting old friend Cynthia right after a fortune cookie had forewarned him of such an occurrence. It was a coincidence, of course, for it could be nothing else. Harry enjoyed reading the messages—written, he always assumed, by coolie labor somewhere in Hong Kong—but he did not believe them to contain the absolute truth.

Not just then, he didn't.

The meeting places of himself and Cynthia were, needless to say, Chinese restaurants. Her husband, she told him, was a beast who made her life miserable. His wife, he informed her, was a bitch with whom he was quite unhappy. On one of these occasions, after a delicious meal of sweet-and-sour spareribs, Harry cracked open his fortune cookie to discover this message:

WATCH OUT! SOMEONE IS FOLLOWING YOU!

He looked up to discover Cynthia's irate husband entering the restaurant. There was barely time enough to spirit her out the rear exit. There would have been no time at all if the Chinese fortune cookie hadn't alerted Harry to the imminent danger.

Coincidence again, Harry decided—until he received a similarly worded message an instant before his wife (who hated Chinese food) entered the restaurant where he and Cynthia were eating, and once again Harry escaped in the nick of time.

As a result, Harry began taking the messages more seriously. He was hoping for some invaluable tip on the stock market or some winning horse in Saturday's race, but none came. For the most part, except for emergencies, the messages were bland bits of wisdom and random advice.

With one noticeable exception.

It occurred as he and Cynthia (who, like him, loved Chinese food) were finishing off the remaining morsels of Mandarin duck and she was telling how suspicious her husband was getting and how sure she was that Harry's own wife must not be blind to the secret rendezvous. At that precise moment, Harry cracked open a crisp fortune cookie, pulled out the slip of paper and read:

YOU ARE GOING TO DIE!

Harry gulped and almost choked on the piece of cookie in his mouth. It was ridiculous, of course. Then his attitude changed abruptly to one of indignation. What the hell kind of message was that for some underpaid coolie in Hong Kong to stuff into a fortune cookie? He thought of complaining to the manager, but he changed his mind. Instead, he decided he didn't feel well. He took Cynthia home, letting her off in front of her apartment.

As he was about to drive off, he heard a noise at the opposite window. He looked to see Cynthia's husband pointing a gun at him. He gasped, flung open the car door and scrambled out, bumping into his wife, who also had a gun in her hand.

Harry ran. He was vaguely aware that two guns fired simultaneously, but he felt no pain and was not about to stop his flight. He ran, not pausing for breath until he was a good four blocks away. Then he leaned against a building, dragging in lungfuls of air, to take inventory. There didn't seem to be any holes in him, nor was there any sign of blood.

Thank God, he thought, for the lousy aim of the two irate spouses.

Even so, he was shaking uncontrollably. He had to go someplace and relax. They might still be after him, and he'd be safer in a crowded place. He looked up at the building to see where he was.

He was standing in front of a Chinese restaurant.

It was one he'd never been to before, and his curiosity was aroused. Also his appetite, although he'd eaten a Chinese meal only an hour before. Besides, he always felt secure in such a place.

Harry Folger walked in, sat at a table. Surprisingly, he was the only person there. When a waiter appeared, Harry ordered the number-two dinner. He ate it, enjoying each mouthful, forgetting the unpleasant episode in the street. Then he cracked open his fortune cookie and read the message that had been tucked inside.

The words didn't register at first. When they did, he looked up in sudden panic—to see the waiter grinning derisively with a skull face. Harry looked around wildly for a way out, but there were no doors or windows in the restaurant, no way to get out now or ever.

He started screaming.

When he tired of that, he felt hungry again. He ordered another meal, ate it. The message in the fortune cookie this time was exactly as the first.

He had another meal after that one, and another after that, and another after that—and each time the message in the fortune cookie was the same. It said:

YOU'RE DEAD!

YESTERDAY WAS MONDAY
Theodore Sturgeon

TELEPLAY BY ROCKNE S. O'BANNON

AIRED JANUARY 24, 1986, AS "A MATTER OF MINUTES"

STARRING ADAM ARKIN, KAREN AUSTIN, ADOLPH CAESAR

HARRY WRIGHT ROLLED OVER AND SAID SOMETHING spelled "Bzzzzhha-a-aw!" He chewed a bit on a mouthful of dry air and spat it out, opened one eye to see if it really would open, opened the other and closed the first, closed the second, swung his feet onto the floor, opened them again and stretched. This was a daily occurrence, and the only thing that made it remarkable at all was that he did it on a Wednesday morning, and—

Yesterday was Monday.

Oh, he knew it was Wednesday, all right. It was partly that, even though he knew yesterday was Monday, there was a gap between Monday and now; and that must have been Tuesday. When you fall asleep and lie there all night without dreaming, you know, when you wake up, that time has passed. You've done nothing that you can remember; you've had no particular thoughts, no way to gauge time, and yet you know that some hours have passed. So it was with Harry Wright. Tuesday had gone wherever your eight hours went last night.

But he hadn't slept through Tuesday. Oh no. He never slept, as a matter of fact, more than six hours at a stretch, and there was no particular reason for him doing so now. Monday was the day before yesterday; he had turned in and slept his usual stretch, he had awakened, and it was Wednesday.

It *felt* like Wednesday. There was a Wednesdayish feel to the air.

Harry put on his socks and stood up. He wasn't fooled. He knew what day it was. "What happened to yesterday?" he muttered. "Oh— yesterday was Monday." That sufficed until he got his pajamas off. "Monday," he mused, reaching for his underwear, "was quite a while back, seems as though." If he had been the worrying type, he would have started then and there. But he wasn't. He was an easygoing sort, the kind of man that gets himself into a rut and stays there until he is pushed out. That was why he was an automobile mechanic at twenty-three dollars a week; that's why he had been one for eight years now, and would be from now on, if he could only find Tuesday and get back to work.

Guided by his reflexes, as usual, and with no mental effort at all, which was also usual, he finished washing, dressing, and making his bed. His alarm clock, which never alarmed because he was of such regular habits, said, as usual, six twenty-two when he paused on the way out, and gave his room the once-over. And there was a certain something about the place that made even this phlegmatic character stop and think.

It wasn't finished.

The bed was there, and the picture of Joe Louis. There were the two chairs sharing their usual seven legs, the split table, the pipe-organ bedstead, the beige wallpaper with the two swans over and over and over, the tiny corner sink, the tilted bureau. But none of them were finished. Not that there were any holes in anything. What paint there had been in the first place was still there. But there was an odor of old cut lumber, a subtle, insistent air of building, about the room and everything in it. It was indefinable, inescapable, and Harry Wright stood there caught up in it, wondering. He glanced suspiciously around but saw nothing he could really be suspicious of. He shook his head, locked the door and went out into the hall.

On the steps a little fellow, just over three feet tall, was gently stroking the third step from the top with a razor-sharp chisel, shaping up a new scar in the dirty wood. He looked up as Harry approached, and stood up quickly.

"Hi," said Harry, taking in the man's leather coat, his peaked cap, his wizened, bright-eyed little face. "Whatcha doing?"

"Touch-up," piped the little man. "The actor in the third floor front has a nail in his right heel. He came in late Tuesday night and cut the wood here. I have to get it ready for Wednesday."

"This is Wednesday," Harry pointed out.

"Of course. Always has been. Always will be."

Harry let that pass, started on down the stairs. He had achieved his amazing bovinity by making a practice of ignoring things he could not understand. But one thing bothered him—

"Did you say that feller in the third floor front was an actor?"

"Yes. They're all actors, you know."

"You're nuts, friend," said Harry bluntly. "That guy works on the docks."

"Oh yes—that's his part. That's what he acts."

"No kiddin'. An' what does he do when he isn't acting?"

"But he— Well, that's all he does do! That's all any of the actors do!"

"Gee— I thought he looked like a reg'lar guy, too," said Harry. "An actor? 'Magine!"

"Excuse me," said the little man, "but I've got to get back to work. We mustn't let anything get by us, you know. They'll be through Tuesday before long, and everything must be ready for them."

Harry thought: this guy's crazy nuts. He smiled uncertainly and went down to the landing below. When he looked back, the man was cutting skillfully into the stair, making a neat little nail scratch. Harry shook his head. This was a screwy morning. He'd be glad to get back to the shop. There was a '39 sedan down there with a busted rear spring. Once he got his mind on that, he could forget this nonsense. That's all that matters to a man in a rut. Work, eat, sleep, payday. Why even try to think anything else out?

The street was a riot of activity, but then, it always was. But not quite this way. There were automobiles and trucks and buses around, aplenty, but none of them were moving. And none of them were quite complete. This was Harry's own field; if there was anything he didn't know about motor vehicles, it wasn't very important. And through that medium he began to get the general idea of what was going on.

Swarms of little men who might have been twins of the one he had spoken to were crowding around the cars, the sidewalks, the stores and buildings. All were working like mad with every tool imaginable. Some were touching up the finish of the cars with fine wire brushes, laying on networks of microscopic cracks and scratches. Some, with ball peens and mallets, were denting fenders skillfully, bending bumpers in an artful crash pattern, spiderwebbing safety-glass windshields. Others were aging top dressing with high-pressure, needlepoint sandblasters. Still others were pumping dust into upholstery, sandpapering the dashboard finish around light switches, throttles, chokes, to give a finger-worn appearance. Harry stood aside as a half dozen of the workers scampered down the street bearing a fender which they riveted to a 1930 coupé. It was freshly bloodstained.

Once awakened to this highly unusual activity, Harry stopped, slightly openmouthed, to watch what else was going on. He saw the same process being industriously accomplished with the houses and stores. Dirt was being laid on plate-glass windows over a coat of clear sizing. Woodwork was being cleverly scored and the paint peeled to make it look correctly weather-beaten, and dozens of leather-clad laborers were on their hands and knees, poking dust and dirt into the cracks between the paving blocks. A line of them went down the sidewalk, busily chewing gum and spitting it out; they were followed by another crew who carefully placed the wads according to diagrams they carried, and stamped them flat.

Harry set his teeth and muscled his rocking brain into something like its normal position. "I ain't never seen a day like this or crazy people like this," he said, "but I ain't gonna let it be any of my affair. I got my job to go to." And trying vainly to ignore the hundreds of little, hard-working figures, he went grimly on down the street.

When he got to the garage, he found no one there but more swarms of stereotyped little people climbing over the place, dulling the paint work, cracking the cement flooring, doing their hurried, efficient little tasks of aging. He noticed, only because he was so familiar with the garage, that they were actually *making* the marks that had been there as long as he had known the place. "Hell with it," he gritted, anxious to submerge himself into his own world of wrenches and grease guns. "I got my job; this is none o' my affair."

He looked about him, wondering if he should clean these interlopers out of the garage. Naw—not his affair. He was hired to repair cars, not to police the joint. Long as they kept away from him—and, of course, animal caution told him that he was far, far outnumbered. The absence of the boss and the other mechanics was no surprise to Harry; he always opened the place.

He climbed out of his street clothes and into coveralls, picked up a tool case and walked over to the sedan, which he had left up on the hydraulic rack yester— that is, Monday night. And that is when Harry Wright lost his temper. After all, the car was his job, and he didn't like having anyone else mess with a job he had started. So when he saw his job—his '39 sedan—resting steadily on its wheels over the rack, which was down under the floor, and when he saw that the rear spring was repaired, he began to burn. He dived under the car and ran deft fingers over the rear wheel suspensions. In spite of his anger at this unprecedented occurrence, he had to admit to himself that the job had been done well. "Might have done it myself," he muttered.

A soft clank and a gentle movement caught his attention. With a roar he reached out and grabbed the leg of one of the ubiquitous little men, wriggled out from under the car, caught his culprit by his leather collar, and dangled him at arm's length.

"What are you doing to my job?" Harry bellowed.

The little man tucked his chin into the front of his shirt to give his windpipe a chance, and said, "Why, I was just finishing up that spring job."

"Oh. So you were just finishing up on that spring job," Harry whispered, choked with rage. Then, at the top of his voice, "Who told you to touch that car?"

"Who told me? What do you— Well, it just had to be done, that's all. You'll have to let me go. I must tighten up those two bolts and lay some dust on the whole thing."

"You must *what?* You get within six feet o' that car and I'll twist your head offn your neck with a Stillson!"

"But— It has to be done!"

"You won't do it! Why, I oughta—"

"Please let me go! If I don't leave that car the way it was Tuesday night—"

"When was Tuesday night?"

"The last act, of course. Let me go, or I'll call the district supervisor!"

"Call the devil himself. I'm going to spread you on the sidewalk outside; and heaven help you if I catch you near here again!"

The little man's jaw set, his eyes narrowed, and he whipped his feet upward. They crashed into Wright's jaw; Harry dropped him and staggered back. The little man began squealing, "Supervisor! Supervisor! Emergency!"

Harry growled and started after him; but suddenly, in the air between him and the midget workman, a long white hand appeared. The empty air was swept back, showing an aperture from the garage to blank, blind nothingness. Out of it stepped a tall man in a single loose-fitting garment literally studded with pockets. The opening closed behind the man.

Harry cowered before him. Never in his life had he seen such noble, powerful features, such strength of purpose, such broad shoulders, such a deep chest. The man stood with the backs of his hands on his hips, staring at Harry as if he were something somebody forgot to sweep up.

"That's him," said the little man shrilly. "He is trying to stop me from doing the work!"

"Who are you?" asked the beautiful man, down his nose.

"I'm the m-mechanic on this j-j— Who wants to know?"

"Iridel, supervisor of the district of Futura, wants to know."

"Where in hell did you come from?"

"I did not come from hell. I came from Thursday."

Harry held his head. "What *is* all this?" he wailed. "Why is today Wednesday? Who are all these crazy little guys? What happened to Tuesday?"

Iridel made a slight motion with his finger, and the little man scurried back under the car. Harry was frenzied to hear the wrench busily tightening bolts. He half started to dive under after the little fellow, but Iridel said, "Stop!" and when Iridel said, "Stop!" Harry stopped.

"This," said Iridel calmly, "is an amazing occurrence." He regarded Harry with unemotional curiosity. "An actor onstage before the sets are finished. Extraordinary."

"What stage?" asked Harry. "What are you doing here anyhow, and what's the idea of all these little guys working around here?"

"You ask a great many questions, actor," said Iridel. "I shall answer them, and then I shall have a few to ask you. These little men are stage-hands—I am surprised that you didn't realize that. They are setting the stage for Wednesday. Tuesday? That's going on now."

"Arrgh!" Harry snorted. "How can Tuesday be going on when today's Wednesday?"

"Today isn't Wednesday, actor."

"Huh?"

"Today is Tuesday."

Harry scratched his head. "Met a feller on the steps this mornin'— one of these here stagehands of yours. He said this was Wednesday."

"It *is* Wednesday. Today is Tuesday. Tuesday is today. 'Today' is simply the name for the stage set which happens to be in use. 'Yesterday' means the set that has just been used; 'Tomorrow' is the set that will be used after the actors have finished with 'today.' This is Wednesday. Yesterday was Monday; today is Tuesday. See?"

Harry said, "No."

Iridel threw up his long hands. "My, you actors are stupid. Now listen carefully. This is Act Wednesday, Scene 6:22. That means that everything you see around you here is being readied for 6:22 A.M. on Wednesday. Wednesday isn't a time; it's a place. The actors are moving along toward it now. I see you still don't get the idea. Let's see . . . ah. Look at that clock. What does it say?''

Harry Wright looked at the big electric clock on the wall over the compressor. It was corrected hourly and highly accurate, and it said 6:22. Harry looked at it amazed. "Six tw— but my gosh, man, that's what time I left the house. I walked here, an' I been here ten minutes already!''

Iridel shook his head. "You've been here no time at all, because there is no time until the actors make their entrances."

Harry sat down on a grease drum and wrinkled up his brains with the effort he was making. "You mean that this time proposition ain't something that moves along all the time? Sorta—well, like a road. A road don't go no place— You just go places along it. Is that it?''

"That's the general idea. In fact, that's a pretty good example. Suppose we say that it's a road; a highway built of paving blocks. Each block is a day; the actors move along it, and go through day after day. And our job here—mine and the little men—is to . . . well, pave that road. This is the cleanup gang here. They are fixing up the last little details, so that everything will be ready for the actors."

Harry sat still, his mind creaking with the effects of this information. He felt as if he had been hit with a lead pipe, and the shock of it was being drawn out infinitely. This was the craziest-sounding thing he had ever run into. For no reason at all he remembered a talk he had had once with a drunken aviation mechanic who had tried to explain to him how the air flowing over an airplane's wings makes the machine go up in the air. He hadn't understood a word of the man's discourse, which was all about eddies and chords and cambers and foils, dihedrals and the Bernoulli effect. That didn't make any difference; the things flew whether he understood how or not; he knew that because he had seen them. This guy Iridel's lecture was the same sort of thing. If there was nothing in all he said, how come all these little guys were working around here? Why wasn't the clock telling time? Where was Tuesday?

He thought he'd get that straight for good and all. "Just where is Tuesday?'' he asked.

"Over there," said Iridel, and pointed. Harry recoiled and fell off the drum; for when the man extended his hand, it *disappeared!*

Harry got up off the floor and said tautly, "Do that again."

"What? Oh— Point toward Tuesday? Certainly." And he pointed. His hand appeared again when he withdrew it.

Harry said, "My gosh!" and sat down again on the drum, sweating and staring at the supervisor of the district of Futura. "You point, an' your hand—ain't," he breathed. "What direction is that?"

"It is a direction like any other direction," said Iridel. "You know yourself there are four directions—forward, sideward, upward; and—" he pointed again, and again his hand vanished "—*that* way!"

"They never tole me that in school," said Harry. "Course, I was just a kid then, but—"

Iridel laughed. "It is the fourth dimension—it is *duration*. The actors move through length, breadth, and height, anywhere they choose to within the set. But there is another movement—one they can't control—and that is duration."

"How soon will they come . . . eh . . . here?" asked Harry, waving an arm. Iridel dipped into one of his numberless pockets and pulled out a watch. "It is now eight thirty-seven Tuesday morning," he said. "They'll be here as soon as they finish the act, and the scenes in Wednesday that have already been prepared."

Harry thought again for a moment, while Iridel waited patiently, smiling a little. Then he looked up at the supervisor and asked, "Hey—this 'actor' business—what's that all about?"

"Oh—that. Well, it's a play, that's all. Just like any play—put on for the amusement of an audience."

"I was to a play once," said Harry. "Who's the audience?"

Iridel stopped smiling. "Certain— Ones who may be amused," he said. "And now I'm going to ask you some questions. How did you get here?"

"Walked."

"You *walked* from Monday night to Wednesday morning?"

"Naw— From the house to here."

"Ah— But how did you get to Wednesday, six twenty-two?"

"Well I— Damfino. I just woke up an' came to work as usual."

"This is an extraordinary occurrence," said Iridel, shaking his head in puzzlement. "You'll have to see the producer."

"Producer? Who's he?"

"You'll find out. In the meantime, come along with me. I can't leave you here; you're too close to the play. I have to make my rounds anyway."

Iridel walked toward the door. Harry was tempted to stay and find himself some more work to do, but when Iridel glanced back at him and motioned him out, Harry followed. It was suddenly impossible to do anything else.

Just as he caught up with the supervisor, a little worker ran up, whipping off his cap.

"Iridel, sir," he piped, "the weather makers put .006 of one percent too little moisture in the air on this set. There's three sevenths of an ounce too little gasoline in the storage tanks under here."

"How much is in the tanks?"

"Four thousand two hundred and seventy-three gallons, three pints, seven and twenty-one thirty-fourths ounces."

Iridel grunted. "Let it go this time. That was very sloppy work. Someone's going to get transferred to Limbo for this."

"Very good, sir," said the little man. "Long as you know we're not responsible." He put on his cap, spun around three times and rushed off.

"Lucky for the weather makers that the amount of gas in that tank doesn't come into Wednesday's script," said Iridel. "If anything interferes with the continuity of the play, there's the devil to pay. Actors haven't sense enough to cover up, either. They are liable to start whole series of miscues because of a little thing like that. The play might flop and then we'd all be out of work."

"Oh," Harry oh-ed. "Hey, Iridel—what's the idea of that patchy-looking place over there?"

Iridel followed his eyes. Harry was looking at a corner lot. It was tree-lined and overgrown with weeds and small saplings. The vegetation was true to form around the edges of the lot, and around the path that ran diagonally through it; but the spaces in between were a plane surface. Not a leaf nor a blade of grass grew there; it was naked-looking, blank, and absolutely without any color whatever.

"Oh, that," answered Iridel. "There are only two characters in Act Wednesday who will use that path. Therefore it is as grown-over as it should be. The rest of the lot doesn't enter into the play, so we don't have to do anything with it."

"But— Suppose someone wandered off the path on Wednesday," Harry offered.

"He'd be due for a surprise, I guess. But it could hardly happen. Special prompters are always detailed to spots like that, to keep the actors from going astray or missing any cues."

"Who are they—the prompters, I mean?"

"Prompters? G.A.'s—Guardian Angels. That's what the script writers call them."

"I heard o' them," said Harry.

"Yes, they have their work cut out for them," said the supervisor. "Actors are always forgetting their lines when they shouldn't, or remembering them when the script calls for a lapse. Well, it looks pretty good here. Let's have a look at Friday."

"Friday? You mean to tell me you're working on Friday already?"

"Of course! Why, we work years in advance! How on earth do you think we could get our trees grown otherwise? Here—step in!" Iridel put out his hand, seized empty air, drew it aside to show the kind of absolute nothingness he had first appeared from, and waved Harry on.

"Y-you want me to go in there?" asked Harry diffidently.

"Certainly. Hurry, now!"

Harry looked at the section of void with a rather weak-kneed look, but could not withstand the supervisor's strange compulsion. He stepped through.

And it wasn't so bad. There were no whirling lights, no sensations of falling, no falling unconscious. It was just like stepping onto another room—which is what had happened. He found himself in a great round chamber, whose roundness was touched a bit with the indistinct. That is, it had curved walls and a domed roof, but there was something else about it. It seemed to stretch off in that direction toward which Iridel had so astonishingly pointed. The walls were lined with an amazing array of control machinery—switches and ground-glass screens, indicators and dials, knurled knobs, and levers. Moving deftly before them was a crew of men, each looking exactly like Iridel except that their garments had no pockets. Harry stood wide-eyed, hypnotized by the enormous complexity of the controls and the ease with which the men worked among them. Iridel touched his shoulder. "Come with me," he said. "The producer is in now; we'll find out what is to be done with you."

They started across the floor. Harry had not quite time to wonder how long it would take them to cross that enormous room, for when they had taken perhaps a dozen steps, they found themselves at the opposite wall. The ordinary laws of space and time simply did not apply in the place.

They stopped at a door of burnished bronze, so very highly polished that they could see through it. It opened and Iridel pushed Harry through. The door swung shut. Harry, panic-stricken lest he be separated from the only thing in this weird world he could begin to get used to, flung himself against the great bronze portal. It bounced him back, head over heels, into the middle of the floor. He rolled over and got up to his hands and knees.

He was in a tiny room, one end of which was filled by a colossal teakwood desk. The man sitting there regarded him with amusement. "Where'd you blow in from?" he asked; and his voice was like the angry bee sound of an approaching hurricane.

"Are you the producer?"

"Well, I'll be darned," said the man, and smiled. It seemed to fill the whole room with light. He was a big man, Harry noticed; but in this deceptive place, there was no way of telling how big. "I'll be most verily darned. An actor. You're a persistent lot, aren't you? Building houses for me that I almost never go into. Getting together and sending requests for better parts. Listening carefully to what I have to say and then ignoring or misinterpreting my advice. Always asking for just one more chance, and when you get it, messing that up too. And now one of you crashes the gate. What's your trouble, anyway?"

There was something about the producer that bothered Harry, but he could not place what it was, unless it was the fact that the man awed him and he didn't know why. "I woke up in Wednesday," he stammered, "and yesterday was Tuesday. I mean Monday. I mean—" He cleared his throat and started over. "I went to sleep Monday night and woke up Wednesday, and I'm looking for Tuesday."

"What do you want me to do about it?"

"Well—couldn't you tell me how to get back there? I got work to do."

"Oh—I get it," said the producer. "You want a favor from me. You know, someday, some one of you fellows is going to come to me wanting to give me something, free and for nothing, and then I am going to drop quietly dead. Don't I have enough trouble running this show without taking up time and space by doing favors for the likes of you?" He drew a couple of breaths and then smiled again. "However—I have always tried to be just, even if it is a tough job sometimes. Go on out and tell Iridel to show you the way back. I think I know what happened to you; when you made your exit from the last act you played in, you somehow managed to walk out behind the wrong curtain when you reached the wings. There's going to be a prompter sent to Limbo for this. Go on now—beat it."

Harry opened his mouth to speak, thought better of it and scuttled out the door, which opened before him. He stood in the huge control chamber, breathing hard. Iridel walked up to him.

"Well?"

"He says for you to get me out of here."

"All right," said Iridel. "This way." He led the way to a curtained doorway much like the one they had used to come in. Beside it were two dials, one marked in days, and the other in hours and minutes.

"Monday night good enough for you?" asked Iridel.

"Swell," said Harry.

Iridel set the dials for 9:30 P.M. on Monday. "So long, actor. Maybe I'll see you again sometime."

"So long," said Harry. He turned and stepped through the door.

He was back in the garage, and there was no curtained doorway behind him. He turned to ask Iridel if this would enable him to go to bed again and do Tuesday right from the start, but Iridel was gone.

The garage was a blaze of light. Harry glanced up at the clock—It said fifteen seconds after nine-thirty. That was funny; everyone should be home by now except Slim Jim, the night man, who hung out until four in the morning serving up gas at the pumps outside. A quick glance around sufficed. This might be Monday night, but it was a Monday night he hadn't known.

The place was filled with the little men again!

Harry sat on the fender of a convertible and groaned. "Now what have I got myself into?" he asked himself.

He could see that he was at a different place-in-time from the one in which he had met Iridel. There, they had been working to build, working with a precision and nicety that was a pleasure to watch. But here—

The little men were different, in the first place. They were tired-looking, sick, slow. There were scores of overseers about, and Harry winced with one of the little fellows when one of the men in white lashed out with a long whip. As the Wednesday crews worked, so the Monday gangs slaved. And the work they were doing was different. For here they were breaking down, breaking up, carting away. Before his eyes, Harry saw sections of paving lifted out, pulverized, toted away by the sackload by lines of trudging, browbeaten little men. He saw great beams upended to support the roof, while bricks were pried out of the walls. He heard the gang working on the roof, saw patches of roofing torn away. He saw walls and roof both melt away under that driving, driven onslaught, and before he knew what was happening, he was standing alone on a section of the dead white plain he had noticed before on the corner lot.

It was too much for his overburdened mind; he ran out into the night, breaking through lines of laden slaves, through neat and growing piles of rubble, screaming for Iridel. He ran for a long time, and finally dropped down behind a stack of lumber out where the Unitarian church used to be, dropped because he could go no farther. He heard footsteps and tried to make himself smaller. They came on steadily; one of the overseers rounded the corner and stood looking at him. Harry was in deep shadow, but he knew the man in white could see in the dark.

"Come out o' there," grated the man. Harry came out.

"You the guy was yellin' for Iridel?"

Harry nodded.

"What makes you think you'll find Iridel in Limbo?" sneered his captor. "Who are you, anyway?"

Harry had learned by this time. "I'm an actor," he said in a small voice. "I got into Wednesday by mistake, and they sent me back here."

"What for?"

"Huh? Why— I guess it was a mistake, that's all."

The man stepped forward and grabbed Harry by the collar. He was about eight times as powerful as a hydraulic jack. "Don't give me no guff, pal," said the man. "Nobody gets sent to Limbo by mistake, or if he didn't do somethin' up there to make him deserve it. Come clean, now."

"I didn't do nothin'," Harry wailed. "I asked them the way back, and they showed me a door, and I went through it and came here. That's all I know. Stop it, you're choking me!"

The man dropped him suddenly. "Listen, babe, you know who I am? Hey?" Harry shook his head. "Oh—you don't. Well, I'm Gurrah!"

"Yeah?" Harry said, not being able to think of anything else at the moment.

Gurrah puffed out his chest and appeared to be waiting for something more from Harry. When nothing came, he walked up to the mechanic, breathed in his face. "Ain't scared, huh? Tough guy, huh? Never heard of Gurrah, supervisor of Limbo an' the roughest, toughest son of the devil from Incidence to Eternity, huh?"

Now Harry was a peaceable man, but if there was anything he hated, it was to have a stranger breathe his bad breath pugnaciously at him. Before he knew it had happened, Gurrah was sprawled eight feet away, and Harry was standing alone rubbing his left knuckles—quite the more surprised of the two.

Gurrah sat up, feeling his face. "Why, you . . . you hit me!" he roared. He got up and came over to Harry. "You hit me!" he said softly, his voice slightly out of focus in amazement. Harry wished he hadn't—wished he was in bed or in Futura or dead or something. Gurrah reached out with a heavy fist and—patted him on the shoulder. "Hey," he said, suddenly friendly, "you're all right. Heh! Took a poke at me, didn't you? Be damned! First time in a month o' Mondays anyone ever made a pass at me. Last was a feller named Orton. I killed 'im." Harry paled.

Gurrah leaned back against the lumber pile. "Dam'f I didn't enjoy that, feller. Yeah. This is a hell of a job they palmed off on me, but what can you do? Breakin' down—breakin' down. No sooner get through one job, workin' top speed, drivin' the boys till they bleed, than they give you the devil for not bein' halfway through another job. You'd think I'd been in the business long enough to know what it was all about, after more than eight hundred an' twenty million acts, wouldn't you? Heh. Try to tell *them* that. Ship a load of doghouses up to Wednesday, sneakin' it past backstage nice as you please. They turn right around and call me up. 'What's the matter with you, Gurrah? Them doghouses is no good. We sent you a list o' worn-out items two acts ago. One o' the items was doghouses. Snap out of it or we send someone back there who can read an' put you on a tote-line.' That's what I get—act in and act out. An' does it do any good to tell 'em that my aide got the message an' dropped dead before he got it to me? No. Uh-uh. If I say anything about that, they tell me to stop workin' 'em to death. If I do that, they kick because my shipments don't come in fast enough."

He paused for breath. Harry had a hunch that if he kept Gurrah in a good mood, it might benefit him. He asked, "What's your job, anyway?"

"Job?" Gurrah howled. "Call this a job? Tearin' down the sets, shippin' what's good to the act after next, junkin' the rest?" He snorted.

Harry asked, "You mean they use the same props over again?"

"That's right. They don't last, though. Six, eight acts, maybe. Then they got to build new ones and weather them and knock 'em around to make 'em look as if they was used."

There was silence for a time. Gurrah, having got his bitterness off his chest for the first time in literally ages, was feeling pacified. Harry didn't know how to feel. He finally broke the ice. "Hey, Gurrah— How'm I goin' to get back into the play?"

"What's it to me? How'd you— Oh, that's right, you walked in from the control room, huh? That it?"

Harry nodded.

"An' how," growled Gurrah, "did you get inta the control room?"

"Iridel brought me."

"Then what?"

"Well, I went to see the producer, and—"

"Th' *producer!* Holy— You mean you walked right in and—" Gurrah mopped his brow. "What'd he say?"

"Why—he said he guessed it wasn't my fault that I woke up in Wednesday. He said to tell Iridel to ship me back."

"An' Iridel threw you back to Monday." And Gurrah threw back his shaggy head and roared.

"What's funny?" asked Harry, a little peeved.

"Iridel," said Gurrah. "Do you realize that I've been trying for fifty thousand acts or more to get something on that pretty ol' heel, and he drops you right in my lap. Pal, I can't thank you enough! He was supposed to send you back into the play, and instead o' that, you wind up in yesterday! Why, I'll blackmail him till the end of time!" He whirled exultantly, called to a group of bedraggled little men who were staggering under a cornerstone on their way to the junkyard. "Take it easy, boys!" he called. "I got ol' Iridel by the short hair. No more busted backs! No more snotty messages! *Haw haw haw!*"

Harry, a little amazed at all this, put in a timid word, "Hey—Gurrah. What about me?"

Gurrah turned. "You? Oh. *Tel-e-phone!*" At his shout, two little workers, a trifle less bedraggled than the rest, trotted up. One hopped up and perched on Gurrah's right shoulder; the other draped himself over the left, with his head forward. Gurrah grabbed the latter by the neck, brought the man's head close and shouted into his ear. "Give me Iridel!" There was a moment's wait, then the little man on his other shoulder spoke in Iridel's voice, into Gurrah's ear, "Well?"

"Hiyah, fancy pants!"

"Fancy— I beg your— Who is this?"

"It's Gurrah, you futuristic parasite. I got a couple things to tell you."

"Gurrah! How—*dare* you talk to me like that! I'll have you—"

"You'll have me in your job if I tell all I know. You're a wart on the nose of progress, Iridel."

"What is the meaning of this?"

"The meaning of this is that you had instructions sent to you by the producer an' you muffed them. Had an actor there, didn't you? He saw the boss, didn't he? Told you he was to be sent back, didn't he? Sent him right over to me instead of to the play, didn't you? You're slippin',

Iridel. Gettin' old. Well, get off the wire. I'm callin' the boss, right now.''

"The boss? Oh—don't do that, old man. Look, let's talk this thing over. Ah—about that shipment of three-legged dogs I was wanting you to round up for me; I guess I can do without them. Any little favor I can do for you—''

"—you'll damn well do, after this. You better, Goldilocks.'' Gurrah knocked the two small heads together, breaking the connection and probably the heads, and turned grinning to Harry. "You see," he explained, "that Iridel feller is a damn good supervisor, but he's a stickler for detail. He sends people to Limbo for the silliest little mistakes. He never forgives anyone and he never forgets a slip. He's the cause of half the misery back here, with his hurry-up orders. Now things are gonna be different. The boss has wanted to give Iridel a dose of his own medicine for a long time now, but Irrie never gave him a chance.''

Harry said patiently, "About me getting back now—''

"My fran'!" Gurrah bellowed. He delved into a pocket and pulled out a watch like Iridel's. "It's eleven-forty on Tuesday," he said. "We'll shoot you back there now. You'll have to dope out your own reasons for disappearing. Don't spill too much, or a lot of people will suffer for it— you the most. Ready?''

Harry nodded; Gurrah swept out a hand and opened the curtain to nothingness. "You'll find yourself quite a ways from where you started," he said, "because you did a little moving around here. Go ahead.''

"Thanks," said Harry.

Gurrah laughed. "Don't thank me, chum. You rate all the thanks! Hey—if, after you kick off, you don't make out so good up there, let them toss you over to me. You'll be treated good; you've my word on it. Beat it; luck!''

Holding his breath, Harry Wright stepped through the doorway.

He had to walk thirty blocks to the garage, and when he got there, the boss was waiting for him.

"Where you been, Wright?''

"I—lost my way.''

"Don't get wise. What do you think this is—vacation time? Get going on the spring job. Damn it, it won't be finished now till tomorra.''

Harry looked him straight in the eye and said, "Listen. It'll be finished tonight. I happen to know." And, still grinning, he went back into the garage and took out his tools.

TO SEE THE
INVISIBLE MAN
Robert Silverberg

TELEPLAY BY STEVEN BARNES

AIRED JANUARY 31, 1986

STARRING COTTER SMITH, KARLENE CROCKETT

AND THEN THEY FOUND ME GUILTY, AND THEN THEY pronounced me invisible, for a span of one year beginning on the eleventh of May in the year of Grace 2104, and they took me to a dark room beneath the courthouse to affix the mark to my forehead before turning me loose.

Two municipally paid ruffians did the job. One flung me into a chair and the other lifted the brand.

"This won't hurt a bit," the slab-jawed ape said, and thrust the brand against my forehead, and there was a moment of coolness, and that was all.

"What happens now?" I asked.

But there was no answer, and they turned away from me and left the room without a word. The door remained open. I was free to leave, or to stay and rot, as I chose. No one would speak to me, or look at me more than once, long enough to see the sign on my forehead. I was invisible.

You must understand that my invisibility was strictly metaphorical. I still had corporeal solidity. People *could* see me—but they *would not* see me.

An absurd punishment? Perhaps. But then, the crime was absurd too. The crime of coldness. Refusal to unburden myself for my fellow man. I was a four-time offender. The penalty for that was a year's invisibility. The complaint had been duly sworn, the trial held, the brand duly affixed.

I was invisible.

I went out, out into the world of warmth.

They had already had the afternoon rain. The streets of the city were drying, and there was the smell of growth in the Hanging Gardens. Men and women went about their business. I walked among them, but they took no notice of me.

The penalty for speaking to an invisible man is invisibility, a month to a year or more, depending on the seriousness of the offense. On this the whole concept depends. I wondered how rigidly the rule was observed.

I soon found out.

I stepped into a liftshaft and let myself be spiraled up toward the nearest of the Hanging Gardens. It was Eleven, the cactus garden, and those gnarled, bizarre shapes suited my mood. I emerged on the landing

194

stage and advanced toward the admissions counter to buy my token. A pasty-faced, empty-eyed woman sat back of the counter.

I laid down my coin. Something like fright entered her eyes, quickly faded.

"One admission," I said.

No answer. People were queuing up behind me. I repeated my demand. The woman looked up helplessly, then stared over my left shoulder. A hand extended itself, another coin was placed down. She took it, and handed the man his token. He dropped it in the slot and went in.

"Let me have a token," I said crisply.

Others were jostling me out of the way. Not a word of apology. I began to sense some of the meaning of my invisibility. They were literally treating me as though they could not see me.

There are countervailing advantages. I walked around behind the counter and helped myself to a token without paying for it. Since I was invisible, I could not be stopped. I thrust the token in the slot and entered the garden.

But the cacti bored me. An inexpressible malaise slipped over me, and I felt no desire to stay. On my way out, I pressed my finger against a jutting thorn and drew blood. The cactus, at least, still recognized my existence. But only to draw blood.

I returned to my apartment. My books awaited me, but I felt no interest in them.. I sprawled out on my narrow bed and activated the energizer to combat the strange lassitude that was afflicting me. I thought about my invisibility.

It would not be such a hardship, I told myself. I had never depended overly on other human beings. Indeed, had I not been sentenced in the first place for my coldness toward my fellow creatures? So what need did I have of them now? *Let* them ignore me!

It would be restful. I had a year's respite from work, after all. Invisible men did not work. How could they? Who would go to an invisible doctor for a consultation, or hire an invisible lawyer to represent him, or give a document to an invisible clerk to file? No work, then. No income, of course, either. But landlords did not take rent from invisible men. Invisible men went where they pleased, at no cost. I had just demonstrated that at the Hanging Gardens.

Invisibility would be a great joke on society, I felt. They had sentenced me to nothing more dreadful than a year's rest cure. I was certain I would enjoy it.

But there were certain practical disadvantages. On the first night of my invisibility, I went to the city's finest restaurant. I would order their most lavish dishes, a hundred-unit meal, and then conveniently vanish at the presentation of the bill.

My thinking was muddy. I never got seated. I stood in the entrance half an hour, bypassed again and again by a maître d'hôtel who had clearly been through all this many times before. Walking to a seat, I realized, would gain me nothing. No waiter would take my order.

I could go into the kitchen. I could help myself to anything I pleased. I could disrupt the workings of the restaurant. But I decided against it. Society had its ways of protecting itself against the invisible ones. There could be no direct retaliation, of course, no intentional defense. But who could say no to a chef's claim that he had seen no one in the way when he hurled a pot of scalding water toward the wall? Invisibility was invisibility, a two-edged sword.

I left the restaurant.

I ate at an automated restaurant nearby. Then I took an autocab home. Machines, like cacti, did not discriminate against my sort. I sensed that they would make poor companions for a year, though.

I slept poorly.

The second day of my invisibility was a day of further testing and discovery.

I went for a long walk, careful to stay on the pedestrian paths. I had heard all about the boys who enjoy running down those who carry the mark of invisibility on their foreheads. Again, there is no recourse, no punishment for them. My condition has its little hazards by intention.

I walked the streets, seeing how the throngs parted for me. I cut through them like a microtome passing between cells. They were well trained. At midday I saw my first fellow Invisible. He was a tall man of middle years, stocky and dignified, bearing the mark of shame on a domelike forehead. His eye met mine only for a moment. Then he passed on. An invisible man, naturally, cannot see another of his kind.

I was amused, nothing more. I was still savoring the novelty of this way of life. No slight could hurt me. Not yet.

Late in the day I came to one of those bathhouses where working girls can cleanse themselves for a couple of small coins. I smiled wickedly and went up the steps. The attendant at the door gave me the flicker of a startled look—it was a small triumph for me—but did not dare to stop me.

I went in.

An overpowering smell of soap and sweat struck me. I persevered inward. I passed cloakrooms where long rows of gray smocks were hanging, and it occurred to me that I could rifle those smocks of every unit they contained, but I did not. Theft loses meaning when it becomes too easy, as the clever ones who devised invisibility were aware.

I passed on, into the bath chambers themselves.

Hundreds of women were there. Nubile girls, weary wenches, old crones. Some blushed. A few smiled. Many turned their backs on me. But they were careful not to show any real reaction to my presence.

Supervisory matrons stood guard, and who knew but that she might be reported for taking undue cognizance of the existence of an Invisible?

So I watched them bathe, watched five hundred pairs of bobbing breasts, watched naked bodies glistening under the spray, watched this vast mass of bare feminine flesh. My reaction was a mixed one, a sense of wicked achievement at having penetrated this sanctum sanctorum unhalted, and then, welling up slowly within me, a sensation of—was it sorrow? Boredom? Revulsion?

I was unable to analyze it. But it felt as though a clammy hand had seized my throat. I left quickly. The smell of soapy water stung my nostrils for hours afterward, and the sight of pink flesh haunted my dreams that night. I ate alone, in one of the automatics. I began to see that the novelty of this punishment was soon lost.

In the third week I fell ill. It began with a high fever, then pains of the stomach, vomiting, the rest of the ugly symptomatology. By midnight I was certain I was dying. The cramps were intolerable, and when I dragged myself to the toilet cubicle, I caught sight of myself in the mirror, distorted, greenish, beaded with sweat. The mark of invisibility stood out like a beacon in my pale forehead.

For a long time I lay on the tiled floor, limply absorbing the coolness of it. Then I thought: What if it's my appendix? That ridiculous, obsolete, obscure prehistoric survival? Inflamed, ready to burst?

I needed a doctor.

The phone was covered with dust. They had not bothered to disconnect it, but I had not called anyone since my arrest, and no one had dared call me. The penalty for knowingly telephoning an invisible man is invisibility. My friends, such as they were, had stayed far away.

I grasped the phone, thumbed the panel. It lit up and the directory robot said, "With whom do you wish to speak, sir?"

"Doctor," I gasped.

"Certainly, sir." Bland, smug mechanical words! No way to pronounce a robot invisible, so it was free to talk to me!

The screen glowed. A doctorly voice said, "What seems to be the trouble?"

"Stomach pains. Maybe appendicitis."

"We'll have a man over in—" He stopped. I had made the mistake of upturning my agonized face. His eyes lit on my forehead mark. The screen winked into blackness as rapidly as though I had extended a leprous hand for him to kiss.

"Doctor," I groaned.

He was gone. I buried my face in my hands. This was carrying things too far, I thought. Did the Hippocratic Oath allow things like this? Could a doctor ignore a sick man's plea for help?

Hippocrates had not known anything about invisible men. A doctor was not required to minister to an invisible man. To society at large, I simply was not there. Doctors could not diagnose diseases in nonexistent individuals.

I was left to suffer.

It was one of invisibility's less attractive features. You enter a bathhouse unhindered, if that pleases you—but you writhe on a bed of pain equally unhindered. The one with the other, and if your appendix happens to rupture, why, it is all the greater deterrent to others who might perhaps have gone your lawless way!

My appendix did not rupture. I survived, though badly shaken. A man can survive without human conversation for a year. He can travel on automated cars and eat at automated restaurants. But there are no automated doctors. For the first time, I felt truly beyond the pale. A convict in a prison is given a doctor when he falls ill. My crime had not been serious enough to merit prison, and so no doctor would treat me if I suffered. It was unfair. I cursed the devils who had invented my punishment. I faced each bleak dawn alone, as alone as Crusoe on his island, here in the midst of a city of twelve million souls.

How can I describe my shifts of mood, my many tacks before the changing winds of the passing months?

There were times when invisibility was a joy, a delight, a treasure. In those paranoid moments I gloried in my exemption from the rules that bound ordinary men.

I stole. I entered small stores and seized the receipts while the cowering merchant feared to stop me, lest in crying out, he make himself liable to my invisibility. If I had known that the State reimbursed all such losses, I might have taken less pleasure in it. But I stole.

I invaded. The bathhouse never tempted me again, but I breached other sanctuaries. I entered hotels and walked down the corridors, opening doors at random. Most rooms were empty. Some were not.

Godlike, I observed all. I toughened. My disdain for society—the crime that had earned me invisibility in the first place—heightened.

I stood in the empty streets during the periods of rain, and railed at the gleaming faces of the towering buildings on every side. "Who needs you?" I roared. "Not I! Who needs you in the slightest?"

I jeered and mocked and railed. It was a kind of insanity, brought on, I suppose, by the loneliness. I entered theaters—where the happy lotus eaters sat slumped in their massage chairs, transfixed by the glowing tridim images—and capered down the aisles. No one grumbled at me. The luminescence of my forehead told them to keep their complaints to themselves, and they did.

Those were the mad moments, the good moments, the moments when I towered twenty feet high and strode among the visible clods with contempt oozing from every pore. Those were insane moments—I admit that freely. A man who has been in a condition of involuntary invisibility for several months is not likely to be well balanced.

Did I call them paranoid moments? Manic-depressive might be more to the point. The pendulum swung dizzily. The days when I felt only contempt for the visible fools all around me were balanced by days when the isolation pressed in tangibly on me. I would walk the endless streets, pass through the gleaming arcades, stare down at the highways with their streaking bullets of gay colors. Not even a beggar would come up to me. Did you know we had beggars, in our shining century? Not till I was pronounced invisible did I know it, for then my long walks took me to the slums, where the shine has worn thin, and where shuffling stubble-faced old men beg for small coins.

No one begged for coins from me. Once a blind man came up to me.

"For the love of God," he wheezed, "help me to buy new eyes from the eye bank."

They were the first direct words any human being had spoken to me in months. I started to reach into my tunic for money, planning to give him every unit on me in gratitude. Why not? I could get more simply by taking it. But before I could draw the money out, a nightmare figure hobbled on crutches between us. I caught the whispered word, "Invisible," and then the two of them scuttled away like frightened crabs. I stood there stupidly holding my money.

Not even the beggars. Devils, to have invented this torment!

So I softened again. My arrogance ebbed away. I was lonely, now. Who could accuse me of coldness? I was spongy soft, pathetically eager for a word, a smile, a clasping hand. It was the sixth month of my invisibility.

I loathed it entirely, now. Its pleasures were hollow ones and its torment was unbearable. I wondered how I would survive the remaining six months. Believe me, suicide was not far from my mind in those dark hours.

And finally I committed an act of foolishness. On one of my endless walks I encountered another Invisible, no more than the third or the fourth such creature I had seen in my six months. As in the previous encounters, our eyes met, warily, only for a moment. Then he dropped his to the pavement, and he sidestepped me and walked on. He was a slim young man, no more than forty, with tousled brown hair and a narrow, pinched face. He had a look of scholarship about him, and I wondered what he might have done to merit his punishment, and I was seized with the desire to run after him and ask him, and to learn his name, and to talk to him, and embrace him.

All these things are forbidden to mankind. No one shall have any contact whatsoever with an Invisible—not even a fellow Invisible. Especially not a fellow Invisible. There is no wish on society's part to foster a secret bond of fellowship among its pariahs.

I knew all this.

I turned and followed him, all the same.

For three blocks I moved along behind him, remaining twenty to fifty paces to the rear. Security robots seemed to be everywhere, their scanners quick to detect an infraction, and I did not dare make my move. Then he turned down a side street, a gray, dusty street five centuries old, and began to stroll, with the ambling, going-nowhere gait of the Invisible. I came up behind him.

"Please," I said softly. "No one will see us here. We can talk. My name is—"

He whirled on me, horror in his eyes. His face was pale. He looked at me in amazement for a moment, then darted forward as though to go around me.

I blocked him.

"Wait," I said. "Don't be afraid. Please—"

He burst past me. I put my hand on his shoulder, and he wriggled free.

"Just a word," I begged.

Not even a word. Not even a hoarsely uttered "Leave me alone!" He sidestepped me and ran down the empty street, his steps diminishing from a clatter to a murmur as he reached the corner and rounded it. I looked after him, feeling a great loneliness well up in me.

And then a fear. *He* hadn't breached the rules of Invisibility, but I had. I had seen him. That left me subject to punishment, an extension of my term of invisibility, perhaps. I looked around anxiously, but there were no security robots in sight, no one at all.

I was alone.

Turning, calming myself, I continued down the street. Gradually I regained control over myself. I saw that I had done something unpardonably foolish. The stupidity of my action troubled me, but even more the sentimentality of it. To reach out in that panicky way to another Invisible—to admit openly my loneliness, my need—no. It meant that society was winning. I couldn't have that.

I found that I was near the cactus garden once again. I rode the liftshaft, grabbed a token from the attendant, and bought my way in. I searched for a moment, then found a twisted, elaborately ornate cactus eight feet high, a spiny monster. I wrenched it from its pot and broke the angular limbs to fragments, filling my hands with a thousand needles. People pretended not to watch. I plucked the spines from my hands and, palms bleeding, rode the liftshaft down, once again sublimely aloof in my invisibility.

The eighth month passed, the ninth, the tenth. The seasonal round had made nearly a complete turn. Spring had given way to a mild summer, summer to a crisp autumn, autumn to winter with its fortnightly snowfall, still permitted for aesthetic reasons. Winter had ended, now. In the parks, the trees sprouted green buds. The weather control people stepped up the rainfall to thrice daily.

My term was drawing to its end.

In the final months of my invisibility I had slipped into a kind of torpor. My mind, forced back on its own resources, no longer cared to consider the implications of my condition, and I slid in a blurred haze from day to day. I read compulsively but unselectively. Aristotle one day, the Bible the next, a handbook of mechanics the next. I retained nothing; as I turned a fresh page, its predecessor slipped from my memory.

I no longer bothered to enjoy the few advantages of invisibility, the voyeuristic thrills, the minute throb of power that comes from being able to commit any act with only limited fears of retaliation. I say *limited* because the passage of the Invisibility Act had not been accompanied by an act repealing human nature; few men would not risk invisibility to protect their wives or children from an invisible one's molestations; no one would coolly allow an Invisible to jab out his eyes; no one would tolerate an Invisible's invasion of his home. There were ways of coping with such infringements without appearing to recognize the existence of the Invisible, as I have mentioned.

Still, it was possible to get away with a great deal. I declined to try. Somewhere Dostoyevski has written, "Without God, all things are possible." I can amend that. "To the invisible man, all things are possible— and uninteresting." So it was.

The weary months passed.

I did not count the minutes till my release. To be precise, I wholly forgot that my term was due to end. On the day itself, I was reading in my room, morosely turning page after page, when the annunciator chimed.

It had not chimed for a full year. I had almost forgotten the meaning of the sound.

But I opened the door. There they stood, the men of the law. Wordlessly, they broke the seal that held the mark to my forehead. The emblem dropped away and shattered.

"Hello, citizen," they said to me.

I nodded gravely. "Yes. Hello."

"May 11, 2105. Your term is up. You are restored to society. You have paid your debt."

"Thank you. Yes."

"Come for a drink with us."

"I'd sooner not."

"It's the tradition. Come along."

I went with them. My forehead felt strangely naked now, and I glanced in a mirror to see that there was a pale spot where the emblem had been. They took me to a bar nearby, and treated me to synthetic whiskey, raw, powerful. The bartender grinned at me. Someone on the next stool clapped me on the shoulder and asked me who I liked in tomorrow's jet races. I had no idea, and I said so.

"You mean it? I'm backing Kelso. Four to one, but he's got terrific spurt power."

"I'm sorry," I said.

"He's been away for a while," one of the government men said softly.

The euphemism was unmistakable. My neighbor glanced at my forehead and nodded at the pale spot. He offered to buy me a drink too. I accepted, though I was already feeling the effects of the first one. I was a human being again. I was visible.

I did not dare snub him, anyway. It might have been construed as a crime of coldness once again. My fifth offense would have meant five years of Invisibility. I had learned human humility.

Returning to visibility involved an awkward transition, of course. Old friends to meet, lame conversations to hold, shattered relationships to renew. I had been an exile in my own city for a year, and coming back was not easy.

No one referred to my time of invisibility, naturally. It was treated as an affliction best left unmentioned. Hypocrisy, I thought, but I accepted it. Doubtless they were all trying to spare my feelings. Does one tell a man whose cancerous stomach has been replaced, "I hear you had a narrow escape just now?" Does one say to a man whose aged father has tottered off toward a euthanasia house, "Well, he was getting pretty feeble anyway, wasn't he?"

No. Of course not.

So there was this hole in our shared experience, this void, this blankness. Which left me little to talk about with my friends, in particular since I had lost the knack of conversation entirely. The period of readjustment was a trying one.

But I persevered, for I was no longer the same haughty, aloof person I had been before my conviction. I had learned humility in the hardest of schools.

Now and then I noticed an Invisible on the streets, of course. It was impossible to avoid them. But, trained as I had been trained, I quickly glanced away, as though my eyes had come momentarily to rest on some shambling, festering horror from another world.

It was in the fourth month of my return to visibility that the ultimate lesson of my sentence struck home, though. I was in the vicinity of the City Tower, having returned to my old job in the documents division of the municipal government. I had left work for the day and was walking toward the tubes when a hand emerged from the crowd, caught my arm.

"Please," the soft voice said. "Wait a minute. Don't be afraid."

I looked up, startled. In our city, strangers do not accost strangers.

I saw the gleaming emblem of invisibility on the man's forehead. Then

I recognized him—the slim man I had accosted more than half a year before on that deserted street. He had grown haggard; his eyes were wild, his brown hair flecked with gray. He must have been at the beginning of his term, then. Now he must have been near its end.

He held my arm. I trembled. This was no deserted street. This was the most crowded square of the city. I pulled my arm away from his grasp and started to turn away.

"No—don't go," he cried. "Can't you pity me? You've been there yourself."

I took a faltering step. Then I remembered how I had cried out to him, how I had begged him not to spurn me. I remembered my own miserable loneliness.

I took another step away from him.

"Coward!" he shrieked after me. "Talk to me! I dare you! Talk to me, coward!"

It was too much. I was touched. Sudden tears stung my eyes, and I turned to him, stretched out a hand to his. I caught his thin wrist. The contact seemed to electrify him. A moment later, I held him in my arms, trying to draw some of the misery from his frame to mine.

The security robots closed in, surrounding us. He was hurled to one side, I was taken into custody. They will try me again—not for the crime of coldness, this time, but for a crime of warmth. Perhaps they will find extenuating circumstances and release me; perhaps not.

I do not care. If they condemn me, this time I will wear my invisibility like a shield of glory.

DEAD RUN
Greg Bear

TELEPLAY BY ALAN BRENNERT

AIRED FEBRUARY 21, 1986

STARRING STEVEN RAILSBACK, BARRY CORBIN, JOHN DELANCIE

THERE AREN'T MANY HITCHHIKERS ON THE ROAD TO
Hell.

I noticed this dude from four miles away. He stood where the road is
straight and level, crossing what looks like desert except it has all these
little empty towns and motels and shacks. I had been on the road for
about six hours, and the folks in the cattle trailers behind me had been
quiet for the last three—resigned, I guess—so my nerves had settled a
bit and I decided to see what the dude was up to. Maybe he was one of
the employees. That would be interesting, I thought.

Truth to tell, once the wailing settled down, I got pretty bored.

The dude was on the right-hand side of the road, thumb out. I piano-
keyed down the gears, and the air brakes hissed and squealed at the tap
of my foot. The semi slowed and the big diesel made that gut-deep
dinosaur-belch of shuddered-downness. I leaned across the cab as everything came to a halt and swung the door open.

"Where you heading?" I asked.

He laughed and shook his head, then spit on the soft shoulder. "I
don't know," he said. "Hell, maybe." He was thin and tanned with
long, greasy black hair and blue jeans and a vest. His straw hat was dirty
and full of holes, but the feathers around the crown were bright and new-
looking, pheasant, if I was any judge. A worn gold chain hung out of
his vest going into his watch pocket. He wore old Frye boots with the
toes turned up and soles thinner than my spare's retread. He looked an
awful lot like I had when I hitchhiked out of Fresno, broke and unemployed, looking for work.

"Can I take you there?" I asked.

"Sho'." He climbed in and eased the door shut behind him, took out
a kerchief and mopped his forehead, then blew his long nose and stared
at me with bloodshot sleepless eyes. "What you hauling?" he asked.

"Souls," I said. "Whole shitload of them."

"What kind?" He was young, not more than twenty-five. He wanted
to sound nonchalant, but I could hear the nerves.

"Usual kind," I said. "Human. Got some Hare Krishnas this time.
Don't look too close anymore."

I coaxed the truck along, wondering if the engine was as bad as it
sounded. When we were up to speed—eighty, eighty-five, no smokies
on *this* road—he asked, "How long you been hauling?"

"Two years."

"Good pay?"

"It'll do."

"Benefits?"

"Union like everyone else."

"I heard about that," he said. "In that little dump about two miles back."

"People live there?" I asked. I didn't think anything lived along the road.

"Yeah. Real down folks. They said Teamster bosses get carried in limousines when they go."

"Don't really matter how you get there, I suppose. The trip's short, and forever is a long time."

"Getting there's all the fun?" he asked, trying for a grin. I gave him a shallow one.

"What're you doing out here?" I asked a few minutes later. "You aren't dead, are you?" I'd never heard of dead folks running loose or looking quite as vital as he did, but I couldn't imagine anyone else being on the road. Dead folks—and drivers.

"No," he said. He was quiet for a bit. Then, slow, as if it embarrassed him, "I came to find my woman."

"Yeah?" Not much surprised me, but that was a new twist. "There ain't no returning, you know."

"Sherill's her name, spelled like sheriff but with two L's."

"Got a cigarette?" I asked. I didn't smoke, but I could use them later. He handed me the last three in a crush-proof pack, not just one but all, and didn't say anything.

"Haven't heard of her," I said. "But then, I don't get to converse with everybody I haul. And there are lots of trucks, lots of drivers."

"I know," he said. "But I heard about them benefits."

He had a crazy kind of sad look in his eye when he glanced at me, and that made me angry. I tightened my jaw and stared straight ahead.

"You know," he said, "back in that town they tell some crazy stories. About how they use old trains for China and India, and in Russia there's a tramline. In Mexico it's old buses along roads, always at night—"

"Listen, I don't use all the benefits," I said. "I know some do, but I don't."

"Sure, I got you," he said, nodding that exaggerated goddamn young folks' nod, his whole neck and shoulders moving along, it's all right everything's cool.

"How you gonna find her?" I asked.

"I don't know. Do the road, ask the drivers."

"How'd you get in?"

He didn't answer for a moment. "I'm coming here when I die. That's pretty sure. It's not so hard for folks like me to get in beforehand. And

. . . my daddy was a driver. He told me the route. By the way, my name's Bill.''

"Mine's John," I said.

"Glad to meet you."

We didn't say much after that for a while. He stared out the right window and I watched the desert and faraway shacks go by. Soon the mountains came looming up—space seems compressed on the road, especially once past the desert—and I sped up for the approach. There was some noise from the back.

"What'll you do when you get off work?" Bill asked.

"Go home and sleep."

"Nobody knows?"

"Just the union."

"That's the way it was with Daddy, until just before the end. Look, I didn't mean to make you mad or nothing. I'd just heard about the perks, and I thought . . ." He swallowed, his Adam's apple bobbing. "Thought you might be able to help. I don't know how I'll ever find Sherill. Maybe back in the annex . . ."

"Nobody in their right minds goes into the yards by choice," I said. "And you'd have to look over everybody that's died in the last four months. They're way backed up."

Bill took that like a blow across the face, and I was sorry I'd said it. "She's only been gone a week," he said.

"Well," I said.

"My mom died two years ago, just before Daddy."

"The High Road," I said.

"What?"

"Hope they both got the High Road."

"Mom, maybe. Yeah. She did. But not Daddy. He knew." Bill hawked and spit out the window. "Sherill, she's here—but she don't belong."

I couldn't help but grin.

"No, man, I mean it, I belong but not her. She was in this car wreck couple of months back. Got pretty badly messed up. I'd dealed her dope at first and then fell in love with her, and by the time she landed in the hospital, she was, you know, hooked on about four different things."

My arms stiffened on the wheel.

"I tried to tell her when I visited that it wouldn't be good for her to get anything, no more dope, but she begged me. What could I do? I loved her." He wasn't looking out the window now. He was looking down at his worn boots and nodding. "She begged me, man. So I brought her stuff. I mean she took it all when they weren't looking. She just took it *all*. They pumped her out, but her insides were just gone. I didn't hear about her being dead until two days ago, and that really burned me. I was the only one who loved her and they didn't even tell me. I had to go up to her room and find her bed empty. Jesus. I hung out at Daddy's union hall. Someone talked to someone else and I found her name on a list. The Low Road.''

I hadn't known it was that easy to find out; but then, I'd never traveled in dopers' territory. Dope can loosen a lot of lips.

"I don't use any of those perks,'' I said, just to make it clear I couldn't help him. "Folks in back got enough trouble without me. I think the union went too far there.''

"Bet they felt you'd get lonely, need company,'' Bill said quietly, looking at me. "It don't hurt the folks back there. Maybe give them another chance to, you know, think things over. Give 'em relief for a couple of hours, a break from the mash—''

"Listen, a couple of hours don't mean nothing in relation to eternity. I'm not so sure I won't be joining them someday, and if that's the way it is, I want it smooth, nobody pulling me out of a trailer and putting me back in.''

"Yeah,'' he said. "Got you, man. I know where that's at. But she might be back there right now, and all you'd have to—''

"Bad enough I'm driving this rig in the first place.'' I wanted to change the subject.

"Yeah. How'd that happen?''

"Couple of accidents. Hot-rodding with an old fart in a Triumph. Nearly ran over some joggers on a country road. My premiums went up to where I couldn't afford payments and finally they took my truck away.''

"You coulda gone without insurance.''

"Not me,'' I said. "Anyway, some bad word got out. No companies would hire me. I went to the union to see if they could help. They told me I was a dead-ender, either get out of trucking or . . .'' I shrugged. "This. I couldn't leave trucking. It's bad out there, getting work. Lots of unemployed. Couldn't see myself pushing a hack in some big city.''

"No, man,'' Bill said, giving me that whole-body nod again. He cackled sympathetically.

"They gave me an advance, enough for a down payment on my rig.'' The truck was grinding a bit but maintaining. Over the mountains, through a really impressive pass like from an old engraving, and down in a rugged rocky valley, was the City. I'd deliver my cargo, get my slip, and take the rig (with Bill) back to Baker. Park it in the yard next to my cottage after letting him out someplace sane.

Get some sleep.

Start over again next Monday, two loads a week.

"I don't think I'd better go on,'' Bill said. "I'll hitch with some other rig, ask around.''

"Well, I'd feel better if you rode with me back out of here. Want my advice?'' Bad habit. "Go home—''

"No,'' Bill said. "Thanks anyway. I can't go home. Not without Sherill. She don't belong here.'' He took a deep breath. "I'll try to work up a trade. I stay, she goes to the High Road. That's the way the game runs down here, isn't it?''

I didn't tell him otherwise. I couldn't be sure he wasn't right. He'd made it this far. At the top of the pass I pulled the rig over and let him out. He waved at me, I waved back, and we went our separate ways.

Poor rotten doping son of a bitch. I'd screwed up my life half a dozen different ways—three wives, liquor, three years at Tehachapi—but I'd never done dope. I felt self-righteous just listening to the dude. I was glad to be rid of him, truth be told.

The City looks a lot like a county full of big white cathedrals. Casting against type. High wall around the perimeter, stretching as far as my eye can see. No horizon but a vanishing point, the wall looking like an endless highway turned on its side. As I geared the truck down for the decline, the noise in the trailers got irritating again. They could smell what was coming, I guess, like pigs stepping up to the man with the knife.

I pulled into the disembarkation terminal and backed the first trailer up to the holding pen. Employees let down the gates and used some weird kind of prod to herd them. These people were past mortal.

Employees unhooked the first trailer and I backed in the second.

I got down out of the cab and an employee came up to me, a big fellow with red eyes and brand-new coveralls. ''Good ones this load?'' he asked. His breath was like the end of a cabbage, bean and garlic dinner.

I shook my head and held a cigarette out for a light. He pressed his fingernail against the tip. The tip flared and settled down to a steady glow. He looked at it with pure lust.

''Listen,'' I said. ''You had anyone named Sherill through here?''

''Who's asking?'' he grumbled, still eyeing the cigarette. He started to do a slow dance.

''Just curious. I heard you guys knew all the names.''

''So?'' He stopped. He had to walk around, otherwise his shoes melted the asphalt and got stuck. He came back and stood, lifting one foot, twisting a bit, then putting it down and lifting the other.

''So,'' I said, with as much sense.

''Like Cherry with an L?''

''No. Sherill, like sheriff but with two L's.''

''Couple of Cheryls. No Sherills,'' he said. ''Now . . .''

I handed him the cigarette. They loved the things. ''Thanks,'' I said. I pulled another out of the pack and gave it to him. He popped both of them into his mouth and chewed, bliss pushing over his seamed face. Tobacco smoke came out his nose and he swallowed. ''Nothing to it,'' he said, and walked on.

The road back is shorter than the road in. Don't ask how. I'd have thought it was the other way around, but barriers are what's important,

not distance. Maybe we all get our chances so the road to Hell is long.
But once we're there, there's no returning. You have to save on the budget
somewhere.

I took the empties back to Baker. Didn't see Bill. Eight hours later I
was in bed, beer in hand, paycheck on the bureau, my eyes wide open.

Shit, I thought. Now my conscience was working. I could have sworn
I was past that. But then, I didn't use the perks. I wouldn't drive without
insurance.

I wasn't really cut out for the life.

There are no normal days and nights on the road to Hell. No matter
how long you drive, it's always the same time when you arrive as when
you left, but it's not necessarily the same time from trip to trip.

The next trip, it was cool dusk and the road didn't pass through desert
and small, empty towns. Instead, it crossed a bleak flatland of skeletal
trees, all the same uniform gray as if cut from paper. When I pulled over
to catch a nap—never sleeping more than two hours at a stretch—the
shouts of the damned in the trailers bothered me even more than usual.
Silly things they said, like:

"You can take us back, mister! You really can!"

"Can he?"

"Shit no, mofuck pig."

"You can let us out! We can't hurt you!"

That was true enough. Drivers were alive, and the dead could never
hurt the living. But I'd heard what happened when you let them out.
There were about ninety of them in back, and in any load there was
always one would make you want to use your perks.

I scratched my itches in the narrow bunk, looking at the Sierra Club
calendar hanging just below the fan. The Devil's Postpile. The load became quieter as the voices gave up, one after the other. There was one
last shout—some obscenity—then silence.

It was then I decided I'd let them out and see if Sherill was there, or
if anyone knew her. They mingled in the annex, got their last socializing
before the City. Someone might know. Then I saw Bill again—

What? What could I do to help him? He had screwed Sherill up royally,
but then, she'd had a hand in it too, and that was what Hell was all
about. Poor stupid sons of bitches.

I swung out of the cab, tucking in my shirt and pulling my straw hat
down on my crown. "Hey!" I said, walking alongside the trailers. Faces
peered at me from the two inches between each white slat. "I'm going
to let you out. Just for a while. I need some information."

"Ask!" someone screamed. "Just ask, goddammit!"

"You know you can't run away. You can't hurt me. You're all dead.
Understand?"

"We know," said another voice, quieter.

"Maybe we can help."

"I'm going to open the gates one trailer at a time." I went to the rear trailer first, took out my keys and undid the Yale padlock. Then I swung the gates open, standing back a little like there was some kind of infected wound about to drain.

They were all naked, but they weren't dirty. I'd seen them in the annex yards and at the City; I knew they weren't like concentration camp prisoners. The dead can't really be unhealthy. Each just had some sort of air about him telling why he was in Hell; nothing specific but subliminal.

Like three black dudes in the rear trailer, first to step out. Why they were going to Hell was all over their faces. They weren't in the least sorry for the lives they'd led. They wanted to keep on doing what had brought them here in the first place—scavenging, hurting, hurting *me* in particular.

"Stupid ass mofuck," one of them said, staring at me beneath thin, expressive eyebrows. He nodded and swung his fists, trying to pound the slats from the outside, but the blows hardly made them vibrate.

An old woman crawled down, hair white and neatly coifed. I couldn't be certain what she had done, but she made me uneasy. She might have been the worst in the load. And lots of others, young, old, mostly old. Quiet for the most part.

They looked me over, some defiant, most just bewildered.

"I need to know if there's anyone here named Sherill," I said, "who happens to know a fellow named Bill."

"That's my name," said a woman hidden in the crowd.

"Let me see her." I waved my hand at them. The black dudes came forward. A funny look got in their eyes and they backed away. The others parted and a young woman walked out. "How do you spell your name?" I asked.

She got a panicked expression. She spelled it, hesitating, hoping she'd make the grade. I felt horrible already. She was a Cheryl.

"Not who I'm looking for," I said.

"Don't be hasty," she said, real soft. She wasn't trying hard to be seductive, but she was succeeding. She was very pretty with medium-sized breasts, hips like a teenager's, legs not terrific but nice. Her black hair was clipped short and her eyes were almost Oriental. I figured maybe she was Lebanese or some other kind of Middle Eastern.

I tried to ignore her. "You can walk around a bit," I told them. "I'm letting out the first trailer now." I opened the side gates on that one and the people came down. They didn't smell, didn't look hungry, they just all looked pale. I wondered if the torment had begun already, but if so, I decided, it wasn't the physical kind.

One thing I'd learned in my two years was that all the Sunday school and horror movie crap about Hell was dead wrong.

"Woman named Sherill," I repeated. No one stepped forward. Then

I felt someone close to me and I turned. It was the Cheryl woman. She
smiled. "I'd like to sit up front for a while," she said.

"So would we all, sister," said the white-haired old woman. The
black dudes stood off separate, talking low.

I swallowed, looking at her. Other drivers said they were real insub-
stantial except at one activity. That was the perk. And it was said the
hottest ones always ended up in Hell.

"No," I said. I motioned for them to get back into the trailers. Whatever she was on the Low Road for, it wouldn't affect her performance in
the sack, that was obvious.

It had been a dumb idea all around. They went back and I returned to
the cab, lighting up a cigarette and thinking what had made me do it.

I shook my head and started her up. Thinking on a dead run was no
good. "No," I said, "goddamn," I said, "good."

Cheryl's face stayed with me.

Cheryl's body stayed with me longer than the face.

Something always comes up in life to lure a man onto the Low Road,
not driving but riding in the back. We all have some weakness. I wondered what reason God had to give us each that little flaw, like a chip in
crystal, you press the chip hard enough, everything splits up crazy.

At least now I knew one thing. My flaw wasn't sex, not this way.
What most struck me about Cheryl was wonder. She was so pretty;
how'd she end up on the Low Road?

For that matter, what had Bill's Sherill done?

I returned hauling empties and found myself this time outside a small
town called Shoshone. I pulled my truck into the cafe parking lot. The
weather was cold and I left the engine running. It was about eleven in
the morning and the cafe was half-full. I took a seat at the counter next
to an old man with maybe four teeth in his head, attacking French toast
with downright solemn dignity. I ordered eggs and hash browns and
juice, ate quickly, and went back to my truck.

Bill stood next to the cab. Next to him was an enormous young woman
with a face like a bulldog. She was wrapped in a filthy piece of plaid
fabric that might have been snatched from a trash dump somewhere.
"Hey," Bill said. "Remember me?"

"Sure."

"I saw you pulling up. I thought you'd like to know . . . This is
Sherill. I got her out of there." The woman stared at me with all the
expression of a brick. "It's all screwy. Like a power failure or something. We just walked out on the road and nobody stopped us."

Sherill could have hid any number of weirdnesses beneath her formi-
dable looks and gone unnoticed by ordinary folks. But I didn't have any
trouble picking out the biggest thing wrong with her: she was dead. Bill
had brought her out of Hell. I looked around to make sure I was in the

World. I was. He wasn't lying. Something serious had happened on the Low Road.

"Trouble?" I asked.

"Lots." He grinned at me. "Pan-demon-ium." His grin broadened.

"That can't happen," I said. Sherill trembled, hearing my voice.

"He's a *driver,* Bill," she said. "He's the one takes us there. We should git out of here." She had that soul-branded air and the look of a pig that's just escaped slaughter, seeing the butcher again. She took a few steps backward. Gluttony, I thought. Gluttony and buried lust and a real ugly way of seeing life, inner eye pulled all out of shape by her bulk.

Bill hadn't had much to do with her ending up on the Low Road.

"Tell me more," I said.

"There's folks running all over down there, holing up in them towns, devils chasing them—"

"Employees," I corrected.

"Yeah. Every which way."

Sherill tugged on his arm. "We got to go, Bill."

"We got to go," he echoed. "Hey, man, thanks. I found her!" He nodded his whole-body nod and they were off down the street, Sherill's plaid wrap dragging in the dirt.

I drove back to Baker, wondering if the trouble was responsible for my being rerouted through Shoshone. I parked in front of my little house and sat inside with a beer while it got dark, checking my calendar for the next day's run and feeling very cold. I can take so much supernatural in its place, but now things were spilling over, smudging the clean-drawn line between my work and the World. Next day I was scheduled to be at the annex and take another load.

Nobody called that evening. If there was trouble on the Low Road, surely the union would let me know, I thought.

I drove to the annex early in the morning. The crossover from the World to the Low Road was normal; I followed the route and the sky muddied from blue to solder-color and I was on the first leg to the annex. I backed the rear trailer up to the yard's gate and unhitched it, then placed the forward trailer at a ramp, all the while keeping my ears tuned to pick up interesting conversation.

The employees who work the annex look human. I took my invoice from a red-faced old guy with eyes like billiard balls and looked at him like I was in the know but could use some updating. He spit smoking saliva on the pavement, returned my look slantwise and said nothing. Maybe it was all settled. I hitched up both full trailers and pulled out.

I didn't even mention Sherill and Bill. Like in most jobs, keeping one's mouth shut is good policy. That and don't volunteer.

It was the desert again this time, only now the towns and tumbledown houses looked bomb-blasted, like something big had come through flushing out game with a howitzer.

Eyes on the road. Push that rig.

Four hours in, I came to a roadblock. Nobody on it, no employees, just big carved-lava barricades cutting across all lanes, and beyond them a yellow smoke which, the driver's unwritten instructions advised, meant absolutely no entry.

I got out. The load was making noises. I suddenly hated them. Nothing beautiful there—just naked Hell-bounders shouting and screaming and threatening like it wasn't already over for them. They'd had their chance and crapped out and now they were still bullshitting the World.

Least they could do was go with dignity and spare me their misery.

That's probably what the engineers on the trains to Auschwitz thought. Yeah, yeah, except I was the fellow who might be hauling those engineers to their just deserts.

Crap, I just couldn't be one way or the other about the whole thing. I could feel mad and guilty and I could think Jesus, probably I'll be complaining just as much when my time comes. Jesus H. Twentieth Century Man Christ.

I stood by the truck, waiting for instructions or some indication what I was supposed to do. The load became quieter after a while, but I heard noises off the road, screams mostly and far away.

"There isn't anything," I said to myself, lighting up one of Bill's cigarettes even though I don't smoke and dragging deep, *"anything* worth this shit."* I vowed I would quit after this run.

I heard something come up behind the trailers and I edged closer to the cab steps. High wisps of smoke obscured things at first, but a dark shape three or four yards high plunged through and stood with one hand on the top slats of the rear trailer. It was covered with naked people, crawling all over, biting and scratching and shouting obscenities. It made little grunting noises, fell to its knees, then stood again and lurched off the road. Some of the people hanging on saw me and shouted for me to come help.

"Help us get this son of a bitch down!"

"Hey, you! We've almost got 'im!"

"He's a driver—"

"Fuck 'im, then."

I'd never seen an employee so big before, nor in so much trouble. The load began to wail like banshees. I threw down my cigarette and ran after it.

Workers will tell you. Camaraderie extends even to those on the job you don't like. If they're in trouble, it's part of the mystique to help out. Besides, the unwritten instructions were very clear on such things, and I've never knowingly broken a job rule—not since getting my rig back—and couldn't see starting now.

Through the smoke and across great ridges of lava, I ran until I spotted the employee about ten yards ahead. It had shaken off the naked people and was standing with one in each hand. Its shoulders smoked and scales stood out at all angles. They'd really done a job on the bastard. Ten or twelve of the dead were picking themselves off the lava, unscraped, unbruised. They saw me.

The employee saw me.

Everyone came at me. I turned and ran for the truck, stumbling, falling, bruising and scraping myself everywhere. My hair stood on end. People grabbed me, pleading for me to haul them out, old, young, all fawning and screeching like whipped dogs.

Then the employee swung me up out of reach. Its hand was cold and hard like iron tongs kept in a freezer. It grunted and ran toward my truck, opening the door wide and throwing me roughly inside. It made clear with huge, wild gestures that I'd better turn around and go back, that waiting was no good and there was no way through.

I started the engine and turned the rig around. I rolled up my window and hoped the dead weren't substantial enough to scratch paint or tear up slats.

All rules were off now. What about the ones in my load? All the while I was doing these things, my head was full of questions, like how could souls fight back and wasn't there some inflexible order in Hell that kept such things from happening? That was what had been implied when I hired on. Safest job around.

I headed back down the road. My load screamed like no load I'd ever had before. I was afraid they might get loose, but they didn't. I got near the annex and they were quiet again, too quiet for me to hear over the diesel.

The yards were deserted. The long, white-painted cement platforms and whitewashed wood-slat loading ramps were unattended. No souls in the pens.

The sky was an indefinite gray. An out-of-focus yellow sun gleamed faintly off the stark white employees' lounge. I stopped the truck and swung down to investigate.

There was no wind, only silence. The air was frosty without being particularly cold. What I wanted to do most was unload and get out of there, go back to Baker or Barstow or Shoshone.

I hoped that was still possible. Maybe all exits had been closed. Maybe the overseers had closed them to keep any more souls from getting out.

I tried the gate latches and found I could open them. I did so and returned to the truck, swinging the rear trailer around until it was flush with the ramp. Nobody made a sound. "Go on back," I said. "Go on back. You've got more time here. Don't ask me how."

"Hello, John." That was behind me. I turned and saw an older man without any clothes on. I didn't recognize him at first. His eyes finally clued me in.

"Mr. Martin?" My high school history teacher. I hadn't seen him in maybe twenty years. He didn't look much older, but then, I'd never seen him naked. He was dead, but he wasn't like the others. He didn't have that look that told me why he was here.

"This is not the sort of job I'd expect one of my students to take," Martin said. He laughed the smooth laugh he was famous for, the laugh that seemed to take everything he said in class and put it in perspective.

"You're not the first person I'd expect to find here," I responded.

"The cat's away, John. The mice are in charge now. I'm going to try to leave."

"How long you been here?" I asked.

"I died a month ago, I think," Martin said, never one to mince words.

"You can't leave," I said. Doing my job even with Mr. Martin. I felt the ice creep up my throat.

"Team player," Martin said. "Still the screwball team player, even when the team doesn't give a damn what you do."

I wanted to explain, but he walked away toward the annex and the road out. Looking back over his shoulder, he said, "Get smart, John. Things aren't what they seem. Never have been."

"Look!" I shouted after him. "I'm going to quit, honest, but this load is my responsibility." I thought I saw him shake his head as he rounded the corner of the annex.

The dead in my load had pried loose some of the ramp slats and were jumping off the rear trailer. Those in the forward trailer were screaming and carrying on, shaking the whole rig.

Responsibility, shit, I thought. As the dead followed after Mr. Martin, I unhitched both trailers. Then I got in the cab and swung away from the annex, onto the incoming road. "I'm going to quit," I said. "Sure as anything, I'm going to quit."

The road out seemed awfully long. I didn't see any of the dead, surprisingly, but then, maybe they'd been shunted away. I was taking a route I'd never been on before, and I had no way of knowing if it would put me where I wanted to be. But I hung in there for two hours, running the truck dead-out on the flats.

The air was getting grayer like somebody turning down the contrast on a TV set. I switched on the high beams, but they didn't help. By now I was shaking in the cab and saying to myself, Nobody deserves this. Nobody deserves going to Hell no matter what they did. I was scared. It was getting colder.

Three hours and I saw the annex and yards ahead of me again. The road had looped back. I swore and slowed the rig to a crawl. The loading docks had been set on fire. Dead were wandering around with no idea what to do or where to go. I sped up and drove over the few that were on the road. They'd come up and the truck's bumper would hit them and I wouldn't feel a thing, like they weren't there. I'd see them in the rearview mirror, getting up after being knocked over. Just knocked over. Then I was away from the loading docks and there was no doubt about it this time.

I was heading straight for Hell.

The disembarkation terminal was on fire, too. But beyond it, the City was bright and white and untouched. For the first time I drove past the terminal and took the road into the City.

It was either that or stay on the flats with everything screwy. Inside, I thought maybe they'd have things under control.

The truck roared through the gate between two white pillars maybe seventy or eighty feet thick and as tall as the Washington Monument. I didn't see anybody, employees or the dead. Once I was through the pillars—and it came as a shock—

There was no City, no walls, just the road winding along and countryside in all directions, even behind.

The countryside was covered with shacks, houses, little clusters and big clusters. Everything was tight-packed, people working together on one hill, people sitting on their porches, walking along paths, turning to stare at me as the rig barreled on through. No employees—no monsters. No flames. No bloody lakes or rivers.

This must be the outside part, I thought. Deeper inside it would get worse.

I kept on driving. The dog part of me was saying let's go look for authority and ask some questions and get out. But the monkey was saying let's just go look and find out what's going on, what Hell is all about.

Another hour of driving through that calm, crowded landscape and the truck ran out of fuel. I coasted to the side and stepped down from the cab, very nervous.

Again I lit up a cigarette and leaned against the fender, shaking a little. But the shaking was running down and a tight kind of calm was replacing it.

The landscape was still condensed, crowded, but nobody looked tortured. No screaming, no eternal agony. Trees and shrubs and grass hills and thousands and thousands of little houses.

It took about ten minutes for the inhabitants to get around to investigating me. Two men came over to my truck and nodded cordially. Both were middle-aged and healthy-looking. They didn't look dead. I nodded back.

"We were betting whether you're one of the drivers or not," said the first, a black-haired fellow. He wore a simple handwoven shirt and pants. "I think you are. That so?"

"I am."

"You're lost, then."

I agreed. "Maybe you can tell me where I am?"

"Hell," said the second man, younger by a few years and just wearing shorts. The way he said it was just like you might say you came from Los Angeles or Long Beach. Nothing big, nothing dramatic.

"We've heard rumors there's been problems outside," a woman said, coming up to join us. She was about sixty and skinny. She looked like she should be twitchy and nervous, but she acted rock-steady. They were all rock-steady.

"There's some kind of strike," I said. "I don't know what it is, but I'm looking for an employee to tell me."

"They don't usually come this far in," the first man said. "We run things here. Or rather, nobody tells us what to do."

"You're alive?" the woman asked, a curious hunger in her voice. Others came around to join us, a whole crowd. They didn't try to touch. They stood their ground and stared and talked.

"Look," said an old black fellow. "You ever read about the Ancient Mariner?"

I said I had in school.

"Had to tell everybody what he did," the black fellow said. The woman beside him nodded slowly. "We're all Ancient Mariners here. But there's nobody to tell it to. Would you like to know?" The way he asked was pitiful. "We're sorry. We just want everybody to know how sorry we are."

"I can't take you back," I said. "I don't know how to get there myself."

"We can't go back," the woman said. "That's not our place."

More people were coming and I was nervous again. I stood my ground, trying to seem calm, and the dead gathered around me, eager.

"I never thought of anybody but myself," one said. Another interrupted with, "Man, I fucked my whole life away, I hated everybody and everything. I was burned out—"

"I thought I was the greatest. I could pass judgment on everybody—"

"I was the stupidest goddamn woman you ever saw. I was a sow, a pig. I farrowed kids and let them run wild, without no guidance. I was stupid and cruel, too. I used to hurt things—"

"Never cared for anyone. Nobody ever cared for me. I was left to rot in the middle of a city and I wasn't good enough not to rot."

"Everything I did was a lie after I was about twelve years old—"

"Listen to me, mister, because it hurts, it hurts so bad—"

I backed up against my truck. They were lining up now, organized, not like any mob. I had a crazy thought they were behaving better than any people on Earth, but these were the damned.

I didn't hear or see anybody famous. An ex-cop told me about what he did to people in jails. A Jesus-freak told me that knowing Jesus in your heart wasn't enough. "Because I should have made it, man, I should have made it."

"A time came and I was just broken by it all, broke myself really. Just kept stepping on myself and making all the wrong decisions—"

They confessed to me, and I began to cry. Their faces were so clear and so pure, yet here they were, confessing, and except maybe for specific things—like the fellow who had killed Ukrainians after the Second World War in Russian camps—they didn't sound any worse than the crazy sons of bitches I called friends who spent their lives in trucks or bars or whorehouses.

They were all recent. I got the impression the deeper into Hell you went, the older the damned became, which made sense; Hell just got bigger, each crop of damned got bigger, with more room on the outer circles.

"We wasted it," someone said. "You know what my greatest sin was? I was dull. Dull and cruel. I never saw beauty. I saw only dirt. I loved the dirt, and the clean just passed me by."

Pretty soon my tears were uncontrollable. I kneeled down beside the truck, hiding my head, but they kept on coming and confessing. Hundreds must have passed, talking quietly, gesturing with their hands.

Then they stopped. Someone had come and told them to back away, that they were too much for me. I took my face out of my hands and a very young-seeming fellow stood looking down on me. "You all right?" he asked.

I nodded, but my insides were like broken glass. With every confession I had seen myself, and with every tale of sin, I had felt an answering echo.

"Someday, I'm going to be here. Someone's going to drive me in a cattle car to Hell," I mumbled. The young fellow helped me to my feet and cleared a way around my truck.

"Yeah, but not now," he said. "You don't belong here yet." He opened the door to my cab and I got back inside.

"I don't have any fuel," I said.

He smiled that sad smile they all had and stood on the step, up close to my ear. "You'll be taken out of here soon anyway. One of the employees is bound to get around to you." He seemed a lot more sophisticated than the others. I looked at him maybe a little queerly, like there was some explaining in order.

"Yeah, I know all that stuff," he said. "I was a driver once. Then I got promoted. What are they all doing back there?" He gestured up the road. "They're really messing things up now, ain't they?"

"I don't know," I said, wiping my eyes and cheeks with my sleeve.

"You go back, and you tell them that all this revolt on the outer circles, it's what I expected. Tell them Charlie's here and that I warned them. Word's getting around. There's bound to be discontent."

"Word?"

"About who's in charge. Just tell them Charlie knows and I warned them. I know something else, and you shouldn't tell anybody about this . . ." He whispered an incredible fact into my ear then, something that shook me deeper than what I had already been through.

I closed my eyes. Some shadow passed over. The young fellow and everybody else seemed to recede. I felt rather than saw my truck being picked up like a toy.

Then I suppose I was asleep for a time.

In the cab in the parking lot of a truck stop in Bakersfield, I jerked awake, pulled my cap out of my eyes and looked around. It was about noon. There was a union hall in Bakersfield. I checked and my truck was full of diesel, so I started her up and drove to the union hall.

I knocked on the door of the office. I went in and recognized the fat old dude who had given me the job in the first place. I was tired and I smelled bad, but I wanted to get it all done with now.

He recognized me but didn't know my name until I told him. "I can't work the run anymore," I said. The shakes were on me again. "I'm not the one for it. I don't feel right driving them when I know I'm going to be there myself, like as not."

"Okay," he said, slow and careful, sizing me up with a knowing eye. "But you're out. You're busted then. No more driving, no more work for us, no more work for any union we support. It'll be lonely."

"I'll take that kind of lonely any day," I said.

"Okay." That was that. I headed for the door and stopped with my hand on the knob.

"One more thing," I said. "I met Charlie. He says to tell you word's getting around about who's in charge, and that's why there's so much trouble in the outer circles."

The old dude's knowing eye went sort of glassy. "You're the fellow got into the City?"

I nodded.

He got up from his seat real fast, jowls quivering and belly doing a silly dance beneath his work blues. He flicked one hand at me, come 'ere. "Don't go. Just you wait a minute. Outside in the office."

I waited and heard him talking on the phone. He came out smiling and put his hand on my shoulder. "Listen, John, I'm not sure we should let you quit. I didn't know you were the one who'd gone inside. Word is, you stuck around and tried to help when everybody else ran. The company appreciates that. You've been with us a long time, reliable driver, maybe we should give you some incentive to stay. I'm sending you to Vegas to talk with a company man . . ."

The way he said it, I knew there wasn't much choice and I better not fight it. You work union long enough and you know when you keep your mouth shut and go along.

They put me up in a motel and fed me, and by late morning I was on my way to Vegas, arriving about two in the afternoon. I was in a black union car with a silent driver and air conditioning and some *Newsweek*s to keep me company.

The limo dropped me off in front of a four-floor office building, glass and stucco, with lots of divorce lawyers and a dentist and small companies with anonymous names. White plastic letters on a ribbed felt background in a glass case. There was no name on the office number I had been told to go to, but I went up and knocked anyway.

I don't know what I expected. A district supervisor opened the door and asked me a few questions and I said what I'd said before. I was adamant. He looked worried. "Look," he said. "It won't be good for you now if you quit."

I asked him what he meant by that, but he just looked unhappy and said he was going to send me to somebody higher up.

That was in Denver, nearer my God to thee. The same black car took me there, and Saturday morning, bright and early, I stood in front of a very large corporate building with no sign out front and a bank on the bottom floor. I went past the bank and up to the very top.

A secretary met me, pretty but her hair done up very tight and her jaw grimly square. She didn't like me. She let me into the next office, though.

I swear I'd seen the fellow before, but maybe it was just a passing resemblance. He wore a narrow tie and a tasteful but conservative gray suit. His shirt was pastel blue and there was a big Rembrandt Bible on his desk, sitting on the glass top next to an alabaster pen holder. He shook my hand firmly and perched on the edge of the desk.

"First, let me congratulate you on your bravery. We've had some reports from the . . . uh . . . field, and we're hearing nothing but good about you." He smiled like that fellow on TV who's always asking the audience to give him some help. Then his face got sincere and serious. I honestly believe he was sincere; he was also well trained in dealing with not-very-bright people. "I hear you have a report for me. From Charles Frick."

"He said his name was Charlie." I told him the story. "What I'm curious about, what did he mean, this thing about who's in charge?"

"Charlie was in Organization until last year. He died in a car accident. I'm shocked to hear he got the Low Road." He didn't look shocked. "Maybe I'm shocked but not surprised. To tell the truth, he was a bit of a troublemaker." He smiled brightly again and his eyes got large and there was a little too much animation in his face. He had on these MacArthur wire-rimmed glasses too big for his eyes.

"What did he mean?"

"John, I'm proud of all our drivers. You don't know how proud we all are of you folks down there doing the dirty work."

"What did Charlie mean?"

"The abortionists and pornographers, the hustlers and muggers and murderers. Atheists and heathens and idol-worshippers. Surely there must be some satisfaction in keeping the land clean. Sort of a giant sanitation squad, you people keep the scum away from the good folks. The plain good folks. Now, we know that driving's maybe the hardest job we have in the company, and that not everyone can stay on the Low Road indefinitely. Still, we'd like you to stay on. Not as a driver—unless you really wish to continue. For the satisfaction of a tough job. No, if you want to move up—and you've earned it by now, surely—we have a place for you here. A place where you'll be comfortable and—"

"I've already said I want out. You're acting like I'm hot stuff and I'm just shit. You know that, I know that. What is going on?"

His face hardened on me. "It isn't easy up here, either, buster." The "buster" bit tickled me. I laughed and got up from the chair. I'd been in enough offices, and this fancy one just made me queasy. When I stood, he held up his hand and pursed his lips as he nodded. "Sorry. There's incentive, there's certainly a reason why you should want to work here. If you're so convinced you're on your way to the Low Road, you can work it off here, you know."

"How can you say that?"

Bright smile. "Charlie told you something. He told you about who's in charge here."

Now I could smell something terribly wrong, like with the union boss. I mumbled, "He said that's why there's trouble."

"It comes every now and then. We put it down gentle. I tell you where we really need good people, compassionate people. We need them to help with the choosing."

"Choosing?"

"Surely you don't think the Boss does all the choosing directly?"

I couldn't think of a thing to say.

"Listen, the Boss . . . let me tell you. A long time ago, the Boss decided to create a new kind of worker, one with more decision-making ability. Some of the supervisors disagreed, especially when the Boss said the workers would be around for a long, long time—that they'd be indestructible. Sort of like nuclear fuel, you know. Human souls. The waste builds up after a time, those who turn out bad, turn out to be chronically unemployable. They don't go along with the scheme, or get out of line. Can't get along with their fellow workers. You know the type. What do you do with them? Can't just let them go away—they're indestructible, and that ain't no joke, so—"

"Chronically unemployable?"

"You're a union man. Think of what it must feel like to be out of work . . . *forever*. Damned. Nobody will hire you."

I knew the felling, both the way he meant it and the way it had happened to me.

"The Boss feels the project half succeeded, so He doesn't dump it completely. But He doesn't want to be bothered with all the pluses and minuses, the bookkeeping."

"*You're* in charge," I said, my blood cooling.

And I knew where I had seen him before.

On television.

God's right-hand man.

And human. Flesh and blood.

We ran Hell.

He nodded. "Now, that's not the sort of thing we'd like to get around."

"You're in charge, and you let the drivers take their perks on the loads, you let—" I stopped, instinct telling me I would soon be on a rugged trail with no turnaround.

"I'll tell you the truth, John. I have only been in charge here for a year, and my predecessor let things get out of hand. He wasn't a religious man, John, and he thought this was a job like any other, where you could compromise now and then. I know that isn't so. There's no compromise here, and we'll straighten out those inequities and bad decisions very soon. You'll help us, I hope. You may know more about the problems than we do."

"How do you . . . how do you qualify for a job like this?" I asked. "And who offered it to you?"

"Not the Boss, if that's what you're getting at, John. It's been kind of traditional. You may have heard about me. I'm the one, when there was all this talk about after-death experiences and everyone was seeing bright light and beauty, I'm the one who wondered why no one was seeing the other side. I found people who had almost died and had seen Hell, and I turned their lives around. The management in the company decided a fellow with my ability could do good work here. And so I'm here. And I'll tell you, it isn't easy. I sometimes wish we had a little more help from the Boss, a little more guidance, but we don't, and somebody has to do it. Somebody has to clean out the stables, John." Again the smile.

I put on my mask. "Of course," I said. I hoped a gradual increase in piety would pass his sharp-eyed muster.

"And you can see how this all makes you much more valuable to the organization."

I let light dawn slowly.

"We'd hate to lose you now, John. Not when there's security, so much security, working for us. I mean, here we learn the real ins and outs of salvation."

I let him talk at me until he looked at his watch, and all the time I nodded and considered and tried to think of the best ploy. Then I eased myself into a turnabout. I did some confessing until his discomfort was stretched too far—I was keeping him from an important appointment— and made my concluding statement.

"I just wouldn't feel right up here," I said. "I've driven all my life. I'd just want to keep on, working where I'm best suited."

"Keep your present job?" he said, tapping his shoe on the side of the desk.

"Lord, yes," I said, grateful as could be.

Then I asked him for his autograph. He smiled real big and gave it to me, God's right-hand man, who had prayed with presidents.

The next time out, I thought about the incredible thing that Charlie Frick had told me. Halfway to Hell, on the part of the run that he had once driven, I pulled the truck onto the gravel shoulder and walked back, hands in pockets, squinting at the faces. Young and old. Mostly old, or in their teens or twenties. Some were clearly bad news . . . But I was looking more closely this time, trying to discriminate. And sure enough, I saw a few that didn't seem to belong.

The dead hung by the slats, sticking their arms through, beseeching. I ignored as much of that as I could. "You," I said, pointing to a pale, thin fellow with a listless expression. "Why are you here?"

They wouldn't lie to me. I'd learned that inside the City. The dead don't lie.

"I kill people," the man said in a high whisper. "I kill children."

That confirmed my theory. I had *known* there was something wrong with him. I pointed to an old woman, plump and white-haired, lacking any of the signs. "You. Why are you going to Hell?"

She shook her head. "I don't know," she said. "Because I'm bad, I suppose."

"What did you do that was bad?"

"I don't know!" she said, flinging her hands up. "I really don't know. I was a librarian. When all those horrible people tried to take books out of my library, I fought them. I tried to reason with them . . . They wanted to remove Salinger and Twain and Baum . . ."

I picked out another young man. "What about you?"

"I didn't think it was possible," he said. "I didn't believe that God hated me, too."

"What did you do?" These people *didn't need to confess.*

"I loved God. I loved Jesus. But, dear Lord, I couldn't help it. I'm gay. I never had a choice. God wouldn't send me here just for being gay, would he?"

I spoke to a few more, until I was sure I had found all I had in this load. "You, you, you and you, out," I said, swinging open the rear gate. I closed the gate after them and led them away from the truck. Then I told them what Charlie Frick had told me, what he had learned on the road and in the big offices.

"Nobody's really sure where it goes," I said. "But it doesn't go to Hell, and it doesn't go back to Earth."

"Where, then?" the old woman asked plaintively. The hope in her eyes made me want to cry, because I just wasn't sure.

"Maybe it's the High Road," I said. "At least it's a chance. You light out across this stretch, go back of that hill, and I think there's some sort of trail. It's not easy to find, but if you look carefully, it's there. Follow it."

The young man who was gay took my hand. I felt like pulling away, because I've never been fond of homos. But he held on and he said, "Thank you. You must be taking a big risk."

"Yes, thank you," the librarian said. "Why are you doing it?"

I had hoped they wouldn't ask. "When I was a kid, one of my Sunday school teachers told me about Jesus going down to Hell during the three days before he rose up again. She told me Jesus went to Hell to bring out those who didn't belong. I'm certainly no Jesus, I'm not even much of a Christian, but that's what I'm doing. She called it Harrowing Hell." I shook my head. "Never mind. Just go," I said. I watched them walk across the gray flats and around the hill, then I got back into my truck and took the rest into the annex. Nobody noticed. I suppose the records just aren't that important to the employees.

None of the folks I've let loose have ever come back.

I'm staying on the road. I'm talking to people here and there, being cautious. When it looks like things are getting chancy, I'll take my rig back down to the City. And then I'm not sure what I'll do.

I don't want to let everybody loose. But I want to know who's ending up on the Low Road who shouldn't be. People unpopular with God's right-hand man.

My message is simple.

The crazy folks are running the asylum. We've corrupted Hell.

If I get caught, I'll be riding in back. And if you're reading this, chances are you'll be there, too.

Until then, I'm doing my bit. How about you?

BUTTON, BUTTON
Richard Matheson

TELEPLAY BY LOGAN SWANSON

AIRED MARCH 7, 1986

STARRING MARE WINNINGHAM, BRAD DAVIS, BASIL HOFFMAN

THE PACKAGE WAS LYING BY THE FRONT DOOR—A CUBE-shaped carton sealed with tape, their name and address printed by hand: "Mr. and Mrs. Arthur Lewis, 217 E. 37th Street, New York, New York 10016." Norma picked it up, unlocked the door and went into the apartment. It was just getting dark.

After she put the lamb chops in the broiler, she made herself a vodka martini and sat down to open the package.

Inside the carton was a push-button unit fastened to a small wooden box. A glass dome covered the button. Norma tried to lift it off, but it was locked in place. She turned the unit over and saw a folded piece of paper Scotch-taped to the bottom of the box. She pulled it off: "Mr. Steward will call on you at eight P.M."

Norma put the button unit beside her on the couch. She sipped the martini and reread the typed note, smiling.

A few moments later, she went back into the kitchen to make the salad.

The doorbell rang at eight o'clock. "I'll get it," Norma called from the kitchen. Arthur was in the living room, reading.

There was a small man in the hallway. He removed his hat as Norma opened the door. "Mrs. Lewis?" he inquired politely.

"Yes?"

"I'm Mr. Steward."

"Oh, yes." Norma repressed a smile. She was sure now it was a sales pitch.

"May I come in?" asked Mr. Steward.

"I'm rather busy," Norma said. "I'll get you your whatchamacallit, though." She started to turn.

"Don't you want to know what it is?"

Norma turned back. Mr. Steward's tone had been offensive. "No, I don't think so," she replied.

"It could prove very valuable," he told her.

"Monetarily?" she challenged.

Mr. Steward nodded. "Monetarily," he said.

Norma frowned. She didn't like his attitude. "What are you trying to sell?" she asked.

"I'm not selling anything," he answered.

Arthur came out of the living room. "Something wrong?"

Mr. Steward introduced himself.

"*Oh,* the—" Arthur pointed toward the living room and smiled. "What is that gadget, anyway?"

"It won't take long to explain," replied Mr. Steward. "May I come in?"

"If you're selling something—" Arthur said.

Mr. Steward shook his head. "I'm not."

Arthur looked at Norma. "Up to you," she said.

He hesitated. "Well, why not?" he said.

They went into the living room and Mr. Steward sat in Norma's chair. He reached into an inside coat pocket and withdrew a small sealed envelope. "Inside here is a key to the bell-unit dome," he said. He set the envelope on the chair-side table. "The bell is connected to our office."

"What's it for?" asked Arthur.

"If you push the button," Mr. Steward told him, "somewhere in the world, someone you don't know will die. In return for which you will receive a payment of fifty thousand dollars."

Norma stared at the small man. He was smiling.

"What are you talking about?" Arthur asked him.

Mr. Steward looked surprised. "But I've just explained," he said.

"Is this a practical joke?" asked Arthur.

"Not at all. The offer is completely genuine."

"You aren't making sense," Arthur said. "You expect us to believe—"

"Who do you represent?" demanded Norma.

Mr. Steward looked embarrassed. "I'm afraid I'm not at liberty to tell you that," he said. "However, I assure you, the organization is of international scope."

"I think you'd better leave," Arthur said, standing.

Mr. Steward rose. "Of course."

"And take your button unit with you."

"Are you sure you wouldn't care to think about it for a day or so?"

Arthur picked up the button unit and the envelope and thrust them into Mr. Steward's hands. He walked into the hall and pulled open the door.

"I'll leave my card," said Mr. Steward. He placed it on the table by the door.

When he was gone, Arthur tore it in half and tossed the pieces onto the table. "*God!*" he said.

Norma was still sitting on the sofa. "What do you think it was?" she asked.

"I don't care to know," he answered.

She tried to smile but couldn't. "Aren't you curious at all?"

"No." He shook his head.

After Arthur returned to his book, Norma went back to the kitchen and finished washing the dishes.

* * *

"Why won't you talk about it?" Norma asked.

Arthur's eyes shifted as he brushed his teeth. He looked at her reflection in the bathroom mirror.

"Doesn't it intrigue you?"

"It offends me," Arthur said.

"I know, but—" Norma rolled another curler in her hair "—doesn't it intrigue you, too?"

"You think it's a practical joke?" she asked as they went into the bedroom.

"If it is, it's a sick one."

Norma sat on her bed and took off her slippers. "Maybe it's some kind of psychological research."

Arthur shrugged. "Could be."

"Maybe some eccentric millionaire is doing it."

"Maybe."

"Wouldn't you like to know?"

Arthur shook his head.

"Why?"

"Because it's immoral," he told her.

Norma slid beneath the covers. "Well, I think it's intriguing," she said.

Arthur turned off the lamp and leaned over to kiss her. "Good night," he said.

"Good night." She patted his back.

Norma closed her eyes. Fifty thousand dollars, she thought.

In the morning, as she left the apartment, Norma saw the card halves on the table. Impulsively, she dropped them into her purse. She locked the front door and joined Arthur in the elevator.

While she was on her coffee break, she took the card halves from her purse and held the torn edges together. Only Mr. Steward's name and telephone number were printed on the card.

After lunch, she took the card halves from her purse again and Scotch-taped the edges together. Why am I doing this? she thought.

Just before five, she dialed the number.

"Good afternoon," said Mr. Steward's voice.

Norma almost hung up but restrained herself. She cleared her throat. "This is Mrs. Lewis," she said.

"Yes, Mrs. Lewis." Mr. Steward sounded pleased.

"I'm curious."

"That's natural," Mr. Steward said.

"Not that I believe a word of what you told us."

"Oh, it's quite authentic," Mr. Steward answered.

"Well, whatever—" Norma swallowed. "When you said someone in the world would die, what did you mean?"

"Exactly that," he answered. "It could be anyone. All we guarantee is that you don't know them. And, of course, that you wouldn't have to watch them die."

"For fifty thousand dollars," Norma said.

"That is correct."

She made a scoffing sound. "That's crazy."

"Nonetheless, that is the proposition," Mr. Steward said. "Would you like me to return the button unit?"

Norma stiffened. *"Certainly not."* She hung up angrily.

The package was lying by the front door; Norma saw it as she left the elevator. Well, of all the nerve, she thought. She glared at the carton as she unlocked the door. I just won't take it in, she thought. She went inside and started dinner.

Later, she carried her vodka martini to the front hall. Opening the door, she picked up the package and carried it into the kitchen, leaving it on the table.

She sat in the living room, sipping her drink and looking out the window. After a while, she went back into the kitchen to turn the cutlets in the broiler. She put the package in a bottom cabinet. She'd throw it out in the morning.

"Maybe some eccentric millionaire is playing games with people," she said.

Arthur looked up from his dinner. "I don't understand you."

"What does *that* mean?"

"Let it go," he told her.

Norma ate in silence. Suddenly, she put her fork down. "Suppose it's a genuine offer?" she said.

Arthur stared at her.

"Suppose it's a genuine offer?"

"All right, suppose it is?" He looked incredulous. "What would you like to do? Get the button back and push it? *Murder* someone?"

Norma looked disgusted. *"Murder."*

"How would you define it?"

"If you don't even *know* the person?" Norma said.

Arthur looked astounded. "Are you saying what I think you are?"

"If it's some old Chinese peasant ten thousand miles away? Some diseased native in the Congo?"

"How about some baby boy in Pennsylvania?" Arthur countered. "Some beautiful little girl on the next block?"

"Now you're loading things."

"The point is, Norma," he continued, "what's the difference who you kill? It's still murder."

"The point *is,*" Norma broke in, "if it's someone you've never seen in your life and never *will* see, someone whose death you don't even have to *know* about, you *still* wouldn't push the button?"

Arthur stared at her, appalled. "You mean *you would?*"

"Fifty thousand dollars, Arthur."

"What has the amount—"

"Fifty thousand dollars, Arthur," Norma interrupted. "A chance to take that trip to Europe we've always talked about."

"Norma, no."

"A chance to buy that cottage on the Island."

"Norma, *no.*" His face was white. "For God's sake, *no.*"

She shuddered. "All right, take it easy," she said. "Why are you getting so upset? It's only talk."

After dinner, Arthur went into the living room. Before he left the table, he said, "I'd rather not discuss it anymore, if you don't mind."

Norma shrugged. "Fine with me."

She got up earlier than usual to make pancakes, eggs and bacon for Arthur's breakfast.

"What's the occasion?" he asked with a smile.

"No occasion." Norma looked offended. "I wanted to do it, that's all."

"Good," he said. "I'm glad you did."

She refilled his cup. "Wanted to show you I'm not—" She shrugged.

"Not what?"

"Selfish."

"Did I say you were?"

"Well—" she gestured vaguely "—last night . . ."

Arthur didn't speak.

"All that talk about the button," Norma said. "I think you—well, misunderstood me."

"In what way?" His voice was guarded.

"I think you felt—" she gestured again, "—that I was only thinking of myself."

"Oh."

"I wasn't."

"Norma—"

"Well, I *wasn't.* When I talked about Europe, a cottage on the Island—"

"Norma, why are we getting so involved in this?"

"I'm not involved at all." She drew in shaking breath. "I'm simply trying to indicate that—"

"What?"

"That I'd like for *us* to go to Europe. Like for *us* to have a cottage on the Island. Like for *us* to have a nicer apartment, nicer furniture, nicer clothes. Like for us to finally have a *baby,* for that matter."

"Norma, we will," he said.

"When?"

He stared at her in dismay. "Norma—"

"When?"

"Are you—" he seemed to draw back slightly "—are you really saying—"

"I'm saying that they're probably doing it for some research project!" she cut him off. "That they want to know what average people would do under such a circumstance! That they're just *saying* someone would die, in order to study reactions, see if there'd be guilt, anxiety, whatever! You don't really think they'll *kill* somebody, do you?"

Arthur didn't answer. She saw his hands trembling. After a while, he got up and left.

When he'd gone to work, Norma remained at the table, staring into her coffee. I'm going to be late, she thought. She shrugged. What difference did it make? She should be home, anyway, not working in an office.

While she was stacking dishes, she turned abruptly, dried her hands and took the package from the bottom cabinet. Opening it, she set the button unit on the table. She stared at it for a long time before taking the key from its envelope and removing the glass dome. She stared at the button. How ridiculous, she thought. All this over a meaningless button.

Reaching out, she pressed it down. For *us,* she thought angrily.

She shuddered. Was it *happening?* A chill of horror swept across her.

In a moment, it had passed. She made a contemptuous noise. *Ridiculous,* she thought. To get so worked up over nothing.

She threw the button unit, dome and key into the wastebasket and hurried to dress for work.

She had just turned over the supper steaks and was making herself another vodka martini when the telephone rang. She picked up the receiver. "Hello?"

"Mrs. Lewis?"

"Yes?"

"This is the Lenox Hill Hospital."

She felt unreal as the voice informed her of the subway accident—the shoving crowd, Arthur pushed from the platform in front of the train. She was conscious of shaking her head but couldn't stop.

As she hung up, she remembered Arthur's life insurance policy for $25,000, with double indemnity for—

"No." She couldn't seem to breathe. She struggled to her feet and

walked into the kitchen numbly. Something cold pressed at her skull as she removed the button unit from the wastebasket. There were no nails or screws visible. She couldn't see how it was put together.

Abruptly, she began to smash it on the sink edge, pounding it harder and harder, until the wood split. She pulled the sides apart, cutting her fingers without noticing. There were no transistors in the box, no wires or tubes. The box was empty.

She whirled with a gasp as the telephone rang. Stumbling into the living room, she picked up the receiver.

"Mrs. Lewis?" Mr. Steward asked.

It wasn't her voice shrieking so; it couldn't be. *"You said I wouldn't know the one that died!"*

"My dear lady," Mr. Steward said. "Do you really think you knew your husband?"

THE EVERLASTING CLUB
Arthur Gray

TELEPLAY BY ROBERT HUNTER

AIRED MARCH 28, 1986, AS "DEVIL'S ALPHABET"

STARRING BEN CROSS, HYWELL BENNETT, OSMOND BULLOCK

THERE IS A CHAMBER IN JESUS COLLEGE THE EXISTENCE of which is probably known to few who are now resident, and fewer still have penetrated into it or even seen its interior. It is on the right hand of the landing on the top floor of the precipitous staircase in the angle of the cloister next the Hall—a staircase which for some forgotten story connected with it is traditionally called "Cow Lane." The padlock that secures its massive oaken door is very rarely unfastened, for the room is bare and unfurnished. Once it served as a place of deposit for superfluous kitchenware, but even that ignominious use has passed from it, and it is now left to undisturbed solitude and darkness. For I should say that it is entirely cut off from the light of the outer day by the walling up, sometime in the eighteenth century, of its single window, and such light as ever reaches it comes from the door, when rare occasion causes it to be open.

Yet at no extraordinarily remote day this chamber has evidently been tenanted and, before it was given up to darkness, was comfortably fitted, according to the standard of comfort that was known in college in the days of George II. There is still a roomy fireplace before which legs have been stretched and wine and gossip have circulated in the days of wigs and brocade. For the room is spacious, and when it was lighted by the window looking eastward over the fields and common, it must have been a cheerful place for a sociable don.

Let me state in brief, prosaic outline the circumstances that account for the gloom and solitude in which this room has remained now for nearly a century and a half.

In the second quarter of the eighteenth century the University possessed a great variety of clubs of a social kind. There were clubs in college parlors and clubs in private rooms, or in inns and coffee houses; clubs flavored with politics, clubs clerical, clubs purporting to be learned and literary. Whatever their professed particularity, the aim of each was convivial. Some of them, which included undergraduates as well as seniors, were dissipated enough, and in their limited provincial way aped the profligacy of such clubs as the Hell Fire Club of London notoriety.

Among these last was one that was at once more select and of more evil fame than any of its fellows. By a singular accident, presently to be explained, the Minute Book of this club, including the years from 1738 to 1766, came into the hands of a Master of Jesus College, and though, so far as I am aware, it is no longer extant, I have before me a transcript of it which, though it is in a recent handwriting, presents in a bald shape such a singular array of facts that I must ask you to accept them as veracious. The original book is described as a stout duodecimo volume bound in red leather and fastened with red silken strings. The writing in it occupied some forty pages, and ended with the date November 2, 1766.

The club in question was called the Everlasting Club—a name sufficiently explained by its rules, set forth in the pocketbook. Its number was limited to seven, and it would seem that its members were all young men, between twenty-two and thirty. One of them was a Fellow-Commoner of Trinity; three of them were Fellows of Colleges, among whom I should specially mention a Fellow of Jesus, named Charles Bellasis; another was a landed proprietor in the county, and the sixth was a young Cambridge physician. The Founder and President of the club was the Honorable Alan Dermot, who, as the son of an Irish peer, had obtained a nobleman's degree in the University, and lived in idleness in the town. Very little is known of his life and character, but that little is highly in his disfavor. He was killed in a duel at Paris in the year 1743, under circumstances which I need not particularize, but which point to an exceptional degree of cruelty and wickedness in the slain man.

I will quote from the first pages of the Minute Book some of the laws of the club which will explain its constitution:

1. This Society consisteth of seven Everlastings, who may be Corporeal or Incorporeal, as Destiny shall determine.

2. The rules of the Society, as herein written, are immutable and Everlasting.

3. None shall hereafter be chosen into the Society and none shall cease to be members.

4. The Honourable Alan Dermot is the Everlasting President of the Society.

5. The Senior Corporeal Everlasting, not being the President, shall be the Secretary of the Society, and in the Book of Minutes shall record its transactions, the date at which any Everlasting shall cease to be Corporeal, and all fines due to the Society. And when such Senior Everlasting shall cease to be Corporeal, he shall, either in person or by some sure hand, deliver this Book of Minutes to him who shall be next Senior and at the time Corporeal, and he shall in like manner record the transactions therein and transmit it to the next Senior. The neglect of these provisions shall be visited by the President with fine or punishment according to his discretion.

6. On the second day of November in every year, being the Feast of All Souls, at ten o'clock *post meridiem,* the Everlastings shall meet at supper in the place of residence of that Corporeal member of the Society to whom it shall fall in order of rotation to

entertain them, and they shall all subscribe in this Book of Minutes their names and present place of abode.

7. It shall be the obligation of every Everlasting to be present at the yearly entertainment of the Society, and none shall allege for excuse that he has not been invited thereto. If any Everlasting shall fail to attend the yearly meeting, or in his turn shall fail to provide entertainment for the Society, he shall be mulcted at the discretion of the President.

8. Nevertheless, if in any year, in the month of October and not less than seven days before the Feast of All Souls, the major part of the Society, that is to say, four at the least, shall meet and record in writing in these Minutes that it is their desire that no entertainment be given in that year, then, notwithstanding the two rules last rehearsed, there shall be no entertainment in that year, and no Everlasting shall be mulcted on the ground of his absence.

The rest of the rules are either too profane or too puerile to be quoted here. They indicated the extraordinary levity with which the members entered on their preposterous obligations. In particular, to the omission of any regulation as to the transmission of the Minute Book after the last Everlasting ceased to be "Corporeal," we owe the accident that it fell into the hands of one who was not a member of the society, and the consequent preservation of its contents to the present day.

Low as was the standard of morals in all classes of the University in the first half of the eighteenth century, the flagrant defiance of public decorum by the members of the Everlasting Society brought upon it the stern censure of the authorities, and after a few years it was practically dissolved and its members banished from the University. Charles Bellasis, for instance, was obliged to leave the college, and though he retained his fellowship, he remained absent from it for nearly twenty years. But the minutes of the society reveal a more terrible reason for its virtual extinction.

Between the years 1738 and 1743, the minutes record many meetings of the club, for it met on other occasions besides that of All Souls Day. Apart from a great deal of impious jocularity on the part of the writers, they are limited to the formal record of the attendance of the members, fines inflicted, and so forth. The meeting on November 2nd in the latter year is the first about which there is any departure from the stereotyped forms. The supper was given in the house of the physician. One member, Henry Davenport, the former Fellow-Commoner of Trinity, was absent from the entertainment, as he was then serving in Germany, in the Dettingen campaign. The minutes contain an entry, "Mulctatus propter absentiam per Presidentem, Hen. Davenport." An entry on the next page of the book runs, "Henry Davenport by a Cannon-shot became an Incorporeal Member, November 3, 1743."

The minutes give in their own handwriting, under date November 2, the names and addresses of the six other members. First in the list, in a large, bold hand, is the autograph of "Alan Dermot, President, at the Court of His Royal Highness." Now, in October Dermot had certainly been in attendance on the Young Pretender at Paris, and doubtless the address that he gave was understood at the time by the other Everlastings to refer to the fact. But on October 28, five days *before* the meeting of the Club, he was killed, as I have already mentioned, in a duel. The news of his death cannot have reached Cambridge on November 2, for the Secretary's record of it placed below that of Davenport, and with the date November 10: "This day was reported that the President was become an Incorporeal by the hands of a French chevalier." And in a sudden ebullition, which is in glaring contrast with his previous profanities, he has dashed down, "The Good God shield us from ill."

The tidings of the President's death scattered the Everlastings like a thunderbolt. They left Cambridge and buried themselves in widely parted regions. But the Club did not cease to exist. The Secretary was still bound to his hateful records; the five survivors did not dare to neglect their fatal obligations. Horror of the presence of the President made the November gathering once and forever impossible; but horror, too, forbade them to neglect the precaution of meeting in October of every year to put in writing their objection to the celebration. For five years, five names are appended to that entry in the minutes, and that is all the business of the Club. Then another member died, who was not the Secretary.

For eighteen more years, four miserable men met once each year to deliver the same formal protest. During those years we gather from the signatures that Charles Bellasis returned to Cambridge, now, to appearance, chastened and decorous. He occupied the rooms that I have described on the staircase in the corner of the cloister.

Then in 1766 comes a new handwriting and an altered minute: "Jan. 27, on this day Francis Witherington, Secretary, became an Incorporeal Member. The same day this Book was delivered to me, James Harvey." Harvey lived only a month, and a similar entry on March 7 states that the book has descended, with the same mysterious celerity, to William Catherston. Then, on May 18, Charles Bellasis writes that on that day, being the date of Catherston's decease, the Minute Book has come to him as the last surviving Corporeal of the club.

As it is my purpose to record fact only, I shall not attempt to describe the feelings of the unhappy Secretary when he penned that fatal record. When Witherington died, it must have come home to the three survivors that after twenty-three years' intermission, the ghastly entertainment must be annually renewed, with the addition of fresh incorporeal guests, or that they must undergo the pitiless censure of the President. I think it likely that the terror of the alternative, coupled with the mysterious delivery of the Minute Book, was answerable for the speedy decease of the two first successors to the Secretaryship. Now that the alternative was offered to Ballasis alone, he was firmly resolved to bear the consequences, whatever they might be, of an infringement of the club rules.

The graceless days of George II had passed way from the University. They were succeeded by times of outward respectability, when religion and morals were no longer publicly challenged. With Bellasis, too, the petulance of youth had passed: he was discreet, perhaps exemplary. The scandal of his early conduct was unknown to most of the new generation, condoned by the few survivors who had witnessed it.

On the night of November 2nd, 1766, a terrible event revived in the older inhabitants of the College the memory of those evil days. From ten o'clock to midnight, a hideous uproar went on in the chamber of Bellasis. Who were his companions, none knew. Blasphemous outcries and ribald songs, such as had not been heard for twenty years past, aroused from sleep or study the occupants of the court; but among the voices was not that of Bellasis. At twelve a sudden silence fell upon the cloisters. But the Master lay awake all night, troubled at the relapse of a respected colleague and the horrible example of libertinism set to his pupils.

In the morning, all remained quiet about Bellasis's chamber. When his door was opened, soon after daybreak, the early light creeping through the drawn curtains revealed a strange scene. About the table were drawn seven chairs, but some of them had been overthrown, and the furniture was in chaotic disorder, as after some wild orgy. In the chair at the foot of the table sat the lifeless figure of the Secretary, his head bent over his folded arms, as though he would shield his eyes from some horrible sight. Before him on the table lay pen, ink and the red Minute Book. On the last inscribed page, under the date of November 2nd, were written, for the first time since 1742, the autographs of the seven members of the Everlasting Club, but without address. In the same strong hand in which the President's name was written, there was appended below the signatures the note, "Mulctatus per Presidentem propter neglectum obsonii, Car. Bellasis."

The Minute Book was secured by the Master of the College, and I believe that he alone was acquainted with the nature of its contents. The scandal reflected on the College by the circumstances revealed in it caused him to keep the knowledge rigidly to himself. But some suspicion of the nature of the occurrences must have percolated to students and servants, for there was a long-abiding belief in the College that annually on the night of November 2, sounds of unholy revelry were heard to issue from the chamber of Bellasis. I cannot learn that the occupants of the adjoining rooms have ever been disturbed by them. Indeed, it is plain from the minutes that owing to their improvident drafting, no provision was made for the perpetuation of the All Souls entertainment after the last Everlasting ceased to be Corporeal. Such superstitious belief must be treated with contemptuous incredulity. But whether for that cause or another, the rooms were shut up, and have remained tenantless from that day to this.

THE LAST DEFENDER
OF CAMELOT
Roger Zelazny

Teleplay by George R. R. Martin

Aired April 11, 1986

Starring Richard Kiley, Jenny Agutter, Norman Lloyd

THE THREE MUGGERS WHO STOPPED HIM THAT OCTOBER
night in San Francisco did not anticipate much resistance from the old
man, despite his size. He was well dressed, and that was sufficient.

The first approached him with his hand extended. The other two hung
back a few paces.

"Just give me your wallet and your watch," the mugger said. "You'll
save yourself a lot of trouble."

The old man's grip shifted on his walking stick. His shoulders straightened. His shock of white hair tossed as he turned his head to regard the
other.

"Why don't you come and take them?"

The mugger began another step, but he never completed it. The stick
was almost invisible in the speed of its swinging. It struck him on the
left temple and he fell.

Without pausing, the old man caught the stick by its middle with his
left hand, advanced and drove it into the belly of the next nearest man.
Then, with an upward hook as the man doubled, he caught him in the
softness beneath the jaw, behind the chin, with its point. As the man
fell, he clubbed him with its butt on the back of the neck.

The third man had reached out and caught the old man's upper arm
by then. Dropping the stick, the old man seized the mugger's shirtfront
with his left hand, his belt with his right, raised him from the ground
until he held him at arm's length above his head and slammed him against
the side of the building to his right, releasing him as he did so.

He adjusted his apparel, ran a hand through his hair and retrieved his
walking stick. For a moment he regarded the three fallen forms, then
shrugged and continued on his way.

There were sounds of traffic from somewhere off to his left. He turned
right at the next corner. The moon appeared above tall buildings as he
walked. The smell of the ocean was on the air. It had rained earlier and
the pavement still shone beneath streetlamps. He moved slowly, pausing
occasionally to examine the contents of darkened shop windows.

After perhaps ten minutes, he came upon a side street showing more
activity than any of the others he had passed. There was a drugstore,
still open, on the corner, a diner farther up the block, and several well-
lighted storefronts. A number of people were walking along the far side
of the street. A boy coasted by on a bicycle. He turned there, his pale
eyes regarding everything he passed.

Halfway up the block, he came to a dirty window on which was painted the word READINGS. Beneath it were displayed the outline of a hand and a scattering of playing cards. As he passed the open door, he glanced inside. A brightly garbed woman, her hair bound back in a green kerchief, sat smoking at the rear of the room. She smiled as their eyes met and crooked an index finger toward herself. He smiled back and turned away, but . . .

He looked at her again. What was it? He glanced at his watch.

Turning, he entered the shop and moved to stand before her. She rose. She was small, barely over five feet in height.

"Your eyes," he remarked, "are green. Most gypsies I know have dark eyes."

She shrugged.

"You take what you get in life. Have you a problem?"

"Give me a moment and I'll think of one," he said. "I just came in here because you remind me of someone and it bothers me—I can't think who."

"Come into the back," she said, "and sit down. We'll talk."

He nodded and followed her into a small room to the rear. A threadbare oriental rug covered the floor near the small table at which they seated themselves. Zodiacal prints and faded psychedelic posters of a semireligious nature covered the walls. A crystal ball stood on a small stand in the far corner beside a vase of cut flowers. A dark, long-haired cat slept on a sofa to the right of it. A door to another room stood slightly ajar beyond the sofa. The only illumination came from a cheap lamp on the table before him and from a small candle in a plaster base atop the shawl-covered coffee table.

He leaned forward and studied her face, then shook his head and leaned back.

She flicked an ash onto the floor.

"Your problem?" she suggested.

He sighed.

"Oh, I don't really have a problem anyone can help me with. Look, I think I made a mistake coming in here. I'll pay you for your trouble, though, just as if you'd given me a reading. How much is it?"

He began to reach for his wallet, but she raised her hand.

"Is it that you do not believe in such things?" she asked, her eyes scrutinizing his face.

"No, quite the contrary," he replied. "I am willing to believe in magic, divination and all manner of spells and sendings, angelic and demonic. But—"

"But not from someone in a dump like this?"

He smiled.

"No offense," he said.

A whistling sound filled the air. It seemed to come from the next room back.

"That's all right," she said, "but my water is boiling. I'd forgotten it was on. Have some tea with me? I do wash the cups. No charge. Things are slow."

"All right."

She rose and departed.

He glanced at the door to the front but eased himself back into his chair, resting his large, blue-veined hands on its padded arms. He sniffed then, nostrils flaring, and cocked his head as at some half-familiar aroma.

After a time, she returned with a tray, set it on the coffee table. The cat stirred, raised her head, blinked at it, stretched, closed her eyes again.

"Cream and sugar?"

"Please. One lump."

She placed two cups on the table before him.

"Take either one," she said.

He smiled and drew the one on his left toward him. She placed an ashtray in the middle of the table and returned to her own seat, moving the other cup to her place.

"That wasn't necessary," he said, placing his hands on the table.

She shrugged.

"You don't know me. Why should you trust me? Probably got a lot of money on you."

He looked at her face again. She had apparently removed some of the heavier makeup while in the back room. The jawline, the brow . . . He looked away. He took a sip of tea.

"Good tea. Not instant," he said. "Thanks."

"So you believe in all sorts of magic," she asked, sipping her own.

"Some," he said.

"Any special reason why?"

"Some of it works."

"For example?"

He gestured aimlessly with his left hand.

"I've traveled a lot. I've seen some strange things."

"And you have no problems?"

He chuckled.

"Still determined to give me a reading? All right. I'll tell you a little about myself and what I want right now, and you can tell me whether I'll get it. Okay?"

"I'm listening."

"I am a buyer for a large gallery in the East. I am something of an authority on ancient work in precious metals. I am in town to attend an auction of such items from the estate of a private collector. I will go to inspect the pieces tomorrow. Naturally, I hope to find something good. What do you think my chances are?''

"Give me your hands."

He extended them, palms upward. She leaned forward and regarded them. She looked back up at him immediately.

"Your wrists have more rascettes than I can count!"

"Yours seem to have quite a few, also."

She met his eyes for only a moment and returned her attention to his hands. He noted that she had paled beneath what remained of her makeup, and her breathing was now irregular.

"No," she finally said, drawing back, "you are not going to find here what you are looking for."

Her hand trembled slightly as she raised her teacup. He frowned.

"I asked only in jest," he said. "Nothing to get upset about. I doubted I would find what I am really looking for, anyway."

She shook her head.

"Tell me your name."

"I've lost my accent," he said, "but I'm French. The name is DuLac."

She stared into his eyes and began to blink rapidly.

"No . . ." she said. "No."

"I'm afraid so. What's yours?"

"Madam Le Fay," she said. "I just repainted that sign. It's still drying."

He began to laugh, but it froze in his throat.

"Now—I know—who—you remind me of . . ."

"You reminded me of someone, also. Now I, too, know."

Her eyes brimmed, her mascara ran.

"It couldn't be," he said. "Not here . . . Not in a place like this . . ."

"You dear man," she said softly, and she raised his right hand to her lips. She seemed to choke for a moment, then said, "I had thought that I was the last, and yourself buried at Joyous Gard. I never dreamed . . ." Then, "This?" gesturing about the room. "Only because it amuses me, helps to pass the time. The waiting—"

She stopped. She lowered his hand.

"Tell me about it," she said.

"The waiting?" he said. "For what do you wait?"

"Peace," she said. "I am here by the power of my arts, through all the long years. But you—How did you manage it?"

"I—" He took another drink of tea. He looked about the room. "I do not know how to begin," he said. "I survived the final battles, saw the kingdom sundered, could do nothing—and at last departed England. I wandered, taking service at many courts, and after a time under many names, as I saw that I was not aging—or aging very, very slowly. I was in India, China—I fought in the Crusades. I've been everywhere. I've spoken with magicians and mystics—most of them charlatans, a few with the power, none so great as Merlin—and what had come to be my own belief was confirmed by one of them, a man more than half charlatan, yet . . .'' He paused and finished his tea. "Are you certain you want to hear all this?'' he asked.

"I want to hear it. Let me bring more tea first, though.''

She returned with the tea. She lit a cigarette and leaned back.

"Go on.''

"I decided that it was—my sin,'' he said, "with . . . the Queen.''

"I don't understand.''

"I betrayed my Liege, who was also my friend, in the one thing which must have hurt him most. The love I felt was stronger than loyalty or friendship—and even today, to this day, it still is. I cannot repent, and so I cannot be forgiven. Those were strange and magical times. We lived in a land destined to become myth. Powers walked the realm in those days, forces which are now gone from the earth. How or why, I cannot say. But you know that it is true. I am somehow of a piece with those gone things, and the laws that rule my existence are not normal laws of the natural world. I believe that I cannot die; that it has fallen my lot, as punishment, to wander the world till I have completed the Quest. I believe I will only know rest the day I find the Holy Grail. Giuseppe Balsamo, before he became known as Cagliostro, somehow saw this and said it to me just as I had thought it, though I never said a word of it to him. And so I have traveled the world, searching. I go no more as knight, or soldier, but as an appraiser. I have been in nearly every museum on Earth, viewed all the great private collections. So far, it has eluded me.''

"You *are* getting a little old for battle.''

He snorted.

"I have never lost,'' he stated flatly. "Down ten centuries, I have never lost a personal contest. It is true that I have aged, yet whenever I am threatened, all of my former strength returns to me. But, look where I may, fight where I may, it has never served me to discover that which I must find. I feel I am unforgiven and must wander like the Eternal Jew until the end of the world.''

She lowered her head.

". . . And you say I will not find it tomorrow?''

"You will never find it,'' she said softly.

"You saw that in my hand?''

She shook her head.

"Your story is fascinating and your theory novel,'' she began, "but Cagliostro was a total charlatan. Something must have betrayed your thoughts, and he made a shrewd guess. But he was wrong. I say that you will never find it, not because you are unworthy or unforgiven. No, never that. A more loyal subject than yourself never drew breath. Don't you

know that Arthur forgave you? It was an arranged marriage. The same
thing happened constantly elsewhere, as you must know. You gave her
something he could not. There was only tenderness there. He understood. The only forgiveness you require is that which has been withheld
all these long years—your own. No, it is not a doom that has been laid
upon you. It is your own feelings which led you to assume an impossible
quest, something tantamount to total unforgiveness. But you have suffered all these centuries upon the wrong trail.''

When she raised her eyes, she saw that his were hard like ice or
gemstones. But she met his gaze and continued: "There is not now, was
not then, and probably never was, a Holy Grail.''

"I saw it," he said, "that day it passed through the Hall of the Table.
We all saw it.''

"You thought you saw it," she corrected him. "I hate to shatter an
illusion that has withstood all the other tests of time, but I fear I must.
The kingdom, as you recall, was at that time in turmoil. The knights
were growing restless and falling away from the fellowship. A year—six
months, even—and all would have collapsed, all Arthur had striven so
hard to put together. He knew that the longer Camelot stood, the longer
its name would endure, the stronger its ideals would become. So he made
a decision, a purely political one. Something was needed to hold things
together. He called upon Merlin, already half-mad, yet still shrewd
enough to see what was needed and able to provide it. The Quest was
born. Merlin's powers created the illusion you saw that day. It was a lie,
yes. A glorious lie, though. And it served for years after to bind you all
in brotherhood, in the name of justice and love. It entered literature, it
promoted nobility and the higher ends of culture. It served its purpose.
But it was—never—really—there. You have been chasing a ghost. I am
sorry, Launcelot, but I have absolutely no reason to lie to you. I know
magic when I see it. I saw it then. That is how it happened.''

For a long while he was silent. Then he laughed.

"You have an answer for everything," he said. "I could almost believe
you, if you could but answer me one thing more—Why am I here? For
what reason? By what power? How is it I have been preserved for half
the Christian era while other men grow old and die in a handful of years?
Can you tell me now what Cagliostro could not?''

"Yes," she said, "I believe that I can.''

He rose to his feet and began to pace. The cat, alarmed, sprang from
the sofa and ran into the back room. He stooped and snatched up his
walking stick. He started for the door.

"I suppose it was worth waiting a thousand years to see you afraid,''
she said.

He halted.

"That is unfair," he replied.

"I know. But now you will come back and sit down," she said.

He was smiling once more as he turned and returned.

"Tell me," he said. "How do you see it?"

"Yours was the last enchantment of Merlin, that is how I see it."

"Merlin? Me? Why?"

"Gossip had it the old goat took Nimue into the woods and she had to use one of his own spells on him in self-defense—a spell which caused him to sleep forever in some lost place. If it was the spell that I believe it was, then at least part of the rumor was incorrect. There was no known counterspell, but the effects of the enchantment would have caused him to sleep not forever but for a millennium or so, and then to awaken. My guess now is that his last conscious act before he dropped off was to lay this enchantment upon you, so that you would be on hand when he returned."

"I suppose it might be possible, but why would he want me or need me?"

"If I were journeying into a strange time, I would want an ally once I reached it. And if I had a choice, I would want it to be the greatest champion of the day."

"Merlin . . ." he mused. "I suppose that it could be as you say. Excuse me, but a long life has just been shaken up, from beginning to end. If this is true . . ."

"I am sure that it is."

"If this is true . . . A millennium, you say?"

"More or less."

"Well, it is almost that time now."

"I know. I do not believe that our meeting tonight was a matter of chance. You are destined to meet him upon his awakening, which should be soon. Something has ordained that you meet me first, however, to be warned."

"Warned? Warned of what?"

"He is mad, Launcelot. Many of us felt a great relief at his passing. If the realm had not been sundered finally by strife, it would probably have been broken by his hand, anyway."

"That I find difficult to believe. He was always a strange man—for who can fully understand a sorcerer?—and in his later years he did seem at least partly daft. But he never struck me as evil."

"Nor was he. His was the most dangerous morality of all. He was a misguided idealist. In a more primitive time and place and with a willing tool like Arthur, he was able to create a legend. Today, in an age of monstrous weapons, with the right leader as his cat's-paw, he could unleash something totally devastating. He would see a wrong and force his man to try righting it. He would do it in the name of the same high ideal he always served, but he would not appreciate the results until it was too late. How could he—even if he were sane? He has no conception of modern international relations."

"What is to be done? What is my part in all of this?"

"I believe you should go back, to England, to be present at his awakening, to find out exactly what he wants, to try to reason with him."

"I don't know . . . How would I find him?"

"You found me. When the time is right, you will be in the proper place. I am certain of that. It was meant to be, probably even a part of his spell. Seek him. But do not trust him."

"I don't know, Morgana." He looked at the wall, unseeing. "I don't know."

"You have waited this long and you draw back now from finally finding out?"

"You are right—in that much, at least." He folded his hands, raised them and rested his chin upon them. "What I would do if he really returned, I do not know. Try to reason with him, yes—Have you any other advice?"

"Just that you be there."

"You've looked at my hand. You have the power. What did you see?" She turned away.

"It is uncertain," she said.

That night he dreamed, as he sometimes did, of times long gone. They sat about the great Table, as they had on that day. Gawaine was there and Percival. Galahad . . . He winced. This day was different from other days. There was a certain tension in the air, a before-the-storm feeling, an electrical thing . . . Merlin stood at the far end of the room, hands in the sleeves of his long robe, hair and beard snowy and unkempt, pale eyes staring—at what, none could be certain . . .

After some timeless time, a reddish glow appeared near the door. All eyes moved toward it. It grew brighter and advanced slowly into the room—a formless apparition of light. There were sweet odors and some few soft strains of music. Gradually, a form began to take shape at its center, resolving itself into the likeness of a chalice . . .

He felt himself rising, moving slowly, following it in its course through the great chamber, advancing upon it, soundlessly and deliberately, as if moving underwater . . .

. . . Reaching for it.

His hand entered the circle of light, moved toward its center, neared the now blazing cup and passed through . . .

Immediately, the light faded. The outline of the chalice wavered, and it collapsed in upon itself, fading, fading, gone . . .

There came a sound, rolling, echoing about the hall. Laughter.

He turned and regarded the others. They sat about the table, watching him, laughing. Even Merlin managed a dry chuckle.

Suddenly, his great blade was in his hand, and he raised it as he strode toward the Table. The knights nearest him drew back as he brought the weapon crashing down.

The Table split in half and fell. The room shook.

The quaking continued. Stones were dislodged from the walls. A roof beam fell. He raised his arm.

The entire castle began to come apart, falling about him, and still the laughter continued.

He awoke damp with perspiration and lay still for a long while. In the morning, he bought a ticket for London.

Two of the three elemental sounds of the world were suddenly with him as he walked that evening, stick in hand. For a dozen days, he had hiked about Cornwall, finding no clues to that which he sought. He had allowed himself two more before giving up and departing.

Now the wind and the rain were upon him, and he increased his pace. The fresh-lit stars were smothered by a mass of cloud, and wisps of fog grew like ghostly fungi on either hand. He moved among trees, paused, continued on.

"Shouldn't have stayed out this late," he muttered, and after several more pauses, *"Nel mezzo del cammin di nostra vita mi ritrovai per una selva oscura, che la diritta via era smarrita,"* then he chuckled, halting beneath a tree.

The rain was not heavy. It was more a fine mist now. A bright patch in the lower heavens showed where the moon hung veiled.

He wiped his face, turned up his collar. He studied the position of the moon. After a time, he struck off to his right. There was a faint rumble of thunder in the distance.

The fog continued to grow about him as he went. Soggy leaves made squishing noises beneath his boots. An animal of indeterminate size bolted from a clump of shrubbery beside a cluster of rocks and tore off through the darkness.

Five minutes . . . ten . . . He cursed softly. The rainfall had increased in intensity. Was that the same rock?

He turned in a complete circle. All directions were equally uninviting. Selecting one at random, he commenced walking once again.

Then, in the distance, he discerned a spark, a glow, a wavering light. It vanished and reappeared periodically, as though partly blocked, the line of sight a function of his movements. He headed toward it. After perhaps half a minute, it was gone again from sight, but he continued on in what he thought to be its direction. There came another roll of thunder, louder this time.

When it seemed that it might have been illusion or some short-lived natural phenomenon, something else occurred in that same direction. There was a movement, a shadow-within-shadow shuffling at the foot of a great tree. He slowed his pace, approaching the spot cautiously.

There!

A figure detached itself from a pool of darkness ahead and to the left. Manlike, it moved with a slow and heavy tread, creaking sounds emerging from the forest floor beneath it. A vagrant moonbeam touched it for a moment, and it appeared yellow and metallically slick beneath moisture.

He halted. It seemed that he had just regarded a knight in full armor in his path. How long since he had beheld such a sight? He shook his head and stared.

The figure had also halted. It raised its right arm in a beckoning gesture, then turned and began to walk away. He hesitated for only a moment, then followed.

It turned off to the left and pursued a treacherous path, rocky, slippery, heading slightly downward. He actually used his stick now, to assure his footing, as he tracked its deliberate progress. He gained on it, to the point where he could clearly hear the metallic scraping sounds of its passage.

Then it was gone, swallowed by a greater darkness.

He advanced to the place where he had last beheld it. He stood in the lee of a great mass of stone. He reached out and probed it with his stick.

He tapped steadily along its nearest surface, and then the stick moved past it. He followed.

There was an opening, a crevice. He had to turn sidewise to pass within it, but as he did, the full glow of the light he had seen came into sight for several seconds.

The passage curved and widened, leading him back and down. Several times, he paused and listened, but there were no sounds other than his own breathing.

He withdrew his handkerchief and dried his face and hands carefully. He brushed moisture from his coat, turned down his collar. He scuffed the mud and leaves from his boots. He adjusted his apparel. Then he strode forward, rounding a final corner, into a chamber lit by a small oil lamp suspended by three delicate chains from some point in the darkness overhead. The yellow knight stood unmoving beside the far wall. On a fiber mat atop a stony pedestal directly beneath the lamp lay an old man in tattered garments. His bearded face was half-masked by shadows.

He moved to the old man's side. He saw then that those ancient dark eyes were open.

"Merlin . . . ?" he whispered.

There came a faint hissing-sound, a soft croak. Realizing the source, he leaned nearer.

"Elixir . . . in earthen rock . . . on ledge . . . in back," came the gravelly whisper.

He turned and sought the ledge, the container.

"Do you know where it is?" he asked the yellow figure.

It neither stirred nor replied, but stood like a display piece. He turned away from it then and sought further. After a time, he located it. It was more a niche than a ledge, blending in with the wall, cloaked with shadow. He ran his fingertips over the container's contours, raised it gently. Something liquid stirred within it. He wiped its lip on his sleeve after he had returned to the lighted area. The wind whistled past the entranceway and he thought he felt the faint vibration of thunder.

Sliding one hand beneath his shoulders, he raised the ancient form. Merlin's eyes still seemed unfocused. He moistened Merlin's lips with the liquid. The old man licked them, and after several moments opened his mouth. He administered a sip, then another, and another . . .

Merlin signalled for him to lower him, and he did. He glanced again at the yellow armor, but it had remained motionless the entire while. He looked back at the sorcerer and saw that a new light had come into his eyes and he was studying him, smiling faintly.

"Feel better?"

Merlin nodded. A minute passed, and a touch of color appeared upon his cheeks. He elbowed himself into a sitting position and took the container into his hands. He raised it and drank deeply.

He sat still for several minutes after that. His thin hands, which had appeared waxy in the flamelight, grew darker, fuller. His shoulders straightened. He placed the crock on the bed beside him and stretched his arms. His joints creaked the first time he did it, but not the second. He swung his legs over the ledge of the bed and rose slowly to his feet. He was a full head shorter than Launcelot.

"It is done," he said, staring back into the shadows. "Much has happened, of course . . ."

"Much has happened," Launcelot replied.

"You have lived through it all. Tell me, is the world a better place or is it worse than it was in those days?"

"Better in some ways, worse in others. It is different."

"How is it better?"

"There are many ways of making life easier, and the sum total of human knowledge has increased vastly."

"How has it worsened?"

"There are many more people in the world. Consequently, there are many more people suffering from poverty, disease, ignorance. The world itself has suffered great depredation, in the way of pollution and other assaults on the integrity of nature."

"Wars?"

"There is always someone fighting, somewhere."

"They need help."

"Maybe. Maybe not."

Merlin turned and looked into his eyes.

"What do you mean?"

"People haven't changed. They are as rational—and irrational—as they were in the old days. They are as moral and law-abiding—and not—as ever. Many new things have been learned, many new situations evolved, but I do not believe that the nature of man has altered significantly in the time you've slept. Nothing you do is going to change that. You may be able to alter a few features of the times, but would it really be proper to meddle? Everything is so interdependent today that even you would not be able to predict all the consequences of any actions you take. You might do more harm than good; and whatever you do, man's nature will remain the same.''

"This isn't like you, Lance. You were never much given to philosophizing in the old days."

"I've had a long time to think about it."

"And I've had a long time to dream about it. War is your craft, Lance. Stay with that."

"I gave it up a long time ago."

"Then what are you now?"

"An appraiser."

Merlin turned away, took another drink. He seemed to radiate a fierce energy when he turned again.

"And your oath? To right wrongs, to punish the wicked . . . ?"

"The longer I lived, the more difficult it became to determine what was a wrong and who was wicked. Make it clear to me again and I may go back into business."

"Galahad would never have addressed me so."

"Galahad was young, naive, trusting. Speak not to me of my son."

"Launcelot! Launcelot!" He placed a hand on his arm. "Why all this bitterness for an old friend who has done nothing for a thousand years?"

"I wished to make my position clear immediately. I feared you might contemplate some irreversible action which could alter the world balance of power fatally. I want you to know that I will not be party to it."

"Admit that you do not know what I might do, what I can do."

"Freely. That is why I fear you. What *do* you intend to do?"

"Nothing, at first. I wish merely to look about me, to see for myself some of these changes of which you have spoken. Then I will consider which wrongs need righting, who needs punishment, and who to choose as my champions. I will show you these things, and then you can go back into business, as you say."

Launcelot sighed.

"The burden of proof is on the moralist. Your judgment is no longer sufficient for me."

"Dear me," the other replied, "it is sad to have waited this long for an encounter of this sort, to find you have lost your faith in me. My powers are beginning to return already, Lance. Do you not feel magic in the air?"

"I feel something I have not felt in a long while."

"The sleep of ages was a restorative—an aid, actually. In a while, Lance, I am going to be stronger than I ever was before. And you doubt that I will be able to turn back the clock?"

"I doubt you can do it in a fashion to benefit anybody. Look, Merlin, I'm sorry. I do not like it that things have come to this either. But I have lived too long, seen too much, know too much of how the world works now to trust any one man's opinion concerning its salvation. Let it go. You are a mysterious, revered legend. I do not know what you really are. But forgo exercising your powers in any sort of crusade. Do something else this time around. Become a physician and fight pain. Take up painting. Be a professor of history, an antiquarian. Hell, be a social critic and point out what evils you see for people to correct themselves."

"Do you really believe I could be satisfied with any of those things?"

"Men find satisfaction in many things. It depends on the man, not on the things. I'm just saying that you should avoid using your powers in any attempt to effect social changes as we once did, by violence."

"Whatever changes have been wrought, time's greatest irony lies in its having transformed you into a pacifist."

"You are wrong."

"Admit it! You have finally come to fear the clash of arms! An appraiser! What kind of knight are you!"

"One who finds himself in the wrong time and the wrong place, Merlin."

The sorcerer shrugged and turned away.

"Let it be, then. It is good that you have chosen to tell me all these things immediately. Thank you for that, anyway. A moment."

Merlin walked to the rear of the cave, returned in moments attired in fresh garments. The effect was startling. His entire appearance was more kempt and cleanly. His hair and beard now appeared gray rather than white. His step was sure and steady. He held a staff in his right hand but did not lean upon it.

"Come walk with me," he said.

"It is a bad night."

"It is not the same night you left without. It is not even the same place."

As he passed the suit of yellow armor, he snapped his fingers near its visor. With a single creak, the figure moved and turned to follow him.

"Who is that?"

Merlin smiled.

"No one," he replied, and he reached back and raised the visor. The helmet was empty. "It is enchanted, animated by a spirit," he said. "A trifle clumsy, though, which is why I did not trust it to administer my draft. A perfect servant, however, unlike some. Incredibly strong and swift. Even in your prime you could not have beaten it. I fear nothing when it walks with me. Come, there is something I would have you see."

"Very well."

Launcelot followed Merlin and the hollow knight from the cave. The rain had stopped, and it was very still. They stood on an incredibly moonlit plain where mists drifted and grasses sparkled. Shadowy shapes stood in the distance.

"Excuse me," Launcelot said. "I left my walking stick inside."

He turned and reentered the cave.

"Yes, fetch it, old man," Merlin replied. "Your strength is already on the wane."

When Launcelot returned, he leaned upon the stick and squinted across the plain.

"This way," Merlin said, "to where your questions will be answered. I will try not to move too quickly and tire you."

"Tire me?"

The sorcerer chuckled and began walking across the plain. Launcelot followed.

"Do you not feel a trifle weary?" he asked.

"Yes, as a matter of fact, I do. Do you know what is the matter with me?"

"Of course. I have withdrawn the enchantment which has protected you all these years. What you feel now are the first tentative touches of your true age. It will take some time to catch up with you, against your body's natural resistance, but it is beginning its advance."

"Why are you doing this to me?"

"Because I believed you when you said you were not a pacifist. And you spoke with sufficient vehemence for me to realize that you might even oppose me. I could not permit that, for I knew that your old strength was still there for you to call upon. Even a sorcerer might fear that, so I did what had to be done. By my power was it maintained; without it, it now drains away. It would have been good for us to work together once again, but I saw that that could not be."

Launcelot stumbled, caught himself, limped on. The hollow knight walked at Merlin's right hand.

"You say that your ends are noble," Launcelot said, "but I do not believe you. Perhaps in the old days they were. But more than the times have changed. You are different. Do you not feel it yourself?"

Merlin drew a deep breath and exhaled vapor.

"Perhaps it is my heritage," he said. Then, "I jest. Of course I have changed. Everyone does. You yourself are a perfect example. What you consider a turn for the worse in me is but the tip of an irreducible conflict which has grown up between us in the course of our changes. I still hold with the true ideals of Camelot."

Launcelot's shoulders were bent forward now and his breathing had deepened. The shapes loomed larger before them.

"Why, I know this place," he gasped. "Yet I do not know it. Stone-

henge does not stand so today. Even in Arthur's time it lacked this per-
fection. How did we get here? What has happened?''

He paused to rest, and Merlin halted to accommodate him.

"This night we have walked between the worlds," the sorcerer said.
"This is a piece of the land of Faërie and that is the true Stonehenge, a
holy place. I have stretched the bounds of the worlds to bring it here.
Were I unkind I could send you back with it and strand you there forever.
But it is better that you know a sort of peace. Come!''

Launcelot staggered along behind him, heading for the great circle of
stones. The faintest of breezes came out of the west, stirring the mists.

"What do you mean—know a sort of peace?''

"The complete restoration of my powers and their increase will require a sacrifice in this place.''

"Then you planned this for me all along!''

"No. It was not to have been you, Lance. Anyone would have served,
though you will serve superbly well. It need not have been so, had you
elected to assist me. You could still change your mind.''

"Would you want someone who did that at your side?''

"You have a point there.''

"Then why ask—save as a petty cruelty?''

"It is just that, for you have annoyed me.''

Launcelot halted again, when they came to the circle's periphery. He
regarded the massive stands of stone.

"If you will not enter willingly,'' Merlin stated, "my servant will be
happy to assist you.''

Launcelot spat, straightened a little and glared.

"Think you I fear an empty suit of armor, juggled by some hell-born
wight? Even now, Merlin, without the benefit of wizardly succor, I could
take that thing apart.''

The sorcerer laughed.

"It is good that you at least recall the boasts of knighthood when all
else has left you. I've half a mind to give you the opportunity, for the
manner of your passing here is not important. Only the preliminaries are
essential.''

"But you're afraid to risk your servant?''

"Think you so, old man? I doubt you could even bear the weight of a
suit of armor, let alone lift a lance. But if you are willing to try, so be
it!''

He rapped the butt of his staff three times upon the ground.

"Enter," he said then. "You will find all that you need within. And
I am glad you have made this choice. You were insufferable, you know.
Just once, I longed to see you beaten, knocked down to the level of
lesser mortals. I only wish the Queen could be here, to witness her
champion's final engagement.''

"So do I," said Launcelot, and he walked past the monolith and entered the circle.

A black stallion waited, its reins held down beneath a rock. Pieces of armor, a lance, a blade and a shield leaned against the side of the dolmen. Across the circle's diameter, a white stallion awaited the advance of the hollow knight.

"I am sorry I could not arrange for a page or a squire to assist you," Merlin, said, coming around the other side of the monolith. "I'll be glad to help you myself, though."

"I can manage," Launcelot replied.

"My champion is accoutered in exactly the same fashion," Merlin said, "and I have not given him any edge over you in weapons."

"I never liked your puns either."

Launcelot made friends with the horse, then removed a small strand of red from his wallet and tied it about the butt of the lance. He leaned his stick against the dolmen stone and began to don the armor. Merlin, whose hair and beard were now almost black, moved off several paces and began drawing a diagram in the dirt with the end of his staff.

"You used to favor a white charger," he commented, "but I thought it appropriate to equip you with one of another color, since you have abandoned the ideals of the Table Round, betraying the memory of Camelot."

"On the contrary," Launcelot replied, glancing overhead at the passage of a sudden roll of thunder. "Any horse in a storm, and I am Camelot's last defender."

Merlin continued to elaborate upon the pattern he was drawing as Launcelot slowly equipped himself. The small wind continued to blow, stirring the mist. There came a flash of lightning, startling the horse. Launcelot calmed it.

Merlin stared at him for a moment and rubbed his eyes. Launcelot donned his helmet.

"For a moment," Merlin said, "you looked somehow different . . ."

"Really? Magical withdrawal, do you think?" he asked, and he kicked the stone from the reins and mounted the stallion.

Merlin stepped back from the now-completed diagram, shaking his head, as the mounted man leaned over and grasped the lance.

"You still seem to move with some strength," he said.

"Really?"

Launcelot raised the lance and couched it. Before taking up the shield he had hung at the saddle's side, he opened his visor and turned and regarded Merlin.

"Your champion appears to be ready," he said. "So am I."

Seen in another flash of light, it was an unlined face that looked down at Merlin, clear-eyed, wisps of pale gold hair fringing the forehead.

"What magic have the years taught you?" Merlin asked.

"Not magic," Launcelot replied. "Caution. I anticipated you. So, when I returned to the cave for my stick, I drank the rest of your elixir."

He lowered the visor and turned away.

"You walked like an old man . . ."

"I'd a lot of practice. Signal your champion!"

Merlin laughed.

"Good! It is better this way," he decided, "to see you go down in full strength! You still cannot hope to win against a spirit!"

Launcelot raised the shield and leaned forward.

"Then what are you waiting for?"

"Nothing!" Merlin said. Then he shouted, "Kill him, Raxas!"

A light rain began as they pounded across the field; and staring ahead, Launcelot realized that flames were flickering behind his opponent's visor. At the last possible moment, he shifted the point of his lance into line with the hollow knight's blazing helm. There came more lightning and thunder.

His shield deflected the other's lance while his went on to strike the approaching head. It flew from the hollow knight's shoulders and bounced, smouldering, on the ground.

He continued on to the other end of the field and turned. When he had, he saw that the hollow knight, now headless, was doing the same. And beyond him, he saw two standing figures, where moments before there had been but one.

Morgan Le Fay, clad in a white robe, red hair unbound and blowing in the wind, faced Merlin from across his pattern. It seemed they were speaking, but he could not hear the words. Then she began to raise her hands, and they glowed like cold fire. Merlin's staff was also gleaming, and he shifted it before him. Then he saw no more, for the hollow knight was ready for the second charge.

He couched his lance, raised the shield, leaned forward and gave his mount the signal. His arm felt like a bar of iron, his strength like an endless current of electricity as he raced down the field. The rain was falling more heavily now and the lightning began a constant flickering. A steady rolling of thunder smothered the sound of the hoofbeats, and the wind whistled past his helm as he approached the other warrior, his lance centered on his shield.

They came together with an enormous crash. Both knights reeled and the hollow one fell, his shield and breastplate pierced by a broken lance. His left arm came away as he struck the earth; the lance-point snapped and the shield fell beside him. But he began to rise almost immediately, his right hand drawing his long sword.

Launcelot dismounted, discarding his shield, drawing his own great blade. He moved to meet his headless foe. The other struck first and he parried it, a mighty shock running down his arms. He swung a blow of his own. It was parried.

They swaggered swords across the field, till finally Launcelot saw his opening and landed his heaviest blow. The hollow knight toppled into the mud, his breastplate cloven almost to the point where the spear's shaft protruded. At that moment, Morgan Le Fay screamed.

Launcelot turned and saw that she had fallen across the pattern Merlin had drawn. The sorcerer, now bathed in a bluish light, raised his staff and moved forward. Launcelot took a step toward them and felt a great pain in his left side.

Even as he turned toward the half-risen hollow knight who was drawing his blade back for another blow, Launcelot reversed his double-handed grip upon his own weapon and raised it high, point downward.

He hurled himself upon the other, and his blade pierced the cuirass entirely as he bore him back down, nailing him to the earth. A shriek arose from beneath him, echoing within the armor, and a gout of fire emerged from the neck hole, sped upward and away, dwindled in the rain, flickered out moments later.

Launcelot pushed himself into a kneeling position. Slowly then, he rose to his feet and turned toward the two figures who again faced one another. Both were now standing within the muddied geometries of power, both were now bathed in the bluish light. Launcelot took a step toward them, then another.

"Merlin!" he called out, continuing to advance upon them. "I've done what I said I would! Now I'm coming to kill you!"

Morgan Le Fay turned toward him, eyes wide.

"No!" she cried. "Depart the circle! Hurry! I am holding him here! His power wanes! In moments, this place will be no more. Go!"

Launcelot hesitated but a moment, then turned and walked as rapidly as he was able toward the circle's perimeter. The sky seemed to boil as he passed among the monoliths.

He advanced another dozen paces, then had to pause to rest. He looked back to the place of battle, to the place where the two figures still stood locked in sorcerous embrace. Then the scene was imprinted upon his brain as the skies opened and a sheet of fire fell upon the far end of the circle.

Dazzled, he raised his hand to shield his eyes. When he lowered it, he saw the stones falling, soundless, many of them fading from sight. The rain began to slow immediately. Sorcerer and sorceress had vanished along with much of the structure of the still-fading place. The horses were nowhere to be seen. He looked about him and saw a good-sized stone. He headed for it and seated himself. He unfastened his breastplate and removed it, dropping it to the ground. His side throbbed and he held it tightly. He doubled forward and rested his face on his left hand.

The rains continued to slow and finally ceased. The wind died. The mists returned.

He breathed deeply and thought back upon the conflict. This, this was the thing for which he had remained after all the others, the thing for which he had waited, for so long. It was over now, and he could rest.

There was a gap in his consciousness. He was brought to awareness again by a light. A steady glow passed between his fingers, pierced his eyelids. He dropped his hand and raised his head, opening his eyes.

It passed slowly before him in a halo of white light. He removed his sticky fingers from his side and rose to his feet to follow it. Solid, glowing, glorious and pure, not at all like the image in the chamber, it led him on out across the moonlit plain, from dimness to brightness to dimness, until the mists enfolded him as he reached at last to embrace it.

HERE ENDETH THE BOOK OF LAUNCELOT,
LAST OF THE NOBLE KNIGHTS OF THE
ROUND TABLE, AND HIS ADVENTURES
WITH RAXAS, THE HOLLOW KNIGHT,
AND MERLIN AND MORGAN LE FAY,
LAST OF THE WISE FOLK OF CAMELOT,
IN HIS QUEST FOR THE SANGREAL.

QUO FAS ET GLORIA DUCUNT.

A SAUCER OF LONELINESS
Theodore Sturgeon

Teleplay by David Gerrold

Aired September 27, 1986

Starring Shelley Duvall, Richard Libertini, Nan Martin

IF SHE'S DEAD, I THOUGHT, I'LL NEVER FIND HER IN THIS
white flood of moonlight on the white sea, with the surf seething in and
over the pale, pale sand like a great shampoo. Almost always, suicides
who stab themselves or shoot themselves in the heart carefully bare their
chests; the same strange impulse generally makes the sea-suicide go naked.

A little earlier, I thought, or later, and there would be shadows for the
dunes and the breathing toss of the foam. Now the only real shadow was
mine, a tiny thing just under me, but black enough to feed the blackness
of the shadow of a blimp.

A little earlier, I thought, and I might have seen her plodding up the
silver shore, seeking a place lonely enough to die in. A little later and
my legs would rebel against this shuffling trot through sand, the mad-
dening sand that could not hold and would not help a hurrying man.

My legs did give way then and I knelt suddenly, sobbing—not for her;
not yet—just for air. There was such a rush about me: wind, and tangled
spray, and colors upon colors and shades of colors that were not colors
at all but shifts of white and silver. If light like that were sound, it would
sound like the sea on sand, and if my ears were eyes, they would see
such a light.

I crouched there, gasping in the swirl of it, and a flood struck me,
shallow and swift, turning up and outward like flower petals where it
touched my knees, then soaking me to the waist in its bubble and crash.
I pressed my knuckles to my eyes so they would open again. The sea
was on my lips with the taste of tears and the whole white night shouted
and wept aloud.

And there she was.

Her white shoulders were a taller curve in the sloping foam. She must
have sensed me—perhaps I yelled—for she turned and saw me kneeling
there. She put her fists to her temples and her face twisted, and she
uttered a piercing wail of despair and fury, and then plunged seaward
and sank.

I kicked off my shoes and ran into the breakers, shouting, hunting,
grasping at flashes of white that turned to sea-salt and coldness in my
fingers. I plunged right past her, and her body struck my side as a wave
whipped my face and tumbled both of us. I gasped in solid water, opened
my eyes beneath the surface and saw a greenish-white distorted moon

hurtle as I spun. Then there was sucking sand under my feet again and my left hand was tangled in her hair.

The receding wave towed her away and for a moment she streamed out from my hand like steam from a whistle. In that moment I was sure she was dead, but as she settled to the sand, she fought and scrambled to her feet.

She hit my ear, wet, hard, and a huge, pointed pain lanced into my head. She pulled, she lunged away from me, and all the while my hand was caught in her hair. I couldn't have freed her if I had wanted to. She spun to me with the next wave, battered and clawed at me, and we went into deeper water.

"Don't . . . don't . . . I can't swim!" I shouted, so she clawed me again.

"Leave me alone," she shrieked. "Oh, dear God, why can't you *leave*" (said her fingernails) "me . . ." (said her snapping teeth) *"alone!"* (said her small, hard fist).

So by her hair I pulled her head down tight to her white shoulder; and with the edge of my free hand I hit her neck twice. She floated again, and I brought her ashore.

I carried her to where a dune was between us and the sea's broad, noisy tongue, and the wind was above us somewhere. But the light was as bright. I rubbed her wrists and stroked her face and said, "It's all right," and, "There!" and some names I used to have for a dream I had long, long before I ever heard of her.

She lay still on her back with the breath hissing between her teeth, with her lips in a smile which her twisted-tight, wrinkle-sealed eyes made not a smile but a torture. She was well and conscious for many moments and still her breath hissed and her closed eyes twisted.

"Why couldn't you leave me alone?" she asked at last. She opened her eyes and looked at me. She had so much misery that there was no room for fear. She shut her eyes again and said, "You know who I am."

"I know," I said.

She began to cry.

I waited, and when she stopped crying, there were shadows among the dunes. A long time.

She said, "You don't know who I am. Nobody knows who I am."

I said, "It was in all the papers."

"That!" She opened her eyes slowly and her gaze traveled over my face, my shoulders, stopped at my mouth, touched my eyes for the briefest second. She curled her lips and turned away her head. "Nobody knows who I am."

I waited for her to move or speak, and finally I said, "Tell me."

"Who are you?" she asked, with her head still turned away.

"Someone who . . ."

"Well?"

"Not now," I said. "Later, maybe."

She sat up suddenly and tried to hide herself. "Where are my clothes?"

"I didn't see them."

"Oh," she said. "I remember. I put them down and kicked sand over them, just where a dune would come and smooth them over, hide them as if they never were . . . I hate sand. I wanted to drown in the sand, but it wouldn't let me . . . You mustn't look at me!" she shouted. "I hate to have you looking at me!" She threw her head from side to side, seeking. "I can't stay here like this! What can I do? Where can I go?"

"Here," I said.

She let me help her up and then snatched her hand away, half turned from me. "Don't touch me. Get away from me."

"Here," I said again, and walked down the dune where it curved in the moonlight, tipped back into the wind and down and became not dune but beach. "Here," I pointed behind the dune.

At last she followed me. She peered over the dune where it was chest-high, and again where it was knee-high. "Back there?"

I nodded.

"I didn't see them."

"So dark . . ." She stepped over the low dune and into the aching black of those moon-shadows. She moved away cautiously, feeling tenderly with her feet, back to where the dune was higher. She sank down into the blackness and disappeared there. I sat on the sand in the light. "Stay away from me," she spat.

I rose and stepped back. Invisible in the shadows, she breathed, "Don't go away." I waited, then saw her hand press out of the clean-cut shadows, "There," she said, "over there. In the dark. Just be a . . . Stay away from me now . . . Be a—voice."

I did as she asked, and sat in the shadows perhaps six feet from her.

She told me about it. Not the way it was in the papers.

She was perhaps seventeen when it happened. She was in Central Park, in New York. It was too warm for such an early spring day, and the hammered brown slopes had a dusting of green of precisely the consistency of that morning's hoarfrost on the rocks. But the frost was gone and the grass was brave and tempted some hundreds of pairs of feet from the asphalt and concrete to tread on it.

Hers were among them. The sprouting soil was a surprise to her feet, as the air was to her lungs. Her feet ceased to be shoes as she walked, her body was consciously more than clothes. It was the only kind of day which in itself can make a city-bred person raise his eyes. She did.

For a moment she felt separated from the life she lived, in which there was no fragrance, no silence, in which nothing ever quite fit nor was quite filled. In that moment the ordered disapproval of the buildings around the pallid park could not reach her; for two, three clean breaths it no longer mattered that the whole wide world really belonged to images projected on a screen; to gently groomed goddesses in these steel-and-glass towers; that it belonged, in short, always, always to someone else.

So she raised her eyes, and there above her was the saucer.

It was beautiful. It was golden, with a dusty finish like that of an unripe Concord grape. It made a faint sound, a chord composed of two tones and a blunted hiss like the wind in tall wheat. It was darting about like a swallow, soaring and dropping. It circled and dropped and hovered like a fish, shimmering. It was like all these living things, but with that beauty it had all the loveliness of things turned and burnished, measured, machined, and metrical.

At first she felt no astonishment, for this was so different from anything she had ever seen before that it had to be a trick of the eye, a false evaluation of size and speed and distance that in a moment would resolve itself into a sun-flash on an airplane or the lingering glare of a welding arc.

She looked away from it and abruptly realized that many other people saw it—saw *something*—too. People all around her had stopped moving and speaking and were craning upward. Around her was a globe of silent astonishment, and outside it, she was aware of the life-noise of the city, the hard-breathing giant who never inhales.

She looked up again, and at last began to realize how large and how far away the saucer was. No: rather, how small and how very near it was. It was just the size of the largest circle she might make with her two hands, and it floated not quite eighteen inches over her head.

Fear came then. She drew back and raised a forearm, but the saucer simply hung there. She bent far sideways, twisted away, leaped forward, looked back and upward to see if she had escaped it. At first she couldn't see it; then as she looked up and up, there it was, close and gleaming, quivering and crooning, right over her head.

She bit her tongue.

From the corner of her eye, she saw a man cross himself. *He did that because he saw me standing here with a halo over my head,* she thought. And that was the greatest single thing that had ever happened to her. No one had ever looked at her and made a respectful gesture before, not once, not ever. Through terror, through panic and wonderment, the comfort of that thought nestled into her, to wait to be taken out and looked at again in lonely times.

The terror was uppermost now, however. She backed away, staring upward, stepping a ludicrous cakewalk. She should have collided with people. There were plenty of people there, gaping and craning, but she reached none. She spun around and discovered to her horror that she was the center of a pointing, pressing crowd. Its mosaic of eyes all bulged, and its inner circle braced its many legs to press back and away from her.

The saucer's gentle note deepened. It tilted, dropped an inch or so.

Someone screamed, and the crowd broke away from her in all directions, milled about, and settled again in a new dynamic balance, a much larger ring, as more and more people raced to thicken it against the efforts of the inner circle to escape.

The saucer hummed and tilted, tilted . . .

She opened her mouth to scream, fell to her knees, and the saucer struck.

It dropped against her forehead and clung there. It seemed almost to lift her. She came erect on her knees, made one effort to raise her hands against it, and then her arms stiffened down and back, her hands not reaching the ground. For perhaps a second and a half the saucer held her rigid, and then it passed a single ecstatic quiver to her body and dropped it. She plumped to the ground, the backs of her thighs heavy and painful on her heels and ankles.

The saucer dropped beside her, rolled once in a small circle, once just around its edge, and lay still. It lay still and dull and metallic, different and dead.

Hazily, she lay and gazed at the gray-shrouded blue of the good spring sky, and hazily she heard whistles.

And some tardy screams.

And a great stupid voice bellowing, "Give her air!" which made everyone press closer.

Then there wasn't so much sky because of the blue-clad bulk with its metal buttons and its leatherette notebook. "Okay, okay, what's happened here stand back figods sake."

And the widening ripples of observation, interpretation and comment: "It knocked her down." "Some guy knocked her down." "He knocked her down." "Some guy knocked her down and—" "Right in broad daylight this guy . . ." "The park's gettin' to be . . ." onward and outward, the adulteration of fact until it was lost altogether because excitement is so much more important.

Somebody with a harder shoulder than the rest bulling close, a notebook here, too, a witnessing eye over it, ready to change ". . . a beautiful brunet . . ." to "an attractive brunet" for the afternoon editions, because "attractive" is as dowdy as any woman is allowed to get if she is a victim in the news.

The glittering shield and the florid face bending close: "You hurt bad, sister?" And the echoes, back and back through the crowd, "Hurt bad, hurt bad, badly injured, he beat the hell out of her, broad daylight . . ."

And still another man, slim and purposeful, tan gabardine, cleft chin and beard-shadow: "Flyin' saucer, hm? Okay, Officer, I'll take over here.

"And who the hell might you be, takin' over?"

The flash of a brown leather wallet, a face so close behind that its chin was pressed into the gabardine shoulder. The face said, awed: "FBI"

and that rippled outward, too. The policeman nodded—the entire policeman nodded in one single bobbing genuflection.

"Get some help and clear this area," said the gabardine.

"Yes, *sir!*" said the policeman.

"FBI, FBI," the crowd murmured, and there was more sky to look
at above her.

She sat up and there was a glory in her face. "The saucer talked to
me," she sang.

"You shut up," said the gabardine. "You'll have lots of chance to
talk later."

"Yeah, sister," said the policeman. "My God, this mob could be full
of Communists."

"You shut up, too," said the gabardine.

Someone in the crowd told someone else a Communist beat up this
girl, while someone else was saying she got beat up because she was a
Communist.

She started to rise, but solicitous hands forced her down again. There
were thirty police there by that time.

"I can walk," she said.

"Now, you just take it easy," they told her.

They put a stretcher down beside her and lifted her onto it and covered
her with a big blanket.

"I can walk," she said as they carried her through the crowd.

A woman went white and turned away moaning, "Oh, my God, how
awful!"

A small man with round eyes stared and stared at her and licked and
licked his lips.

The ambulance. They slid her in. The gabardine was already there.

A white-coated man with very clean hands: "How did it happen,
miss?"

"No questions," said the gabardine. "Security."

The hospital.

She said, "I got to get back to work."

"Take your clothes off," they told her.

She had a bedroom to herself then for the first time in her life. Whenever the door opened, she could see a policeman outside. It opened very
often to admit the kind of civilians who were very polite to military
people, and the kind of military people who were even more polite to
certain civilians. She did not know what they all did nor what they
wanted. Every single day they asked her four million five hundred thousand questions. Apparently they never talked to each other, because each
of them asked her the same questions over and over.

"What is your name?"

"How old are you?"

"What year were you born?"

"What is your name?"

Sometimes they would push her down strange paths with their questions.

"Now, your uncle. Married a woman from Middle Europe, did he? Where in Middle Europe?"

"What clubs or fraternal organizations did you belong to? Ah! Now, about that Rinkeydinks gang on Sixty-third Street. Who was *really* behind it?"

But over and over again, "What did you mean when you said the saucer talked to you?"

And she would say, "It talked to me."

And they would say, "And it said—"

And she would shake her head.

There would be a lot of shouting ones, and then a lot of kind ones. No one had ever been so kind to her before, but she soon learned that no one was being kind to *her*. They were just getting her to relax, to think of other things, so they could suddenly shoot that question at her. "What do you mean it talked to you?"

Pretty soon it was just like Mom's or school or anyplace, and she used to sit with her mouth closed and let them yell. Once they sat her on a hard chair for hours and hours with a light in her eyes and let her get thirsty. Home, there was a transom over the bedroom door and Mom used to leave the kitchen light glaring through it all night, every night, so she wouldn't get the horrors. So the light didn't bother her at all.

They took her out of the hospital and put her in jail. Some ways it was good. The food. The bed was all right, too. Through the window she could see lots of women exercising in the yard. It was explained to her that they all had much harder beds.

"You are a very important young lady, you know."

That was nice at first, but as usual, it turned out they didn't mean her at all. They kept working on her. Once they brought the saucer in to her. It was inside a big wooden crate with a padlock, and a steel box inside that with a Yale lock. It only weighed a couple of pounds, the saucer, but by the time they got it packed, it took two men to carry it and four men with guns to watch them.

They made her act out the whole thing just the way it happened, with some soldiers holding the saucer over her head. It wasn't the same. They'd cut a lot of chips and pieces out of the saucer, and, besides, it was that dead gray color. They asked her if she knew anything about that, and for once, she told them.

"It's empty now," she said.

The only one she would ever talk to was a little man with a fat belly who said to her the first time he was alone with her, "Listen, I think the way they've been treating you stinks. Now, get this: I have a job to do. My job is to find out *why* you won't tell what the saucer said. I don't

want to know what it said and I'll never ask you. I don't even want you
to tell me. Let's just find out why you're keeping it a secret.''

Finding out why turned out to be hours of just talking about having
pneumonia and the flower pot she made in second grade that Mom threw
down the fire escape and getting left back in school and the dream about
holding a wineglass in both hands and peeping over it at some man.

And one day she told him why she wouldn't say about the saucer, just
the way it came to her: "Because it was talking to *me,* and it's just
nobody else's business.''

She even told him about the man crossing himself that day. It was the
only other thing she had of her own.

He was nice. He was the one who warned her about the trial. "I have
no business saying this, but they're going to give you the full dress treatment. Judge and jury and all. You just say what you want to say, no less
and no more, hear? And don't let 'em get your goat. You have a right to
own something.''

He got up and swore and left.

First a man came and talked to her for a long time about how maybe
this Earth would be attacked from outer space by beings much stronger
and cleverer than we are, and maybe she had the key to a defense. So
she owed it to the whole world. And then even if Earth wasn't attacked,
just think of what an advantage she might give this country over its
enemies. Then he shook his finger in her face and said that what she was
doing amounted to working *for* the enemies of her country. And he turned
out to be the man that was defending her at the trial.

The jury found her guilty of contempt of court, and the judge recited
a long list of penalties he could give her. He gave her one of them and
suspended it. They put her back in jail for a few more days, and one fine
day they turned her loose.

That was wonderful at first. She got a job in a restaurant, and a furnished room. She had been in the papers so much that Mom didn't want
her back home. Mom was drunk most of the time and sometimes used
to tear up the whole neighborhood, but all the same she had very special
ideas about being respectable, and being in the papers all the time for
spying was not her idea of being decent. So she put her maiden name
on the mailbox downstairs and told her daughter not to live there anymore.

At the restaurant she met a man who asked her for a date. The first
time. She spent every cent she had on a red handbag to go with her red
shoes. They weren't the same shade, but anyway, they were both red.
They went to the movies, and afterward he didn't try to kiss her or
anything, he just tried to find out what the flying saucer told her. She
didn't say anything. She went home and cried all night.

Then some men sat in a booth talking and they shut up and glared at
her every time she came past. They spoke to the boss, and he came and

told her that they were electronics engineers working for the government and they were afraid to talk shop while she was around—wasn't she some sort of spy or something? So she got fired.

Once she saw her name on a jukebox. She put in a nickel and punched that number, and the record was all about "the flyin' saucer came down one day, and taught her a brand-new way to play, and what it was I will not say, but she took me out of this world." And while she was listening to it, someone in the juke joint recognized her and called her by name. Four of them followed her home and she had to block the door shut.

Sometimes she'd be all right for months on end, and then someone would ask for a date. Three times out of five, she and the date were followed. Once the man she was with arrested the man who was tailing them. Twice the man who was tailing them arrested the man she was with. Five times out of five, the date would try to find out about the saucer. Sometimes she would go out with someone and pretend that it was a real date, but she wasn't very good at it.

So she moved to the shore and got a job cleaning at night in offices and stores. There weren't many to clean, but that just meant there weren't many people to remember her face from the papers. Like clockwork, every eighteen months, some feature writer would drag it all out again in a magazine or a Sunday supplement; and every time anyone saw a headlight on a mountain or a light on a weather balloon, it had to be a flying saucer, and there had to be some tired quip about the saucer wanting to tell secrets. Then for two or three weeks she'd stay off the streets in the daytime.

Once she thought she had it whipped. People didn't want her, so she began reading. The novels were all right for a while until she found out that most of them were like the movies—all about the pretty ones who really own the world. So she learned things—animals, trees. A lousy little chipmunk caught in a wire fence bit her. The animals didn't want her. The trees didn't care.

Then she hit on the idea of the bottles. She got all the bottles she could and wrote on papers which she corked into the bottles. She'd tramp miles up and down the beaches and throw the bottles out as far as she could. She knew that if the right person found one, it would give that person the only thing in the world that would help. Those bottles kept her going for three solid years. Everyone's got to have a secret little something he does.

And at last the time came when it was no use anymore. You can go on trying to help someone who *maybe* exists; but soon you can't pretend there's such a person anymore. And that's it. The end.

"Are you cold?" I asked when she was through telling me.

The surf was quieter and the shadows longer.

"No," she answered from the shadows. Suddenly she said, "Did you think I was mad at you because you saw me without my clothes?"

"Why shouldn't you be?"

"You know, I don't care? I wouldn't have wanted . . . wanted you to see me even in a ball gown or overalls. You can't cover up my carcass. It shows; it's there whatever. I just didn't want you to see me. At all."

"Me, or anyone?"

She hesitated. "You."

I got up and stretched and walked a little, thinking. "Didn't the FBI try to stop you throwing those bottles?"

"Oh, sure. They spent I don't know how much taxpayers' money gathering 'em up. They still make a spot check every once in a while. They're getting tired of it, though. All the writing in the bottles is the same." She laughed. I didn't know she could.

"What's funny?"

"All of 'em—judges, jailers, jukeboxes—people. Do you know it wouldn't have saved me a minute's trouble if I'd told 'em the whole thing at the very beginning?"

"No?"

"No. They wouldn't have believed me. What they wanted was a new weapon. Super-science from a super-race, to slap hell out of the super-race if they ever got a chance, or out of our own if they don't. All those brains," she breathed, with more wonder than scorn, "all that brass. They think 'super-race' and it comes out 'super-science.' Don't they ever imagine a super-race has super-feelings, too—super-laughter, maybe, or super-hunger?" She paused. "Isn't it time you asked me what the saucer said?"

"I'll tell you," I blurted.

> *"There is in certain living souls*
> *A quality of loneliness unspeakable,*
> *So great it must be shared*
> *As company is shared by lesser beings.*
> *Such a loneliness is mine; so know by this*
> *That in immensity*
> *There is one lonelier than you."*

"Dear Jesus," she said devoutly, and began to weep. "And how is it addressed?"

"To the loneliest one . . ."

"How did you know?" she whispered.

"It's what you put in the bottles, isn't it?"

"Yes," she said. "Whenever it gets to be too much, that no one cares, that no one ever did . . . you throw a bottle into the sea, and out goes a part of your own loneliness. You sit and think of someone somewhere finding it . . . learning for the first time that the worst there is can be understood."

The moon was setting and the surf was hushed. We looked up and out to the stars. She said, "We don't know what loneliness is like. People thought the saucer was a saucer, but it wasn't. It was a bottle with a message inside. It had a bigger ocean to cross—all of space—and not much chance of finding anybody. Loneliness? We don't know loneliness."

When I could, I asked her why she had tried to kill herself.

"I've had it good," she said, "with what the saucer told me. I wanted to . . . pay back. I was bad enough to be helped; I had to know I was good enough to help. No one wants me? Fine. But don't tell me no one, anywhere, wants my help. I can't stand that."

I took a deep breath. "I found one of your bottles two years ago. I've been looking for you ever since. Tide charts, current tables, maps and . . . wandering. I heard some talk about you and the bottles hereabouts. Someone told me you'd quit doing it, you'd taken to wandering the dunes at night. I knew why. I ran all the way.

I needed another breath now. "I got a club foot. I think right, but the words don't come out of my mouth the way they're inside my head. I have this nose. I never had a woman. Nobody ever wanted to hire me to work where they'd have to look at me. You're beautiful," I said. "You're beautiful."

She said nothing, but it was as if a light came from her, more light and far less shadow than ever the practiced moon could cast. Among the many things it meant was that even to loneliness there is an end, for those who are lonely enough, long enough.

LOST AND FOUND
Phyllis Eisenstein

TELEPLAY BY GEORGE R. R. MARTIN

AIRED OCTOBER 18, 1986

STARRING AKOUSA BUSIA, CINDY HARRELL, LESLIE ACKERMAN

IT STARTED ONE WINTER NIGHT WHEN I COULDN'T FIND the screwdriver.

I told my roommate Cath, "I'm sure I left it on top of the refrigerator. I used it to put the light fixture back together, and then I laid it on top of the fridge while I made a snack. That wasn't more than three hours ago, and now it's gone."

"The roaches borrowed it," said Cath, who was washing the week's accumulation of dirty dishes. "You always say they'll walk off with the place someday."

"Be serious."

"Poltergeists, then."

I poked her shoulder. "Did you take it?"

"I was in the living room reading Freud. Do I need a screwdriver for that?"

"Well, what happened to it, then?"

"Honest to God, Jenny, I don't know. It'll turn up. What thief would climb three flights of stairs just to steal a lousy screwdriver?"

I wondered about that. For several minutes I'd felt that someone was standing behind me, watching me. Not Cath; someone else, someone I couldn't see. The suggestion of a burglar struck too close to my own suspicions. I resisted the impulse to peek into the broom closet, but I did check the back door; it was securely locked.

I shook off my uneasiness and returned to my room, determined to study through the rest of the evening. I'd been loafing a lot lately; with exams a week away, I played solitaire at my desk rather than review my chemistry notes. It helped dispel the tension. I sat down and picked up the deck. After half a dozen poor rounds, I promised myself I'd play only one more, and I dealt it out with vicious slaps. When the game turned sour, I began cheating, but no matter what I did, I couldn't win. No wonder: pawing through the cards, I realized that the ace of spades and the ten of clubs were missing. I peered under the desk; there was the ten, but no ace. I checked the drawers, the bookcase, the floor beneath the bed, the dart board. Nowhere. I'd won a game earlier in the day—how could I have done that without the ace of spaces?

If Cath was playing a joke on me, I'd wring it out of her.

She must have heard me step into the living room, for she looked up from her book. "Jenny, you look terrible. What's the matter? You *can't* be studying too hard."

"Did you take a card from my desk?"

"Card? What kind of card?"

"A playing card."

"Today?"

"A little while ago."

"I haven't been in your room today."

"The ace of spades is gone."

Cath shut her book and shook her head. "That's terribly symbolic," she said. With her green pen, she added small horns to the portrait of Freud gracing the dust jacket. "I'd say you were getting absentminded, Jenny." She meditated a moment. "Knowing you, of course, you couldn't have used it as a bookmark."

I sat on the arm of the chair. "Cath," I said very seriously, "have you ever thought you might be a kleptomaniac?"

She looked me in the eye. "No, but I guess *you* have. Couldn't you use your time a little more constructively?"

Growling under my breath, I took the hint and stalked back to my room. I sat down at my desk, put my feet up, and let my eyes and mind roam. Something was odd about the bookshelf in front of me. My university mug was gone. My quartz paperweight was gone. My leather-bound copy of *Othello* was gone. I turned in my chair and looked at the rest of the room, wondering where I could have put the stuff. Was I sleepwalking? My tennis racket was missing from its peg above the bed; the stack of records on the floor had shrunk by half. I looked into the wastebasket, wondering if I had unconsciously thrown anything there, but it was empty. That wasn't right: hadn't I thrown away some old English papers this afternoon?

Where *was* everything?

Again, the creepy feeling of being secretly observed stole over me. Someone was staring at my back, perhaps waiting for me to leave so he could come in and get more. More what? None of my stuff was particularly valuable.

I heard a muffled shuffling noise behind me. I turned and looked at the closet door. I didn't have the nerve to open it.

I shouted, "Cath!"

Suddenly I felt naked and weaponless. What if it was a burglar? He was trapped in there, probably desperate, maybe armed. Even though there were two of us, it might be wiser to call the cops and let them handle it.

Cath came in. "What do you want?"

"The closet," I whispered.

"What?"

"I think there's someone inside."

We stood there a moment. I could feel my guts twisting. The last thing on earth I wanted to do was open that door. I wanted to run out of the room, out of the apartment, as fast as I could.

Cath shrugged, stepped forward, turned the doorknob, and yanked the closet door open.

My heart, and everything under it, suddenly pressed at the top of my throat.

There was nothing in the closet but clothing.

I had a mild case of jitters for the next couple of minutes. Cath clucked her tongue, then led me to the kitchen and poured me a cup of tea.

"Take it easy, Jenny," she said, forcing me into a chair by the table. "You can't crack up till after exams are over."

"I . . . I . . . thought . . . someone was in the closet." I gulped some tea; the cup clattered as I set it down in its saucer.

"We've been home all afternoon and evening. How could anyone have gotten in?"

I attempted a nonchalant shrug, but it turned into a shudder. "I don't know."

Cath pulled me into the living room after I finished my tea, and she handed me a paperback sex novel. "You sit in this nice soft chair and read something light, to relax. I'll sit over there and study."

I read, but I couldn't concentrate; I was too nervous to string the words and phrases together.

Then I heard something. A scuffling, rustling sound.

"Did you hear something?" I asked. "From my room?"

"Roaches," Cath said without looking up. "Or mice. Forget it."

I heard it again. "Cath!" I gasped hoarsely, springing across the room. She caught my arm as I passed her. "Maybe we'd better go to a movie."

Then there was another noise, louder this time.

"I hear something in your room," she said.

"Roaches," I whispered.

"Okay, let's see what it is. Wait here a minute." She went to the kitchen and returned with two long, sharp carving knives. She gave one to me.

"What do you think it is?" I murmured.

"Some nut trying to get in a third-floor window."

But when we stepped into my room, we saw that the window was closed and locked, as it had been for several months. Outside, silent snow fell vertically through the darkness; the thick white frosting it had slathered on the windowsill remained velvet-smooth, undisturbed. The closet door, however, was slightly ajar, although Cath had shut it firmly just a little while ago.

"There can't be anyone in the closet," Cath said. "There simply can't be." Still, she went to the closet and threw open the door.

Someone was in the closet, all right. Two someones, both young and muscular, one male, one female. They were fair-haired and evenly tanned, and they wore only scanty metallic briefs and weblike sandals. We stared; they stared back.

"Are you Jennifer Erica Templeton?" the man demanded of Cath.

"Not me," said Cath. "Her." The tip of her knife wavered in my direction.

"Jennifer Erica Templeton?" he asked me. "Born June 3, 1958, in Chicago, to Albert and Sara Templeton; student at the University of Chicago from 1977 to 1985, B.A., M.A., Ph.D. Anthropology?" He rattled off the data as if it were name, rank and serial number, and then he paused expectantly.

His friend nudged him. "I told you this was only '79, dear. She doesn't have any degrees yet, and her field is still chemistry."

I found myself nodding.

The man lunged, grabbing at my head. As I elbowed him in the solar plexus, I heard a snipping sound behind my right ear, and then he reeled away, clutching a handful of my hair. "Authentic souvenir!" he croaked.

"All right, all right," the woman said, hauling him back into the oddly deep space of the closet. "Now that you've got one, too, let's go home!" She slammed the door, and for several seconds a rummaging noise sounded beyond it. Then there was silence.

Cath stared at me, her mouth agape. She reached out and very slowly and gingerly pulled open the door. The strangers had vanished; once again, the closet was shallow and inhabited only by my clothes.

"Jenny," Cath whispered, "what's going on?"

I looked at her for a minute, and then I looked at the closet. I fingered my scalp where the spray of stubble interrupted the smooth flow of hair. "I'm not sure," I replied, "but tomorrow I think I'm going to transfer to the Anthropology Department."

INFLUENCING THE HELL OUT OF TIME AND TERESA GOLOWITZ

GOLOWITZ

Parke Godwin

TELEPLAY BY ALAN BRENNERT

AIRED JULY 10, 1987,

AS "TIME AND TERESA GOLOWITZ"

STARRING GENE BARRY, PAUL SAND, KRISTI LYNES,

GRANT HESLOV

THE FIRST CONSCIOUS SHOCK AFTER THE CORONARY WAS staring down at my own body huddled on the floor by the piano. The next was the fiftyish, harmless-looking total stranger helping himself to my liquor. His cordial smile matched the Brooks Brothers tailoring. An urbane Cecil Kellaway toasting me with my own scotch.

"Cheers, Mr. Bluestone. Hope you don't mind."

I found what passed for a voice. "The hell I don't. Who are you, and—and what's happened to me?"

For all the portly bulk of obvious good living, he moved lightly, settling in a Danish modern chair to sip at his purloined drink. "Glenmorangie single malt—one doesn't find much of it in the States. One: my friends call me the Prince. Two: you've just had your second and final heart attack."

Right so far: my first was two seasons back, just after finishing the score for *Huey.*

"You've made the big league." The alleged Prince gestured with his drink at my inert form; rich gold links gleamed against snowy cuffs. "No more diets, no more pills, backers' auditions, or critics. You've crossed over."

I goggled at my corpulent residue. "Dead?"

"As Tutankhamen."

At first blush, there didn't seem much change. My penthouse living room, the East River, Roosevelt Island framed in the picture window with late winter sun. My score on the piano with Ernie Hammil's new lyrics. My wife Sarah's overpriced and underdesigned furniture. Even the records I was listening to after lunch: Pete Rugolo and Stan Kenton, discs on the turntable, jackets on the shelf. For difference—me, very dead at the worst time.

"It couldn't wait? We open in two weeks, the second act needs three new songs, and God gives me this for *tsouris?*" I collapsed on the piano bench as my mind did a double take. "Wait a minute. Prince of what?"

His smile was too benign for the answer. "Darkness—or light, it depends on the translation. We do get deplorable press."

I took his point, not very reassured. "I'm not . . . under arrest or something?"

"Of course not." He seemed to regard the question as gauche.

"Will anyone come?"

"Why should they?"

"Well, what do I do? Where do I go?"

The Prince opened his arms to infinite possibilities. "Where would you like to go? Before you answer hastily—" He sipped his scotch, sighing in savory judgment. "Oh, that *is* good. You see, you've cut your spiritual teeth on misconceptions. Good, bad, I'm in heaven, it's pure hell, all of which rather begs the distinction. We're familiarly known as Topside and Below Stairs."

"Below Stairs," I swallowed. "That's hell?"

"Eternity is an attitude. Some say it looks like Queens. You have free choice, Mr. Bluestone, bounded only by imagination and your own will to create—and that, for far too many, is living hell. For you: *carte blanche* to the past, present, or future. Though I did have some small personal motive in dropping by."

"I thought so.'

"Nonono. Not a collection but a request. We adore your music Below Stairs. Now that you're eligible, we hoped you'd visit for as long as you like. We've quite an art colony, hordes of theater folk. Wilksey Booth would like to do a musical, and this very night there's a grand party at Petronius's house."

Adventure was not my long suit. "Thanks just the same. I'll stay here."

The Prince pursed his lips and frowned. "You never liked unpleasant scenes. You won't be found until Sarah gets back from Miami, and by then not even the air conditioning will help. There's going to be some abysmal *Grand Guignol* with the mortuary men, a rubber bag, and your wife weeping buckets into a handkerchief."

Not likely. Sarah bought them at Bergdorf's, Belgian lace. For me she'd use Kleenex—the story of our marriage. We never even had children. Sarah was a real princess. Her only bedtime activities were fighting and headaches. For grief, she'd be spritzing the place with Airwick before they got the rubber bagful of me down the elevator. On the other hand, my last will and testament might get a Bergdorf's hanky. The Actors Fund would see a windfall. Sarah wouldn't.

The Prince nudged delicately at the elbow of my thoughts. "Pensive, Mr. Blaustein. It was Blaustein once."

"Not for thirty-five years. Didn't look good on a marquee."

"No fibbing."

"Okay. Four years in an upper-class Washington high school. I used to dream I was a tall blond WASP. On bad days even an Arab."

Memories and reasons dissolved to another dusty but undimmed image. My Holy of Holies. Mary Ellen Cosgrove, supershiksa.

Wheat-blond hair brushed thick and shining in a long pageboy, good legs, tight little boobs succinctly defined by an expensive sweater, sorority pin bobbling provocatively over the left one like Fay Wray hanging from the Empire State Building. I think my eyes really went from fol-

lowing the undulations of her tush. She was my first lust, aridly unre-
quited, but I played the piano well enough to be invited to all her Lambda
Pi parties, Oscar Levant among the Goldwyn Girls with weak, horn-
rimmed eyes, pimpled, and factory-reject teeth. Not much hope against
jocks like Bob Bolling, who was born in a toothpaste ad.

But I could dream; beside me, Portnoy was a eunuch. My lust burned
eternal in the secrecy of my bedroom as, near nightly, I plowed a fistful
of ready, willing, and totally unliberated Mary Ellen Cosgrove and panted
to my pillow, *Why don't you love me?*

Because you're a nebbish, my pillow said.

The Prince apparently read the thought; his response was tinged with
sympathy. "Yes. Mary Ellen."

"It's been forty years. I don't even know if she's still alive."

"More or less."

I was surprised to find how important it was. Past, present, or future,
the man said. Why not?

The Prince's brows lifted in elegant question. "A decision?"

"You won't believe this."

"Try me, I'm jaded."

"I want to *shtup* Mary Ellen Cosgrove."

His urbane tolerance palled to disappointment. "That's all?"

"I've missed a lot of things in my life. She was the first, we'll start
there."

"My talented friend: *Faust,* for all its endurance, is pure propaganda.
I should have thought, at the very least, an introduction to Mozart or
Bach—"

"Look, for bar mitzvah I got ten bucks and a pen that leaked on white
shirts. Now I'm dead. For door prize you want me to klatch with harp-
sichord players? Later with the music; I want to ball Mary Ellen Cosgrove."

The Prince regarded me with cosmic weariness, steepling manicured
fingernails under his chin. "I wonder. If memory serves, you last saw
this Nordic nymphet in graduation week, 1945."

The growing eagerness made me tremble. "What happened to her?"

"You really want to know?"

"Maybe she's not a big deal after forty years, buddy. But she was the
first. That's entitled."

"Let me think." The Prince leaned back, concentrating. "Cosgrove . . .
From high school she wafted to a correct junior college, married a correct
young man with a correctly promising future. Bob Bolling."

"I knew it! That horny bastard just wanted to score. Not just her,
anybody."

"A fact Mr. Bolling belatedly appreciates; at eighteen he considered
himself in love when he only needed to go to the bathroom. He spends
less time on his libido now than his gall bladder. Nevertheless, for his

better days there is a pliant secretary who understands on cue. Mary Ellen has been relatively faithful.''

''Relatively?''

The Prince's hands arced in graceful deprecation. ''The usual. First affair at forty when her children were grown and no one seemed to need her anymore. An aftermath of delicious guilt followed by anticlimax when no one found out, and one expensive face-lift. The last liaison, predictably, just after her younger daughter's wedding. Relatively, I say. She doesn't care that much now. Ennui is always safer than principles; it locks from the inside. Currently into est, vodka, vague malaise about the passage of time and what she imperfectly recalls as her 'golden, best years.' There are millions like her, Mr. Bluestone, perhaps billions. She never found much in herself beyond what men expected of her. For such people, youth ought to be bright. It's their end.''

His voice, cultivated with overtones of Harvard and Westminster, carried all the ineffable sadness of being alive, growing up, growing older. But I knew what I wanted.

''Not Mary Ellen now, but *then*. A night in October 1944, the start of our senior year. There was a party at her house.''

The Prince's eyes flickered with new interest. ''Oh, yes. A fateful evening.''

''I kissed her. The first and only time.''

Memories like that stay with you. Somehow she was in my arms, fabulous boobs and all, Fay Wray enfolded by Kong Blaustein, and all futures were possible. But I retreated into embarrassment; in the middle of paradise, I thought of my bad teeth and wondered if she noticed. ''I blew it.''

''By an odd coincidence, the merest chance,'' the Prince said, ''Teresa Golowitz was there that night.''

''Who?''

''You don't remember her? Nobody does. Sad child, always faded into the wallpaper. Won't you say hello for me?''

Golowitz . . . No, not a clue for memory. Old acquaintance was definitely forgot. She would have paled under the beacon of Mary Ellen, in any case. ''Will I be able to make it with her, change the way things happened?''

''I certainly hope so,'' the Prince purred, rising and making for the whiskey again. ''If not change, a definite influence.''

''Then I'm going to influence the hell out of her.''

''I'm counting on it, Mr. Bluestone.'' For an instant I sensed more in his eyes than weary omniscience. ''Remember, you'll be sixteen years old with fifty-odd years of experience. That's not a blessing. Perhaps you can make it one.''

Already in a fever to depart, I stopped, agonized by a detail. ''I don't remember the exact date.''

The Prince flourished like a banner headline. "October 3, 1944! Paris liberated! Allied armies roll across France! Binky Blaustein encircles *la belle* Cosgrove! Why not take the bus for old times' sake?"

"It'll be packed."

"Weren't they all then?" He raised the refilled glass to me. "Good hunting, Binky. And say hello to Teresa."

Again with Golowitz, when my soaring purpose strained at the bit. "Who the hell is—?"

But the Prince, the room, and the year were gone.

Sixteen feels so different from fifty-five. An unsettling mix of fear and intoxication. A well of nervous energy, health, and fluttering insecurity based on the hard certainty that you're the homeliest, most unworthy and unwanted, least redeemable *schlemiel* in the universe. God may love you, but girls don't, and life is measured to that painful priority.

Even after forty years, I knew the route in my sleep. From my father's jewelry store down Fourteenth Street to Eleventh and E. Catch the Walker Chapel bus through Georgetown over Key Bridge into Virginia, up Lee Highway to Cherrydale and Mary Ellen's house on Military Road.

The bus pulled out at seven-ten; I'd be there at seven forty-five. Just a little more than half an hour! Dropping my real-silver Columbia dime into the paybox, I quivered despite the double exposure of age/youth, glowing with the joyful pain that always churned my blood whenever I was going to see her. It was beginning, would be as it was *then* before time turned into nostalgia and faded both of us into what passed for maturity.

The ancient bus was wartime-jammed with tired government workers and young soldiers in olive drab with shoulder patches no one remembers now: ASTP, Washington Command, the Wolverine Division, Seventh Expeditionary Force. Baby-faced sailors with fruit salad on their winter blues, patient and stoic Negroes in the still-Jim-Crowed back seats. Two working housewives from the Government Printing Office in upswept hairdos and square-shouldered jackets, bitching about their supervisors and the outlandish price of beef: you wouldn't need ration stamps soon, but *sixty* cents a pound, who could pay that? Bad enough you couldn't get cigarettes now even if you ran a drug store.

The bus lumbered up the spottily repaired blacktop of Lee Highway toward Cherrydale. Grimy windows and the outside dark made a passable mirror to show me Richard Blaustein—Binky—in his rumpled reversible box coat from Woodward & Lothrop. Bushy brown hair neither efficiently combed nor recently cut, unformed mouth and chin still blurred with baby fat. Not Caliban, not even homely; merely embryonic. I winked at him from forty years of forgiveness. *Hey, kid, I fixed the teeth.*

Next to me in the crowded aisle, two sailors compared the sultry charms of Veronica Lake with an upstart pinup newcomer named Bacall. I felt dizzy, godlike. It's October 1944. Veronica Lake is box office in four starring Paramount vehicles, besides spawning the peekaboo hairstyle that gave eyestrain to a million American girls. *To Have and Have Not* isn't released yet. I might be smoking my hoarded Pinehursts with three fingers along the butt like Bogart, but Lauren Bacall is just a lanky new whosis named Betty Perske.

I looked closer at my mirror-Binky. The liquid brown eyes behind the glasses were not completely naive even then, wary-humorous with an ancient wisdom not yet renamed Murphy's Law. What can go wrong will, but—a little patience, a little hope. In four years we'll raise our own flag over Jerusalem; for the blacks in the rear of bus, it'll be longer. Veronica Lake was a waitress before she died. Bacall opened her second Broadway show in 1981. They were both nice girls, but Perske and me, we lasted. Don't ask: there are survivors and others.

Cherrydale. I pulled the buzzer cord and wormed through the press toward the rear door as the bus slowed. It rattled open with a wheeze of fatigued hydraulics, then I was out of the smell of sweat, stale perfume, wool, and monoxide, standing on the corner of Military Road under clear October stars.

"Oh, it's you. Come in."

Mary Ellen stood in the open door, one slender hand on the knob, backed by music and chatter. My Grail, the Ark of my libido's own Covenant—and yet different, a subtle gap between my memory and the fact of her.

"Melly?"

"Well, don't stare at me. Come in, hang up your coat. Bo-*ub!*" And she was off paging Bob Bolling. I hung my coat in the familiar closet and stepped into the large living room. Smaller than I remembered it. Gracious, comfortable chairs and sofa, French doors at the rear leading to the yard, Mason & Hamlin grand piano in the far corner. Boys in trousers that seemed baggy and ill cut to me, girls in pleated skirts and bobby sox. And faced I recalled with a pang: Bill Tait, Frankie Maguerra. And willowy Laura Schuppe, always inches taller than her escorts.

"It's old Blaustein!"

And of course, Bob Bolling with his unwrinkled Arrow collar and hair that stayed combed. He steered around two girls catting to a record of Tommy Dorsey's "Boogie Woogie," stroking one on the hips—"Shake it but don't break it"—to tower over me with an intimidating sunburst of thirty-two straight teeth.

"Big night, Blaustein," he confided. "Melly's folks are away and I brought some grade-A hooch. Bourbon, Blaustein." He always pronounced it *steen* despite my repeated corrections. He patted me on the cowlick. "If you got a note from your mother, I might put some in your

Coke. Heh-heh. Come in the kitchen.'' He disappeared through the hall arch.

"Skip the bourbon." The unsolicited advice came from an owlish, bespectacled boy curled in a chair with a thick book. "It's a gift from Mrs. Bolling's third cousin, a distant relative in the process of retreating even further. Try the scotch.''

I edged over to him. A great disguise, but there was no hiding those velvet overtones. "Prince?''

"Even he.'' He turned a page and giggled. "I love *Paradise Lost*. Milton gave me such marvelous lines. The scotch is under the sink.''

The record ended; couples shuffled about, awkward, faced with the need for conversation until the music started again. Bill Tait bummed one of my Pinehursts, and I took the first puff. They tasted awful, but you couldn't find real butts anywhere. I segued to the kitchen in time to hear Mary Ellen, coy, sibilant, and not really angry:

"Bob, now *quit* that! Honest, you're all hands tonight. Grab, grab.''

When they saw me, I felt only a phantom of jealousy. " 'Scuse me. Thought I'd get a drink or something.''

"Sure, Binky.'' Mary Ellen switched her pert tush to the icebox. "Coke or Pepsi? Bink, what are you staring at? Coke or Pepsi?''

"Scotch, please.''

She made a face at me, strained patience. "You don't drink. Stop putting on.''

Bob whinnied. "Little man had a ha-a-rd day?''

"You wouldn't believe—the death of me.''

"Mama and Daddy don't even drink scotch.''

"Under the sink.''

"See, smarty?'' Mary Ellen yanked open the cabinet door. *Voilà:* Glenmorangie, the bottle collared with a small handwritten tag: *Against mixed blessings.*

"I never saw that." She shrugged. "Anyway, aspirin and Coke are your speed.''

The bottle looked like an oasis. "Ice?''

"Sure, it's your funeral. Just don't get sick on the furniture.''

I dropped three ice cubes in a jigger with a decent lack of haste, christened them with three fat fingers of whiskey, and inhaled half of it in a gulp. "Jesus, that's good!''

"Don't curse, Binky. And stop showing off.''

I winced in spite of myself at the sound of that thin, plaintive voice. Once it must have been aphrodisiac, especially when she sang. Now it merely grated.

"It's good to see you again, Melly.''

"You drip, you saw me in school today.'' She peered closer at me. "But—gee, I don't know—you look different.''

"So do you." It came out flat and not too gracious.

"Well, you don't have to be so sad about it. Bob, let's go dance."

That evidently concluded her obligations as a hostess. Abandoned, I leaned against the sink and watched that little ass, the centerfold of a thousand steamy fantasies, bounce out of the kitchen with Bolling in tow. Thank God for the drink; the rest of me was deflating fast. Memory was definitely suspect. I remembered her prettier, even beautiful, and much more mature. She was as unformed as myself. The eyes, to which I once wrote saccharine verse, were merely blue with a patina of intolerance over ignorance. The figure was child-cute, but after thirty-five years of grown women and a regiment of Broadway dancers, it retreated now as the half-realized first draft of an ordinary, mesomorphic female body. So far from a resurgence of passion, I felt more pity and understanding than anything else, like suffering the gauche sophistication of a daughter struggling to be grown-up. The idea of sleeping with Melly was more than absurd, even faintly incestuous. My overblown lust went flat as a bride's biscuit, and from the shadows of Shubert Alley I heard the mournful laughter of Rick Bluestone, who would never call a spade a heart. Mary Ellen Cosgrove at sixteen was interesting as a clam. But then, so was I.

More kids arrived, conversation got louder, high and giddy on youth alone. Melly and Bob danced with glum precision. Suffering from total recall, Frankie Maguerra regaled anyone in earshot with Hope-Crosby jokes from *The Road to Morocco*. My bookish buddy had vanished, but Laura Schuppe over at the piano gave me an X-rated wink and a little beckoning toss of her head. I joined her on the bench.

"Find the scotch?"

"Huh? Yeah. Where's the little guy who was sitting over there?"

"Nelson Baxley, class of '46. Korea, Bronze Star and Purple Heart. Later: television production, five children, one Emmy, one duodenal ulcer."

I might have known. Laura would never even look at me, let alone wink. "Prince?"

"Nelson left, so I borrowed Laura."

"It doesn't bother her, having you in residence?"

"No, it's all rather split-screen. On her side she's drooling over that varsity jock in the maroon sweater. Nice girl, somewhat confused, poor self-image. Top model for *Vogue* and *Harper's*, 1949–55. One therapist, two nervous breakdowns, serial affairs with lovers of mixed gender. Cocaine, anorexia, born-again Christianity. Married a fundamentalist; currently works for the Moral Majority. Depressing. And Mary Ellen?"

"The booze is better. Thanks."

Laura sighed with a wisdom eons beyond her. "Nostalgia is always myopic. By the way, there's Miss Golowitz: trying to be invisible as usual."

Even as I recognized and remembered the fat, homely girl, my older heart went out to her. Teresa Golowitz—a dark, shapeless smudge among blondish altos in the school choral section. Coarse, frizzy hair, unplucked eyebrows that aspired to meet over her nose, and a faint but discernible mustache line. Thick legs blotched with unshaved hair under laddered nylons, and—insult to injury—a dress that would look better on Aunt Jemima. Among the relatively svelte Lambda Pi girls, she fit in like pork chops at a seder. I wondered why she'd been invited.

"That's why." The Prince read my thought casually. "Cast your mind back: Mary Ellen always had a few plain girls around to make her look good. And tonight is Teresa's turn in the barrel."

Memory sharpened to cruel clarity. My own family was conservative enough, but Teresa's orthodox parents made mine look like atheists. She came to school in *shmotte* dresses and no makeup. She'd done her face for the party, no doubt on the bus in a bad light. I watched Teresa trying to press herself through the wall, fiddling with her hands, carmined mouth frozen in a stiff smile. I always avoided her in school; she was all the things I wanted to escape. Now I could see how much she might have wanted it, too.

"You're big on futures, Prince. What happened to her?" Two to one she married the kind of guy who wears his yarmulke to the office.

"Don't you remember?"

"Memory, I'm learning not to trust."

"She committed suicide."

"No! She didn—" but in the breath of denial I knew it was true, a sensation at school for a day or two. When Frankie Maguerra told me, I said something like "Gee!" and briefly pondered the intangibles of life before getting on with adolescence.

"When?"

"Tonight."

Yes . . . it was about this month. The Prince stroked soft chords with Laura's long fingers. "Took the bus back to town reflecting on accumulated griefs and loneliness, and the fact that no one at this golden gathering even said hello to her, not even Blaustein. She got off the bus and waited at the curb—as she is now, tearing at her cuticles, multiplying this night by so many others and so many more to come. She didn't like the product. When the next bus came along—behind schedule and traveling too fast—she stepped in front of it."

I shook my head, foggily mournful. "What a sad waste."

"Sad but academic." The Prince stood up. "Excuse me, Laura has to go to the little girls' room. Had the immortal embrace yet?"

"No. Who needs it?"

Dismally true; the whole purpose of my flashback was on the cutting room floor. I was pondering whether to talk to Teresa or just leave now when Bill Tait roared away from a dirty-joke session to drape himself over the piano. "Bink! Give us 'Boogie Woogie.' "

"No!" someone else demanded. "Do 'Blue Lights.' "

"Hey, Bink's gonna play."

"Yay!"

I swung into "House of Blue Lights" to a chorus of squealed approval. It sounded fantastic, too good, until I realized I was playing with forty-five years of practice behind me and basic ideas still unknown outside of Fifty-second Street: steel rhythm under a velvet touch, block chords out of Monk, Powell, and Kenton that wouldn't be heard for years yet. The crowd began to collect around the piano. Mary Ellen got set to sing, her big thing at parties. Teresa Golowitz edged in next to her, almost apologetically, pudgy fingers dancing on the piano top. Melly took the vocal on the second verse; not a bad voice, but it wouldn't go past the fifth row without a mike.

Fall in there, where the blue light's lit,
Down at the house, the House of Blue Lights.

And then I heard it, rising over Mary Ellen's sweet, whitish soprano like a great big bird, that smoky alto soaring into the obligato release. Yah-duh-dee-duh-DAH-duh-duh-duh-DEE-dah-dah, bouncing twice around the electrified room and sliding back into the lyric like she was born there. The hair rose on my head and arms; everyone stared at Teresa Golowitz, who, perhaps for the first time and on the last night of her life, had decided to leave her mark. I rocked into another coda for her alone, begging.

"Take it, girl!"

Teresa did; together we worked things on that basic boogie that weren't invented yet. And what a voice—not pure, not classical, but a natural for jazz. Teresa straightened out of her usual slump, closed her eyes, and let the good riffs roll. Sixteen years old; you could teach her a little about phrasing and breath control, but the instrument was incredible. She played with the notes, slurring over and under the melodic line with a pitch and rhythm you couldn't break with dynamite. All the greats had this for openers: Lutcher, Fitzgerald, Stafford, June Christy, Sassy Vaughan, all of them. Under the excitement, the Prince's voice whispered into my mind: *Of course she's beautiful. It's her requiem.*

It could well be. When we finished the number, I bounced up and smeared her lipstick with an off-center kiss. "Baby, you're gorgeous. Don't ever think you're not."

"Hey, lookit old Blaustein the wolf!"

Mary Ellen snickered; as a vocalist, her nose was a little out of joint— say about a mile. "Oh, it's a *love* match!"

Teresa blushed crimson; I doubt if she was kissed much at home, let alone at parties. She started to retreat, but I grabbed her hand. "Don't go, I need you. You know 'Opus One'?"

She hesitated, then made her decision. She glared with fierce pride at Mary Ellen and stood even straighter. "Hit it, Blaustein."

I zapped into the machine-gun opening with pure joy. "Opus One" is a real catting number. Most of the kids started to dance, the rest jiggling and beating time on the piano top. From Teresa, we hadn't heard anything yet. She vocalized the soprano sax break from the Dorsey orchestration with a scatty-doo riff that wailed like Nellie Lutcher's "Lake Charles." She shouldn't end like this. In four years or less there'd be recording techniques able to put that voice on the moon, and she wants to off herself in an hour or two. The hell with it all, if I could just keep her from that.

We rolled up the wall-shaking finish, both of us out of breath. Teresa parked herself on the bench beside me, guzzling sloppily at her drink. "You are reet, Blaustein. You are definitely a groove."

"Me! Where'd you pick up jazz like that?"

"Who picks up? You feel it. The first time is like remembering."

"Feeling good, Terri?"

"Yeah, kinda." She grinned shyly. "I always wanted to be called that."

"Terri it is. And take advice: tomorrow we start working together." Her eyes clouded. "Tomorrow . . ."

"Unless you're not around, you know what I mean? Go home, take a *shvitz*. Tomorrow things will look pure gold. And when I call New York about you—"

I talked fast, promising, conning, cajoling, speaking of agents and record producers not even born yet, anything to get her mind off the loser track and that fatal bus. Still talking, I steered her into the kitchen, spiked her a little Pepsi in a lot of bourbon, a new scotch for me. I'd bomb the suicide out of her if I could, sing it out: one hour when she and everybody in range knew Teresa Golowitz was a person, a talent, and worth the future.

We were literally dragged back to the piano. Play more. Sing, Teresa. Please sing, Teresa. She didn't know how to handle it all, never opened up like this before. I ruffled a big fanfare chord on the piano.

"Ladies and gentlemen—the fourteen karats of Miss Terri Gold!"

"Yay!"

"Huh?" said Teresa. "What's with Gold?"

"Just like Blaustein. I yell 'Golowitz!'—who'd come? Hang on, Terri. We are going to the moon."

I launched into music so far beyond eight-to-the-bar that the kids were mystified. Way-out Monk, Shearing riffs, Charlie Ventura stuff, bop sounds most of the world hadn't heard yet, like "The Man from Minton's" and the clean, hard-rocking Previn-Manne "I Could Have Danced All Night," still twelve years in the future. Terri's eyes were moons of discovery before she dug it. Like she said, a kind of remembering. On artist like yourself, a sculptor of possibilities. What could you change with Mary Ellen, who was cast and immutable by the age of ten?''

I stared at him, unbelieving. ''Dead one day and already I need a lawyer.''

''And you shall have the best,'' the Prince conciliated. ''For services rendered. Darrow loves cases like this.''

''I'll bet. No wonder you get lousy reviews Topside.''

''Topside!'' he flared in disgust. ''Stodgy, pragmatic conservatives. Liszt should die of fever before he's thirty, Schubert before he could write the glorious Ninth? Never! It's not all fun, believe me. Win some, lost some. Lose a Shelley, lose a Byron, a Kapell. Lose a Radiguet before he's twenty-one, a Gershwin at thirty-nine. But a Terri Gold at sixteen? No, the world is threadbare enough. And no one Topside, not even my celestial Brother—the white sheep of an otherwise brilliant family—has ever understood the concept of *creative* history. What in the cosmos does it matter if I make a mess of their records? I create! Like any artist, I need to be recognized. I need to be understood. Most of all,'' the Prince concluded wearily, ''I need another drink.''

I didn't understand half of it, but—you know?—I couldn't really stay mad at him. Whatever else, bad press or no, the guy has *chutzpah*. And there are all those years of Terri Gold.

''How long has Terri got?''

''Ages, Mr. Bluestone. Dogs' years. More records, more men, more grandchildren. She'll be roaring drunk when she goes, and happy as a bee among flowers. And the last drink will be her best.'' The Prince polished off his own, neat. ''Shall we?''

''Uh . . . where to?''

''As advertised: your choice. But till the heat's off, I'd suggest Petronius's party. There's someone positively seething to meet you, that clever little woman from the Algonquin set. Which reminds me.''

The Prince swept up the Glenmorangie in one protective arm, the other through mine. ''Dottie said to bring you *and* the scotch. *Allons,* Mr. Bluestone. The night is young!''